MW01124412

for all the lovers
but most especially
Fritz

ACKNOWLEDGEMENTS

Godspeed, Lovers is the product of lots of love, not all of it my own.

Fritz Westenberger, you've given me so much support to follow my heart. Thank you for the inspiration and encouragement I needed. And thanks for the typography wizardry on the cover!

Laura Hassenstein, Maxwell Ciardullo, Sylvia Caitlin Burn, and Doug Spearman, thank you for reading earlier, messier versions of this story. Your feedback helped me polish the gems. I'm so grateful to have you in my life.

Steve Clayton, Bill Thames, and T Duncan, thank you for the endless encouragement and support.

Grant Sutton, while I enlisted your help on a different story, your feedback will continue to influence me, especially your advice to "make it gayer."

Colette Bennett, thank you for helping me fine-tune how Casey and Oscar's story would be read. Every writer's editor should be as skilled, efficient, compassionate, and enthusiastic as you!

Joel Luna, the cover image is absolutely perfect! Gracias.

And to all the lovers, godspeed.

GODSPEED, LOVERS

A LOVERS UNIVERSE NOVEL

TQ SIMS

ARCHWAY PUBLISHING

Archway Publishing books may be ordered through booksellers or by contacting:

Archway Publishing
1663 Liberty Drive
Bloomington, IN 47403
www.archwaypublishing.com
844-669-3957

ISBN: 978-1-6657-5156-8 (sc)
ISBN: 978-1-6657-5157-5 (e)

Library of Congress Control Number: 2023919491

Print information available on the last page.

Archway Publishing rev. date: 10/13/2023

CASEY

"Casey!" Franxis shakes my arm, where my hair stands on its end. They strengthen their accompaniment, reach into my mind to see what I see, what I feel. When they sense the dark, cold stare peering through the extradimensional rift to look for me, they gasp.

That's it, isn't it? Franxis transfers psychically.

(People scream and break everything around them, including other people, including themselves. My lover attacks me–his face twisted in rage. Our SkyDrive crashes. I watch my open wounds heal in seconds, but my mind is torn open…)

It glares at me.

No amount of mental training or psychic assistance can stop the flood of fragmented memories from coming back. My trauma has been triggered. Flashes of the past race through my mind. Though we cannot stop the memories from crowding in, together my comp and I order the memories. Franxis dials up our psybridge, reaches into my mind, and assists me in piecing the fragments together.

The rebound from the gravity wave rocks the station, knocking others to the floor. Sparks fly from service panels. Klaxons sound. Mumbles of confusion come from others beginning to right themselves.

"Did the cannon hit us?" I ask.

"It hit the asteroid as planned," Franxis replies. They kneel next to me and help me sit up. They send a quick, bolstering force into my mind to steady me, but even with their psychic accompaniment, something feels off.

The amplified voice of Station Scire's Captain Commander Gala N'guwe sounds throughout the station. "Attention Scire, an interdimensional breach has opened nearby. All visiting and independently contracted divs and comps activate emergency EDB engagement protocols. All unRisen personnel to shelter units."

Breathless, I turn toward the gallery window. A short distance from the station, where the asteroid met the sardonyx blast of the cannon-wings, like a massive lens flare with a hidden light source, glows a rip in our reality. Light curves around it, refusing to enter. An extra-dimensional rift.

I feel it staring into me. A fear I haven't felt in one hundred years grips me.

Others are scrambling to right themselves, but I'm frozen.

The klaxons, the chaos—even the threat is not enough to keep me present. My mind goes back to the day I encountered my first sentient storm. Franxis is with me, a felt presence, and together we watch as—

(The unpredicted storm descends over South Los Angeles.)

Inside the half-glow of the rift near Station Scire, a thunderhead glowing with purple-black, intercloud lightning creeps toward our world.

(The dingy storm cloud's thin vortexes creep down like tentacles. It reaches into the heads of tens of thousands of people, altering their perception.)

Boots hit the floor around us as the crowd runs to their assigned battle stations. They run, dodging me where I sit.

(I'm fighting my neighbors, wondering why such nice people have suddenly attacked me.)

Franxis lays a hand on my shoulder, and I flinch.

"Casey," Franxis urges. "You're not there! Be here now!"

I stand and stumble. Franxis catches me and puts their arm around me.

Heavy chunks of the remaining asteroid crash against the station's prismatic shield with pounding explosions and brilliant sparks.

(I'm running with my lover Usain from our apartment building, which is exploding behind us.)

The first of the clash-wings and crux-wings pull into view, heading for the rift and the sentient storm beginning to invade our world. The urge to be with them swells in me, and for a moment, I'm free of the memories.

It peers through the storm, and Franxis and I turn back to gaze toward the rift again. My body trembles, and Franxis squeezes their arm around me. They stomp their foot on the floor, sending grounding energy into my being, stabilizing me.

They ask, "That's what you felt the day of Bakkeaux's First Assault, your day of Rising. Isn't it?"

"It's looking for me."

"Then Rise up to meet the fucker."

Their eyes meet mine, and a charge of energy swells within me as Franxis anchors me so I can reach up through my Levels, pulling power down from my access at Level Three. (I feel its cold stare,) and I slip. My levels misalign, and a torrent of divination flows from a higher level that I'm not prepared to receive. I remember my training. I try to remain calm, but the killer storm approaching the station has triggered my trauma. The flood of divination moves through my body. My mind pulses with the influx of power. I begin to see wisps of Franxis' aura turning red as they stabilize me.

Franxis nods. "I got you, Casey! Go!"

I turn to run, dodging others. Each stride pushes me further and faster as power from Level Three rushes through me. Streams of luminous divination course through my body, giving me supernatural speed. I run faster than I've ever run, faster than anyone else around me as they rush to defense or safety positions.

Hangar-1 is buzzing with engines burning, docks being lowered, and wings moving through the airlock channel. Scores of ships move through the series of plasma-grid airlocks, toward the rift and the invading storm.

A pilot runs past me toward a crux-wing.

(I'm running with Usain toward our SkyDrive. He flings open the door to the flying car, and I yell at him that I'm a better pilot. I yell at him, and—)

I still feel guilty a century later. I try to push away the memory, the guilt. As I was trained to, I focus on my breath, rein my senses in, dial them in until the past is not so intense.

The surge of memories is quelled.

There's a problem with the scanner. I try it several times before someone behind me urgently says, "Come on, look at the screen, mate!"

The screen displays my face-rec, official marks, but also in big red letters: UNAUTHORIZED.

I step aside and watch the other pilots getting scanned and into their assigned light-wings, clash-wings, a few dozen pouring into each DSV. Rookies climb aboard the deep space V-wing, a ship not so different from what I flew commercially back on Earth. I could fly a DSV half asleep, yet I'm not authorized for any wings, not even as a power channel to send divination through the DSV's weaponry. Pilots climb into the crux-wings, and I feel a flush of jealousy as they take off in a ship that I helped design. Others brush past me, their auras flowing in vibrant colors of fear or excitement.

"Divinator Casey Isaac," says a voice from my comm, "to the operations bridge."

"EDB emergencies override my restrictions! Why am I not going out?"

The voice from Ops replies, "Operations bridge now, Div Isaac!"

As more wings leave the harbor, I turn away. I run through corridors, weaving around people getting in place for the encounter with the storm. Their auras are distracting. My mind flashes to the violent crowds in South Los Angeles. I'm tapped into more divination than I can handle.

As I pass through the comp deck, I notice that Franxis is absent from their console. When the doors to the command bridge security check slide open, Franxis is there waiting for me.

"There's a good reason," they say before I can open my mouth to complain. "Apparently, the final decision was made less than a few minutes ago. Ops is making assessments, since they've registered that you've pulled down from above your Levels. That may complicate things—."

"Franxis, what are you talking about?"

"You're going up to the Haven."

"Did my div-enhanced hearing deceive me?" Hunter Bolden says as he rushes ahead of us. "No way is Casey Isaac, famed slow learner, going to the Haven for an actual EDB encounter. Only Fours and up, little lady."

Before I can say anything, Franxis quickens their step and shoves Hunter forward. He catches himself quickly and sneers back with anger and surprise.

"Misgender me when we're not under attack, Hunter." Franxis' eyes are scary-calm in the face of Hunter's aggression. "I'll kick your rude ass."

"Kinda hard for a comp to match div-strength though, right tough guy?"

Franxis lunges at him, but I catch their arm. He's right. His enhanced strength would give him an advantage over Franxis' small frame. I speak to the back of Hunter's head. "They meant to say: we'll kick your rude ass."

Hunter snickers but quickens his step.

He wouldn't've dared to be so rude if we were still with the UNAF, Franxis transfers. *Our new corporate overlords have let these assholes get away with a lot.*

I signal a reminder that there is a sentient storm positioning itself to attack us.

Got it. And with an audible snort, Franxis adds, *But I can support all my divs while complaining about assholes like Hunter. I'm a master multi-tasker.*

The doors to the station's operation and command deck slide open, and we enter. Chatter from Operations surrounds us as everyone scrambles to shift from a low-risk asteroid dusting into full defense against whatever is coming through the extra-dimensional rift. A group of Ops gather around a holographic model of the station with a fleet of wings pouring from each harbor.

I am having a hard time getting past the fact that I am here and not out there where I'm at my most useful.

Hunter scoffs. "No Level Three has ever been up there, and the idea that they'd call you up when we're all at risk doesn't make sense."

I psychically signal to Franxis that Hunter is right.

Something's up. Let's try and calm your nerves, they reply.

"They might not mind that you've accessed some extra divination. What's new since it poured in?" Franxis asks.

They could easily scan my mind for the answers. However, getting me to talk makes it easier for Franxis to help ease my frustration, to help me refocus.

"I'm faster. A lot. Heightened awareness, attention. Also, auras. By the way, yours is the prettiest I've seen."

Hunter scoffs at my lightheartedness.

Franxis smiles lightly. "Sounds like everything is yours from being so close to Four, except the auras. That's probably pulled down from a higher Level. Probably won't stick, so don't get used to it."

"Close to Four?" Hunter asks.

Captain Commander Gala N'guwe and her scheduled replacement, Captain Arianne Holt, stand at the door to the lift. N'guwe holds her hand out to me, calling me across the command bridge. "Div Isaac, this way."

Franxis walks alongside me as we move through the action all around us. I hear Ops talking to divs in wings, and I feel a pull at my heart, hoping they're okay out there. At another panel, Ops confirms that the sentient storm is moving through the breach, spilling into our world with lightning striking at the wings.

One of the comm operators' aura shifts from orange to red as she announces to N'guwe, "We've received confirmation of backup from all three other stations, ma'am. Their first wings arrive in fourteen minutes."

"Helixx Corp can handle this. We don't need the UNAF getting involved," Holt says to N'guwe.

N'guwe turns to the operative. "Tell them to punch it and call in assistance from Luna." She turns to Holt. "I'm still in command, and I won't take that risk with the skeleton crew left from this foolish corporate takeover."

An operative from the science panel addresses everyone on the command deck.

"Launching probes into the storm."

"Units planetside awaiting classification," the officer next to her says as murky red flares sweep through her aura.

The science operative leans toward the holoscreen in front of her and I watch her shoulders tense. "Scanning quantum signatures—" A pleasant ding rings out from her monitors, momentarily putting the flurry of activity on pause.

Everyone goes still, listening.

She announces the quantum signature classification of the EDB, and we hear the word none of us want to hear: "Haddyc."

"Fuck," Hunter mumbles.

"The worst of the worst." Franxis puts a hand on my arm. "But we've beat them before. You've got this, and I've got you." Franxis psychically anchors me again, but I feel my traumatic memories on the periphery of my mind.

Captain Holt taps a button, and the lift doors slide open.

Hunter steps toward the lift, then turns toward N'guwe.

"Captain Commander, I urge you to reconsider sending up a Level Three."

I assert, "Sages have confirmed that I am close to Four, ma'am."

Hunter steps onto the lift. "He's only recently at Three. No way the guy who spent fifty years each at One and Two is already close to Four."

Holt looks up from a holoscreen and raises an eyebrow. "His emo-spec grade does show that he's scattered, showing signs of triggered trauma. Could cause major blocks to accessing divination."

Hunter adds, "He's a liability."

N'guwe calmly steps to the panel on the wall. "Div Bolden, no one asked you. Go do your job." She pushes the button, and before Hunter can protest, the lift doors close.

Franxis says, "If you don't send him to the Haven, put him in a crux. Let him fight."

I look down at their hand holding mine and see their emerald aura fading into sky blue as it integrates into my golden glow. As I let go of their hand, this connection persists, wisps of emerald and gold dancing across it to touch.

"Div Isaac," N'guwe says. "The Sages didn't have time to tell me what their plan is. I don't know what you're walking into. If you feel you're not ready…"

The doors of the empty lift slide open again.

"They asked for me." I step into the lift. "I'm here."

The captain commander nods, and Franxis beams at me, filling me with energetic support.

Across the operations deck, someone in Analysis calls out "genus strange," a first encounter.

Holt looks at N'guwe again. "We don't know how the storm will attack us. If it gets past us, we don't know how it will affect the unRisen on Earth. We're humanity's first line of defense against the storm's psychic assault. Are you really sending up a Level Three?"

"Good luck, Div Isaac." N'guwe says as she closes the lift door.

Something moves in my periphery. The mysterious movement without a mover, that accompanies significant, often stressful moments, flickers and is gone, leaving me fearful of what lies ahead.

A flash of memory brings back the confusion I felt when Usain started attacking me, his face twisted. It's not enough to yank my mind back to the past, but it's enough to make me doubt myself. I failed Usain. I could fail again.

I slam my hand on the panel to halt the lift. Why am I on the station—not in a wing, doing what I do well? The question lands in my mind, and a flash moves into my mind as if to answer. I'm jolted by the fear that the light is the Haddyc invading my mind. Franxis anchors me as I reach up to pull down from my Levels. The light folds. I've only heard of the folding light of prescient visions.

Like origami made of light, radiant edges become shapes. The shapes shift into curves. The vision emerges. A bright, green light, a star at the center of my chest. Within the glow of my heart is a felt sense of someone I love. Some wordless suggestion hints at romantic love, and I shatter the vision with my familiar doubt and self-depreciation. An unfamiliar song echoes in my head.

A persistent spark of the light voices, *It's going to be okay.*

Annoyed with the seeming irrelevance, I dismiss the vision as nonsense.

My doubt leads to frustration.

Deep breaths.

Was that prescience? Franxis transfers. *You've never...*

I signal that it was nothing, that I saw the flicker which Sages tell me is missed prescience just before.

Franxis wants to know more but respectfully drops it.

I drop to my knees, toes tucked, and sit back on my heels. The intense stretch in my soles is an anchor for my awareness. I focus on the sensation, and it brings presence. I bring my middle and ring fingers in to touch the tips of my thumbs, and I splay the index and little fingers out. I turn my palms up and rest the backs of my hands on my lap. The creation of the mudra helps me focus on disarming my trauma.

From across our comp-bridge, Franxis observes as I restabilize my mind.

The soft voice of a Sage awaiting my arrival in the Haven lands in my mind. *Are you in the wrong place?*

Meaning is layered. Am I in the wrong place by not being in the Haven already? Am I in the wrong place emotionally? Am I not present, but hung up in the past?

From their station on the comp deck, Franxis psychically signals confidence, a reminder of assurance.

I'm here. I'm where I should be.

The Sage transfers again, offering their psybridge. *Welcome.*

I meet the invitation to integrate with humility. I discharge and dispel my frustration, not wanting to meet the Sage with it still echoing. I dial in the heightened sense of perception and expand around it, dropping the impressions from the activity I've been in since the gallery, the hangar, the command deck. The Sage watches me from across our psychic bridge.

"To the Haven," I command the lift.

The doors slide open, and I stay on my knees, toes tucked. The stretch in the soles of my feet grows stronger, more intense, but I feel I cannot focus fully. I open my eyes slowly to find that the elevator itself has disappeared into what appears to be endless, effulgent white light.

Five Sages sit in varying meditation positions within the light, which is enhanced by the Haven technology but accessed through the Sages psychically reaching to the highest known Level.

They hold me in their gaze with neutral expressions, except for one. Yahima smiles gently, as if careful not to stun me with their beauty. I bow my head, unable to hide a thought that I want to stare at their beautiful features—a balance of feminine and masculine that somehow elevates and transcends both—if only we were not in imminent danger.

Yahima's voice moves in me as it does through all present. *Welcome, Casey Isaac.*

I'm staring at their beautiful oval face, high cheekbones, prominent nose, and brows. Their silky hair is parted down the center and braided over one shoulder, wrapped tightly in a cloth over the other shoulder. Their dark, almond shaped eyes seem to peer deep into me, so much that it almost unnerves me until their gentle smile widens.

I'm somehow getting my awareness hung up on the Sages' faces, meditation positions, and saffron and orange uniforms, forgetting the danger coming through the rift. The Haven and the energy from above Level Three are amplifying my mind too much. I close my eyes. I try to make my focus more easeful.

"Allow me," Sage Murtagh says, lifting a mudra on one hand, and a wave expands through the effulgent light and lands in me. The effect of her psychic reach diminishes my confusion and anger, eases trauma's grip on me bringing calm to my body and mind. She siphons away the overload of divination from above Three.

Murtagh says, "You will integrate, learn, and retain more this way." She speaks with calm certainty as if we are not currently threatened by a dangerous being from some type of hell.

As my mind calms, the effulgent light appears to fade from endlessness. The boundaries defining the spacious room we call Haven emerge. The Sages are each seated on tech-embedded crystal plinths of various heights. There are others behind me, a group of divs, all Levels Four and higher.

Murtagh looks at me, expression neutral. "Sit," she says.

I move to the small group of divs, who all sit with their eyes closed. I recognize several of them. Aside from Hunter, I know none of them personally even though there are two that I've had sex with. There seems to be maybe a dozen or so divs here. I notice that two of the divs are in black and pink uniforms. The independent contractors brought in to take transfers off-station have been called to the Haven to assist. The other indie divs are probably out in wings approaching the maelstrom.

I sit, legs crossed, and the crystal floor lifts underneath me, adapting to whatever the embedded tech senses to be my optimal meditation seat.

I close my eyes like the other divs, and the Sages open their psybridge wider, integrating our psychic connections into one mindfield. I sense movement around me. With assistance from the Sages, we diminish barriers, shift boundaries, set aside our obscurations. We cannot draw from our Levels through obstructions. Instead, each of our individual obscurations are held low in the periphery of our awareness, shifting like ferrofluid blobs underneath the shimmering edges of the psybridge, keeping our secrets private.

Confusion interwoven with something else begins to arise within me, soon unraveling and revealing something about being Level Three while everyone else who has ever been here has been more skilled, more adept than me. Stowaway doubt, fear, inadequacies are unwoven from the confusion. I get a sense of Yahima's delight in my detection of these sour vibes that could hinder me here. Yahima shines as I disentangle wonder and curiosity, discharging and dispelling the rest.

I'm in the right place.

We turn up our collective power. We pour from our bodies, minds, spaces—the field around us. Above each one of us, a glowing ring or disc brightens into view and expands as it ascends. Our nimbuses integrate into concentric circles highlighting their sacred geometry to shine together. The Haven vibrates as our Levels harmonize. Subtle vibrations from the union of various Levels rains down on us. We open our eyes simultaneously, one sight, seeing into both the Haven and the mindfield.

Projectors spin beams of blue light into holograms of the station, wings, and rift.

The breach half-glows where the Cannon-wing broke the rock, perhaps contributing to the extradimensional breach but also ensuring that the asteroid would not crash into the station, opening the rift on top of us. A menacing grey storm cloud with purple-black flashes of intracloud lightning billows through the gaping rift. The Haddyc appears to be hesitant to move towards the growing flock of wings.

Crystal ngars along the wings flash brightly, channeling the pilots' divination. Beams of the powerful force cut into the storm, locking segments of the cloud's body in cascades of sparkling crystals. Long, thin needles of tightened storm cloud suddenly jab out from the depths of the storm. A spear whips out and connects with a cluster of wings. It breaches their prismatic shields with incredible force. The holographic wings flash red before being replaced with fireballs that flash and become wreckage.

The wings move into another formation. Purple-black lightning crawls through the maelstrom. The storm attacks again and again, and each lightning bolt is skirted by the wings, a lightning-dodging murmuration. Another larger blast flies out of the storm, electrical leaders step outward in several directions spreading toward the wings. Some of the wings are knocked around or fall out of formation completely, their shields scraping each other. Several are hit, disabled, or destroyed in purple-black flashes and orange fireballs.

While the Haddyc is occupied with the wings, we collectively astral project ourselves, and like stowaways riding on its thoughts, we rise into the extra-dimensional being's mindfield. Our bodies remain present in the Haven, witnessing the skirmish via hologram, but we are also in the mind of the storm. We are met with the scent of brine and burning sulfur.

The scent of a Haddyc, Yahima transfers, seemingly to me alone. *Takes some getting used to.*

I try to silence my disgust and urge to turn away.

I get the sense that Yahima is watching over me because of my limited experience with stepping into the mindfield of such a powerful being. Yahima directs my awareness, and I notice that the space we have astral-projected into, the EDB's mind, is textured. Semi-transparent, rippling waves of resistance hang in the space around us, brushing forcefully against our astral projections. The waves grind against our astral projections trying to prevent us from moving through the EDB's psychic barrier. We push against the waves of resistance, and they succumb to our insistence. We break through them, moving further into the storm's mind.

We feel something else building in the Haddyc: fear and rage. The being senses uninvited guests and immediately attacks us. A blast rushes toward us through the mindfield and somehow into the physical space of the Haven. Ripples of metal and ash rip through the air around our bodies.

An EDB has never been able to physically reach into the Haven. Until today.

The flying debris cuts through the air and into skin. All hold fast, repelling the assault. Three of us are injured. Our concern finds their pain and soothes them as their healing factors begin repairing their bodies. A sphere grows from the Sages to cover and shield our physical bodies from the swirling debris.

Low-thunder crashes down on us in the EDB's mindfield. Alone we would be shaken, but together, we find steadiness and begin to disarm the thunder. We disable the lightning attacks on the ships. The next blast is course redirected into implosion through the gaseous colony of organisms that make up the storm's body.

It roars in response.

Near the rift, wings sweep past any ebbs of the storm invading our world. Their chargers flash, making direct hits, and the remaining cloud jerks away as its crystalized remains drift out into open space. In spite of the storm pulling itself through the rift, the murmuration of wings corrals the otherworldly tempest.

The Sages call forth from us, and we give our divination to them. A cascade of spectral radiance pours from us, into the Sages. Their skin lights up as the light bounces around in their bodies, where they redirect it down into the crystal plinths and into the Scire's primary charger. The effulgence around the Sages shifts to become a spectral wheel of all light, sorting beams of ruby, saffron, gold, jade, azure, indigo, violet, and white. All lights swirl as they are reordered around and within the Sages.

The station's shield parts over the primary charger, a transforming network of crystal ngars opening like the layered petals of a lotus. Ops opens the channel. The Sages release. We open a brilliant vortex of swirling divination shot from the primary charger, across space, towards the killer storm. Wings part as the beam of colorful divination surrounds the Haddyc, forcing the maelstrom into the channel.

The atmosphere of the Haven is filled with effulgent white light again. The debris that had been bouncing off of our shield has disappeared, yet we maintain the sphere as a precaution. One of the Level Fours seems as if they are about to fall away. It's an independent contractor who was injured before we could get shielded. She starts to drop, and we all feel a collective lurch before two of the other Level Fours catch her and assist her stabilization. With the help of our comps at their stations, we re-settle ourselves.

We watch the maelstrom still trying to pull its way through the rift, even with the channel of light surrounding it. We reach into its mindfield again, agitating its desire to push free. From the other end of the channel, we reach vibrant multi-colored threads of divination into the storm, where they hook into its body. It struggles to push the rest of its cloud-body through the rift. We pull, using its own momentum against it. A golden ring of light flashes through the Haddyc's mindfield, and suddenly, it billows away from the rift towards the station. Ops hits the charger again, and bolts of white light, our divination channeled from the Haven, spread across the borders of our light-channel. A magnificent fractal pattern spreads across and crystalizes the light. The two ends of the channel are sealed, trapping the raging sentient storm inside a giant crystal chamber, floating in space.

Comps and Ops hail all crew.

"Haddyc contained."

A wave of joyful release moves through us. It almost topples me. Yahima rests their gaze on me, and I follow them, as they teach me to ride the wave. I'm reminded of catching my first ocean wave, learning to surf on the California coast. When it passes, we refocus our astral projections in the Haddyc's mindfield.

Others around me quell their elation and relief, but my excitement lingers.

Interesting, the youngest of the Sages, Arun, gently transfers to me. *Level Three?* There's something coming from him that I cannot gather, so I open wider to him. He transfers the amazing sound and feeling of his laughter.

He transfers to me, *Look there and there.*

I see within me building impressions of excitement tinged with aggression.

Arun watches as Franxis' support anchors me and allows me to clear the impressions which have shifted my obscurations up where they could disrupt the flow of my divination.

You are uncertain? I'm not sure what he means. *Still?*

My insecurities flash before me, and I see Usain, his face soft and sweet, his face poisoned and enraged, his neck bent and broken.

I feel this pain too. He means my pain.

I'm afraid he will quell it, but instead, he gently highlights it, sending compassion.

As the Sages lengthen the psybridge, the pale effulgent light around us flickers with as we move deeper into the mind of the extra-dimensional threat. I worry that the Haddyc will reach its physical storm of sharp debris back into the Haven, but Yahima assures me that the physical threat is contained.

We move our consciousness, our psychic avatars, along the psybridge, astral-projecting into the crystal chamber to face the Haddyc. With the storm at one end of the crystal chamber, we gather at the other. The foul smell of rot seems to penetrate my brain.

Yahima transfers, *Stay close, our minds are still at risk here.*

Amidst the glimmering facets of huge crystals extending in from the chamber borders, the violent cloud draws into itself. Thunder rocks the crystal, and purple-black lightning breaks through an eddy. Three bolts hit our prismatic shield where they are absorbed, momentarily tinting the shield purple-black. Three of the Level Fours guide me in with them to learn. They shift the charge, repack it, confirm that I see how this is done, and we hold the glowing lightning bolt in wait.

Shards of metal bounce off the sphere as the whirlwind comes toward us. It sounds almost like rain until the vortex pulls the shards back into the space around the densest parts of the maelstrom to reshape them into larger chunks which come down with crashes. The bombardment continues again and again. Each time the rocks are reshaped bigger and bigger. The storm cloud seems smaller and smaller, until giant, pointed stone columns crash and break against the sphere. The broken storm falls to the base of the crystal, perhaps too big to rise up again having spent so much energy.

As much of its mass lies immobilized below us the whirlwind slows, and we see into its center.

An ashen humanoid body of dense substance hovers near the top of the crystal chamber. Aside from a crown of starfire, most light somehow bends around it as if it is unable to touch the surface of the body.

What is this? one of the Sages whispers.

Never has an extra-dimensional being present as humanoid.

Even the Sages are afraid.

A collective jolt of sharp terror unsettles us, as the ashen body shrieks. The mind-piercing sound is like bending and breaking metal, coarse and alarming. The shriek amplifies our fears, agitating our connections to our comps. I feel Franxis straining to anchor me.

The astral projections of three divs fall away, and their nimbuses clatter against the collective above as they tumble out of place and vanish. A vacuum is created in the broken formation. The lurch unsettles someone else. Hunter drops away, and part of me envies his departure. That same part of me wishes I didn't have this horror in my mind.

It peers at me and tilts its head slightly, and I'm gripped by the fear of an EDB looking into me. There is more to the being standing before us. Its shadow lands in a dimension far away, and it is the shadow of the storm that threatens our world. The Shadow looks into my mind with familiarity. It sees something it wants, something I have.

No one else seems to sense the monster's cold stare. I feel alone and afraid.

Franxis reaches for me. *You're not alone,* they transfer.

I focus on my breath and shape my hands into a mudra to release distraction. I quell the noise and signal to Franxis that I'm stabilizing. Franxis reaches for me and pulls, anchoring me within myself. I project my gaze up as the Haddyc's shriek dwindles.

It looms, as if hooked onto the rays of the starfire crown piercing through the dome of its head. Something moves within the starfire.

I glimpse ornaments floating amongst the starfire. Most of them are obscured by the light. A golden ring around something like a festoon orbits the crown. Movement in the periphery of my vision! A familiar wavering of space, a flicker of movement minus mover, distracts me. A prick of light from the crown flashes, and sears into my forearm like a molten needle.

I realize that I was reaching for the ring.

I fall, clutching my arm, almost losing my hold helping keep the lightning bolt in place. The pain burns away a part of me, making space for something else.

I glean a thought from one of the other divs: *Why do we have a Three in here?*

The ornaments! I hail everyone in the sphere, Sages too—I gather that they did not see them. *Don't reach for them!*

Nearby divs and Franxis stabilize me with tenderness.

Yahima turns toward me, eyes wide, assessing any damage, any risk. They aid me in shielding the other divs from my pain. Yahima's support is enough to encourage me to be with the pain to let it bring me focus.

I look toward the being's face, and all my stability is lost. Like stretched to breaking skin, the ash and dust peel away from its no-face. A mirror-mask of reflective gold turns down on me.

Some force yanks my mind, sending a painful jolt through my astral projection and into my physical body. The mirror-mask. Terror swells in me as I watch my screaming reflection slip around the curve of the reflective surface.

Don't look at its face! both of the Elder Sages yell in unison.

Through the dull aura around the Haddyc, several of us have already caught glimpses of our faces in its mirror mask, and we are being vexed.

Pain flares. My tortured memories surge. Usain, neck twisted, face enraged, our home crumbling. Fighting. Arguing. Pushing him away but wanting to keep him close. Screaming. Patterns from previous relationships overlap. Fighting. Drug misuse. My father's hatred and hands in fists pummeling my head. His grip on my neck, spit on his lips, "Oughtta break your fucking neck! You don't belong in my house!" Hatred within me.

The mirror mask pulls at my history, exploits my wounds, my hurt. The trauma that remains in my body is alive and amplified. I am overwhelmed with the burden of carrying that pain. I wish only to be free of it.

Some force reaches in, I sense not the relief of resolving that pain, but a tearing away of the mental structures built to begin healing. My reality is pulled apart by the wicked force. Perception of the world built on personal justification cracks, nearly collapses. I begin to feel lost within my own mind. I watch aspects of my identity-matrix slipping away. Any orientation made from experience is in danger of being stolen. Awareness of myself begins to slide away.

Comps, divs, the Sages move to protect those of us being vexed. They reach towards me, offering care. Franxis. My heart aches.

The mirror brings to the surface my most painful memories, heaviest impressions, most unwieldy barriers. I've cleared them so many times, ignoring the hurt in them, fabricating details, burying them again and again.

I am failing, flailing.

The weight of loss buries me.

Moments and memories which had come to a halt, leaving the treads and waves in my mind to grind against them, start to loosen and become permeable. The thoughts, the wonder, the questioning, the sadness shaking my mindfield, the Sages, the divinators, the connections, Franxis, the Haven, all drop away from me suddenly.

No one is with me. For a brief moment, I am alone.

Space opens. Again I am at the center of all space. I'm shielded, supported, but this is not the Sages or my comp. It's simply there. I have felt this before.

I am Held.

From above and within, I hear the voice of Truth. This is not the last time that painful memories will seem too heavy, but I am not alone with the pain. The light-threads around my heart begin to glow, illuminating connections of my heart.

The distorted reflection of my face curves around the mirror.

I bring forth an awareness of myself, flawed, talented—a lovable loner. My potential lying in the space of my lack. My complexity. My love and appreciation of who I am. Self-compassion becomes armor. I reclaim my growth rooted in my hurt. I let my broken heart open, gaping wide.

My reflection is cast away from the mirror mask. I pour the energy of my realizations outward through the light rays of my heart. Others integrate my realizations and use them to bolster their own. They pull themselves away from the mask. Our collective power is increased as we share the energy coming from our hearts.

Deeper within myself, I see a radiant array of light beams coming together in a star at the center of my chest. Prismatic sparks glide along each light-thread. Each brilliant ray extends to other luminous hearts. My heartstar bursts into radiant light.

The being's fingers spread wide and curl in with rage as it shrieks.

What bits of crumbled stone, shards of metal, ash, and grime that can be lifted from the floor are pulled up into the hurricane gathering around its crown. Its hands tighten into fists, and a grey light swells behind the mirror. The eye of the hurricane opens and the sound of conquered worlds screaming shakes the crystal.

The injured amongst us waver, and the psybridge quivers. Above us, our nimbuses begin to slip out of formation.

As the Sages move to brace us, we reach toward each other. Empathy moves in and out of me along the beams of my heartstar. From the center of my being, synchronizing divination spirals out from me. I feel, see, and hear Franxis, people in other parts of the station or out in the wings, even the birds in the station's Avifaun Gardens. Brilliant light-threads pour from my heart to theirs. It all surges back. Ecstasy.

Franxis anchors me. I reach up for the vivid, flowing energy of Level Four. Divination pours into me.

I Rise.

Everything pulses with a low thunder *AUM*.

Others briefly Rise with me to glean divination from the upper Levels. Our power fills everything within the prismatic sphere.

Yahima transfers a call to presence and an order to release, *NOW!*

We release the divination-charged lightning bolt. Air around the energy pops as it sails through the crystal chamber. It cuts deep into the ashen being. The movement of the storm stops suddenly. Bits of metal and ash fall. Lodged within its floating body, the multi-colored lightning rages. The being tries to hold itself aloft. It screams, blaring sounds of metal bending, snapping, grinding in on itself. Its body slackens and falls.

The mirror mask cracks against the rocks of the broken storm. Grey light, like small waves of distorted reality, seep from the crack. The light of the crown flickers out like a dying fire, ornaments vanishing.

A shared impulse moves through us, and Arun very sternly calls to us, *Does it really need to be said again? Do not look at its face.*

As if it is too heavy to lift itself, the injured EDB struggles at the base of the crystal. Our attacker is defeated.

All around the crystal, the wings begin to blink their lights. They've been there the whole time, ready to crystalize as much as they could, should the storm escape the crystal chamber. I was in their position decades ago. I know they can't see our astral projections. I don't know if they see the weakly writhing humanoid body of the Haddyc. Perhaps only we see it through our astral projections inside the being's mindfield. Their lights signal to us that they see that the storm is contained and unmoving.

They signal Ops, herald comps, and we receive another rush of celebration. Franxis' joy rushes through me. Again, we ride the wave. The wave is more energy, recharging us.

We are not done.

We step back on the psybridge and look down into the crystal chamber at the being below us. A quiet, atmospheric song grows from within the two Elder Sages, the song of uncommon compassion. Only the Sages know the song. It's measured out in fractions, slowly, carefully affecting our attacker, which seems to struggle against it.

A question about healing the being we just defended ourselves against begins to arise but is appeased by Arun's smirk and narrowed eyes. He transfers a whisper: *Seriously???*

Its turns its face toward us, and we look away from the mask as a broken piece falls away. Grey light bleeds out and into the space around its face. It tries to transfer something to us, something wordless, and I glean from the Sages that they recognize the sound of Truth amidst the Shadow's commitment to devouring our world. Moments later, its head rocks to the side, and its body slowly writhes.

The Elder Sages continue calling forth the hymn of uncommon compassion.

In agony below us, amidst the fallen storm, lies the broken prince of the maelstrom.

ꝏ

"Div Casey Isaac, long time no see," Nala Young the counsel technician greets me, wheeling her chair closer. "Happy to see that you finally made it back to therapy."

"I've been given orders to be here."

"By Ops?"

"By Franxis."

Franxis and Nala exchange looks and laugh. "Well done, Franxis."

"Our old strategy of pushing aside and burying his trauma according to the old UNAF strategy has finally come back to bite us in the ass," Franxis quips.

I add, "And apparently aligning a resolution to that trauma might just help me lock in Four."

"It most likely will." Nala gestures to the suspensor chair, inviting me to lie back. "I'm glad you finally took the order. I'm required to tell you what you already know. The memory machine will force a recall of the traumatic memories that you got hung up on when the rift opened." When I'm lying back in the chair, she adds, "We'll recall the day of the First Assault by the extradimensional being known as Bakkeaux. Won't be fun."

"Never is," I sigh.

The rosy quartz dome comes down over my head. The counsel technician's deliberately calming voice and the white noise of the room's operation systems drop away. For a few moments, probably not even a full minute, the voice of expectation and hesitation, the accidental psychic interception buzzing on the periphery, even the trauma that I'm here to address, are all gone. It's quiet in my mind. It usually takes some time sitting with my legs crossed, my mind focused to get to this meditative place. Here in counsel, it happens instantly.

For just a few moments, I am pleasantly alone. But it doesn't last.

"Comfortable?" The Counselor asks, her voice tinny and distant from the old comm.

I gaze up at the wires, lights, sensors, disruptors, and emulators embedded into the quartz. Through the rosy crystal, I see the counsel technician wheel her chair away from my seat. Inside the dome, I nod and breathe deep.

Nala sets Franxis up across from my chair. She lowers another crystal dome over their head, and I gaze up into the embedded tech, growing brighter as the technician powers up the machine.

I don't want to be here. I don't want to relive the day a fucking sentient cloud ripped my life apart. But I can't have another hang up like before. My hang ups could put the entire planet at risk.

Nala says, "Most divs spend quite some time at Three."

I sigh, "That's what I keep hearing."

"You might've uncovered some things you weren't ready to by getting to Four so quickly."

"But getting to Four kinda saved the day."

"And now you have to deal with it." Her gentle hand pats my shoulder again before her wheelchair rolls back. She scans a holoscreen, taking in my emo-spec grade. "Casey, this will be easier if you just relax."

"I've heard that before. Many times," I quip with a hint of innuendo.

Franxis chuckles and shakes their head, but the joke is either lost on our counsel tech or ignored.

In her calming, counsel technician voice, Nala reminds, "You can stop this at any time. While the memories become very clear with a counsel channeler, they are only enhanced echoes of how you saw things based on who you were, giving perspective on who you are now. This will give us insights on what work still needs to be done."

"I know. I'm ready."

She nods, taps a few buttons on her holoscreen. As the power increases in the memory machine, its pull strengthens. Across from me, Franxis nods.

From the projector in the crystal dome, blue lights spin, and their beams land across my face, shining softly into my eyes.

"Spinning memory selection into view in five—" As Nala counts backwards, the machine hums louder. "Four—" I feel its pull. "Three…" The building energy sways my brainwaves. "Two…" I barrel through the hesitation, tune my mind to the memory despite the pain it will bring up. "One."

(I'm just inside the door of our apartment. We're arguing.)

The projected world around me glitches. The scene suddenly appears flat, and a blue line moves from my lower to upper periphery. I'm not sure I can hold the memory. Maybe it's too painful.

"Try to focus," the technician says. "Allow the memory recall."

I breathe deep, dive into the memory, allow the machine to pull it out and put it in front of my face. Everything around me begins to shift. Shapes lift and settle with inadequate depth. It all feels a fragile. As if I'm reaching through time to peer through my own eyes again, I see Usain. My heart aches. I know what's coming. I'll watch it happen again.

(He tells me to go. I hesitate.)

You don't have to do this alone, buddy.

Franxis is with me, watching the memory replay, offering support.

(I walk out in the open-air hallway. The light coming through the dim clouds is dingy.)

The machine hums louder. The sound keeps me anchored to the present moment, as I allow my mind to get pulled toward the past.

(A massive thunderhead rolls across the sky. It stops above the city.)

((An echo of Dr. Kavali's voice surfaces. The UNAF agents who tracked me down stand nearby, and the doctor speaks, "South Los Angeles. You were there in one of the first cities attacked. You saw the city getting torn apart—"))

Not that memory, Franxis transfers. *It's just tethered. Go back to the day of the First Attack. You were at your apartment…*

I quell the memory of my interrogation. The machine hums as flashes of audible memory pass through me. (Something like thunder tears through the sky. Broken glass, gunshots, cars crashing, wreckage falling from the sky, screaming—terrible, human, but horrified, and other screams, human, but devolved. Then, explosions, distant at first.)

You saw your neighbors. They had changed.

I bow my head and signal Franxis for more support. I encourage them to stay with me, and the machine reconstructs the scene around me. As Franxis guides, and I lean in, the visions grow strong and clear for both of us.

"What did you do when you heard your neighbors' argument become violent?" Nala asks through the comm.

"I knocked on their door."

"Even as the world was falling down around you?"

"It had just started to get weird."

(My neighbor throws their door open. They turn the unhinged rage they had for each other on me. I cannot stop them.)

"My lover, Usain, was at our door down the hall. He was on the phone with domestic violence responders, and... he closed the door. He shut me out." My stomach hollows.

(He leaves me in the hallway with raging monsters.)

"What happened then?"

"They attacked me." (I try to dodge them. These people who had been so mild mannered, so welcoming, are foaming at the mouth, clawing at me. They tear at my clothes, spitting, cursing.) "I finally punched them, trying to get them to stop, trying to get away from them." (His nose gushes blood. She swings at me, but I push her down. He grabs me from behind. He has an arm around my throat. As she is getting up, I kick her, and she falls back and hits her head. His arm around my throat tightens. I struggle to break free, to breathe. The edges of my vision go dark. He screams in pain. He drops me.)

(From my knees, I look up, gasping for air as the periphery of my sight comes back. My lover stands there with a chopping knife from our kitchenette. Blood drips down the edge of the blade. The man lunges towards Usain. Usain thrusts the knife forward. The man slumps down to the floor. He stays down.)

(As Usain helps me onto my feet, the man grabs at me again, and I kick—out of anger and frustration this time. My shoe connects with enough force behind it to crack his jaw. The sound is imprinted in my memory. His neck is gushing blood. He lays there twitching. A strange tendril, a clear sinuous vortex flows from his crown through the ceiling of the hallway. She has one too.)

(Usain is hysterical. "What is that? What the fuck is that?")

(An explosion knocks us against the exterior wall of our apartment as several floors of the building next door explode. I think that it must have been a gas leak. But there isn't much time to think when the rest of the shoddy construction starts to come down.)

(We run.)

(Usain's vehicle is parked on the platform across the street. He slings open the pilot-side door, and I yell at him. He looks hurt because of the way I yelled—as if he was foolish to think he should pilot. I feel guilty for making him feel stupid while we're running for our lives.)

I almost pull away. I clear my throat. "Everything happened so fast. We got into the SD and took off."

Franxis urges me on, sending support through our psybridge. "What did you see from your SkyDrive?"

(Bodies falling from buildings, buildings on fire. Intentional crashes on the street, SkyBikes flying into trees, buildings, people.)

(He's yelling at me. I scream at him to stop.)

I open my eyes again to find Franxis looking at me through their crystal dome. The pull of the psychic channel slows, and Nala taps the keypad to adjust the amplifier. The channel eases down.

Franxis asks, "Casey, do you want to keep going?"

I hesitate because I know what's coming, but I assent.

"Let's go back just a little. I noticed a little snag." Franxis says. *Back to the hallway and Usain.*

The snag is there preceding the violent attack. I loosen my conviction, and watch the memory smooth out, releasing tension. Usain didn't close the door and shut me out. He ran inside (the door closes behind him) to get something he could use to protect me.

Guilt floors me. I created the fabrication in an attempt to justify what I did to him.

I resist the pull of the machine, and Franxis coaxes me to continue while reminding me that I can stop if I have to.

I stop resisting and let the memory machine push me back into the story that has been so heavy that I created false memories to buffer the pain.

"He said to stay low." (I try keeping the SkyDrive closer to the street, but people are losing their minds. Crowds gather into roaring brawls. People throw things at us. Cars crash right below us. I'm afraid there will be another explosion.)

(Usain yells at me to stay low, away from the stormcloud. Other SkyDrives are flying too close. One of them clips us and we spin.)

(Against his protests, I pull up.)

(Vortexes funnel down from the cloud, reaching like tentacles. I realize what is happening. The cloud is poisoning people. It tears into their minds, and they tear into the world.)

(I see another SkyDrive in the rearview scans. A prominent vortex reaches down into the roof. I tell Usain to strap in. I bank left hard, sweep over the river, try to put some space between us and the other SD. It banks left too. It's much faster and catches us in minutes.)

(He bumps us twice, like he's toying with us.)

(I try to fly under the bridge, and he slams us. The drive rotor shields get caught on one another, and we start spinning, spiraling down.)

(Usain curses at me.)

(I think he's distressed and afraid, but when I look over, there's a vortex going down into his head. His eyes are bloodshot. His mouth is foaming. Spit flies from his lips with his vitriol, "Fucking not worth the effort! I deserve better! You don't belong with me!" He punches me hard, and I cannot quite believe it's happening—)

((My father punches me from the driver's seat. He hits me again. I try to block him. He's so much bigger than me. With one hand he drives. His other hand is on the back of my head, and he shoves it into the dash. "You don't belong in my house!"))

I hear a chime from the emo-spec monitor, and the channel shifts, moves within me, and I'm back to the day of Bakkeaux's first attack. For the first time, I remember clearly.

(Some darkness moves across my mind, and a novel fear fills me. I look up past the swirling vortexes into the cloud. The cloud looks back at me, into me. But it's not just the cloud that sees into me. Something sinister, made of shadows, looks into me from worlds away... and it sees something it wants.)

(Usain slams my face before I think to put my arm up and block. The knife! He jabs the knife at me repeatedly, and I try to deflect it away from my chest with my arm. My forearm is sliced, then my shoulder, then behind my ear. I think he's going to get my neck next.)

(I struggle to defend myself and pilot the SkyDrive.)

(Usain hisses strained vitriol, and I fumble with the controls.)

(I have to get away from him—or get him away from me.)

There's an obscuration. It won't budge.

(The roof blows. His seat shoots out and away. Usain's head hits the side of the bridge, bending his neck too far. The vortex is whipped back into the cloud. His limp body, strapped into the chair, falls, and sinks into the river. The parachute slips underwater behind him.)

(I strain to scream, but it's lodged in my throat.)

(Hung up on each other, the SkyDrives spin towards a massive pillar supporting the bridge.)

(I unbuckle my seat belts, and careful to not get bumped by the spiraling wreckage, I slide out of the SkyDrive.)

I resist going further. I open my eyes to meet Franxis' compassionate gaze.

Our counsel tech lifts the crystal domes back away from our heads.

My third eye tingles lightly. I pinch my brow, tighten my eyes enough to hold back tears. "I can't. I know there's an obscuration, but I can't move it."

Franxis hands me another tissue. "We should ease you down."

I take the tissue, but the usual tears don't come. I feel steady, as if I can let the weight of the memories fall behind me.

They already know the answer, but to prep me for the next session, Franxis asks me, "How long did it take to get out of the city?"

I smile softly. "Three tough days."

They wink at me. "You were lucky to find me, buddy. Happy we made it out together, and that you've made it to where you are now." Franxis layers multiple meanings into their words: where I am… on the station, my role in protecting the planet, my orientation towards post-traumatic growth. I gather all of this not from transference, but through the tone of their voice, through the mutual understanding between us.

To ease me out of the memory recall process, Franxis and I refrain from transference or signaling. The counsel emulators near my head hum, soothing my brain with shifting frequencies.

Nala shifts the conversation to current concerns. "What will you do if you don't lock in Four?"

"Maybe work with div-tech on another ship that Ops won't let me fly."

More scrolling sounds on the screens behind me.

"Not everyone can pull tech-specific knowledge down from the upper levels."

"Truthfully, I would get bored if I was stuck with tech the whole time. Maybe everyone feels that way about their secondary assignments." With each honest answer the counseling technology, soothes our minds.

"Are you bored in your current position?" Nala prods me, trying to nudge me past my tendencies to deflect or crack jokes or direct the conversation.

Franxis grins as they sense all the jokes coming up in my mind, and it amuses me.

I answer honestly. "More like worried. Lots of people getting transferred off station lately. And I've been getting passed up for assignments for a long time. Probably because it took so long for me to even get to Three."

"Are you still worried now that you're at Four?" Nala asks.

Franxis' expression is neutral.

I shrug as emphasis. "I've been messed up a long time. I'm dragging a lot of my past around with me."

Franxis nods gently. "You're not the only one."

Our psybridge hums, and the Counsel technology chimes to signal the strength of our psychic connection.

As Nala refills my tea, she asks, "Casey, does having Franxis as your comp ever bring up any memories of the day you met? Any trauma that might stall you?"

I hesitate. "Sometimes. But I power through."

She slightly winces at my answer while typing on her holoscreen. "And has it been that way for all one hundred and eight years?"

"Yes, but like I said, only sometimes." I smile towards Franxis, and they smile back. "It's not a problem."

Nala nods and forces a smile. "Divs and comps with strong bonds often process trauma together. It often helps to have other assistance as well. That's what Counsel is here for. I am happy you took the recommendation—or orders, as you say."

Franxis laughs.

I drink my tea, grateful for the taste and the feeling of the warm cup.

Nala begins a series of personal, casual questions designed to help further dial down the effect of the memory machine.

"Are you dating anyone, Casey?" she asks.

Franxis snorts.

I again dismiss the prescient vision I had before the Haddyc encounter, and I answer, "Not going to any time soon."

Nala's smile is unguarded. "It can be nice to have someone who cares about you."

"I thought you do care," I try to look hurt. "You care, don't you, Franxis?"

Franxis gives me a sardonic shrug, and I feign insult.

Nala smiles too. "I mean not just Franxis or me. Someone not assigned—"

"Up here?"

"—to a specific capacity of relationship. Someone who is not filing reports on you. Someone who helps you see yourself—just because they see you."

I laugh lightly, shake my head, and change the subject. "Why didn't you go into defense?" I ask, unsure if it's too personal for the first personal question to ever ask a person. Multiple sessions and I know so little about her.

She wheels her chair closer. "I worked as a therapist before Bakkeaux. I volunteered to help Risen survivors, and because I had Risen as well, I could understand what they were going through. I had a chance to go into defense, but Sages determined I only had potential to reach Two. The new space program wasn't accepting any combat divs predicted to top off on such a low level, so I put in a request to join as a counselor. Central accepted. And here we are."

I smile, nodding. "They probably wouldn't have accepted me if they knew it would take me so long to level up. Not sure Helixx Corp will keep me around."

She leans forward, and I'm surprised by the amount of compassion in her eyes. "Casey, no one goes through what you've been through without a considerable amount of trauma. It will get better."

I nod again, just once. "Sure."

Franxis smiles softly, and I feel the steadiness of Level Four. I glimpse a glimmering thread of light between Franxis and me, connecting our glowing hearts at the center of our chests. I glimpse another glimmering light-thread from my heart to Nala's. I see that she cares, and I decide to tell her something I've been holding back.

"There is this moment after I hit the water and sank down, right before I pulled myself back towards the surface. I'm weightless. Space around me opens. I am at the center of all spaciousness, not held by the water. Just… held."

I pause there.

"That's something you kept out of your file…" Counselor's eyes scan behind me, and I hear the spinning and scribing sound of the display projector, scanning documents, probably personal info, communications. "No mention of that at all in Central's records."

"First time I've told anyone other than Franxis."

Franxis nods encouraging me to continue.

"At first, I wondered if I had imagined it. There wasn't time to really process every little detail. Then I thought it was just the moment my body stopped moving down, before I swam back up, buoyancy resisting downward force… Later, I couldn't shake the feeling of being held… There was nothing around me, no water, no chaos. Just being held. And I heard a voice. Not speaking in language… but in Truth."

"What did the voice… say?" She shrugs.

"No words, no visions, just Truth poured into me, through me. Knowing that I was here." I point to the spot under my feet.

Nala lifts her eyebrows. "With me? On Station Scire orbiting the Earth?"

Franxis sends me the essence of a full embrace through our psybridge.

"More like, I knew I was far away from that day and all that was happening. I knew I would not only survive, but that I would go on to live in a way very different than before… Without seeing details, I knew that I would live a greater purpose... as a divinator."

ꝏ

My delight in having reached Level Four is tempered by a light sense of dread over the recent corporate purchase of the station. This place has been more of a home than almost anywhere planetside ever was.

I look at my comm, staring blankly at the message that I had been dreading opening all day. I berate myself for opening it now instead of later. The first line of the message underneath the Helixx Corp logo makes my mind spin: "Divinator Casey Isaac, your upcoming performance and positioning assessment is scheduled..."

I look up and see a group of twenty divinators and comps walking side by side down the corridor towards the nearest shuttle harbor. I recognize every single man from their Joynr profiles, although I don't know their names. I only know that their profiles say that they are interested in dating men.

A few of the women and enbies are vaguely familiar. I think I met them briefly through Franxis during one of their attempts to help me make friends. I suspect all twenty folks are Queer. Their civilian clothes and carryalls are sure signs that they're leaving Station Scire and not coming back.

There are rumors that Helixx Corp is getting rid of Station Scire's Queer population. Never mind they've defended the planet from this station for a long time. A lot of people suspect homophobia, but there is one rumor that it has nothing to do with it. Some say that a Helixx Sage has predicted catastrophe folding out from a group of Queer divinators.

I sigh, power off the comm, try to ignore the message. I'm ready for my distraction to open his door.

I catch a glimpse of my face in the window reflection. I brush the swoop of ruddy, brown hair back from my forehead. My pale skin needs more sun, even artificial, but I look pretty good for a hundred and forty years old. Physically, my face looks much the same as it did when I was thirty-two. Somehow, my divination keeps entropy at bay while allowing refinement.

My mind drifts toward the First Assault, and I feel Level Four lurch as if it is inches from slipping away. I tell myself to be present and calm. From far away, Franxis helps me stabilize my Levels. I worry that Four will slip away before I can lock it into place.

As I look out the window, down at the night-side surface of the planet, I sigh heavily. I feel both impatient and annoyed with myself for repeating this pattern which I've realized is not entirely satisfying. It's a distraction from my worries, a quick relief from the painful memories. It's an easy fix but very temporary.

I check the time on my comm, wondering when he's going to open the door. What is his name? Fuck. I swipe through the comm, looking for the Joynr app, trying to access his profile quickly.

Just when I don't want it to, his door slides open.

Whatever his name is sticks his very attractive face out, looks up and down the busy hallway. He sees me and grins. When I step into the doorframe, I see him in a robe held tight in front so none of the late shift technicians or tourist distans bots might get a peek.

The door slides closed behind me.

He dims the lights as I step towards him. A genuine grin slowly stretches across his lips as he drops his robe to the floor. His cologne is probably expensive, but I've never been a fan of synthetic commercial fragrances. "Hello again, Casey Isaac."

Shit, he even remembers my last name. "Hey," I say, extremely grateful that I'm close enough to him to bring my lips toward his and end our conversation.

He weaves his face aside, dodging my lips, even as he lets me pull him closer. "Not on the lips. It's in my profile. Remember?" He runs his hands under my shirt as he presses his naked body against me. His hands slip down below my waist band. "Told you what I want. Remember?"

Just in case, I raise my obscurations. I don't want him to accidentally glean any of the thoughts I'm trying to avoid or hear me trying to recall his name.

I tell myself again, just like I've told myself over and over. This is purely physical pleasure, a bit of fun. But it's not. I've known for a long time that this is my avoidance pattern. But that doesn't stop me. I want to avoid the stirred up memories, the worry about my future on the station.

I would say he helps me out of my clothes, but really, he just pulls my pants down around my ankles. I start to step out of the pants, but he's already on his knees. He reminds me of what he said he wanted, what I said I wanted, and I begin to appreciate his wordless reminder. I drop my shirt to the floor. I tell him that his mouth feels fucking amazing, but it sounds performative.

After only a few minutes, he's up, grinning, guiding me towards the nearby bed, pulling me down on top of him, between his legs. He brings his legs up but not around me, and I give him what we both want until we don't want it anymore.

"That was good," he says flatly as he gets up and steps into the lavatory.

Level Four tips ever so slightly, and I psychically reach to catch it, accidentally accessing an urge for a heart-felt connection. "Do you think the good sex has something to do with our divination? Maybe this job too? Feels good to fuck a hero." My heart feels open, and I'm compelled to share. "Even if I don't see myself that way. Just another guy who helped save humanity." Level Four has my heartstar glowing, feeling eager for a connection that I don't actually want... Wait. Do I want it?

He comes back with his comm in hand, scrolling through Joynr. "Sorry, I wasn't listening."

"Oh, good." I feel a rush of connection between our hearts as Level Four begins pouring down more power, and he looks at me with a smile. "Ooh. No." I do not want to amplify anything between our hearts. I scramble to get dressed.

He stops paying attention to me. He's focused on Joynr, potentially finding another match for tonight. Maybe neither of us is satisfied.

I know I'm nowhere near contentment. Contentment could help lock in Level Four, giving me more control of how to connect, avoiding this sudden, risky flush of feeling between my heart and what's his name's. The key is to be content with just about everything: the Level I'm on, where I am in personal relationships, with slowly realizing that maybe I'm done with the sex-feast and ready for a sex-fast.

I'm finally out the door, pulling on my shirt while a couple of women down the hallway laugh sympathetically in my direction. They think I'm dashing out after a quickie, which isn't untrue. But it's Level Four messing with my heart that's got me on the run.

I reach towards Franxis, who moves their psychic energy through my mind with joy. They laugh as they stabilize me, and my heart feels less vulnerable again. Just as quickly, they move back into a subtle presence, giving me space and privacy.

For some time, I've been ignoring the idea of a sex-fast that has been coming together at the edges of my mind. But the idea persists.

I can smell his synthetic fragrance on my skin.

I cannot deny that I feel unsatisfied. It's always the same with anyone lately. "Lately" is mis-leading, I realize. It's been this way for a while, for years. The sex-fast idea moves further into place, becomes a decision.

"This is for the best," I tell myself, as I take out my comm. I temporarily suspend my Joynr profile.

I decide to not have sex with anyone for at least three months. I tell myself I can go to the meditation halls more than required, work out more, start running on the outer rings of the station. Maybe I can lock in Level Four before my worries and unresolved trauma cause me to regress. Maybe I'll put in a transfer to one of the UNAF stations.

But first I need to shower off what's his name's cologne.

The hallway quietly buzzes with activity. Talk is kept to a minimum and none of the noisier remodeling is taking place during the night cycle. Dozens of technicians work to upgrade, modify, remove, or replace the station's old systems. None of them wear the circlets that would spare their minds from a sudden EDB attack. Then again, this station is usually the last called into action, and it's been that way for a long time. Emblazoned across the back and over the heart of each uniform are the words Helixx Corp. Each x is a double helix—hence the two x's.

I remember the moment when I stepped away from Franxis and the crowd huddled around giant screens, looking at the livestream of giant architecture being locked together between the Earth and the moon. I had stepped outside alone onto the tarmac and looked up into the night sky to see the cluster of bright lights shine down the moment Scire went online. I knew then where I wanted to be.

Down the hallway, the technicians have most of the wall panels open, exposing wires. Floating holographic screens in front of one of the technicians get swiped aside as he grumbles, "Why didn't Helixx just build their own station?"

The tech next to him tugs at a conduit plug stuck in a socket. "I hear GHF's coming back to the sector," she sighs. "Maybe no time to build another station."

"She ain't livin' in this dump. I wouldn't even live here." They laugh.

The comment shifts my perception of the place. I see the station as if I haven't really looked at it in seventy years. The design is retro-futuristic but happening right now. It's outdated. It's what we used to think the future would look like long ago. I pass by the empty planters which once held vibrant greenery, now, sealed with a dull cap. The colored lines along the floor with red directing anyone following it to medical, green to the agriculture and parks areas, blue to domestic quarters, yellow to Ops, and so on, all look scuffed and faded under seventy years of foot traffic. The irony makes me smile. Div-tech can set a small floating city—more like a village—into the Earth's orbit, but they forgot to create durable colored markings for direction.

Ultra-high definition screens are being taken out of the walls. They'll soon all be replaced with holoscreens, which the other three stations have had for decades. One of the technicians glances towards me as he and his coworker toss the perfectly fine screen into a large trash bin. I hear it crack, and almost stop to tell them how dangerous broken glass could be if we have to go into low or no gravity mode, but I hear them lock the lid down on the bin.

One of them cocks his head in my direction and whispers to the other. "A little swish in his step?"

I speak loudly so he can hear me down the hallway. "Swish?" I smirk and tilt my head towards their surprised faces. "You know, most divs have enough enhanced hearing to pick up on your musty homophobia."

They grumble and quickly turn back to their work.

I'm not even sure why I said anything. It's not like I care what they think, but maybe the rumors about Helixx Corp firing divs just because they're Queer have gotten me fired up. It's the fucking future. We should've been done with this shit long ago.

I keep my head up, but the mockery, the audacity, the insinuation—albeit correct, all get my head spinning. I can hear my father sneering at me for the swish in my childhood gait.

(I want to be alone.)

Technicians have the shade switched off the big window ahead. The moon floats silently nearby. Lights of the industrial cities, mining colonies, shipyards, crystal generation facilities, glitter the cratered lunar surface.

"Lilly?" I call to my personal AI in my housing unit.

Her chipper voice comes through my comm. "I'm here to help."

I lift my forearm and launch a small holoscreen. "Show personal images, 2029." I scroll through the photos, knowing what's coming, and will my mind to stay calm.

The holoscreen displays Usain's handsome face, big nose, dark eyes, thick lashes. His lips, his smile. As I gaze at his face, many memories get triggered, and most of them are unwieldy.

"You seem sad, Casey." Lilly says.

I quip, "Well, it's only been a little over a century."

The recall is difficult, but after counseling, it feels easier to move through. I notice my heartstar expanding above my hollowed gut. A hint of forgiveness. The past is allowed to land and settle with grace. I inhale slowly; sigh deeply.

We took the picture ourselves, both of our faces are close to the camera, to each other, doesn't matter where we were. He looks so happy and carefree, relaxed in our closeness.

The pattern of self-incrimination occupies my mind. I feel the urge to turn away from these feelings, open the dating app, find someone to fuck just to feel something other than this unwieldiness. I'd been so complacent about my avoidance pattern only months ago. It makes its lines from one emotion-laden thought to another and back around, having been reinforced by avoiding the past over and over.

Something is different. My heartstar glows as I realize that I don't want the avoidance pattern, and I see the old pattern beginning to dissolve in places. There's a strong appreciation for the feeling of sexual energy and the pleasure of giving it away. There's absolutely no shame for my past landing into this pattern, but I feel a healthy regret for having used sex to avoid my hurt and myself.

I gaze down at the picture again. This time, I notice the smile on my own face, the happiness in my own eyes, but there is a tightness, a discomfort in being so close to Usain. There's no way to stop the oncoming memories. All I can do is hide the emotions, prevent my reactions. My mind is a whirlwind. I tell myself that it's okay, I can't control the weather.

"Fuck." I say the word louder than I wanted to. The technicians working nearby jerk their heads towards me, but unlike the last two, their eyes seem kind. "Sorry," I mumble.

I sigh, taking one more look at the picture, and I find within myself mercy and forgiveness. My heartstar is glowing, and I am almost afraid of the unfamiliar feelings.

There's a pull, a shift, as I realize that my heart is open to myself, and my mind moves into a space of clarity. I know I'm done with the avoidance pattern for a bit. I'm not interested in getting close to anyone, even just for sex. I'm shifting my strategy to be even more of a loner, another avoidance technique, but I also see potential. It's a faster track to what I want. Without the distraction, I can train harder, refine my div-enhanced abilities, lock in Four—that way I'm more likely to get a transfer to another station.

I'll give the sex-fast three months, maximum.

If I'm not on assignment or leveled up to Four after that, at least breaking the fast will be fun.

A new before and after is coming.

I close the holoscreen and gaze out the window, staring at the lunar surface. With all of the industrial lights on its surface, I can no longer see the man in the moon.

ꝏ

In the Avifaun Gardens while watching some warblers play, Franxis nudges my arm. "This isn't what you want to hear, but Ops won't likely be putting you back on assignment soon."

"Not surprising considering I stopped going to counseling weeks ago."

"I thought counseling was working."

"Seeing Usain that way… With the memory recall tech, it's like I'm there. It's too much. Besides, I'm at Four now. I've done enough trauma work to get here, and I just need a break from the heavy lifting."

"Ops is concerned that there is something off because you moved through Three at ten times the rate that you moved through One and Two. Also, the Sages have confirmed what Ops is picking up on: your Level Four is far from locked in." Franxis shrugs their narrow shoulders.

"Don't you love accompanying an anomaly?" I look back at Franxis and flash a cartoonish smile. "I move through Levels unlike any other divs. I take the fast ones slowly, the slow ones fast. No wonder Ops doesn't know what to do with me."

"Let's not let that bring you down. You're at Level Four, buddy! Maybe you're catching up. This sex-fast might be working after all." We stroll past several other divs and comps. Franxis waves to some of them, but I don't recognize anyone. "It's been a whole month and not even a quickie. How is life as a celibate monk?"

"Well, I still jerk off, so I'm not a monk," I say, smiling before I remember who I'm talking to and how quickly they'll see the deflection. "Yet."

"Pretty sure a lot of monks jerk off, but you're less fun lately, for sure."

"Monks can be fun."

"Not if you want to get under their robes."

"Do you want to get under my robes, Franxis?"

"No. Emphatically. I was referring to your general mood. You've been more closed off than usual."

"I can get robes…"

"Get back in counseling instead."

"Now, who's no fun?"

The ends of their thin mustache curve up with their sweet smile. Their mullet—which they insist is a modern update on a classic hairstyle—is freshly coiffed. Through their comp-bridge, Franxis catches me admiring them, seeing them as cute, and they raise an eyebrow, fold their arms across their small breasts.

"Stop trying to distract me. Your charms can work on a lot of folks, but for the asexual crowd, we're just annoyed."

"Oh! Do you speak for all aces now, buddy?" I quip.

With a sigh, Franxis sees right through my second attempt at changing the subject.

Their comp-bridge divulges the subtle thoughts in my mind.

"Can't hide anything from you," I say with admiration.

"Nope. Even if I weren't your comp with access to your mind, I'm your friend. I'm here to walk alongside you, steadying you, helping you discern your next best step."

I cheerily quip, "Lucky me."

"I know."

I smile, but it fades quickly. "I am lucky to have you."

"Right? So… more counseling." Franxis looks typically insistent about this subject. "Most divs spend decades moving from Three to Four. It's usually the transition that takes the longest. And you just might be able to lock in Four if you work through that obscuration around Usain's death."

I wince. "Maybe I can lock it in despite the obscuration."

Several bright yellow birds land on a nearby branch. The chirp to each other playfully. The gardens are meant to be a place of respite and calm, but I feel anxious.

Franxis continues their campaign, "You've gotten to Level Four—even if it's not locked in—after only a few years at Three. That's probably, most likely–okay definitely because you've been working with your trauma. I know counseling sessions can be intense, buddy. But you really seem happier when you do the work. If you work through even a little bit of your trauma…"

"If I hadn't, I wouldn't be here with you on this lovely day." I turn my face up again to the very convincing but holographic blue sky and false sun rays. I notice the net, thin but present, keeping the birds from flying into what looks like a blue sky. I feel a hint of heartache for the birds in this enclosed space. Their ancestors never volunteered for a space program, and yet, here they are helping bio-diversify the green space and therefore helping make all life on the station more sustainable. They are pretty prisoners, possibly unaware of their cage.

"You've come a long way from where you were. You helped save the world multiple times."

"Just Earth. No biggie," I say sarcastically.

"Think of how much further you could go if you'd just unburden yourself a bit."

"Easier said than done, my comp." Using their job description makes this less casual, but I'd rather we call it like it is at this moment. This isn't just a conversation between two friends. This is our work: invasive, but loyally accepted.

"Yes, dear div, but also, easier done with help." Franxis is calling it like it is. They have a job to do, but they also care. As Franxis takes my hand, I glimpse a trace of a light-thread from their heart to mine becoming luminous blue with compassion.

Franxis psychically reaches toward me, disarms my sarcasm and my diversions just by being present. The small tears that hang in the corners of my eyes can't get wiped away, because Franxis holds both of my hands, and also, I'm trying my damnedest to ignore them. I look aside and blink a few times. Our light-thread highlights a hint of our shared experience, our shared trauma. Franxis proves their point by wordlessly reminding me that they have worked with their own trauma, becoming more confident for it. We both signed up for these roles to prevent that trauma from happening to other people.

I sigh, but Franxis keeps holding my hands and gazing into my eyes until I speak. "I'm afraid of counsel, because going in with you means certain memories might be more intense. I don't know if I can handle it." I speak faster: "Also, I've worked hard to avoid those memories for a hundred years, and I've gotten pretty good at it."

"Have you though?"

Can't hide anything from Franxis.

We step across the bridge over the water. Song-birds glide across our path, and watching them move seemingly with so little effort, I know it is time to take Franxis' advice.

"Want to walk to the gallery?" Franxis asks.

"Let's go before you make me cry again," I joke as I put an arm around their shoulder.

ꝏ

We walk quietly, closely towards the long ringed gallery between the residential levels and work areas. We stop for coffee along the way.

"In my personal session, Counsel said she thinks it would be beneficial for us to chat one on one about when we met."

"Y'all talk about me when I'm not there?" I say with mock flattery.

Franxis pretends to be annoyed with me. At least, I think they're pretending. "Not just about you. She's my Counsel too. Although, I hadn't seen her for a while until your sessions started. After that, I started going solo."

We take our coffees down the gallery to one of the long settees. Several other small groups or pairs are there as well. All of the metaglass windows are unshaded, and despite the heavenly bodies all around us, we're all looking at only two things: the rift that hangs open like none other ever recorded and the giant crystal that contains a yet unkillable, extradimensional threat.

"Didn't know you've been seeing counsel solo. You okay, buddy?"

"Oh, yeah, I'm fine." They pause, glance away, and quip. "It's more you."

"As long as you didn't talk about my romantic life."

They laugh.

"Romantic is not the word I'd use for it."

They change the subject. "A lot more people here than I expected."

"Few of us have ever seen a rift, much less one that won't close." I sit back on the bench and hold our coffees as Franxis reconfigures settings on the new floating holoscreen. We gaze ahead through the metaglass that separates us from outer space, a dense but clear barrier between us and the mysterious opening between worlds.

Along the gallery, several other small groups are using the new holoscreens to get a better view of the rift or the crystal chamber. I look around at the gathering crowd and notice that our numbers have significantly dwindled since the corporate takeover.

A group of four independent contractors in black and pink uniforms gather together at one of the screens. A tall, heavyset fellow with red hair and freckles looks back over his shoulder at me, and I turn away. When I glance back, a woman with grey tribal tattoos across her ruddy, dark skin sneers at me.

"Who are the indies in black and pink?" I ask.

"Crew of The Queen. Contracted for all of the transfers. They refuse to leave without their crewmate, the Level Four injured during the Haddyc encounter." Franxis casually adds, "The Queen is S-class if you want to go check it out later."

"So I can see the empty docking stations? No thank you. I'd rather not see the glaring reminder of my failure to design working pod-ships." I sip my bitter coffee. "Thought S-class was decommissioned."

"No, production stopped because no one wanted to buy them without the pod ships and hyperspeed CEA."

"Guess there's not a lot of demand for incomplete ship designs."

"That's not all on you. Scire tech has been working on hyperspeed engines for a while. Last month, they announced that they're very close, but hyperspeed is still not a thing yet."

"But even when it is, my Halos won't be. Without the pod-ships, the highliner still has two missing pieces."

"Maybe you'll pull down the missing pieces of the puzzle soon."

I don't have the heart to verbalize that I gave up on trying to access the knowledge of how to build the ship I could see in my mind but could never quite succeed at designing.

"Yeah, you were close," Franxis says, picking up on my thoughts. "So was Scire's div-tech with the hyperspeed engine. So close that they built the ship in advance. You'll get it eventually."

I quiet my mind. I don't want to think or talk about failures. Each reminder makes me feel like my performance review will end with me being asked to leave the station, my home.

"Looks like the wings are already out," Franxis says, pulling up the radar display to see the exact distance of the ships.

Two light-wings and a crux, float in space several kilometers out, engines thrusting occasionally as they approach the crystal.

"They're still doing analysis on the Haddyc?"

"Helixx Corp has been running all kinds of secret tests all month. Probably trying to figure out why they can't kill it."

"Wish I was out there now."

"Careful what you wish for." Franxis says looking towards space beyond the ships, to the rift.

"I'm nervous about my performance assessment. I want to get back in some wings and prove myself."

"You might not have to prove anything if they keep postponing your review."

"They've rescheduled three times now."

"Probably because you moved through Three faster than anyone they've ever seen. They're maybe waiting to see how else you impress them."

"They don't seem to be keeping the best around. They've got N'guwe training her own replacement. After all her experience and dedication to this station and crew, they're sending her packing and putting a less experienced white woman in her place." I snort. "Do you think Helixx Corp is really letting go of folks like us?"

Franxis looks around and their eyes land on Hunter Bolden. "It's definitely looking more cis-white-hetero around here."

"I thought queerphobia and racism were behind the society we swore to protect."

"Maybe things are different for giant corporations in bed with the UNAF.

Helixx isn't held to the same standards out here as they would be on Earth." Franxis sighs. "Helixx wouldn't get away with this shit planetside."

"When you're as rich as Griselda Harris Ferand you can steer free of consequences." A flash of memory from my confrontation with the Helixx Corp engineers passes, and Franxis expresses concern that I wave away. "I'm fine."

"Maybe it has more to do with the other rumor."

"Which one? The one about death and destruction around a group of Queer divinators?"

"If they're following a prescient vision like that, maybe they're not queerphobic, but they are idiots. I mean, all divs face down death and destruction with every encounter. Occupational hazards."

"I can see myself fucking up so bad the world ends."

"Give me a break." They scan my mind quickly. "And stop self-depreciating. You're an excellent div. And you're at Four now."

"Is it worth it to stick with Station Scire? Maybe you should put in for a transfer to another station. They only take divs locked in at Five, but maybe if you get in, you can bring all of your divs with you, even me."

"You're my main Div, buddy. I'm not going anywhere without you."

I'm reminded of the day we met, and Franxis senses the memory too. We smile thinking of how they started stitching up my wounds only to watch them heal before their eyes. They were shocked, and I was terrified. I cried on their shoulder, and they let me. Even then, as strangers, they held me close.

Franxis and I turn our gazes back towards the glittering lights of the moon's industrial cities. Both of us feel the need for something beautiful to cushion the coming conversation, and from this far away, the lights look like glittering stardust across the lunar surface. Never mind that those lights are all over those craters so miners can strip the moon and build ships from the materials.

"Yeah, so when we met," Franxis says, sensing my need to talk about it.

"And how we met. You've seen the stories; it's been in books—"

They groan. "Conspiracy shit."

"—and there's even a UNAF file, which I'm sure you know is marked... do you ever feel or wonder that we didn't just happen to luck up and meet that day? Maybe we had been guided by someone, something... some force?"

"Oh, Casey, you're my destiny, for sure," Franxis says, raising their coffee to toast.

I usually love when they tease me.

"I'm serious."

"I'm not."

"You never question?"

"No," they say emphatically. "As you know, I was there to answer an emergency call—"

"A call I made about my neighbors."

"That was my job as a domestic disturbance responder. I wasn't there to answer a call from the Heavens—if so, why would it take people brutalizing each other to get me to you? My de-escalation training, my capacity to be present in conflict, and my meditation practice—everything that made me good for that job—was what protected me from that thing, and it was self-defense training that made it possible to defend myself from my partner when he was infected."

"And then, after your partner killed himself and left you stranded, you happened to come across an injured pilot who could fly your SkyVan."

"But that wasn't luck. It wasn't divine influence. That was… us." They look at me and smile. "Even after all that we've seen, I am still very much an atheist."

"Okay, fine." I keep prodding. "But maybe karma? Maybe the influence of some more benevolent EDB?"

"Yet to see hard evidence of either."

"Yet!" I shrug. "Stranger things, you know… We both know we were altered. Our bodies and minds were changed that day."

Franxis' voice is steady and casual even though I sense them moderating their annoyance. "I agree with the jump in evolution theory. Something kicked in when all of humanity was threatened. Like a mom lifting a car off a kid or something."

"We've been up here doing this for over a century, and we haven't aged a day since then."

Their thin mustache curves down with their exaggerated frown. "An aspect of the evolutionary jump we don't quite understand yet, but we will… much the same way we didn't understand how to make a decent coffee up here for centuries. And now?" Franxis raises their cup, winks at me, and takes a sip. "It's half-decent, we're progressing."

"Helixx Corp does have good coffee." I lift my cup as well. Cheers. I note their attempt to steer the conversation elsewhere, but I can't let it go. "But what if someone or something did the altering that day? We know it started then. Who put us on this path?"

"We put ourselves here, buddy. No doubt." Franxis squeezes my hand. "Even if you'd love to believe someone intentionally froze your handsome face at 32 to preserve your good looks."

"I'm a hundred and forty years old, and no one calls me daddy."

Franxis' deep belly laugh bounces out of them. "See. No god," Franxis says through the last waves of laughter, and I laugh loudly.

The three ships' engines brighten hot-blue with the burn off from their crystal energy arrays. The light-wings brighten their burn and pull ahead of the crux. They approach the crystal, scanners raised.

There's a moment of silence as every face in the gallery turns to watch the ships.

Franxis whispers. "Communal silence. Nice."

"Was until you broke it," I whisper sarcastically.

Franxis snorts and shakes their head.

"This is the same thing they do every day." Franxis leans forward, elbows propped on their knees, fists under their chin. "What are they scanning for?"

Fans of light spread out from the scanners and sweep across the glimmering surface of the crystal. Everyone around is quiet as they watch.

A wavering of the half-glow within the distant rift catches my eye. I question if I saw something and tell myself that the drones and wings stationed around the rift would've alerted us all if there was anything moving within the rift.

"After all this time, they finally landed on a name for the EDB," Franxis says, but it's as if their voice is falling away.

My mind zeroes in on the rift. The feeling creeps in slowly. I have felt the Shadow looking for me, into me, only a few times. This feels a bit like that, but this time, it doesn't sense my awareness. It's as if I am looking into the Shadow unseen. It stirs in the depths of a darkened dimension, and like a puppet master, it pulls strings.

Franxis says its name. "MaalenKun."

Someone nearby gasps, and we turn to see one of the Level Sevens wince and pinch the bridge of her nose.

"Hey, are you okay?" Franxis asks her.

Someone else cries out. Hunter's hands go to his head, and the pain in his uncontrolled exhalation brings sympathy from me. His comp Nicholas braces him.

Someone behind us screams. Franxis and I stand as several divs fall to their knees. We rush to them. As Franxis calls for a medical response team, I realize that more and more people are crying out, holding their heads, slumping to the floor as if a sudden collective pain has gripped them all.

The independent crew of The Queen catches the tall ginger before he hits the floor. It takes both of his friends to hold him up. His eyes lock onto the crystal, and his head trembles. He's trying to resist. He can't. He screams.

A jagged line of warmth builds within my arm. The heat spreads quickly. I wince and Franxis looks at me with concern. Where the Haddyc's crown stung me is a roaring flame. As the pain glows hot through my arm, my face tightens, and my breath shortens.

(More screaming.)

I tell myself to stay present, not to slip into the past. Several divs nearby stumble, and I move to catch an enby before they fall. It's the Level Eight from the Haven. They lose consciousness while screaming.

I look around. Everyone who went into the Haddyc's mindfield is screaming in pain and falling unconscious. Except me.

ꝏ

Excerpt from personal communications to Griselda Harris Ferand, President Helixx Corp, from Captain Commander Arianne Holt
March 23, 2138
(file encrypted; sent through stealth signal)
(receipt confirmation noted)

In light of recent events, we must work with the UNAF to study the Haddyc. After it manipulated the crystal in which it is imprisoned to attack those who channeled the divination which created its prison, we are very short-staffed on divinators with clearance for duty in the Haven. This has given the Sages an upper hand in station politics. They have demanded the delay of N'guwe's removal. This will only make the transition of station control to Helixx Corp more difficult than it already is. There is also greater risk of an EDB attack from Still Rift-2138. Helixx Corp will be blamed if another storm comes through and isn't stopped before it attacks planetside.

I am requesting additional assistance in studying the EDB which, although contained in the crystal chamber, remains a threat.

There is also the extremely concerning matter of the extradimensional rift which has yet to diminish. The station remains out of orbit and in position to guard the rift. Again, we are understaffed as this event occurred during the months-long transition of station control required by Central.

I recommend you come back quickly from the Martian sector, Dr. Ferand.

ꝏ

∞

OSCAR

We see wings from Stations Yerum and Eagle heading towards our shared destination. We stay on course and increase speed. We're all answering the emergency call to Station Scire.

I set Old Girl to autopilot and sit back.

"I wouldn't get too comfortable. Scire's not been doing much beyond monitoring the sector for years," Captain Carmel says.

I reply, "Yes, but with three more advanced stations and watchtower satellites, the 5,000 kilometers around Earth are well guarded."

With a raised eyebrow, she adds, "It was before that rift that won't close. And that Haddyc that won't die." She smirks. "And since Helixx took over, they're a much smaller crew. Lot of room for mistakes."

From behind us at the communications console, Thiia says, "Helixx Corp announced that their top scientists, some of the best in the world, are in route aboard The Eminent, but they've kept the request for additional Sages and UNAF science crews like ours." She laughs lightly, "They remind us that they're the best, but they still want our help."

"I can't foresee anything around the rift," Mira announces before returning back to her meditative position at the navigation console.

"Obscurations?" I ask.

"More like the rift itself is inhibiting prescience."

"That's one hell of a psychic disruptor if it can't be read by the most prescient div in the sector," Captain Carmel immediately replies.

"I'm not the most prescient," Mira says through her smile.

"I knew you'd say that. Maybe I'm the most prescient."

Her delivery is quick and sharp, and meant to break the tension.

"What do you think they'll do about this unkillable demon—assuming that's what it is?"

Carmel snorts. "Come on, Oscar. It's Haddyc! When has a Haddyc ever not been a demon?"

We both hold a finger aloft holding our breath, and then point at each other as Thiia predictably cuts in.

"'Demon' is a problematic term for a lot of reasons. EDB, extradimensional being, always. Whether they cause problems or not."

"They only ever cause problems," Captain says, voice firm (or stubborn). "One way or another, they wind up fucking with humanity. Even the ones we thought were benign have contributed to the hysteria, the conspiracy theories, the extremism. Planet is full of nut jobs even if they aren't violent."

Mira quips, "Let's just not save the planet today, Captain."

The captain smirks and looks back at her wife. "No, dogs there."

"Aw, dogs," we all gush at a favorite of our running jokes, genuinely missing those earthlings. We joke often that we're up here risking our lives to protect the animals, not the humans. I'm not sure Carmel is always joking about it.

"Pick up on anything, Mira?" I spin my co-pilot's seat around to face her.

She doesn't answer right away, but "looks ahead" for us, closing her eyes and tuning in her prescient attainments from Level Six. "Massive obscurations inside that crystal from any angle I look," she says. "It's either something I've never seen anything the likes of before, something I can't comprehend—"

"Or someone is obscuring it intentionally," Carmel says, looking back at her wife.

"It'd take a team of Sages to block me out," Mira reminds us.

I look both of them in their eyes. "It's just something new. Also, Captain, I thought you weren't into the whole conspiracy vibe."

"I'm not, but I also don't trust Helixx Corp." She reaches up and switches on the music. cello, predictable, soothing.

I launch a holoscreen of Station Scire. Three large rings with the center ring extending further out sit atop the tower, looking much like a massive torch floating in space near the dull light of the open rift. A large aubergine and pink S-class highliner docked along the shaft is the only ship at the station too big to fit into a harbor. As a fleet of wings return to the harbors, another small group of wings, mostly clash-wings, fly out of the harbor's plasma-grid air locks toward the crystal. There is very little activity for a station that is monitoring an extradimensional rift, and I worry that the station is understaffed and unprepared.

Sunlight glistens along the edge of the massive crystal ahead of us. The tugs attached to the crystal fire a bit every few minutes to keep the crystal in place, invisibly leashed to Scire. Two crimson crux-wings stand guard by the crystal. The fractal pattern on the crystal surface makes it difficult to see inside, but we're close enough to get images of the crystal. Scoping the image in further, we see a steady iridescent glow in the base. It may be storm lightning, but it shimmers like divination energy. Repeated scans indicate no other movement or significant changes in quantum signatures. I'm concerned about it, but as far as I can tell, there is no imminent threat.

Carmel launches a holoscreen and begins studying a report on the Haddyc's psychic attack on those who made the crystal chamber. Thiia texts a few contacts on Scire, but I haven't bothered to ask what they're saying. Mira quietly meditates. The temp crew further back, including the Sage, are either resting or meditating.

Along the atmospheric edge of the Earth, the sun's rays are beginning to show. The blue beginning of Earth's sky meets the edges of space. I watch the dawn light growing across the blue, inviting it into my mind where it spreads. So still. Awe shifts into a reverence which rises and fills the space around me, and I can feel myself settling into the center of profound beauty.

"You steeped?" Captain says, sitting up and leaning forward to gaze out with me.

"Could steep in that glow all day," I say.

"I requested our return to Mani, but they want us to work with Helixx Corp. We might be on Scire for a while."

"Not surprising. With my secondary role and your wife's rare attainment, the UNAF's probably going to need us there to keep them in the loop." I smile as she grumbles. "Besides, we've got a Sage to deliver."

"Even if we drop back, the Sages coming over from Eagle and Yerum will give them seven."

"Ah, I think there's a reason they want one of ours though." I swipe across the glowing blue holoscreen back to the files on the Scire Sages. I tap the image of the man who appears to be the youngest, a lithe, Bharatian man. If not for the orange and saffron uniform, he looks like he might front a punk band with his hair buzzed close into a single strip over his crown. I shift the screen over to Carmel. "Him."

She lifts her eyebrows and snorts. "Arun. Didn't know he was on Scire. Makes sense that they want an extra Sage. They're probably not so sure about the 'young' Sage who shot from none to Nine being stable."

Slight tension builds around her eyes from the grudge she holds.

I remind, "That was over a hundred years ago."

"Yeah, but what if he slips from Nine to none dealing with that Haddyc?"

"Let's hope that doesn't happen." We both know what might happen if he slips, but I sense that she doesn't want to talk about it.

"And what is it that you do?" Our friendly, local escort Sahil asks, having made his rounds through the group and turning to me last.

"Mostly just fly this thing." I nod towards the SkyVanXL where Thiia and Mira are now unloading the last of their camera and sound equipment. That answer is not entirely true. Neither Mira nor I tell him that we also provide security to protect the crew. "But I'm also nice to look at, and I make a decent joke every now and then."

Carmel, the boss, throws a backpack towards me and I have to think fast to catch it. "He also carries stuff," she says with a smirk. As she turns her face up, her aviators reflect the thick grey smog blanketing the sky. "My god, it's hot."

"Yes, mid-summer is not the best time to visit Thiruvanaikaval, but with the river shifting and longer monsoon seasons, who knows how much longer any of us can be here?"

"Exactly why we're here," Carmel says with a gentle smile.

Sahil turns back to me. "Are your parents Bharatian—at least one? Maybe immigrated when Bharat was still India?"

"No," I smile. He's not the first to ask about my heritage. It often comes up on location. "My parents are Dutch and Moroccan, but my great, great grandmother was Pakistani."

"Jai!" He claps me on the shoulder. "Welcome home, cousin!"

After a sympathetic wink and a smile about not having her own mixed-race heritage questioned, Thiia redirects Sahil's attention. "Isn't the temple quite old?" she asks him. "I wonder how the structure is fairing with the shifting river and development around it?"

"Oh, just cleaned." He says proudly. "We've washed the smog residue away from the exterior, so it will look nice for your film."

Carmel doesn't attempt to hide her chagrin. Shiny temples do not fit into the narrative of ancient practices being threatened by capitalism and climate change. This keeps happening, leaving us feeling that the documentary we're making will be less convincing.

I wheel the drone case behind everyone else, taking in the street scene. It's the same as anywhere else we've been to recently. All the devices around us—old televisions, Comms, laptops, radios—are for the most part tuned into one thing: that dirty space-cloud that's been hanging around for months, just outside of the atmosphere.

Some theories suggest that the dingy cloud is the Earth ejecting the toxic smog we've pumped into the sky. No science backs up that theory, and I don't think we get off the hook so easily. Scientists haven't been much help at all. They say that it's a mix of dust and dirt not unlike the rest of the universe. At least, that's what they're telling us. Plenty of conspiracy theorists have gone so far as to call it a poison that the Russians are going to drop down on the United

States; other conspiracies go off the rails about aliens—the usual. Others, especially in communities like the one we're here to visit, seem to think it's divine. Or the opposite.

It's been there long enough for most people back home in the States to have moved on to the next media sensation. I probably would have too if I didn't keep encountering its images in every city we visit.

"How far from here, Sahil?" Carmel asks. Her skin glistens with sweat.

"Short distance. We will catch a few buggies ahead. No cars, no SkyDrives in the old neighborhood." There is a bit of delight in his voice. He seems pleased that the gentrifying area around the temple is more protected from traffic. Sahil takes Carmel's backpack from her. "Please, allow me."

"Thank you," she says, immediately softening her voice.

The buggies weave through the crowd, and we turn the corner to see the temple ahead at the end of the street. The brightly colored tiers rise up from the street much like a pyramid. As we get closer and our eyes can focus enough to see through the low-hanging smog, the bright colors decorating each tier of the temple reveal themselves to be figures of Hindu deities.

Carmel leans over towards me, watching me look up towards the temple. She whispers, "You steeping in the sight of the shiny temple?"

"Nah." I smile at her. In our first week working together, she dubbed my tendency to gaze in awe at beautiful things "steeping."

I too kind of wish the temple looked a bit older, because having not grown up with any religion, aged temples mystify me, leaving me in awe. The temple we see in front of us is bright and shiny, almost like a theme park. I'm charmed, but not in awe. I'm more impressed that someone got up there and power-washed every figure. There is clearly a lot of care going into this temple.

I ask, "We need some drone shots from the street, don't you think?"

Carmel whispers, "Maybe we use file footage? Get the grime so Western audiences aren't distracted by the shiny thing?"

"You're the director. But we can also show how much the community invests in the temple."

"Hope the audience still senses the looming, invisible threats."

She leans forward, asks Sahil if they can fly the drone close to the temple. We've got the permits for the drones which are typically not allowed in this neighborhood, but the ask is a courtesy. Sahil wobbles his head and encourages us to take shots of whatever we'd like.

I'm about to launch one of the smaller drones when I notice that the daylight has gotten much dimmer. Craning my neck, I look towards the sky wondering how the smog could've gotten worse so quickly. In this light, any exterior shots will need retouching.

The buggy breaks hard. The crowd in the street has suddenly stopped.

There's a small gathering ahead of us. Our buggy driver lays on the loud, annoying horn.

"Why are we stopped?" Mira's voice comes through both mine and Carmel's comm watches. They're behind us in the second buggy with most of the gear. "Oscar, can you see what's happening?"

"It's a fight, y'all."

The cluster of onlookers disperses a bit so our buggy can drive past, and we see a young man, buzz cut, old concert t-shirt and dirty jeans, shoving a man in a business suit. The man in the suit falls back into the onlookers who all shout and point at the young man.

Our driver says something else that sounds like more curse words, and I'm equally concerned about the driver's behavior as what's happening on the street. I ask Sahil what he said.

"He said not nice words. They call the boy *Dalit:* 'untouchable.' It is illegal to treat the young man this way, yet the stupid caste system persists."

The buggies slowly move past the scuffle and through the crowd. I re-holster the taser and pull my vest back over it.

I tell the rest of my crew, but mostly Mira who has probably had her hand on her swift as well, "I think we're okay. Keep an eye out though."

Carmel groans.

It could turn into a mob scene if the young man has friends who come in to join the fight. If there's enough of them, they'll target anybody that appears to have money. I worry they might target us and go for the equipment which they could easily sell for what is to them a small fortune.

Our driver grows more aggressive. He rolls down his window and yells something I don't understand. I wish I'd clipped on the translator, but it's in a pack in the hatch behind us. The driver lays on the horn and nudges some legs with the bumper. People push aside enough for us to slowly move through the crowd.

A few more of the younger street kids seem to be making their way through the crowd back to the scuffle. More small clusters gather, more fights—mostly between a street kid or two and someone who looks like they've got money. Some of the street kids are facing down multiple screaming faces.

My hand is back inside my vest on the swift. I look back at the second buggy. Mira is alert, Thiia's head is down. Behind them, a mass of shoving bodies grows. People begin shouting.

"Get us out of here," I tell the driver. Sahil translates.

"How are you, wifey?" Carmel is on the comm with Mira again.

"Did we not get the memo about today's uprising?" she tries to joke.

The sky is getting darker. People are getting off of the street, perhaps expecting rain or because there are more and more people getting rough with each other.

"Yes, yes, move!" Sahil waves them away and pushes on the horn until the driver swats his hand away.

It's that move from the driver that has me bring the taser out and switch on the charge. I keep the swift low so the driver and Sahil don't notice it.

Carmel says, "Honey, we're lively, okay?" Our code, our signal to bring out the tasers, stay alert.

We are only thirty feet from the temple when we hear what sounds a bit like a jet flying low or perhaps some odd thunder.

Thiia's trembling voice comes through our comms, "Sounds like the sky is ripping open."

"Maybe the drought is over!" Sahil says, looking up through the windshield.

"That wasn't thunder," Carmel whispers as she reaches for the door handle.

"Don't open that door, Carmel." My throat is tense. The crowd is running through the street now, away from the temple. "Mira, tell your driver to pull closer to us. Tell her to stay close."

"What was that sound?" Thiia asks Mira.

Then Mira: "No idea, keep recording."

"Fuck," Carmel says, bringing out her phone and starting a livestream.

"Do not get out of this car!" Sahil shouts at the driver.

"Hey!" We shout from the backseat as our driver steps out.

Looking to the sky, the driver takes two steps away, and falls to his knees. Several other people do the same as the rest of the crowd runs around them. They kneel and bring their hands together near their hearts and begin chanting, mumbling something we can't hear.

We see the first vortex spiraling down from the sky, an almost invisible cyclone that bends the smoggy sky and air around it. It reaches down and into the crowd.

We hear screams arising from the crowd near the vortex, and Carmel looks at me, eyes wide. "We need to get out of here." She keeps the phone up, capturing the disruption.

"Sahil, grab that pack. Carmel, the med kit. We're leaving the rest."

Carmel holds up her comm watch closer to her face, "Mira, ditch the gear. We're coming to you and getting the fuck out of here."

"On it." Mira slides the bins out of the back of their buggy, making space for Sahil and Carmel. I get in next to the driver.

"We cannot go back the way we came," our new driver politely says. She points to the rearview mirror and the five of us turn to see more buggies and the crowd packing the street. More thin cyclones come down into the crowd, more screaming, more panicking, more pushing and shoving. The streets' usual commotion is transforming into a riot.

Two men, locked in a brawl, thump against the rear of the buggy. Thiia and our driver both yelp.

"Go!" Sahil yells. "Drive!"

Our driver skillfully winds around the people kneeling, praying in the street. A couple people still on their feet rush the buggy, bang on the glass, before we slip past them. Then, they're attacking the people still on their knees. Behind us, one of the buggies, a thick funnel vortex piercing its roof, backs over people. Carmel sees it and she gasps.

Thiia whispers, "What is happening?" She aims the phone up, livestreaming the strange storm coming down over us. "Why is there no wind?"

"Faster," I tell the driver.

I look up through the windshield. More and more sky-warping whirlwinds spill down from the strange cloud.

Our buggy stops at the barrier of brightly colored posts at the end of the street. There is no one in the space between the end of the road and the temple, which looks like a sanctuary from the chaos building around it.

The six of us run with as little as possible. The driver is the slowest amongst us, so I lag behind her, holding my swift low, scanning nearby brawls. I glance ahead to Mira who is leading everyone across the pavilion towards the temple gates.

An explosion down the street breaks our collective stride momentarily.

Ahead, at the temple gates, are two security guards. My first thought is that they won't let us in, but they're waving to us, telling us to hurry. They close the gate behind us. At the temple door another figure waves us towards him. An old priest in white clothes and an orange sash ushers each of us into the door. We run through the immaculately kept gardens of flowers, fountains of lotuses, elaborate statues of gods and goddesses. As I enter the temple, the priest bows his head, as if offering a blessing.

"Keep your shoes on. I feel we might have to run," he says stopping our driver. He gestures for us to go further inside before turning back to the gate and the security guards.

I call Mira to me, our swifts drawn and charged, and we stand watch behind the priest as the others move further inside. The guards hold the gate closed as someone on the other side pushes against them.

The old priest calls to the guards, but the sound of the sky ripping open makes it hard to hear anything else. The priest runs, orange sash billowing in the wind.

"What—?" Mira asks me. "Are they not letting someone in?"

"I don't understand what is happening," I mumble.

It briefly appears that the old priest doesn't either. He looks from the teenager back at the temple with astonishment, up at the roaring sky, to the guards, and again to the young man at the gate.

It's the young punk, the kid with concert tee and buzz cut. Looks like he is begging. His knees buckle, and he pulls himself back up. But he's not just pleading; his pain is causing him to crumple.

Mira and I step forward but stop when we see the priest open the gate. One of the guards jumps aside as the young man spills onto the cement path. He screams, holding his head. There's a flashing blue light around his head, maybe from an old smartphone or something. As the guards lift him onto his feet, I see the blood dripping down his chin onto his shirt. His nose is smashed in, his eyes rolled back. He stumbles, but they guide him along the path. As they get close, led by the priest who seems to be focused on each step, I see the kid's knuckles are broken and bloody. He is missing a shoe. His foot is bleeding.

The guards pass the young man to Mira and me before returning to the gate. We hold the kid close to us to steady him, and I see that he does not have a phone after all. The flashing lights are coming from inside his head, blue light spills out of his ears, nose, mouth. His eyes are shut tight, but flashes appear behind the lids as he throws his head back, crying through clenched teeth.

We carry him inside and set him down against one of the huge columns.

Carmel already has the med kit open on the ground. Her hands are frozen above it when she notices the flashing lights. She shakes off her astonishment, picks up the bacta-spray and aerosol bandages, and gets ready to treat his cuts.

The kid opens his mouth and screams like his mind is breaking. It's deep, painful, and layered with what sounds like several tortured voices.

He opens his eyes, blue light fills the room, and he turns his head towards the priest. He glances down at the priest's clothing.

The fight on the street. The caste skirmish. Chills run over my skin.

Mira and I aim our tasers at the kid. I don't want to hurt him, but I am afraid he could literally explode in a violent flash of blue.

"No," the priest says to us. His face is serene as he steps towards the young man whose eyes are glaring with blue light. We lower our swifts halfway.

Our driver has dropped to her knees and is praying, repeating a mantra I am vaguely familiar with from our documentary research. Sahil joins her. "*Amma amma tāye.*"

Somehow, I not only clearly hear the words foreign to my ears, but I feel the meaning. *Mother… Provides…*

How do I know what the words mean?

I shake my head and lower the taser.

The young man brings himself to his feet, falling back against the massive column. He looks taller. His clothes look smaller. He speaks, and this one word from Tamil, a language I do not speak, slowly dances in my mind and lands as English, German, French. The language unravels to translate itself in my head, "You..."

I hear more language that I do not understand on the edge of my awareness, undecipherable.

Sahil and our driver continue chanting, *"Akhilānd eshware nīye."*

Universal consciousness... Guide us...

More language turns over itself in my mind, shifting into multiple ways of understanding. Some words remain out of my grasp, just beyond interpretation. I hear Spanish and understand it, although I don't speak Spanish. The rest of the crew does.

The priest steps closer to the young man, who has grown so much in size that his clothes are being ripped apart. He stumbles back against the column as his large head brushes the high ceiling and dust showers down on us all. He struggles to stand upright, to fit. Fear lodges in my throat. His body is enormous, he has to crouch to not push through the ceiling and bring the temple down on us.

He seethes at the priest and speaks in Tamil, "You... call us... untouchable."

I understand every word. The last word lands in my mind with divisive words from other languages. It pulls up language used to demean and diminish entire groups of people. The slur triggers my memory, words I've been called, insults about my sexuality, my mixed-race heritage. I feel the slurs being pulled at in Mira and Carmel. Doubling over, twisting themselves in Thiia, violent words used to diminish both races of her heritage swell like a wave. I look at her through my heart, and within Thiia, transgender slurs come down like an avalanche.

"Annapūrṇ eshware tāye." Provides... nurtures...

Thiia cries. As I realize that the insulting words aren't here to hurt us, but only to remind us of some commonality, some connection through our suffering, she looks over at me, as if she has heard my thoughts. She wipes her eyes and lifts her chin towards me, a sign of supportive solidarity. I'm reminded of the instant bond we had over our mixed race heritages.

"No, no, child," the priest says in whatever language the young man speaks, a language I don't speak, but can in this moment, somehow, understand. The priest reaches up toward the young man's hand which is several times the size of his own. The giant hand trembles and instantly begins to return to a size easier to comprehend. "You are not untouchable." As the young man shrinks down from above us, the priest caresses his face in his hand. The blue lights in the young man's head dim. He falls back against the column, exhausted, becoming a normal sized human being once again.

"Oh ādi para Shakti nīye." The meaning of several words from the mantra

float on the edge of my awareness, not quite discernable. They repeat the mantra again. Some words remain beyond my comprehension.

"Amma amma tāye."

Mother… Provides…

The priest unwraps his sash and drapes it over the sobbing, naked teenager. Carmel approaches with the med-kit and soothes him as she begins treating his bloody hands.

"Akhilānd eshware nīye,"

Universal consciousness… Guide us…

Something moves in the air, space, ether above us. And within us.

Suddenly, the room is full of sound and light. The resonance and brilliant rays of gold move deep within us.

"Annapūrṇ eshware tāye."

Provides… nurtures…

We are all closer to the young man now without having taken any steps, as if the space folded us in to be near each other. He wails again, the lights in his head blaze, and he opens his eyes to the sky. When he screams, a bolt of blue light spreads through his body, and a pulse knocks us off of our feet, into the air.

The mantra continues as I drift.

"Oh ādi para Shakti nīye."

Transcend… Guide us.

A light is poured into me. It folds, becoming shapes. My mind turns, and I see someone ahead of me. This person is a part of my future, I realize. My body is flying through the air in a temple where the world has gone mad, but I'm at ease when he turns his handsome face towards me. The light folds in around him, and I see only his beautiful eyes. Green ringed in grey. Because I see him, my future, I know I'll make it out of this temple, this chaos. I know I'll find him. The vision is dashed, leaving unfamiliar music in my head, a harmonizing of two songs.

We crash against the stone walls, the hard floors. Pain racks my body. I look up, searching for Carmel, Mira, Thiia. The driver, the priest, Sahil—all lie pushed against the walls, still. The young man slumps forward and collapses on his side.

The sound and light rushes out of the space, down the corridor, and out of the temple. The sounds of the world tearing itself apart seep through the temple walls.

I feel like I'm slowly extracting my awareness from a dream. I can't quite wake up, open my eyes, or move my body. I'm aware that my eyes are closed, that my body is still. I hear someone moving around nearby, I see the image on a tablet: more chaos. More images of people losing their minds, tearing apart everything around them, including each other. More images of that storm but elsewhere. I want the images to stop, and I feel like I can't turn away or understand what is happening, and I hear myself and Mira telling Sahil to "Please, turn it off."

And I'm watching Sahil switch off the device and hand it back to Thiia and I feel the device in my hands, but I'm still trying to move them, still trying to wake up. And I'm about to freak out, but Mira and Carmel are holding each other, and I'm being comforted, and I hear Mira's breath near me, but she is across the room, and I feel Carmel holding me as she softens from within herself as she only does with Mira.

I jerk and sit up with my hands over my mouth, a strange cry already having escaped me as I woke up. They all look over at me. Thiia holds the tablet. Mira and Carmel hold each other.

"Hey, Oscar." Thiia brings a thermos over and kneels down next to me. "Hydrate. It'll help."

Her words echo as if I am the one speaking. I take the thermos and gulp the water. "How long was I out?"

"About nine hours."

"What? My head..." My awareness seems spread too wide, foggy in places. Feels very open but unclear. I sense things emerging within the fog. Patterns like memories or imagination reshaping into reality, perception. The feeling of the stone floor. The soreness from getting thrown across the room.

"Us too when we woke up. Drink." Her voice is a sweet sound. Gentle, controlled. There is a musicality to her voice that I hear more clearly.

I drink, and I feel my body coming more alive. The fog begins to lift, and the patterns, turnings of thought move into place quicker.

Carmel and Mira join us.

"The kid... did he...?" I hesitate to ask.

"He's a normal sized human now." Carmel says. We all look across the room at him sleeping under the priest's orange shawl.

Carmel turns back to me. "You okay?"

"Yes, just a bit... confused." I shake my head and sip more water.

Thiia puts a hand on my shoulder, and instantly, I feel steadier.

"What is happening outside?" I ask.

Thiia holds up the tablet before setting it aside. "It's happening in other cities too: South Los Angeles, Barcelona. Complete chaos. People are losing their minds, killing each other, themselves. Mass hysteria or something."

"What?"

"It's all over social. People are livestreaming what they can. It's a horror movie." Carmel takes a small flashlight from her pocket. "Look at me." She shines the light in each eye. She sets the light down and holds up her index finger moves it, right to left and back. She seems confident that I don't have a concussion.

"The storm…"

"It's not a storm," Mira says, shaking her head in disbelief.

"Fucking space-cloud." Carmel stares deep into my eyes. "It broke up, moved over three cities, including the one we're in, yesterday."

"That wasn't on the news—"

Her tone is casual. "No shit. Pentagon Five just debriefed. The cloud broke up, came down over the cities—like here, and… did something to people."

Frustrated, I groan. I rub a palm across my forehead and down my face, stroking my beard.

"What about here? Do we know anything?"

"Bharat officials have quarantined the area and have started looking for survivors. It's bleak out there. There's a lot that's burning. Bodies everywhere."

"You went out there?" I ask.

"No, drone shots. All over the news."

Thiia's fear is tangible in the space between us. I take her hand and feel the heaviness in her heart. She sniffles, wipes away a tear, and says, "I'm sorry, you guys. It's just… you know I have people in all three cities."

Before I can get the words out, Mira says, "You don't have to be sorry for that."

"Ever." Carmel says. "This shit's upsetting. It's okay."

We all pause and quietly feel the heaviness in the space around and within us.

Thiia hangs her head and closes her eyes. I sense her focusing on her breath to calm her nerves. In my own mind, a sympathetic settling begins in sync with hers. She senses me, our minds bridged. I feel suddenly uncomfortable, worried that I'm disrupting her peace. She juts her chin at me, smiles gently, and my fear is diminished. She puts her arms around me, and I immediately feel more centered and clear-headed.

Mira is the first to speak. "So what do we do now?"

We turn towards Carmel who has been the boss, the director, giving orders to the rest of us for months.

Thiia says, "Don't stop telling us what to do now, captain."

Carmel sits back on her heels, looks back at us, and sighs. She doesn't deflect or shy away from what we're asking of her. She nods. "I think first, we take a look outside, see how bad it is in the temple's immediate vicinity. Thiia, see if Sahil can get you somewhere you can get a signal boost, try the local first responders again."

"Might get a signal on the top floor," Thiia says.

"Production offices in South LA know we're here. They might've already called local authorities," Mira says.

"Remember, SLA's a shit show." Carmel reminds us all.

Thiia helps me onto my feet. As soon as I'm upright, I feel steadier, more energized. My senses are heightened. I tell myself it's just nerves or adrenaline, but I know it's something else. Something has changed within me.

"Do the rest of you feel… great?" Mira asks. "Or just me?"

Any tension is broken as Thiia laughs out loud. Her laugh is always contagious. "I feel pretty fucking amazing for the end the world."

Before we head back to the gardens, Carmel stops to check on the young man. He's still unconscious but appears to be sleeping comfortably. His nose is not smashed, although there is dried blood on his face, his neck, his hands. His knuckles are no longer broken. His wounds have already healed.

Mira and I have our swifts half up as we walk down the corridor. We push the doors open with our shoulders and walk out into the smoky air.

The sky is still dark with that malevolent space-cloud. Its eye swirls like a hurricane but there is no wind down on the ground. Purple-black lights crawl slowly through the swirling mantle as if lightning were stalking something through its eddies. Plumes of black smoke billow up into it from burning buildings all over the city.

There are raging fires only a few blocks away. Helicopters drop tanks of water down on fires even further out. The fires will spread. We won't be able to stay in the temple for long.

Drones sweep through the airspace. We step out into the courtyard and try to flag down a drone, but it does not slow down. Maybe it's unmanned, only recording the damage.

We walk through the smoky courtyard towards the gate and find the guards. One of them still has his hands clasped tight around the other's throat even as the other has driven a pocketknife into his gut several times. Both bodies slump motionless against the gate, faces ashen, drained of color. Even the red berets they wore seem dulled. Their glassy eyes are locked on each other, frozen and hardened.

They had called us inside, gotten us to safety.

My heart aches.

We step around the puddle of blood, gaze down the street. Other than the smoke, nothing moves. Lights blink from overturned buggies. Bodies lie in the street, on the sidewalk. A body hangs from a broken window, and I turn away.

We push the gate open, and Mira and I slip out, swifts still lifted. While Mira checks the buggy, I keep my eyes on the street expecting someone to appear. The buggy's windows are all smashed out, the key is gone, and even if we got it started, the streets are crowded with bodies. There is no way to drive out of here. We find a bottle of water, another of juice, and a box of protein bars under the front seat, so we take those.

As we recross the garden path, Mira asks, "How far away is the SkyVan parked?"

I get the sense that as anyone on a security unit should, she already knows, but she wants us to talk about it in front of Carmel. I know this from having spent years working with her, but also, there is now a deep certainty to this feeling.

"About two hundred yards out. Landing lot is almost a straight shot down the street. We only turned one corner."

Carmel shakes her head. "We don't even know if it's still there. It might be smashed like everything else."

I sense within Mira a flash, a light unravels in her mind, leaving a vision. It's uncomfortable but quick. She says, "The SkyVan's okay. I know it is."

Again, a depth of certainty comes with the words. For a moment, I see the SkyVan in the lot—it's fine, but I feel vaguely as if I am seeing it through Mira.

"I don't want you going out there," Carmel says, but not to me, just Mira.

"I can make it on my own," I say, half sure I actually can.

She opens her mouth to say something else, but we all stop in our tracks. The hair on my arms stands up, and a chill rushes through me, through us. I feel Carmel's fear. Mira's fear. My own. We turn slowly.

"Unless that becomes a problem." The occasional good joke. No laughs this time.

Further down the street, another vortex, bigger than what we saw before, yanks at the elements around it, ripping them apart, pulling blood and water from bodies, fire from the burning buildings, whipping them into a void that drains the color from the spaces it touches and pulls it away, into the sky, into the turbid cloud above us.

The reality-draining cyclone begins to wind down the street towards the temple, towards us, perhaps having sensed living bodies and changed course. It rattles and clanks as it moves through crumbled architecture and toppled buggies. It squelches moving through fallen bodies. It pulls at the bonds of existence around it, leaving behind it a discolored wake, a scar suspended in the air.

We feel a presence moving down the garden path from the temple doors. A crescendo moves through us. Fear is diminished, drawn out, and hung in the space around us like a clear-cut current of somehow thicker air, and then, the fear is destroyed, broken into millions of pieces that drift away.

The young man with the bloody face, neck, and hands stands next us. He is naked, but I am more concerned that he will turn into a giant again, crushing us, and at that moment, that fear is ripped out of me painfully. He destroys the fear in a crackling static as if he has cast it into a fire.

He takes my hand and Carmel's, and I feel Carmel take Mira's hand.

Again, the crescendo. My knees buckle, but he squeezes my hand, willing me to stand by him. A current of energy moves down his arm, into my body, and I stand taller. The cells of my body and the spaces between them are suddenly bright with vibrant energy.

My mind is on fire.

The vortex speeds down the street towards us.

A blazing bright blue above my eyes nearly overwhelms me. It pulls something out of me. The minor crescendo: a swell of feeling, care, love for these people I've been working with for years, seeing them pour their hearts and souls into their work to make film after film, trying to wake the world up. How much they care, about each other, about me.

A major crescendo: deep love coming from Carmel and Mira and waves moving from us into this powerful young man whom we don't know but have seen to his protection and care in spite of and because of his extraordinary circumstance.

The tip of the whirling vortex, like a monstrous tentacle, reaches through the temple gates, and my feet are frozen to the ground. The radiance pulls on some force within us, draws it forth, melding its waves into a glowing and radiant point. The vortex reaches toward us. A spear of bright blue light flies from our bodies, and we scream in pain as it leaves. In a flash, it cuts through the air and plunges deep into the vortex.

Recoiling, the gyre pulls the blue bolt into the sky, where its end splits into three points. The trident soars through the dim sky and pierces the eye of the storm. The tempest wails a terrible sound. Purple-black lightning blasts shatter themselves above us. Remnants of the strange storm heave and billow as it pulls itself up and away, retreating out of the atmosphere.

We fall to the ground, and Carmel turns to the young man. "What did you do to us?"

He is again crying and naked. He shakes his head with shame. His words are not our language, but we understand him. "I don't know."

I pull off my shirt and I drape it over him.

We all three rub his back as he sobs.

"It's okay," we say. "It's gone," we say. "Whatever you did, it's okay." And we know he understands. He sniffles and looks up at us. His tears have left trails through the dried blood on his face.

"Forgive me, please." He speaks in Tamil. "I did not mean to hurt you. I just wanted to get rid of the demon."

"You did, you did," Carmel says implying that he did both, but she continues to soothe him.

In the spaces within me, it feels as though something has been stripped away, but as we comfort the young man, as we help him get back on his feet, as we meet the others in the temple, as we share the food we found in the buggy, as we cry and hold each other and work for each other, those spaces begin to heal. Many of those restored places within me begin to come back far stronger, far brighter.

ꝏ

"I'm sorry," I say approaching the altar. "Sorry to interrupt, but... we've got the SkyVan outside. We should go."

Our driver looks back at me over her shoulder. Soft candlelight illuminates her face, and even though I'm clearly interrupting her meditation or prayer or at least the silence in the room, her eyes appear kind.

"No need to be sorry for that!" she says in English. "Just give me a few moments to make an offering. I won't come back to this temple, and... this feels important."

"The storm is gone, but the fires are spreading."

"A few moments—that is all." She turns back away from me towards the icon on the altar. She begins chanting again. It's the mantra she and Sahil chanted when we came inside. Hearing it brings back images of the kid losing control, almost bringing the temple down on us. The light opening me to something. The blast that came through the kid, knocked us all against the walls. My body doesn't even ache.

"You've healed," she says.

I've decided to stop asking how and why out loud, since I'd just be repeating the question over and over. I'm exhausted by wondering.

"The confusion is another pain though," she says. "Come closer if you'd like."

She pours water from a bottle into a clay cup. A small crack spreads up the side of the cup, and beads of water drip out slowly. She places the cracked cup at the feet of the icon, Parvati dressed in all of her finery. The contrast of the cracked cup and the elegance of the murti stirs something in my heart. I gaze at the cracked cup, watching a bead of water seem through the crack before slipping down the side. I steep in its beauty as I listen to the mantra.

For the first time in hours, my mind feels at ease. The pain of uncertainty aches but somehow beautifully.

Thoughts of the others waiting downstairs bring me out of the moment.

She asks, "Please tell me, not just in trying to understand the unusual things that have happened, but... do you feel that you are different?"

There is a deep knowing in her eyes. She already knows.

"Yes," I answer.

"Same for me. There is more knowing, and quite a bit of unknowing happening within me. Forgive me... I think I feel your thoughts. You're worried about the others. You also don't know where we go from here, but you know we can't stay, and that troubles you."

"I think once we get moving, we'll figure it out."

"You can't really keep everyone safe."

"Not everyone. Just my crew." I realize the list is longer. "And you, Sahil, the kid, the priest. At least until we're out of here."

She laughs lightly, pats my hand. "We're in this together now." She shrugs. "Whatever this is."

As we walk away from the altar, she leans over and whispers conspiratorially, "You know, Parvati is not my favorite."

"Shhh… she's right behind us."

Her laugh is giddy. "Well, my favorite of the goddesses is technically her, but in different form. Do you know Akilandeshwari?"

"I know some of the stories, but I don't know that one."

"Her name literally means 'never not broken.'"

"She's a broken goddess?"

"Yes. And it's her brokenness that keeps her open, but also the reason she cannot be contained." She smiles at me kindly, as if there is nothing strange about us taking shelter in the temple. "This is something you would have learned about at this temple, I feel. But now, you must leave, so I'm compelled to tell you about her myself. Maybe because…"

"The world seems broken now."

"All it takes is one monster storm." She throws her hands up, and I can't help but smile. "Akhilandeshwari also rides a crocodile, which is kinda badass." She picks up her shoes at the bottom of the stairs and carries them with her towards the door. "When I was a girl, my Patti told me this crocodile is swinging its tail, chomping down, breaking the world apart. Meanwhile, Akhilandeshwari: super chill. She knows the world is like her, never not broken."

"If only we could all be so chill."

"Indeed." She puts on her shoes at the door.

"What's your name?"

She answers with a friendly smile, "Pyaar."

"I'm Oscar. I'll be your pilot today."

ꝏ

As we cross the courtyard, I realize that the smoke has gotten thicker, the fires closer. There's no way the helicopters can put out all of the fires in time. The temple that we came to help protect will burn soon. So much will be lost.

Moments after the engines are up, turbines going, the air conditioning sucks out all the smoke and filters in fresh air. We lift off, breaking free of the plumes of smoke, not knowing where we are going.

We are in the air for only a few minutes before three military drones fly alongside us, surely scanning our faces. It would normally be an invasion of privacy, but considering the circumstances, we're happy to be found.

A call comes through the SkyVan comm. UN Armed Forces and Bharat National Guard are setting up emergency response at a school campus across the river. They ask specifically if we were at the temple. They also ask if the young man is with us. We reply that he is.

"Drones must've spotted us in the courtyard," Carmel says leaning forward towards the front seats.

"Doing what?" Thiia keeps her voice low.

I keep one hand on the wheel and stroke my beard with the other. "Well, whatever that storm was—it didn't just go away on its own."

"What do you mean?" Thiia asks. She shakes her head slowly as if she is witnessing my memories. "You shot the storm?"

"Do you think we killed it?" Carmel asks.

"No, but we got rid of it—or at least, he did."

"Wait." Thiia looks toward the kid. "What happened?"

"I don't know how to explain it."

In the rearview screen, I see the kid, half scared but also in awe, seeing the city far below him. He looks even younger in my clothes that are too big for him. His slender frame is nearly swallowed by the gym shorts and t-shirt we pulled out of my bag before we dumped the luggage to make room for him in the SkyVan.

We get another call from the UNAF. They tell us to come to them.

"Sounds like an order," Carmel says, sitting back and taking Mira's hand.

"It is." I tap the location they've sent, and the map shows us the campus' location.

"I think we should go," Pyaar says, voice low. "The young man needs help."

Collective tension and worry fill the cabin. We have no idea what they might have seen, why they have asked specifically for the kid, and we really have no better idea of what to do. The decision is unanimous. Even the kid agrees.

ꝏ

We're met by armed soldiers in the landing lot. There are other SkyDrives, cars, and survivors on foot coming in as well, but we're some of the few met by soldiers.

There is a movement above me, perceived by some means beyond my five senses. I hear Carmel in my head saying, *Looks like we're getting special attention.*

We look at each other, surprised but aware that I picked up on her thoughts. I nod my head ever so slightly. She does the same.

The soldiers escort us past the growing line of survivors registering at the first and largest tent. They take us up the steps of the school and inside, into a large classroom, where we are met by several decorated officers from both the UN and Bharat, a couple of men in suits, and a Bharati woman in a stylish pantsuit.

All the school desks have been pushed to one side of the room. Large screens on mobile mounts display images of the destruction we left on the other side of the river, an image of the storm flashing its purple-black lightning, and a montage of images taken from the street, the thin cyclones moving down into people's heads before they become incredibly violent.

I wonder why we are not with the other survivors, the other evacuees.

We're different, Carmel says in my head. I get the layered meaning. We're not like the other survivors. And we're not the same as we were before the storm.

A Bharat National Guard officer with a tablet steps forward, greets us, confirms that we are all who they think we are. That they've already identified us from the drone scans is not surprising. They don't have the kid's name, and the officer does not ask him, which seems a bit rude.

"How'd you all meet?" the officer asks our group.

Carmel says curtly, "Got caught in the storm."

The Bharati woman steps toward us, smiling warmly. "Hello, my name is Dr. Ana Kavali. I am very happy you are here and safe. We, obviously, have many questions, and we believe you can help us find answers." The officers and suits look back and forth between us and their tablet and laptop screens while Dr. Kavali's assistant checks our vitals, offers us water.

There's a camera on us, recording us. There's another device next to the camera which looks a bit like a dulled, opaque mirror lined with what appears to be some sort of clear crystal; several wires run from the back of the device and into a processor. I have a feeling this device is measuring something normally unseen within or around us.

They don't mean us any harm. Pyaar's voice is in my head.

When Thiia gasps and turns toward Pyaar, I realize, we all received the psychic message.

One of the officers must've realized something happened as well. He looks quickly from his screen, to Thiia, to the rest of us, and back to the screen. He leans over to one of the suits who looks at the screen and nods.

One of the officers leans to whisper in Dr. Kavali's ear, but somehow, I hear him clearly. "Not the priest."

Dr. Kavali asks the priest to go with one of the soldiers, tells him that they will show him to the shelter, and they both agreeably nod. Before leaving us, the priest brings his hands together in front of his heart and bows to each of us individually, thanking us. He turns to the kid last and caresses his face, once more.

The priest's touch triggers the memory of the blue flashes going off inside the kid's head. I feel an echo of the pain which wasn't mine but his; I feel a hint of the fear that he felt. As the priest leaves, the kid puts his face in his hands and sobs.

Thiia puts her arm around him, and Pyaar again transfers to us all, *It's going to be okay.*

"Get him some tissue," Thiia orders a nearby soldier who stares back at her as if frozen.

One of the suits hands over his handkerchief.

Pyaar rubs the kid's shaved head.

I turn back towards Dr. Kavali who is next to one of the officers observing something on a screen. The look from the screen to the kid repeatedly.

"Hey!" I demand their attention. "What's going on here? This is not a typical disaster response."

"Not a typical disaster," one of the UNAF officers replies.

Dr. Kavali looks back at us politely. "I'm not a medical doctor. I'm a scientist. I study psychic energy for the UNAF's Project Ascension. You seven have a lot of it. We don't know why, but maybe that doesn't matter." She nods towards one of the officers who taps his tablet, and an image of the temple courtyard comes up on one of the big screens.

Saw this coming, Mira transfers.

"Oh, is that…?" Thiia says aloud.

"That's us," Carmel says to everyone in the room. The picture on the screen is unclear, shot from above through the smoky haze, bright light streaming from the bodies of four individuals linked hand to hand.

"Oh, my," Sahil says. "I had no idea."

The officer taps the tablet again and the screen shows the scene from another angle, a second drone shot from down the street. The video is slowed down to show the spear of light moving from our bodies and into the vortex where it shoots up into the sky. Another video from a drone higher up recording the storm cloud shows the bolt of light spreading out and piercing the eye. There's the implosion of purple-black lightning cracking through the sky, the bellowing of the cloud. The storm retreats, disappearing higher in the atmosphere.

"Obviously, this was not just a storm," the officer with the tablet says. "We have been watching this cloud orbiting the planet for months, as you all know. What we did not tell the public was that we've been aware that the cloud is a living entity of unknown origin. We brought in Dr. Kavali, and we found that this thing had a high amount of psychic activity whirling through it. And unfortunately, that's about all we knew. We didn't know it could come down on us like it did. We've been trying for some time to get rid of it, but we had no idea of how to do so until we saw this." He points toward the big screen. "We think you can help us."

She lowers the tablet she holds, tilts her head down, and Dr. Kavali speaks as if sharing vital but secret information. "I think what might've happened during the attack is that some individuals gained access to a level of power that allows for these special abilities."

"This might all seem very fast," one of the men in suits says. "But we need to move quickly. This thing is regrouping in orbit. We don't know if it will attack again, but it seems likely."

"Tell us," an officer with a lot of medals says. "How did you do this?" He changes the picture back to the first image of the four of us in the courtyard.

Suddenly, I realize that these soldiers might separate us, and I feel protective, defensive, and I remember Pyaar telling me that I can't really keep everyone safe. I breathe deep and try to let go, but the anxiety grips me.

"I think I did that." The kid says in broken English. He steps forward. Thiia still holds his hand.

They're going to take the kid, Mira transfers.

Not without me, Pyaar replies.

"What's your name, young man?" Dr. Kavali asks.

"Arun."

ꝏ

They keep us in the classroom but take Arun somewhere else. Pyaar insists on staying with the young man. As we say our farewells, Arun hangs his head low. Carmel folds her arms and makes a point of saying goodbye to only Pyaar.

Dr Kavali's team wants to interview us in pairs. Through quick transference, we all agree to tell them everything we can, every little detail, including our new communication skills.

A few of the officers and suits remain monitoring their tablets from across the room. Occasionally, they glance up toward us or Thiia and Carmel.

"I think these things are still on." Mira points at the camera and the strange device with crystals aimed at each of us.

Across the room two officers interview Carmel and Thiia. Carmel consoles Thiia, who has her head in her hands. Carmel leans back out of Thiia's periphery and mouths to the officers, "Fuck. Off."

The officers reluctantly give them a break.

"I love her," I say, laughing a little bit.

The corners of Mira's mouth turn up slowly into a full smile. "She's hard candy."

Thiia sits up and puts her head on Carmel's shoulder.

"Don't worry about the kid." Mira says.

"I can't help but worry," I admit.

The woman interviewing us returns and hands us each a bottled water. I point at the device with the crystal-lined surface. "What is that?"

"Don't know what to call it," she answers sincerely. "One of Dr Kavali's instruments."

"Do you know what it does?"

She pauses, glances over her shoulder. "Measures psychic activity. I'm not so convinced it's picking up anything on you, since you couldn't read my mind for the answer."

I appreciate her joke but shake my head and smirk. "I'm not so sure this works like that."

"Want to test it for us?"

Mira shrugs.

I focus my thoughts on Mira, on the movement that I know is above me, but not picked up by my senses. I "feel" that some connection is made, like a link or bridge.

You okay with all of this? I ask.

She transfers back confidently. *Maybe all this helps in some way.*

The woman looks up from her tablet and says, "We don't know exactly what you're saying to each other, but we can tell there's some sort of transference. Am I right?"

We nod.

She calls the doctor over.

Dr Kavali looks at the tablet and back at us. "I've measured this in many people who have similar abilities, but not at these levels. Would you say the sub-vocal communication is as clear as the words I'm speaking? No distortions or words looping back on themselves?"

"Maybe earlier there was some echoing when I woke up in the temple. But it's clear now," I answer.

"You know other people who do this too?" Mira asks.

"Not here. Not yet anyway. I've got a team reaching out to people I've been studying, people with extraordinary psychic abilities. I believe they can help."

"But you're not really just interested in all the ways we can have a conversation, right?" I ask.

"Exactly, Mr. Kenzari. You—or maybe your new friend, Arun, through you—weaponized this energy against the sentient storm. The energy that came from or through you drove that threat away, but it's still lurking high above us. We need to know what happened. Maybe then, we can figure out how to get rid of this monster for good."

"It all happened pretty fast, but when we went into the temple, something happened with the kid. He had this blue light coming out of his head. Looked like he was in a lot of pain."

"Like flashes going off inside of him." Mira adds.

"We got him calmed down, but then one of those flashes blasted through him, knocked us all out."

"When we woke up, we could hear each other's voices in our heads."

The doctor nods. I sense that she has heard this sort of thing before, so I skip ahead.

"From the courtyard, we saw one of those vortexes. It was bigger than the ones we saw before."

"The smaller ones converged after whomever they were attached to died." Dr. Kavali says. I'm surprised she is so forthcoming with information.

"That big one was... It seemed like maybe it was looking for something. Then it came for us."

"Were you afraid?"

"Of course." Mira squints her eyes at the doctor.

I keep talking to buffer Mira's blunt response. "Then the kid, Arun, is there next to us."

"What happened to his clothes?" one of the officers asks.

"We told you before," Mira says, annoyance creeping into her voice. "He lost them when he was a giant, when his head almost exploded."

"This was in the temple before, correct?" The doctor turns to Mira now.

"Yeah," she answers curtly.

"He shrank back to normal when you comforted him?"

"I didn't say those words, but yeah, he calmed down when Carmel and the priest showed him care."

"Flash forward to the courtyard, the big cyclone..." The doctor waves her hand quickly, suggesting we get to what she wants to hear. "Tell me not just what you saw, but what was in your head, your heart, when that light came out of you."

Mira inhales slowly, squints, and answers, "I felt my wife holding my hand, but also Oscar and the kid. I felt a lot of happiness, like a rush of good memories stacked on top of one another. It was kinda ecstatic for a moment."

"I wanted to protect my team, but also, joy, care—a flood of good feeling." I notice myself sitting more upright as I recall the feeling. "But then, it was ripped out of us. All the goodness was torn out."

Mira nods.

Dr. Kavali sees something on the tablets, some measure of what is moving through us, and she seems concerned. "How do you feel right now?"

"There is this echo inside. It still hurts, but I can tell that I'm going to be okay." My shoulders round forward. My head feels heavier.

"Feels like parts of me are missing but being pulled back in slowly," Mira says.

"Your psychic activity rose quite a bit when you spoke about that moment. How do you feel about Arun?" She looks back at the tablet.

"What do you mean?" I ask.

"I don't think he knows exactly what, but he did something to you."

I cross my arms and sit back. "That's not fair."

"You don't think he did something to you?" The doctor crosses her arms.

I sigh and reply, "I don't think it's fair to say it was him. Maybe something was just moving through him."

I'm getting tired of being grilled. Hearing the frustration in Mira's mind while Thiia still cries on the other side of the room takes me to my limit.

Dr. Kavali glances over her shoulder at one of the officers studying the screen on a tablet. He leans toward her and whispers, "No spikes in power."

The doctor is about to say something else, but I put my hand up to stop her. "Hold on. Are you trying to stir shit up? We're not mad at the kid."

"Speak for yourself, Oscar."

"Mira..."

"Not me, but Carmel is, of course, upset. What he did hurt us. In the temple, that blast seemed to be coming through him, but whatever happened in the courtyard—he was more in control. He might not have intended hurt us, but he caused that to happen."

"No flares," the officer whispers to Dr. Kavali again.

"Yeah, we can disagree without getting angry. We're a highly functional family," I explain. "You're going to have to give me a break though. I'm exhausted, and I've told you all I can remember right now."

"Same," Mira says.

"I understand." Dr. Kavali places a hand over her heart and looks sincere. "We don't mean to press you or make you feel unsafe. Please, be patient with us as we try to protect everyone from this threat." She bows her head slightly before standing and waving her team away. "To tell you the truth, I think people like you are paramount to defeating these sentient storms we've come across."

"You've seen this type of thing before." I can hear it in her voice. "There've been other storms?"

She glances at the UNAF officers. "Yes, Mr. Kenzari. When I began working for the UNAF researching individuals with extraordinary psychic abilities, we were mostly studying prescient people. We called them all divinators. They predicted the sentient storms would come, but their success rate as to when was low. Whenever the storms came, we found people, like you, who suddenly had extraordinary abilities. I suggested that the UNAF keep the name divinators for these gifted individuals who've enlisted to combat the storms. I've suggested that the UNAF create a campaign to redefine the word from those who 'predict the future' to those who 'protect the future.'" She looks us both in the eye. "I think you have that power."

ꝏ

excerpt from interview with Arun (no family name) conducted by UNAF special unit investigating extra-normal phenomena led by Dr. Ana Kavali, UNAF Project Ascension
Thiruvanaikaval School of Math and Sciences,
15 March 2030,
following First Assault by extradimensional being (EDB) known as Bakkeaux,
(Translated from Tamil)

Arun: "After that, I worried they would be upset. I didn't know I would hurt them, but somehow, I knew what to do. When we went back inside, the man came and sat next to me. He was kind. And I could understand him perfectly, but I do not speak much English. He asked if I had ever flown anywhere, and I told him that I had not. He asked if I wanted to, and I told him yes. Then, he asked me to come with him to get their SkyVan. I think he wanted me there to help protect him. I was happy the demon was gone."

Kavali: "Do you think you could do what you did again?"
Arun: "I don't know if I can without hurting people again."
Kavali: "But you could do it again?"

ꝏ

CASEY

"This thing fucking hurts." I point at the small black bar implanted in my temple moments after the Haddyc's psychic attack that left so many of us screaming and writhing on the floor. "There's no reason for me to be in here."

"Ops thought so too for a while, but they changed their minds. Everyone involved in generating the crystal chamber is quarantined," Franxis says.

"Except the Sages, of course."

"Pissed you can't play with your new power set?" Franxis smirks. They shift the obstructor on their head.

I realize they've been here for a while, wearing the obstructor to ensure that we don't accidentally reinstate our accompaniment bridge. I'd rather let them go, let them be free of the obstructor.

"I'm worried this div-bar is going to keep me from locking in Four. I don't want to regress because I couldn't process, you know..." I smile and admit, "But yeah, I can't wait to train with my new power set. It'll be fun."

Franxis' mix of adoration and exasperation is my favorite of their unique expressions. There's a hint of irritability in their eyes, but also a smile under their thin mustache.

"You know..." Franxis raises their eyebrows and lifts one corner of their mouth. Their tone is both playful and serious. "It's kind of a mess in there. I'm honestly surprised you got to Four, but I'm very happy you did. It made a huge difference in defeating that thing."

"Afraid to say its name again?" I smirk.

"MaalenKun," They sigh. "How's your hand, your arm?" With the div-bar and obstructor in place, we can't easily transfer. I realize that for the first time in a long time, Franxis doesn't know how I will answer.

"Feels like it got poked by a psychic needle from hell. At least it won't leave a scar. Not one you can see anyway. I'm used to the invisible kind."

"We've treated similar injuries. That independent contractor Zinwara's injuries are more concerning. She'll be in quarantine a long time, so at least you'll have her nearby."

"Even if I did want to make friends, I'm honestly not in the mood for passing notes on paper." Again, I feel annoyed with Scire's outdated rules limiting technology in the quarantine ward. "You know other stations don't have the same rules against tech in quarantine."

They don't let me change the subject. "Might be nice for Zinwara if you wrote her."

"Psychic needle in my writing hand."

Franxis looks serious. "I talked to her comp, Ehsan. He didn't say exactly what, but there's something weird about her injuries. She's having a hard time."

"I'll see if I can fit it into my busy schedule."

Again, the adoration and exasperation.

"That obstructor is flattening your mullet."

"Sacrificed a good hair day to see you."

"Thanks, buddy."

Their eyes move to the div-bar. "The pain will ease up once the bar adjusts to your personal signature."

"Can't. fucking. wait."

Franxis puts their hand on the thick glass between us. I put mine on the other side of theirs. A wave of compassion moves through the glass, into my hand, a salve for my wound.

Franxis is slightly sarcastic, mocking me lightly when they say, "Stay strong, buddy."

We don't say goodbye. We never have.

The other divs pass by my room on their way out of quarantine. They are nice enough to say hello, but they don't stick around for too long. None of us want to risk an accidental connection, potentially bridging the burning wound that's keeping me in quarantine longer.

Both of the divs that I've slept with—separately, but both months ago—linger for a few moments as the rest of the group walks away. Seems like both of them want to maybe say something. They both seem to realize why they hung back, and it gets awkward for all of us. Awkward for me mostly, just watching them simultaneously figure out that I'm not interested in speaking to either of them. I'm not looking for a connection.

Echoes of the Haddyc sting heat my subtle body, my mind. I try to quell them but can't.

I look at the books on the shelf. All of them are decades old. I've read them all but one. I try to muster an interest in the biography of the world's wealthiest woman, the first multi-trillionaire. I already know the most interesting bits, just like anyone on this station. She's the reason it's still up here.

Griselda Harris Ferand, Helixx Corp President and CEO, bought Scire when the UNAF was ready to decommission it. The three newer stations were thought to be enough, but Ferand announced that added protection would be her gift to the world. Rumor is, she bought the station for greater access to div-tech that she sells to the ultra-rich. She's got a small army of divs working for her, creating a fountain of youth for the richest people. She gets paid to keep their bodies healthy and youthful, their minds sharp, and their mansions, yachts, and private islands protected from not just EDBs but common people. Although, I'm sure all of that isn't in the book.

I set the book back on the shelf.

I meditate for an hour, and when I open my eyes, my lunch is waiting for me. As I eat, I look over my files. Medical examinations confirm that I am physically healthy. The damage was done to my subtle body.

The hallway door opens, and Dr. Liyan approaches the glass wall.

"Not going to sugar-coat this, Div Isaac. We're now quarantining everyone who sustained an injury from the Haddyc. We need you to stay longer, not sure how long. Regardless, we feel that in just a few days we can remove the div-bar. Then, you can train and experiment in the quarantine ward facilities."

"Why am I being held longer than the standard day? We've seen Haddyc stings before, and aside from that pain getting triggered, I wasn't affected by the psychic attack on the other divs post-encounter."

"We've never encountered an EDB like the one that stung you. Also, your situation is unique in that you leveled up during the attack while linked to several other divs and Sages—"

"That's not unheard of, doc." I uncross my arms and put my hands on my hips, an old technique for empathically encouraging someone to open up.

"Div Isaac." She sets her tablet down and adjusts her obstructor. "It's honestly not you. We're more concerned about what's happening to Divinator Zinwara Osei of The Queen. While the other physically injured divs have recovered, we've kept them in quarantine, like you, for monitoring. Osei's wounds seemed to be just physical scratches and cuts—which in itself is unusual, considering she was in the Haven. Once we got her in the quarantine ward, we got a better look. There's something going on that we don't understand. I am not authorized to tell you anything more than that."

Again, the Haddyc sting radiates.

Hundreds of paper lotuses are scattered across the floor, a book on origami lies open amongst them. I'm using everything I can in the room to burn off anxious energy, to occupy my mind so that I won't worry over the unpredictable heat surges in my arm.

I move my body. Asana, handstands. Pull-ups. Push-ups. With div-enhanced duration, I barely break a sweat.

Meditation feels increasingly challenging and less appealing. Maybe my mind is telling me to not even bother with it until I', not so anxious. It's hard to be patient, but I try to be understanding.

I think of Zinwara and how afraid I would be in her place.

I write her a short letter. I don't really know her, and I try not to fill the page with assumptions. Instead, I tell her a bit about myself, express gratitude for the support she and the other divs gave me as I leveled up to Four, and I ask her if she wants to borrow the Griselda Harris Ferand autobiography, because honestly, I can't stomach having it in my room anymore.

After sending the letter, I begin longing for face-to-face (minus thick glass) conversation. I haven't seen Franxis all day. I ask Dr. Liyan if I've had any messages, but she doesn't "handle messages." She tries to assure me that MedOps would've gotten any notes to me. I try to chat up my nurse, but he is apparently not interested in making friends, so I eventually stop trying.

I lose count of my pushups around 265 or so. I lay face down on the sweaty mat. A thought sticks to the forefront my mind: I'm fucking lonely in here.

I haven't felt overwhelmingly lonely in years. For a century, Franxis has been with me for emotional support. Since coming to Scire, it's been easy enough to find someone to hook up with whenever I felt even a hint of longing. Counsel has been helping me sort through the mess I carry with me. Even when I'm at home, I have Lilly.

Fuck, I miss Lilly, the hologram AI cat in my quarters. I'm losing it.

I'm so bored that I actually start reading *Living Beyond,* Griselda Harris Ferand's autobiography. I open the book several chapters in to find a fascinating read about her desire to become living data and inhabit a technological body of her own design.

I test the limits of my endurance doing pull-ups, sit-ups, asana for hours. The effort and repetition are more mentally taxing than physically. Still, I can't avoid feeling lonely. It makes me insecure, and I fall into the pattern of self-condemnation which precedes self-disappointment which borders self-loathing. An intense flare of heat surges as if the psychic wound is reopened.

My mind turns to my upcoming performance review. Central won't let them transfer me until I'm out of quarantine, but I'm growing anxious that Helixx Corp will want me to leave. The fear of being let go, unaccepted by other stations, and sent back down to Earth nags me. I could most likely find work as private security for someone, but I'd rather be up in space. I don't want to be planetside worried about EDBs while dealing with all of the additional man-made threats like economic instability, housing crises, climate emergencies, and more. Psychic heat pulses alongside my thoughts of uncertainty and worry.

I feel trapped inside this small room, trapped with loneliness that I can't quell, a weakness that I was sure I'd pushed past.

I plant my hands and push up again, counting each rep to focus my mind, not the emotion, not the neediness. But it's there, deeply ingrained like an etching in my core.

I remember Usain's raised voice: "Stop living in the past, Casey."

I push hard, lift my hands, clap, come down. I do this only once when the sound for whatever reason, triggers my memory. (My father hits me across the face. A flare of anger surges within me.) Heat glows from the wound. I try to push away the memory. The heat builds. More push-ups. (I push him.) I refuse to let the triggered memories cause me to freeze. Again, I push hard, lift my hands, clap, come down, repeat. (He yells at me.) I push harder. (He pushes me away.) Repeat, repeat, repeat.

The heat pours through my arm like lava. I collapse, holding my arm as it burns within. I lay on my side, curled in on myself, clutching my arm. The heat begins to dissipate. The memories and loneliness wane. For a few moments, I feel only frustration before a numbing question of self-worth occupies my mind. I quell the questions and sense a momentary flicker of heat pulling at the memories, blame, anger, and diminished self-worth.

The Haddyc's sting burns its way into my traumatic memories, prying at them, as if it is looking for more of my pain. As I become aware of it, the prying diminishes and fades into nothing.

I tell myself that it's nothing to worry about, that it's gone.

"Casey, do you need help?" the unseen nurse says over the intercom.

I unclench my teeth and answer, "Just another flare up."

"Scans indicate that it's passing. Do you—?"

"No. I don't."

I crawl onto the bed and hold the kambaba jasper stones held by so many other divs who occupied this room before me. The Terran stones are said to be grounding, centering, but I don't feel them working. I turn towards the window and see space and stars through my own permeable reflection. Thousands of dead stars peek through the darkness of space.

(My lip bleeds. I have no idea why he's taken me to a strange city until that moment. My father kicks me out of his truck. He's taken me there to get rid of me. He slurs familiar insults, and I call him a hick. He tells me not to come back to his house. Part of me is relieved. I no longer have to wonder if he loves me. Now, I know he doesn't.)

I almost throw the stones across the room. Instead, I loosen my grip and allow the weight of them to ground me. I rub my thumbs across their smooth curves and begin to calm down.

I let the tears come. Tears slide across my temples, pooling and sliding down the div-bar. I close my hand around the stone and hold my fist to my chest. I focus on my breath moving my body. I feel the steady pulse of my heart. The div-bar blocks my ability to feel the light-thread connecting me to Franxis, leaving me feeling disconnected.

ꝏ

I rub the quickly fading, pink scar where the blade of the div-bar was inserted into my temple. My head rings from the procedure and the unexpected flood of sound and light that I momentarily lost myself to. The migraine is still fading.

It's going to be okay. The voice that accompanied my dismissed vision of love echoes. Something about it, more about my perception of it, feels off, and that makes it more difficult to dismiss.

Are you sure you don't want to tell anyone about that prescient vision? Franxis asks.

It wasn't prescience, I say. *It was more like a dream. Full of symbols and impossibility.*

Still… Franxis transfers from far away. *The best person to talk to about it is right in front of you.*

Behind the glass wall of my quarantine room, Yahima stands poised and tall as Dr. Liyan and a team from MedOps argues with them. They've switched off the intercom, but they're obviously unhappy with Yahima. MedOps wants Franxis unbridged.

Yahima calmly holds up their hands and dissents again. They fold their arms across their breast and become still like a beautiful mountain.

From the strength of our psybridge, I can feel Franxis observing from their comp deck. They grow quiet, listening to what I am observing.

Yahima patiently lets MedOps realize that they are not going to change their mind.

Yahima has the other Sages on their side. They've already discussed with Ops who has the final call, and not only will the bar not be going back in, but the comp-bridge will remain in place.

I realize I am picking up on all of this by gleaning Yahima's mind.

Yahima acknowledges my accidental gleaning with a nod and smiles gently when they see how relieved I am to hear it.

The doctor once again checks my vitals scan, sighs heavily, switches on the intercom, and departs.

"Hello, Casey Isaac."

"Nice to see you again, Yahima." I wait until they are seated first before sitting across from them.

"This was your first time for a div-bar removal." Almost a question.

"The few times I was in quarantine while at Three, the disruptor circlets were enough. Lucky me, I'm at Four now, so they have to go deeper. Lots of firsts happening around here lately."

"Perhaps we are moving into uncharted territory." Yahima tilts their head and their brow furrows lightly. "You seem stable. How do you feel?"

"Steady. But I'm confused about what happened when the bar was removed. That energy was terrifying yet magnificent."

"Scans indicate you pulled down from above Seven. That would be very difficult to receive at Four. I know of only one other person, now a Sage, who has done something similar. His power was difficult for him to control alone. It took a lot of assistance from others to get him stable. You're fortunate it was just a glimpse."

"I'm also disappointed. Thought I was getting out of here, back to work."

"Soon." Yahima speaks slowly, intentionally. "I have read your recent activity files. Several years ago, one of our more prescient Sages foretold a first encounter with a very powerful and dangerous being coming with the next confrontation, but we did not know when that would come. Along with Ops, we had been following your advancement through Three and felt that because you got so close to Four quickly, you'd have momentum. We requested your presence in the Haven because we felt that during the confrontation, you would rise to Four and possibly lock it in place yourself. Until a divinator moves beyond Seven, that surge that comes with Rising to a new level is strongest moving from Three to Four. We felt that surge would enhance everyone in the Haven. It did. I have to admit that I had reservations. I thought you were too self-absorbed." Ouch. "If you had not been able to hold Four stable during the encounter, we could have been compromised. Instead, you proved to me that you are quite skilled. I am grateful that you were there, Casey." She transfers an acknowledgement that the Sages' AAR left out the fact that I spotted the ornaments before anyone else.

I transfer back that my report said that it was only after I had been stabbed that we all simultaneously noticed the ornaments, and I simply verbalized not to reach for them. I didn't want Ops to feel like the Sages had slipped up by not noticing the ornaments before a div.

They transfer that the warning about the ornaments seemed to flow like a Sage Level transference. They were surprised to realize that it had come from me. "You were in the first era of Rising. Did you have a Sage foretell what Level you would reach?"

"I did. They said I would tap out at Six. Why'd Central stop having prescient Sages do that for new divs?"

"It set up expectations which easily became obstacles." Yahima smirks. "Also, those Sages were only right about 35% of the time."

I start to smirk too but stop myself when I realize that the math means there is a 65% chance that I won't even make it to Six.

Perhaps sensing my thoughts, Yahima smiles and shakes their head. "Maybe you'll go further than Six." They tilt their head and say, "Most divinators have more time with Three than you did."

"Typical Capricorn, very focused, driven," I joke.

Appreciating the humor, Yahima smiles politely but gruffly replies. "And yet, it took one hundred years to get to Three."

I try not to look hurt. "For a few decades, I was more focused on becoming a skilled pilot. I can fly any ship on this station and the station itself. Also spent a good deal of that time working with div-tech in aerospace engineering. Helped develop newer wings. Crux-wings, especially."

Yahima does not seem impressed, even though most people are when I tell them that I designed the crux-wing.

"How long have you been so driven to succeed?" they ask.

"Since my initial Rising."

"First Assault of Bakkeaux, Southern Los Angeles."

"You've read more than my recent activity?"

"That was in recent Counsel logs. How did you find your sessions with Counsel?"

"Good... good..." It's hard to find the right words until I realize there are no right or wrong answers. Yahima only wants me to answer honestly. "I feel like I really made progress. I think I know better how to handle that trauma, those memories. I'm able to admit to myself what actually happened and forgive myself for what I felt guilty about for so long. Success. I'm healed."

"Healing is not a destination, but an orientation." Yahima states, and I look away. "And you have been processing other trauma as well?"

I sigh deeply. "Things I haven't thought about in decades have been coming up when I get lonely—intensely lonely."

Sympathy moves across Franxis' comp-bridge to me.

"Does that increase the urge to leave?"

"Very much so."

"Has it always?"

"What do you mean?"

"I've seen it before. A lot of divs have a pattern of loneliness increasing their urge to leave, to run away, to do their work intensely, to use their lovers to make themselves feel better." Their words feel pointed, but I sense that they are not intended to sting. "Patterns from a century ago still influence most of the Risen." They look into me. "You have a tendency to keep others distant, because you feel that if you do so, there is less chance of those memories coming up." Yahima knows they're right, but I nod anyway. They gaze at me with compassionate eyes. "It will be difficult to lock in Four if you continue those patterns."

I had no idea this would be a Counsel session. I didn't know Yahima knew about my sexual habits, but then again, they're a highly skilled psychic. I feel no shame, but still, I wasn't ready for this. "Thought you were here today to lock in Four for me."

"No." They shake their head slowly. "Another Sage might be willing to, but I am not. That's because I believe in you. You can lock it in yourself. Then, you make yourself more stable, access more power."

"But Yahima." I point toward my head. "Even my comp says it's a mess in here. Doesn't the quick rise from Three to Four make somewhat of a slippery slope?"

"You may digress. If you do, you will have to deal with that. You've been pretty skilled at obscuring early trauma from Counsel, Casey. I think the obscurations your comp helped you put in place long ago when that sort of thing was standard actually kept you from dealing with your trauma, but you had a pattern of avoiding it long before that, long before your initial rising."

I feel ambushed but that's the point. I don't know what to say or think.

"I don't know this from your file or know this from transference. I know this because I know what hurt looks like, even in someone who has ignored their hurt for so long. It always looks the same." They pause and tilt their head again. "I know it because I saw it in myself for so long. In my first community, I was honored as two-spirit. Climate crisis caused southern Louisiana to sink, and I was separated from my community. In the climate refugee camps, I faced a lot of hate for being indigenous and for being intersex. My jaw was broken more than once or twice. I was cast out of so many places that I thought I would die alone."

Yahima meets my eyes with a gentle smile, and mutual compassion runs through our light-thread.

"Then, my initial Rising made it harder to die. A lot of things changed for a lot of people when we started to Rise, but not everything changed. A lot of us brought baggage with us. Those obscurations Ops encouraged in the beginning were very popular. Everyone that put them in place denied a part of themselves or their past, and that denial led to internal struggle. Ops thought if we just ignored or blocked things out, we could be better warriors even if for a short time. They hoped it would be long enough." Yahima gazes deep into my eyes. "If we are busy fighting a battle within ourselves, how can we fight for each other?"

I nod, holding Yahima's gaze. A tremble of emotion runs through me, and I subdue the desperation. "How do I not fight this battle within me?"

"By not fighting with yourself or your past. Take down the obscurations. Destroy the patterns that do not serve you. And please, give yourself now whatever you needed back then."

As I absorb Yahima's advice, I become grateful for quarantine. There is nothing to distract me from doing this deep work within myself.

Before I shed too many tears, I hold the smooth jasper stones and consciously call up that old hurt. I do my best to move through the memories with skill, not avoiding but accepting as much as I can. It's not easy. At times, the images and hurt still overpower me, and I just want to keep the memories in those darker corners, strengthen the binds that keep them at bay. The Haddyc wound glows hot. Instead of running from the pain, enforcing that pattern that doesn't serve me, I steady myself. There is no way for me to know if I am making progress in such a short time, but maybe that is not what it's about. What I do realize is how to accept my past with a bit more ease, with a lot more compassion. The heat of the eldritch wound dims.

My work with Counsel, my conversation with Yahima, even recalling how I pulled myself away from MaalenKun's mirror mask lifts me in a way that develops self-confidence. I realize I will not heal for a long time, but the capacity to do so is within me. Somewhere. I orient myself accordingly.

From my window, I watch the wings that go out, dusting rocks, snagging debris, monitoring StillRift-2138.

The crystal containing the weakened Haddyc floats a short distance from the station. The heat of the wound pulses faintly. There's a monster trapped just outside our door, and there's an opening to the monster's world glowing nearby. In spite of Scire being the least qualified to guard an extradimensional breach, we've been pulled into the position.

"Aw, buddy," Franxis says, picking up on what remains of last night's reorientation work. They strengthen our psybridge with fluent shifts in the subtle atmosphere of my mind. "Tough working on yourself, huh?"

"I've been so focused on leveling up, getting past the trauma of the First

Assault. Might've subconsciously used all that to avoid all the shit that came before."

"Sub-consciously?" They ask sarcastically. Both of us snort. My mood shifts, lightens. "It's okay, buddy. You don't need me to enforce obscurations for that anymore, do you?"

I whisper conspiratorially, "That's not allowed anymore." I shake my head. "I just need your accompaniment."

"I got you."

"You're the best comp there is."

Franxis sits across from me and leans toward the glass wall between us. "I'm here to tell you that you're getting what you want, but not quite the way you wanted it."

"What's happening?"

"The Sages have gone back into MaalenKun's mindfield several times. They report that its body still lies at the base of the crystal chamber, injured, somehow not dying. In short, its defenses are down." Franxis says, tone flat. "Ops wants to bring together the team that took down the monster. Sages suspect that the extradimensional being's energetic signature locked in information assimilated from the team's perception to shape its humanoid body, and if the original team goes back in, it will be easier to study. Other arrangements of teams have gone in but have been unsuccessful in gaining any further insights. Also, they couldn't fully crystalize it. I think you're going back in to find out how to kill it."

Franxis hears my questions about Zinwara and the other injured divs before they can fully form. "Other injured divs Chekov and Giles will be suited and shielded like you. That way, you don't feel special." Franxis winks. "From what MedOps tells me, Zinwara will remain quarantined. Her comp—Ehsan—will be in his station on The Queen, receiving a strengthened connection from his other divs, one in the Haven and another in a wing alongside the crystal. They can't run the risk of bridging Ehsan to Zinwara right now, so this is the next best thing."

"What's happening with her?"

"She's physically stable. I don't know more than that. I'm sure the Sages do, but that'll be obscured from you when you sync up. If he knows, Ehsan doesn't say what's going on with her."

"Must be awful." Light-threads from our hearts towards Zinwara's room glimmer with emerald compassion.

My excitement swells. Franxis senses it and smiles wide.

"There's a drop coming to the closet. It'll have your mission gear in it. It'll all be set from Ops so it won't intuit much from you. Shields will be up the whole time—more to keep things in than out. And you won't see anyone but me and essential Ops in route to Haven. Station is on lockdown."

"Seriously?"

"Even though we've seen wounds like yours, you were attacked and injured by an EDB we don't understand. The fact that your wound still causes mental pain is concerning. Considering what's physically happening with Zinwara, we have to reduce risks where we can. Also, I think Ops doesn't want anyone gleaning from you whatever happened during the attack. The AAR's are still not public."

"It's a bit much though, don't you think?"

"Just go along with it. Even with the shield, I'll kinda be able to hug you."

"Sounds worth it, buddy."

My mission gear smells metallic and sterile. The uplink to Ops activates, although there's no reply like usual coming through the comm in my ear. The gear is not set for psychic interfacing, and Ops has the controls. The suit pulls in snug and fit, and the helmet quickly snaps up from its collar chamber, wraps around and over my head, and seals in place. There's a hiss from the air filter, but no systems check on my heads-up display. A quick flash of colors wraps around me as Ops activates the prismatic shield generator. A faint swirl of rainbow colors occasionally slides across the visible boundary.

When I walk out of the room, Franxis throws their arms around the shield and we're almost touching, which is both comical and annoying. We both laugh but it fades fast. They clap my shield over my shoulder, and we exit the quarantine unit together.

The station is eerily quiet. We see no one else in the halls. The command deck is staffed sparsely. There's no officer opening the elevator door to the Haven this time.

"Ok, Casey. You got this." Franxis pats the shield as if patting my back as I step onto the lift.

I wait as instructed until Franxis is at their console on the comp deck, and I feel our psybridge amplified.

When the lift doors reopen, I immediately notice that the effulgent light that filled the space when I last entered is gone. The five Sages sit in meditation on their crystal plinths, and the divs are waiting quietly, eyes closed. They're in the positions they were in the last time I joined them, with the notable exception of Zinwara. The two other shielded and contained divs, Chekov and Giles, both glance my way, and I give them a sympathetic nod.

I take my place. The shield makes it difficult to feel my seat. My ass floats several inches above any support, my legs don't touch when I cross them. In a different setting, this might be funny. I find the most comfortable seat I can, close my eyes, and focus.

This time, there is far less urgency. I feel far more confident, knowing that I'm at Four, yet I feel slightly aggravated that I've had no time to train or lock it in.

Both Scire and the crystal chamber via tugs rotate to the station's previous positions in relation to the rift when the Haddyc was captured.

At Four, I feel the synchronization of our psybridges more fluidly. The spaces around us widen, my body feels both expansive and minute. We consciously entrain on each other's thoughts. Obstacles and boundaries diminish. As we dial each other in, our personal obscurations shift below the glimmering psybridge. All of this happens with much more ease than before.

I sense from several of the other divs who glimpsed their faces in the mirror mask that they have also been dealing with old hurt and new breakthroughs. The commonality boosts us a little unexpectedly, and we sense Murtagh guiding that energetic wave away from an obscuration the Sages have in place, perhaps preventing us from stumbling into awareness of Zinwara's condition or disrupting the Sages' psybridge to her comp, Ehsan.

I focus and refocus, let go, and give in. Again, Yahima watches me as I discharge and dispel doubts and fears. Working with greater clarity of my past, the familiar vibes are easier to quell, but I don't feel any expected boost from that awareness.

Our nimbuses dilate and rise, bringing their sacred geometry together in concentric rings as our Levels coalesce. The Levels integrate, and divination rains down, between, and within us. Its sweet sound moves around us.

The holographic station and the crystal chamber float down into the room. The shape of Scire's primary charger shifts for more depth, panels raised. Several wings float alongside the crystal. Even in the projection, we can see the dark veins of captured storm moving within the crystal, the glow of the div-charged lightning still lodged in the monster.

The Sages call to us, we give, the charger glows, and again the mind-bridge is made. Our astral projections step across the psybridge into the Haddyc's mindfield. Again, the foul stench of the Haddyc hits us. This time, I'm more capable of quickly stifling my disgust. We push our astral projections through the rippling resistance of the weakened EDB's mental barriers.

Below us at the base of the crystal, lies MaalenKun. The iridescent lightning that we slung back into it radiates like a vibrant wound. The mirror mask is broken and part of it seems to have slid away into the dust that became of the storm. Its crown is dim. The ornaments are faint, maybe caught in a small pocket dimension or behind some energetic barrier. Although weakened, the sight of the fiend sends a shiver through the shield, through our beings.

My memory of the crown's radiance surfaces. The sting of a molten needle re-surges within my arm, and I wince. Yahima and Arun have their eyes on me while maintaining our one sight on the injured Haddyc. I recall Yahima's assistance in shielding the others from my pain, and I create the shields on my own. The pain still radiates within me, but I can continue without it affecting others.

Outside the crystal, a small flock of Scire's crux-wings stand watch over the smaller light wing from The Queen. They direct their lights into the chamber. A few drones emit their scanners, sweeping the crystal with fans of light.

The elder Sages begin their song of uncommon compassion.

Strange groaning which sounds like bending metal comes from MaalenKun. Its body cringes. It stirs in the dust at the base of the chamber, pulling its limbs in as it curls. Its own movement seems to cause it more anguish as it pulls away from us.

A light-thread from each of the five Sages beams into the Div collective. They hint at their compassion for this being which attacked us. The song of uncommon compassion resonates within me as we watch its weakened body squirm.

Murtagh calls to us. Light-threads glow in rainbow beams from within a radiant emerald starburst at her heart. She glides her hands around the light and turns her heartstar. Billions of radiant light-threads spin around an unmoving center, ever interconnected. Murtagh searches for a light beam. She shows it to us, gently holding it between her thumb and index finger. A prismatic glimmer runs the length of the light-thread shining down towards the struggling monster. Unlike the other light-threads we see, the glimmer moves in only one direction.

A sympathy builds in at least two of the other divs. More than anything that I can feel for the monster, I feel surging heat where I was stabbed. Nevertheless, I understand. I respect the divs and Sages that can feel compassion for this violent creature which came into our world and attacked us. Through the light-threads at my heart, I send them honor, which spurs radiance within us all, and although I cannot find compassion for the fiend within it, I do find the light-thread from my heartstar moving towards MaalenKun. I see the light-threads from the other divs, the Sages, extending down, meeting the tip of Murtagh's. The light-threads converge just before the grey light bleeding out of the Haddyc.

As a single beam, the light-threads connect to the grey light, and MaalenKun is suddenly shoved to the other end of the chamber. The rest of the broken mirror mask is flung into the dust. A shock of surprise rushes through us, but we stabilize quickly, shifting Levels above us back into seamless integration. A surge comes from comps. The crystal rocks despite the tugs meant to keep it in place. The wings outside flash their lights three times, pause, and repeat three flashes, a warning sequence.

More tugs are launched from the harbor, and when locked onto the crystal, maintain a steady distance from the station.

We all realize it before the signal from comps. The trajectory would have directed the crystal back towards the rift. We pushed it back in the direction from which it came. Another first.

The dust of the fallen storm ripples toward our end of the chamber. Thunderous pulses from within MaalenKun, growing quicker. Each pulse carries an assault of agitation on our minds. As the pulses strengthen, separation begins to spread.

The Levels above us quiver and our shields waver. The shield thins. As we are forced further apart, we become more susceptible to MaalenKun's attacks. Our astral projections flicker, rippling pain in our physical bodies. With a de-harmonizing clamor, the nimbuses slip out of alignment.

Divs quickly reach for support, for each other, attempting to assist in diminishing our distracting fears, residual anger, rising hatred. We strain to bring us back together. The Sages' obscuration drops ever so slightly, and we see behind it. Zinwara Osei, her beautiful, ebony skin opened by large spectrolite crystal formations growing from her wounds looks to us with shock. Our shock and frustration is amplified by MaalenKun's transferred agitation. A flare rises within us full of distrust for the Sages.

MaalenKun's body trembles. A pulse moves through the being and becomes a thunderclap that rocks the crystal and forces the Sages' psybridge to Zinwara to be revealed.

Light surges within Zinwara's spectrolite crystals, and she screams in pain. Her crewmate, the tall ginger, moves to steady her Levels, and I follow him. I look back over my shoulder to see MaalenKun reaching, clamoring for the light in Zinwara's crystals.

As the thunderous agitation breaks our formation, we pour our empathy into Zinwara. Other divs follow suit. We help her diminish her fears, and the light is pulled from the crystals. We cast the light like arrows across the crystal chamber. The volley chips away at its radiance, sending sparks out of its binds. The ornaments are revealed in their wavering orbit around the dying starfire crown.

Our minds reel with bewilderment and betrayal. The Levels above slide further out of integration.

We couldn't tell you, Arun says, but even he knows it's not true.

A torrent builds from us divs. Anguish builds a chaotic fury that is about to fly from us, but the Sages counter it with a massive boundary.

MaalenKun seizes control of the torrent and knocks it back toward us. Most of us are knocked down or out of the mindfield entirely.

Yahima lifts their hands and beautiful eyes and tries to guide the levels back into place. Murtagh and Arun have both arms lifted toward us, mudras raised. We check our distrust, and all divs follow the Sages lead and bring together, on each hand, the tips of their thumbs, middle, and ring fingers, splaying the index and small fingers out. The fury is sent into the space above us, closer to the nimbuses.

Above us the halos, sacred geometry, and symbols aborning the concentric nimbuses are moved closer to reunion. A radiance pours down from the reintegrated rings of light, into the wave, transforming the muddled fury into a controlled rage akin to righteous anger.

The dulled surface of MaalenKun's body pulls inward around the bones of something that is not human, not of the world we protect. The sunken facade is pulled into hollowed eyes. Its jaw opens behind the tightening barrier, and its scream is more like our own.

We all raise our hands, mudras still in place. We thrust the force across the chamber. The monster collapses under the weight of our force. Its crown splits, its body breaks. The grey light crackles out of existence, or at least this reality. Its body slips below the dust.

The Elder Sages amplify the song of uncommon compassion, sending it into our bodies, including Zinwara, including our comps. A warm glow swells within us as assurance couples with compassion.

We pause within the reunification of space and spheres, protected, steady and strong.

The ornaments rise up slowly. As the last of the ash falls from them, the light from the wings outside the chamber reflect on the surfaces of the ornaments. They drift across the space of the chamber and into the open hands of the Sages.

Zinwara looks up, transfers urgently, *Behind you!*

Down in the ash and dust, something stirs. A faint thunder moves through the crystal chamber, and we brace. The body, reformed and frail, rises from under the dust. The light of the wings bounces off of it. And an urgent call from comps tells us what we already know.

MaalenKun stands crownless, ash of the fallen storm sliding off its body, and it steps toward us, coming across the physical space of the crystal chamber toward our astral projections. Fear that the being could step forward, physically entering Haven, grips each of us. The Sages signal to separate from the mindfield, to withdraw the psybridge quickly.

But we cannot.

We strengthen the shields around us, moving Zinwara to the center of the sphere. She is not amplified by the Haven, and although her synchronization is steady, she is the most vulnerable of us.

Without the mirror mask or the crown, MaalenKun appears smaller. Its dull veneer hangs as if unfastened. It limps closer, trudging through the thick layer of dust.

Its invasive transference is full of clattering sounds we struggle against.

It pulls at our language comprehension. Familiar syllables drift up from the commotion. The only words we can pick up on are Latin.

Ave… Eversor…

Hail, Overthrower.

It speaks of itself. It has come here to overthrow.

It turns its faceless form towards me and transfers. ***You…***

The Shadow peers into me, and the other divs slowly turn towards me with fear in their eyes.

Its discordant voice begins to vex us with an alien language. Zinwara cries out touching the crystals in her face, and as we sync concern for her, Murtagh uses this as an opening. Murtagh broadens all of our hearts with a rush of protective love. In a flash, she turns our heartstars aiming our light-threads at MaalenKun. The beams land, knocking its body back again against the other end of the chamber, and we break free of the trance.

The Sages pull all of us back and quickly close the psybridge.

In the safety of the Haven, we sit stunned. Our nimbuses slip away from each other and back to their places above each of us. They disappear from usual sight, integrating the Levels back into the energy of each individual div and Sage. Personal obscurations and patterns settle back into their spaces.

I listen to the hum of my shield generator providing a barrier meant to keep the others safe from any unexpected contamination. But when I hear the sobbing and the other divs gasping, I know the shield no longer matters. I open my eyes to see Zinwara Osei out of quarantine, at the center of the room. Arun immediately casts a shield around her to quarantine her.

Each Sage holds within their hands one of the five ornaments. When they pulled the physical objects from the crystal through the astral projection, Zinwara came with them. As the crystals growing from her body shimmer, she curls into herself, crying on the floor of Haven.

Franxis meets me at the quarantine ward as I walk out. They give me a long-held, unshielded hug, and as they hold my hand while we walk back to my apartment, my heart lights up.

"Got a priority message before I stepped out the door," I say.

"About your performance review?"

"Not canceled… but postponed indefinitely." My smile widens.

"I guess they appreciate your help in containing MaalenKun." Franxis adds facetiously. "Buuuut…"

"Yeah, but…"

"Well, The Queen refuses to leave without Zinwara, so a lot of transfers have been delayed. Another highliner is scheduled to ship out a lot of folks tomorrow. From the looks of it, the rumors are true." Franxis sighs heavily. "They're sending away a lot of Queers."

"Well, buddy," I put my arm around their small shoulders. "We had a good run here."

"We haven't been asked to leave yet." Franxis' voice is slightly strained.

"If you want to stick around with your other divs—"

"Shut up." They put their arm around my back and squeeze me close. "I'm not leaving you. But I thought maybe you'd want to stay here with Scire tech, maybe complete the S-class hyperdrive, the pod-ships."

"I've had a lot of time to think about it, and really it all comes down to whether or not we want to stay with an organization that is becoming less inclusive, even if they want us to stick around."

"Agreed," Franxis says enthusiastically. "I was willing to stick around if you needed to be here, but if you're done, I'm done. Let's put in a transfer request."

"Maybe we can easily join The Queen, since they're already here."

"They won't leave Zinwara. Ops has her in the training facility daily, trying to replicate the teleportation. They even brought in Helixx Corp trainers, which is surprising since she's not their employee. Ehsan says it felt like she accidentally drew some attainment through the crystals when the Sages accessed what they needed to teleport the ornaments."

"That's weird."

"Yeah, so I don't see Helixx Corp letting her go anytime soon."

As we walk, we talk about our options. We make a list of other stations we most prefer, with Yerum at the top, Mani second, Eagle last. We're both okay with lunar colonies if the stations pass on our request. We'd rather find independent contract work on a ship in the Earth's sector than go to the Martian territory. Going planetside is last on our list.

Lilly is happy to see me; her holographic cat greets us at the door to my quarters. I've got too many Joynr messages to deal with.

I shower quickly, while Lilly entertains Franxis with jokes. Their laughter is like wine, I swear I'm getting a buzz from the sound.

"How'd you feel to be back in your mission gear?"

"Annoying, considering." We're both lit up by each other's good mood. "You know I'm eager to get back to missions. Hell, at this point, I'd be happy to go back down to Earth for a run, just to get off this station for a bit."

"Careful what you wish for, my friend. Rumor has it, they're looking for a team to go to South America."

"For what?"

"No idea."

"Lilly, search the network for any clue as to why they would send a team to South America."

The holographic cat hops onto the bed next to Franxis and turns her head toward me. "On the South American continent, there is only one registered EDB. For three years, a being of unknown origin has occupied a region in the Amazon's UN-protected zone. UNAF monitors the being and the zone from a small base known as Amazonian Amparo-1. News reports show gathering crowds at the patrolled borders of the isolated area. Many of them claim the EDB is a deity being held prisoner by the UNAF."

Lilly shows us a picture from a news report. UNAF soldiers behind the gate stare down a crowd gathered on the other side.

"I would guess that if there is a team leaving from Scire for South America, the team will be going to Amparo-1. Other AI are telling me now that the news reports and rumors on the station have led to searches for more information. There are, however, no statements made publicly available by Ops about such a mission. Reminder: my search capabilities are limited."

We both look at each other with raised eyebrows, and I verbalize what we're thinking. "Another cult brewing."

"Sounds localized, but that's got to be it," Franxis says, and Lilly looks back at them, swishing her tail. "Lilly's amazing and cute. Do I want a Holo-pal now?"

The feline projection turns toward them. "Franxis, I know several delightful AI's looking for homes. I could introduce you if you'd like."

"She likes playing matchmaker," I say.

"That's okay, Lilly. I like having my quarters to myself." Franxis declines the offer, but I'm in the mood.

"Lilly, open Joynr, set something up for tonight. My place. Prioritize anyone I haven't met up with yet."

Franxis smiles up at me. "Finally breaking the sex-fast?"

"I'm done with being pent up." I pause, knowing they can read what's coming up in my mind, but I also know it's to my benefit to verbalize my feelings. "In quarantine, I realized that I'd been using others to avoid dealing with my shit. I still want to fuck… just without doing it to avoid myself."

"Glad you had that insight," Franxis says. "You deserve to be happy."

I have the feeling Franxis is refraining from saying something else.

While we're at lunch, Lilly pings my comm several times with matches, but most of them are familiar faces. I tell myself it's best to find someone new if I'm trying to not fall back into my old patterns. The thought occurs to me that I'm looking for someone that I haven't used before, and I feel a bit of regret dampen my mood. In that heavy space, I pour in the forgiveness Yahima told me to give myself. I forgive myself for feeling that I had to use someone else to get through my own pain.

With a smirk, Franxis asks, "Do you want to go with me to the Avifaun Gardens."

"Sure."

I glean extra enthusiasm about my agreement.

I stop walking. "Why are you so excited?"

Franxis grabs my arm and pulls me along. "The crew from Station Mani are camping in the garden."

"That's weird. They have special permission from Ops for that?"

"Come on. They're really nice. And interesting."

"Why are they sticking around?"

"One of them has a rare attainment in EDB communication. Another has a secondary role in EDB science. Plan is to keep them here for a bit to study MaalenKun. I think you'll really like them."

In the Avifaun Garden, I meet only two of the crew from Mani, and while they are lovely women and very interesting people, I can see that Franxis is disappointed to not be introducing me to one of their divs in particular. There's a little glimmer, a little shine in our psybridge, and I realize what they had been holding back before. They want to play matchmaker as well.

ꝏ

Lilly is far more successful at matchmaking. As requested, messages from guys that I haven't already slept with are prioritized, but there's also a match with someone I've hooked up with several times, one of the divs from the Haddyc encounters. He seems eager to hook up again. He says he wanted to tell me when he had gotten out of quarantine, but he didn't want to make things awkward in front of the other guy I had hooked up with.

I message him back: "That other guy won't be around tonight."

I have Lilly display the proximity tracker on our apps, and I eagerly check it every few minutes.

Lilly blinks her projection and all screens off as I open the door, and as soon as he steps in, before I can say hello, he pulls me to him, and presses his lips against mine. I think maybe he didn't want me to kiss him last time, but as he sucks on my lip, I think I must have him confused with someone else.

Neither of us are really interested in small talk. This is familiar ground, and I find myself focusing more on him and what he wants in an effort to not use him to avoid my own sense of lack. But then, I realize I'm burying my own needs and feeling disconnected from the pleasure. Abandoning the strategy, I pull him closer to my body.

He whispers, "Been wanting this so bad."

"You have no idea," I reply with a smirk. "I've been fasting."

He laughs. "I'd never. I love that contact high from fucking a div who's just leveled up or defeated a hellion. And you're both."

"I won't discourage your enthusiasm."

He is doing the same thing I've done many times before, pursuing someone who's still buzzing from tapping into higher levels, looking for that transferred high through sex. There's a moment of disappointment when I realize it's less about me and more about him getting a thrill through me. This is a new feeling for me. Before, I didn't care what someone used me for when I was using them too. I quell my disappointment. I'm up for the high as well.

He peels off his clothes first, eyes closed, keeping our lips close. My clothes fall to the floor, and we both fall back onto the bed. This is when he stops kissing me. Even during foreplay, even when he is inside of me, he doesn't lean into me for another kiss on my lips, and I want him to, and it's almost thrilling that he makes me wait for another, but he keeps me waiting for it. I realize that it's not going to happen. He's not looking at me. He's lost in the sensation, which is both flattering and frustrating. No idea if he's just lost in the high or if he's actually trying to take me there with him.

Insecurity rises. I'm the one being used. I push the idea away, and just allow myself to use him as well. I want to feel good, and he does. What was once a familiar thrill feels lacking. I focus on the intensity of the psychic energy, the bright currents flowing through my body. It's almost enough.

I trace my hand along the lines of the tattoo on his arm, a giant squid. He smiles, and I realize almost everyone he hooks up with does this. I put my arms around him, pull him closer, run my hand in the hair on the back of his head, but he keeps his eyes mostly closed. I tell him to kiss me, and he finally does, but clumsily and briefly.

His head falls to the side, and he grips the bed and I hold him tighter and soon we're done. He does not kiss me again, and that is fine with me. Coming down from the high is fast and almost a relief.

Through heavy breaths, he chuckles. He sits on the edge of the bed, reaches across the floor for his clothes. "Post-demon-slaying fucks are always the best."

"That's so problematic…" I groan. I prop myself up on my elbows. "How are you at Four and still calling EDBs demons?"

He frowns briefly and dismisses my question with a puff. He walks into the bathroom to clean up but pokes his head out to look at me. "This was fun though, right? Always makes it worth it."

"Not worth a Haddyc sting, but still fun."

"Oh, sorry. I forgot."

I tell myself this hookup wasn't all I wanted, but it was good enough. I'm already going over my avoidance pattern, seeing where I unintentionally enforced it through similar behaviors. Recognizing another pattern which merges with it, a pattern of being too hard on myself, which merges with other patterns of self-abuse, carved deep within me.

He sits on the bed, bringing me out of my thoughts. I'm relaxed, relieved sexually, relieved to notice these patterns. Ready to soon be relieved of my guest. I stare at him, trying to remember the details of his Joynr profile.

I decide to risk the embarrassment. "What's your name again?"

"Harjaz Hassenstein…" he smiles knowingly. "Yours?"

"Casey Isaac." We both laugh a little. It's so easy to forget names once the app is closed and the clothes come off.

"Well, thanks, Casey." He smiles a bit more bashfully than I would expect from him before transforming the expression into a sarcastic smirk. I realize that he's about to confess something, and I withdraw. "I've had a lot of stuff coming up lately. Got some history with the crew of The Queen." We both pause. He maybe senses that I'm not going to inquire further. He laughs lightly. "But I knew I could count on you to put a smile on my face."

I sense that he wants to talk more, but I don't.

He's nice enough, but this moment, is less than what I was expecting from breaking my fast. Something shifts in me. Some awareness of potential, connection. But not with him. With myself.

"Yeah, thanks Harjaz," I say politely. I want something more than this.

When he leaves, I take an ultra-light shower. I miss the feeling of actual water showering over me after sex. I miss the feeling of Usain joining me in the shower. I realize what I'm really feeling, and I'm surprised by my openness to it.

"Lilly."

"Here to help."

"Change Joynr profile, under 'looking for…' Keep what's there now… but add 'relationship.'"

I click open the message before I have too much time to think about it.

"Hey there, Casey. I've heard a lot about you. Franxis has been helping us get settled in while you were in quarantine. Guess I just missed meeting you in person yesterday, but I have a feeling we'll meet soon. Very much looking forward to it. — Oscar"

Compared to the usual, far more direct messages for sex, his short note almost comes across as formal. I wonder if he's being reserved. I'm intrigued.

I switch over to Oscar Kenzari's profile to see his pics. His hair is dark and curly, and his beard is thick but cut close. His eyebrows are bold and expressive. Strong, warm, dark eyes seem to peer at me through the screen. Golden undertones in his tawny skin make it seem as if he is almost glowing from within. He also has a big nose, which I always love. There are three pics, no nudes. Only one pic of him shirtless. I marvel at his dark curls of chest hair, his slightly rounded belly. His profile does say to message him for more pics, which of course means he's got the nudes, he's just more selective with who sees them. I scroll down his profile find: "looking for: casual dating, fuck buddy, relationship."

I'm relieved to see that he's not a prude. I instantly wonder if he sees me "looking for: relationship," and I'm suddenly concerned that will limit my options. I am more than happy to be this man's casual date or fuck buddy. I am actually more comfortable with either.

"You're smiling," Lilly says. Her feline projection stands, tail swishing, as I slide the holoscreen away.

"Lilly… what have we done?"

A holoscreen with a bright red banner appears.

"Urgent message from Ops," Lilly says. The message blinks open, covering the screen. I see the label "priority" glowing red at the top of the message, and I move quickly. Lilly reads it while I get into uniform. "Go immediately to the Action Information Center. They want you there to discuss a plan to send MaalenKun, the Haddyc—"

"An assignment?"

"—back through StillRift-2138. They're putting together a select team."

"Finally!"

"This may be the South America assignment. Sorry."

This actually makes me laugh. "I'll take it!"

I'm halfway to the AIC when I remember Oscar Kenzari's handsome face and hairy chest. I realize I didn't answer his message, and I quickly retrieve my comm to reply before some other guy gets to be his casual date or fuck buddy.

Once I'm in the lift, I try to think of a clever reply. The modesty of his message throws me, and I rack my brain on how to respond in a way that is sexy and clever without being too flirty. Everything I come up with sounds trite, and I type then delete each line except for "Hey, Oscar." I finally give up, delete my last attempt, and step off the lift. As I walk down the hallway, I notice the proximity gauge on his profile is ticking down as I get closer and closer to the AIC.

Another reason to smile.

An operations assistant in the lobby tells me to wait as she messages command in the room. The proximity gauge says he's only a few steps away. I put my comm away, but I can't stop smiling. The assistant raises her eyebrows at me. I probably seem way more excited about this meeting than any of the other divs.

"They're ready for you now," she says, and the doors slide open.

I step into the room. Decorated Ops, including several Captains and Captain

Commanders, and eight Sages occupy a crescent row of seats. A group of divs and comps stand behind the chairs. All of them look towards a presenter gesturing to holographic images of the Haddyc storm as it came through the rift. Oscar pauses his presentation, looks over his shoulder, and my pulse quickens when I see his sexy, crooked smile.

"Hello, Casey Isaac."

He looks at me as if he knows me from long ago, and I wonder if our paths have ever crossed.

He says something else about just getting started, but I am too enamored to get his exact words.

As I make my way over to the other divs and comps, I manage to control my smile, but I feel like a giddy idiot inside. I nod at Harjaz, who nods back. Franxis gives me a quick knowing smile. I nod at the two comps from Oscar's crew who I met yesterday. There are a few others, some from the MaalenKun encounters, some I've never seen before and assume came over with the Sages from other stations.

With a touch of annoyance, Station Eagle's Captain Commander Briggs tells Oscar, "Just pick up where you left off again. Divs coming in late can read the report later."

Captain Commander N'guwe raises a single eyebrow at me, and I turn towards Oscar.

Oscar nods his handsome head, and I have to tell myself to not stare at him but pay attention to what he is saying. "As I was saying, after reading the AARs from Scire's recent encounters with MaalenKun, I had an idea." His voice has a strong but musical quality to it. It's very controlled and intentional, leading me to wonder if he is at Level Five. "I met with our Sage from Mani, Pyaar, and we conferenced with the Sages from Eagle and Yerum before putting this together."

He waves his hand and blue lights from the ceiling spin up a holographic model of Scire, the crystal chamber, and several wings near the glowing rift. Everyone stands, and we all move a bit closer.

"In the last encounter the Scire Sages and a team of divs were in the Haven." The model's Haven glows red. "Divinator Osei was in the quarantine ward, and the station had rotated into the same position of the previous encounter when the Haddyc was captured, putting her quarantine room on the same side of Scire as the crystal." A smaller red light indicates Zinwara's position on the lower ring of the station from the Haven. If I had not seen it myself, I would think her teleportation was impossible. "And then of course, comps—" the comp deck lights up "—and wings with Ehsan's other divs filling in—we thought—for Osei." The models of the wings light up red, and Oscar steps around to the side and stands next to me.

"That is what you had advised, and it put our divs and Sages at risk."

Captain Arianne Holt apparently feels a little touchy about the unexpected teleportation, and I feel a suspicion that the Sages again left something out of their report, but I ignore it.

Arun comes to Oscar's defense, but also to maybe avoid talking about Zinwara being secretly psybridged. "We could also say that it was because of Divinator Osei's presence, we were able to unify through concern for her, and that is what led to defeating the Haddyc. We understood the risks, we always do. That's why we're here."

Oscar bows his head for a moment and continues.

"So..." he waves his hand and the projection changes, the wings move further out and join more wings, including several DSVs. "Our proposed strategy... We know that MaalenKun was captured and defeated by harnessing and making use of a boost from Divinator Casey Isaac's rising to Four."

He turns toward me briefly, and I feel a rush.

"I'm sure we've got many divs in the sector that are close to Leveling up. I'd like to suggest that we get those divs on these wings." The DSVs and other wings glow red. "Sages will assist with Rising where necessary. We can utilize that surge of leveling up energy, create not just a psybridge, but a path." A red line moves from the model crystal to StillRift-2138. "We know from the last encounter that there is a light-thread, a heart-ray, connecting Sages and divs to something in or around MaalenKun. Through that light-thread, our heartstars can create a force that literally pushes it towards the rift." He turns and looks each Captain Commander in the eyes, pausing on N'guwe. "We have your five Sages with your divs in the Haven, bridging us all to the Haddyc, which we can do if we place our other Sages on the comp deck, with Zinwara, and out in the wings. Murtagh can teach any of the other Sages how to spin the heart-rays, how to find that light-thread, and then, we push that thing back into StillRift-2138."

As if it could be that easy. A lot of heads are nodding as they watch the holographic crystal smoothly move away from the station, and as if it is guided by a push coming from the l wings, it disappears into the rift.

Yahima, who is not nodding, tilts their head, gazing at Oscar. "Divinator Kenzari, I believe there is more to consider. As you know, the crystal is a physical manifestation of divination, and many of the upper level divs and Sages who generated it were attacked from the being within it. Even after their recovery, many of them have had troubling dreams and visions since containing MaalenKun. Some of those divs are unavailable for actions at this time, hence our urgent call for more divs to join us in this meeting." Her words sting me again; I was called at the last minute because I'm a last resort. "This being is possibly manipulating the energy of the crystal, affecting the builders of its cage. I cannot approve of sending the crystal into the rift. We don't know if the crystalized divination could be used against the Divs and Sages that created it. It's too risky."

"There is also the matter of StillRift-2138 itself," N'guwe says. "We have repeatedly attempted to send in drones, but they crash against the glowing edge of the rift. It could very well be locked to anything from our world. If we manage to open it, how will we close it once the Haddyc has been sent back?"

Oscar smooths his beard quickly. "No one's ever closed a rift because no one has ever had to. There's no plan for that just yet, but we are on it."

"Is that the end of your presentation, Div Kenzari?" N'guwe asks.

Oscar assents and with a wave of his hand reduces the image of the scene until it is no longer visible.

"Yahima, the floor is yours," N'guwe says.

"Thank you, Captain Commander N'guwe." Yahima steps forward, and with a wave of their hands, calls up another hologram, a view of South America. Yahima parts their hands and zooms in over the upper region, then Ecuador, the Amazon's UN protected zone, and then, through the clouds, and over the edge of the forest. Most of us step in for a better look. Brilliant rays of light shine from within the forest, peeking through the treetops.

"Can you see?" Oscar puts his hand on my shoulder briefly, and my body warms to his touch.

I nod, try not to smile too big, and feel my eyes sparkle when I meet his gaze. He half-smiles before we both turn toward the projection.

Yahima waves their hand, and the satellite image slides to the side. Yahima lifts another image of what looks like a glowing fog blanketing a tree. "This being is known in our records as Vasif. The growing cult that worships it calls it *Diosa en flor.*" Yahima calls up another satellite image of the barrier around the protected zone, enforced by a small number of UNAF troops. The other side of the barrier is crowded with people blocking the road. They're dirty and dusty, wearing tattered clothes. "They demand that the UNAF free this being. To be clear, the UNAF was originally stationed to protect what is left of the rainforest. They found the EDB within that zone years later. They have not restricted the being from leaving. Vasif seems to have settled there some time ago."

"Why is it there?" Harjaz interjects.

Yahima's voice remains stern. "Please, don't get too comfortable in this meeting, Divinators. I will not appreciate another interruption."

Harjaz smirks but bows his head. When he looks up again, his face is stern and focused.

"This being has proven difficult to classify. The UNAF team at Amparo-1 has observed combinations of quantum signatures that are Aphrytian, Dymetian, Aethonic, and Haddyc." Yahima slides the image of the crowded worshipers aside, and calls up another image, an empty village within the rainforest. "Years ago, a team of Ops discovered traces of an energetic signature which we have determined came from this being. The indigenous Waorani, who lived in this village, have vanished. When the team of UN divinators began studying Vasif, it transferred to them in the Waorani's language, Sabela." Yahima slides the image of the crowd at the barrier back to center. "Some of the UNAF divs at Amparo-1 say that Vasif is, in many various ways, demanding worship." Yahima lets that last line land before waving their hands and closing all images. "The UN divs have not called for backup which might make sending in a team from Scire a bit more challenging, now that the operation here is privately owned by Helixx Corp. Central is sending a couple of mixed crews to Amparo-1."

"Why do we need anyone from Scire on this assignment exactly?" Captain Commander Briggs asks. "Why isn't this kept solely to UNAF forces if we're heading to a UNAF facility?"

Yahima smiles patiently but pauses for someone from Ops to answer.

Captain Commander N'guwe turns to face Briggs and says, "Station Scire has pulled out of orbit to guard StillRift-2138. Aside from a few small crews assisting our research departments, we've received little support from the UNAF for this monumental task. We will have a team on every assignment in relation to the rift until Central orders us to rescind the responsibility of guarding the rift."

"To that end," Helixx Corp Captain Arianne Holt adds, "I'd like to send down a team without any ties, former or present, to the UNAF. Since we've taken over Station Scire's responsibilities, we could easily put together a team from Helixx when The Eminent arrives."

N'guwe glares at Holt. "The teams will be working with a UNAF camp, so the UNAF will remain involved regardless. As for the teams, it is already decided. A small group from Scire instrumental in capturing the Haddyc will join experts from Station Mani."

Holt huffs, "I see no need to have former UNAF on that team."

"I do." N'guwe smiles politely. "And I am still Scire's captain commander."

Holt cuts her eyes toward N'guwe, and huffs. "Yes, ma'am. It's your call."

N'guwe gestures to Yahima. "Please, continue."

"We prescient Sages feel Vasif may know how to close the rift, and perhaps we can convince it to leave as well. You divs and comps will escort and support two Sages who'll meet with this being."

Having heard the rumors, I had suspected this, but I had been excited and distracted by the potential of hooking up with Oscar. If they send us to Earth soon, there really won't be time for that. My excitement over the assignment is tempered by my disappointment. Through our connection, Franxis sends a bit of facetious consolation followed by a significant amount of delight.

There is a bit of tension in the room. I am not the only one feeling less than enthusiastic about this.

"Any questions?" Captain Commander Gala N'guwe asks.

"Yeah," Franxis says. "What are our teams?"

ꝏ

"Welcome to the team," Captain Carmel says as Thiia and Mira pat me on the back.

"Happy to be joining you guys," I say.

"You too, Franxis!" Thiia says as we walk through the AIC lobby.

We stop on the observation deck, and Franxis makes formal introductions for Mira and Oscar.

"Nice to officially meet you," Oscar says as he shakes my hand. He is not flirty in any way, which makes it easier for me to act accordingly.

"Officially?" Mira asks.

"Joynr," Carmel says with a smirk. "Not something I gleaned. It's just kind of obvious by how they're looking at each other."

I joke, "I promise, I'm trying to tone down my casually sexy vibes right now."

They're gracious enough to laugh. I'm grateful I can make them smile, especially Oscar.

"Well, you're failing," Carmel says with a wink. "But thanks for trying."

Oscar raises his thick brows, turns one corner of his mouth up, and adds, "She never lies, by the way."

"Should we all go get something half-decent to eat before we ship out?" Carmel asks.

"Let them go do their thing, my love," Mira says, taking Carmel's hand and guiding her away from us.

Thiia juts her chin at Oscar, smiles. Franxis flashes a delighted smile, and they follow Carmel and Mira down the hallway.

"They're onto us," Oscar says.

"Hard to keep secrets around psychics," I tell him. "My place?"

"Sure," he says. His smile is controlled, showing confidence more than eagerness.

I let him step into the elevator first and when the doors slide closed behind us, I step in front of him, a few centimeters from his glorious nose. He does not back away. His gasp says astonishment, his eyes, adoration. The left corner of his mouth lifts higher than the right when he smiles.

"You are very cocky," he says, and I feel his words land on my face.

"I am. Very cocky." He begins to laugh again and actually bites his lower lip to hold my gaze. "I cannot wait to show you how cocky."

"Mm-hmm…" He looks away—a moment of shyness—but forces himself to return my gaze and keep his eyes locked on mine. "I'm not usually so forward."

"I am, especially when there's a short window of opportunity."

Playfully, he says, "Maybe I'm not ready to have you so close just yet."

"Oh," I take a step back, raise my hands, and jokingly say. "My apologies, good sir."

He grabs my hands and pulls me closer, and when he kisses me, he keeps his eyes open until I'm melting into them. Our bodies move closer, and we brace each other.

ꝏ

Lilly does not greet me at the door but stays dormant.

As soon as the door closes, I pull him close to me again. His eyes stay open again when we kiss. It's like he can't look away from my eyes.

My mind turns to last night with Harjaz. This feels much different. Less rushed. It's as if Oscar is immediately tuned into me, sensing what I want. He seems to enjoy the slower, more attentive pace.

I put my arms around him, back up slowly to guide him further into the space, and he steps easily in sync with me.

I will my uniform to loosen, and I slide out of the top which hangs around my waist. My hands reach for the seam down the chest of his uniform. I notice a little hesitation, but he wills the suit to ease away from his body. I pry it open and pull his top down around his waist. The hair on his arms stands up as I trace the line of his neck.

Beauty marks and freckles dot his shoulders, his chest, his abdomen. I run my hand across them, tracing a line down to his waist. At my touch, a slight tremble runs through his body.

His kiss turns into a smile and his voice is low. "Please, get me onto your bed, or I'm going to lose my mind."

"If only to preserve your sanity."

He laughs keeping his eyes locked on mine as we find our way onto the bed.

Again, I'm highly aware of how different I feel with Oscar than I did with Harjaz. Oscar is taking his time, noticing me more, fueling his own desire by moving to meet mine.

There's less of a rush that slams into me like with other divs. With Oscar, we are building it slowly. Our bodies and energies are more synced. The powerful energy is still there but not intensely racing through me. I can follow it coursing through me, on my skin, around me, through him, around us.

Our deployment hour looms too close. I feel a sense of urgency, move for his waistband, and he holds my hand again.

Softly, he says, "There's no rush."

"We leave for Earth soon." Crestfallen, I slump back against the pillow and push my hair out of my face.

"We can wait," he says leaning towards me, kissing my chest twice.

"Oh, what are you doing to me?" I'm almost annoyed, but more intrigued.

He puts his hand in mine and props himself up on his other arm. He interlaces our fingers, pulls the back of my hand to his chest, and rubs it close to his heart.

"Well, sometimes, I meet a guy..." His tone is again playful.

"Not every time?"

"No, not every time, but sometimes... If I feel that I really want to see him again—"

"Sure to happen. Same crew now."

"—and I feel that I really might want to get to know him... And I feel like there's a possibility he wants to get to know me..."

"We can do all of that naked," I whisper.

He laughs a little, "If I get this feeling—this rising interest—and I'm really interested in more than just fucking him... I like—" he kisses my hand. "To take—" again. "My time... Our time."

I prop myself up, so we're face to face. "So we're not fucking... because you like me? You're infuriating." I hope he knows I'm only half-joking, half not. I lean towards him and whisper, "Now, I might lose my mind."

He still has my hand near his heart, and I trace a couple fingers along his neck just to feel him tremble again.

"The anticipation, letting it build, is part of the thrill," he confesses.

I let go of his hand and pull his arm around me so that his hand lands softly on my low back. I slide over until our chests are touching again and bring my face into the spot where his beard begins, the most erogenous place I've found on him. yet. "I am not going to make waiting easy for you."

"Please, don't."

As he kisses me again, eyes open, I realize what the voice in my possibly prescient vision meant. I didn't say *It's going to be okay.* It said, *It's going to be O.K.*

Oscar Kenzari.

ꝏ

excerpt from United News Network,
broadcast: 15 March 2031, 18:00
(translated from Spanish)

"Today, we remember and honor the 2,605,462 lives lost when Bakkeaux simultaneously attacked Thiruvanaikaval in Bharat, South Los Angeles in the United States, and Barcelona in Spain. In the names of those lives lost on that day and during the second assault, we continue the important work of preventing more attacks. UN Armed Forces report that they have had great success in training an elite army of the Risen who will soon be taking the fight to Bakkeaux in the Earth's atmosphere..."

OSCAR

He's staring at my nose, and I'm letting him.

I'm absolutely lost in his eyes. A grey ring circles green. I had not noticed it in his profile pics.

"Your eyes…" I say, wanting to steep in the beauty of the eyes I'd seen in a prescient vision a century ago. I knew he was in my future, and now he is in my arms. I resist coming on too strong by telling him that I glimpsed him when I became Risen. "I know we just met, but please, don't look away right now,"

But then, he looks away. Although I know he is not, he pretends to be shy, which is endearing.

"Yeah, I've heard it before…" he groans. "Yours though."

I raise an eyebrow. "Brown?"

"Mahogany… warm…" He pulls me closer again, and I want to rub my beard all along his neck, his chest, but alas, time.

I sigh. "I need to run diagnostics on our ship."

He looks surprised. "Ops is probably already on it."

"They'd better not. Not until I get there at least. They'll help, but my ship, my responsibility. I'd feel weird if I weren't there to get her prepped."

"'Her?' Still gendering spaceships, I see." He's teasing me now. "Does she have a name?"

I wince dramatically, realize it isn't the best look from up close, and shake my head. "We call her Old Girl."

"This poor ship," he sighs with a laugh.

I'm happy I could make him smile before we let go of each other. We sit on the edge of his bed, and I pull my uniform back up.

"So even if we had more time…" he says, shaking his head in mock disbelief. At least I think it's mocked. "We'd be sitting here, having not had sex, but… building anticipation."

"I think so," I say as I slide my arms into their sleeves. I turn towards him, "We've got time though." I lean in. "Just not now."

When he realizes that I'm holding off on another kiss, he might not be entirely mocking exasperation, but he sighs, smiles, and shakes his head back and forth slowly.

"Ok," he says. "Let's go see Old Girl."

I take in the beauty of his body as he pulls the suit up. Part of me wishes we had gotten out of these uniforms entirely, and a louder part of me is looking forward to when we do.

He sees that I'm watching him. He slides the front of the uniform closed, holds out his arms, raises his eyebrows, and psychically wills the suit to fit to his body. "Let's get fully dressed and spend the rest of our time doing boring checks on Old Girl..." I stand up and hold him closer, his hands slide into the open front of my suit, rubbing my chest hair. "All instead of being naked and on top of each other."

"Top each other?" Now, I can tease him. "Why didn't you say something...?"

And now it's his turn to make me wait for a kiss. He snickers, pulls away, still smiling, genuinely. "Oh... but you want to wait..."

"Something to look forward to."

He doesn't make me wait any longer for his kiss.

I wasn't planning for Old Girl's systems checks to be a test for him, but Casey remains both playfully interested and legitimately helpful. I am happy he's not disappointed and game for letting some anticipation build.

"Shield gen on port side seems a little spotty," Casey says looking up from his holoscreen.

"Yeah, it's been that way for a while. I think the monitor isn't integrating, because we've been out snagging debris and dusting rock and the shield has held just fine."

He looks at me like I'm crazy. "Have you crawled out on that wing lately to check for any scrapes?"

"No," I admit. "That's a good idea though."

"I'll do it, unless you really want to."

I look back at him from the cockpit. "Go ahead. I'll be right here." As he climbs the ladder, I watch his perky butt.

"We might be planetside overnight. Maybe you'll get your chance then," Thiia says as she steps into the flight deck.

I feel my cheeks heat up. After a hundred years of not being able to hide my thoughts from her, she can still make me blush.

She pulls her curly hair back and ties it, smirking at me. "But oh, that's not happening yet, is it?"

"You know how I am when I'm really into someone."

"I do. And he's nice, he's cute. Franxis loves him."

"But..."

She shrugs. "Franxis said he's a bit of a loner."

"A lovable loner."

Her voice is kind. "You know, that's a nice way to describe heart-breakers."

"I'm sure I'll be ok, Thiia."

"Of course, you will. Don't get me wrong, I sense a lot of happiness in there." She circles a finger towards my head. "And that's what we all want. A happy Div—"

"—Is an effective Div." Together we complete the famously mocked catchphrase from old UNAF training videos.

"Status on these checks?" Carmel reminds us of who the captain is as soon she steps foot on the ship.

Thiia launches the comms holoscreens at her console. "I monitored Ops' check on mission gear. All good, but the amp packs from Scire are shockingly old. They haven't received updated gear from Helixx, which is crazy considering. Uplink to stations Scire and Mani is strong, Yerum, good enough. Starting comm checks through cabin, charger stations. Mainframe interface on port wing is still glitchy."

There is the faint sound of footsteps from above us.

"Who the fuck's on my ship?" Carmel asks, looking directly at me. "Did you let Helixx step on Old Girl?"

"It's Casey. He's checking that the shield gen is working ok."

"Is he Tech now?"

"Yeah, secondary role. Specifically with ships." Thiia replies.

Mira shrugs. "It's in his file."

"What about you?" Carmel turns to me. "Status?"

"Almost done. Just running final check on nav, auto, and grav."

"No, I mean with him," she points up.

Thiia and Mira laugh, and all I can do is grin. "I'm not rushing things."

"Oh, it's been a while since you've not rushed." Carmel says as she climbs into the left seat of the cockpit. "He must have potential."

"We'll see, captain." I turn back to the screens floating in front of me, pretending to monitor the numbers ticking away.

Thiia announces, "Scire says we're ready to go when the other ship is cleared. Probably ten at the most."

"Thiia, ping the new temps. Tell them to hustle." She turns back to me and lowers her voice, even though Thiia can certainly feel through our comp-bridge the gist of whatever she says. "So did you at least get to check the goods, make sure they are indeed good?"

I shake my head and can't help but grin. "Yes, his goods are quite good."

"And your sexy psybridge thing? Does he know that's a specialty of yours?" Her smile is mischievous.

I smirk back at her. "I did not mention it."

"He doesn't know?" She exaggerates her mocked surprise. "Hope he doesn't freak out."

"He doesn't seem like the type to shy away."

"Exactly! I hope he's not too excited about banging someone who can loop sensations and pull down from Six so your auras can tickle each other or whatever."

"Some divs get super strength, super speed—" I shrug humbly.

"And you got super-fucking."

I cringe. "Are you jealous?"

"Yes, I'm a little fucking jealous. My wife got foresight. Every move I make is buffered by predictability."

"I like your moves, hon." Mira calls from behind our seats. She meditates in the navigation console behind me. She sits with her legs crossed, eyes closed, looking ahead for anything about the trip down.

Casey descends the ladder. I look back at him, over my shoulder, and our eyes lock and linger on each other. Thiia looks from him to me and smiles.

"How does she look?" Carmel asks, her voice stern.

"Captain—" he heard it in her voice; we're at work now. "Old Girl—" his voice is tinged with a touch of sarcasm "—is looking a little older on her port side wing. The wear and tear are nothing to worry about, but if you've been dusting rock, that means some of it's getting through the shield. Considering we're going in unrequested, if there are hostiles…"

"It's Earth," Carmel grumbles. "There are always hostiles."

"With the unpredictable cult around this EDB, I think it's best to strengthen the shield gen."

"We're clear for go in six minutes," Franxis says, stepping in from behind Casey. They share a smile as they pat him on the back. "Everyone else is in the cabin, captain."

"Thiia, get a techie on that shield gen and fast. Everyone else, cabin."

In the small hull of the cabin, we meet Harjaz, his comp Aaliyah, and a Div from Yerum by the looks of his shiny white gear with reflective silver detailing. I'm surprised to not see a Sage with us but an upper level Div instead. When Carmel steps into the room, they all fall silent.

Carmel meets everyone's eyes as she speaks. "We're out shortly. We're not coming in too hot. Gravity generation won't be necessary, so you'll feel the shift in grav once we're 10 minutes out. Take a grav stabilizer if you feel nauseated, especially if it's been a while since your last trip to Earth. Otherwise, you'll be dragging ass the whole trip, and you might not be able to do your job. For some of you, your Div specialties will mean you don't need the pill. You all should know this, but from my understanding Scire hasn't had a trip down in some time, so just a reminder." She looks over the old Scire mission gear. "Also, Ops will have clearance by the time we get there. We're not expecting any trouble, but I want everyone in battle stations regardless. We're still flying into a zone with an active EDB and an unpredictable cult." She looks around at everyone again as she continues. "Remember we're inviting ourselves, and there are people at this party who probably do not want us there. If things shit goes down, listen to me, listen to first officer Div Kenzari," I nod at the crew. "Listen to second officer Div Adivar." Mira nods. "Our assignment is getting the Sages and specialized divs into the protected zone to see what this…" I glean that she almost called Vasif a demon. "...EDB has to say about the fucking rift. Gonna leave it to the Sages to ask politely. Our priority is keeping everyone safe. Ops might not be, but I am concerned about the crowd of fanatics who think we are keeping them from their goddess. If we come across them, remember we're not there for them. However, if they move to start some shit, don't hesitate. Mission gear is set to combat. Remember, sonics at stun can still break bones, but we don't want to hurt them if we don't have to."

Carmel, Mira, and Thiia step back up front, and Harjaz pats my arm. "Is she always this paranoid?"

Maybe he sees this as an errand run. "Been a while since you've been to Earth, huh?"

He opens his mouth, maybe to say something, but just frowns as he turns away. His comp looks bemused to be on this mission. I accidentally glean her thoughts, and to say the least, he isn't her favorite div.

When I turn around, Casey is there. "Hey," he says. "Thiia came through our comm to let me know the shield is good to go, but I forgot to reply, so tell her thank you for letting me know… since I'm riding in that wing, you know."

"You forgot to tell her?"

"My excuse to catch you before you headed back up front." His eyes sparkle.

I see him looking at the corner of my mouth that turns up more than the other. Backing away, he gives me his overly confident grin again and says, "Looking forward to when we get back."

"Me too," I tell him, trying not to get lost in his eyes and risk looking foolish for doing so.

ꝏ

Back up front, Mira asks me to look at a satellite image. A cluster hurricane with multiple eyes is building off South America's northeast coast. It will add some time to our trip down, but we have to go around it. It is, thankfully, just a mega-storm and not a conscious monster from another dimension. I approve Mira's projected route and she relays the changes to Scire and Mani.

I nod to Carmel looking over her shoulder at me as I climb into the co-pilot seat. She pulls her dark hair back into a small bun that her helmet can slip over. Her hair on the sides of her head is buzzed close, highlighting two thick, dark tattoo lines that wrap around her head and dip below her hair bun. She looks strong and bold, and when I see her now, I'm grateful to also know her as loyal and loving.

"So, we got another div. What happened to the Sage?" I already have an idea but want to hear the details.

The captain waves her hands across the dash and several screens are projected in front of our seats. She doesn't look toward me as I take my seat next to her. "Pyaar is staying to study the Haddyc as assigned. All seven of those Sages are studying the Haddyc as planned."

"And Arun? He was the odd man out, pun intended."

She smiles politely at my joke, but it fades quickly. "He's on board The Arrow. He'll be with us on the ground. I requested he not be sent on this mission, and when that was denied, I demanded that he not fly in my ship."

"Captain, he's been Sage Level for decades. He has more control now."

"You know that?"

"We've chatted a couple times since we've been here. He knows he caused a lot of hurt before—"

"That's putting it mildly." She jams her finger into the keypad to initiate lift off.

"He has a healthy regret about it." I trace a finger across the landing gear screen. The display shows the mag locks release.

We each reach our arms forward slightly, and the crystal piloting discs levitate into our palms. They're cool to the touch, and I feel a rush as the sensation couples with the psychic uplink. My fingers wrap around the discs, and the ship's system tugs at my minds. Old Girl is sometimes a bit cranky with the uplink after she's been asleep for days. The interface smooths out gradually, and Carmel and I receive psychic input about the various details of the ship. Some systems are coming online slowly, but everything syncs up. I will the hover engines to brighten, mag locks to release, and skids to retract. The ship rises in the harbor channel.

"Does he know about Sahil? How he tried to remain active with the UNAF, but after a decade when he still couldn't shake off the trauma, he left? He wasn't the only one. We lost a lot of divs because of him." She swipes away the landing screen projection before I can.

"I haven't mentioned Sahil. Honestly, I haven't thought about him for so long." I feel a tinge of guilt for not keeping up with the man who went through the Rising and the Final Assault with us.

Carmel snorts. "Did he apologize?"

"He doesn't have to. I don't want him to."

"Hundreds of other people feel differently."

"That why you didn't want him on this assignment?"

Thiia calls to us in a loud voice. "Control has us clear. The Arrow is already out."

Carmel and I flex our wrists slightly, tipping the discs forward. Old Girl moves toward the first in a series of plasma-grid airlocks.

"If there's one Sage that should not go face to face with an EDB on the physical plane, it's Arun. But UNAF has loaned us out, and Station Scire has the lead. So here we are, escorting the Sage that killed dozens of divs back to Earth."

Old Girl passes through the plasma grid air locks as small thunderclaps echo behind us.

"Come on, Captain. He didn't intend…" I stop myself, not sure if what I'm saying is actually true. In some way, he had to know that he was hurting people.

"Intention isn't impact. There are people down there who have not forgotten or forgiven." She says as we angle the ship towards Earth. "If you ask me, he's a liability."

ꝏ

As trained, when the sirens go off, we all jump out of our beds and gear up. For a moment, Thiia's head is held low, and I remember how afraid she was during the First Assault.

"It's happening!" someone calls down the paths between rows of bunks.

Thiia looks up, meets my eyes with confidence. A lot has changed since the First Assault.

As we have rehearsed many times, I turn to Thiia, and she reaches up and places her hands on the sides of my head. Her eyes are so focused and clear. She sees a bit of fear in my eyes and smiles at me. I know she is not trying to harm me, but still, it hurts every time. The bolt of pain from my eyes to the back of my skull that comes with her psychic bridge causes me to wince. The pain is so strong that I have to hold her arms to maintain eye contact. This is how we're trained. The bolt transforms into a dull headache which radiates in all directions before dissipating.

You got me? I hear her voice in my mind.

I nod at her.

The sounds of our boots on the tarmac fall into a rhythm. The crowd of one hundred Risen comes together with each divinator alongside their Accompaniment. Forming a line of pairs, we run in sync towards the modified V-wing getting ready for lift off.

We have no idea yet where we're going, but we do know why. Bakkeaux has made its fourth descent. Millions of lives are threatened. We'll be briefed as we ascend.

I look around me, keeping pace, but almost desperate to find Carmel and Mira. I see them a few heads behind us. Carmel nods. Mira, the most prescient of anyone in our camp thus far, flashes a half-smile. It's enough to soothe my nerves.

I look around for Sahil and his comp, but I don't see them.

We've all been training for nearly a year for this. We have no idea if the new tech will even work, but it's our best shot—the planet's best shot a demon that's decimated five major cities and terrorized the globe.

We climb aboard the customized V-wing, taking our seats within the wings which have been outfitted with what they're calling chargers, a combination of new technology and hyper-generated crystals that will not only enhance but direct our psychic energy into the sentient storm.

We pull down our helmets and tighten the straps under our chins. I tell myself that this will work. The cables hanging down from the panels in the ceiling to our helmets rattle against each other like wind chimes making random music as one hundred people get plugged into the chargers.

"We're right behind you." I hear Mira from the second row of seats.

"Can you believe this is us now?" Thiia asks us. "About to fight a space monster with our minds?"

"And fucking crystals," Carmel quips.

"Wouldn't want to fight a demon space-cloud without y'all." I can actually feel my nerves settling as the chargers begin to sync us to each other. There's the subtle but more chaotic cacophony of sound in our heads as our mental barriers and obscurations get shoved around before they're all set aside.

Our bodies jerk as a powerful surge pulls through us, amplifying the chargers. The same green eyes ringed in grey that I glimpsed when I became Risen flash through my mind. Thiia takes my hand and I realize I'd gasped. With her accompaniment, it doesn't hurt quite as much as when they plugged us divs in alone, but the memory of that pain gets triggered even though what I feel now is buffered. I often wonder if it's too much for any of us—if there's an easier way of syncing us.

The plane ascends. Our minds feel steadier when the grounders whirl on and connect us to the energy of the Earth as we soar to a higher altitude.

UNAF Sergeant Dunn stands at the front, tightly gripping a mic. "You might have already heard that this is not a drill." His voice is gruff and hardened, a military man who has a difficult time not yelling at us non-military folks in a battle setting. "Bakkeaux has split into three this time. It appears to be heading towards Kansas City, Mexico City and New Singapore. Being a North American team, we will obviously be heading towards Kansas City along with two other teams. Globally, we've got about six teams in the air already, two more headed to Mexico City, and one to New Singapore. We hope to get an Aussie team on their way to NS soon, but they're having issues with their v-wing... All that to say, New Singapore might not make it through the night. Let's not let that happen to Kansas City. If the nation's new capitol goes down, we could lose a lot of governing officials and organizations that are holding together this operation, our only defense against that thing. We cannot fail, divinators. We kick in hyper in three minutes. Everybody, buckle the fuck up."

Dunn takes his seat and straps in. He studies a monitor and checks the communications link to operations on the ground in Colorado. He's purely tactical. As is the meteorologist-turned-Bakkeaux movement scientist. They appear to be analyzing satellite and drone images, deciding how to coordinate our plan of attack with the other two teams. There's no charger linked helmet for them, but they wear pyrite lined helmets that we are 90% certain will keep Bakkeaux's tentacles out of their heads. If the helmets don't work, there are ten of us on board armed with swifts that will stun them unconscious.

"So sad," Thiia says mournfully. "The team at New Singapore won't be able to do much if they're the only wing in the sky."

I feel heartache move through her, and I couple it with my own. "Let's hope the Aussie team makes it in time." I squeeze her hand. "All we can do right now is focus on here and now."

She lifts her chin and closes her eyes.

We have a different strategy than what some of the leading divs have suggested. Instead of pushing away heavy emotions or distracting memories, we accelerate their processing. Together, we bring the heartache that is here and now, closer, breathe with it, allow it to be, watch it increasing our compassion for each other, for the people of New Singapore, then Kansas City, Mexico City, the teams rushing toward danger. The heartache is transmuted into an awareness, fast moving little threads of connection extending from our hearts.

We're not the only ones who have tuned into these light-threads. We can feel others on board doing the same. Through various glimmering threads, we sense Carmel, Mira, and somewhere along those lines, the familiar feeling of Sahil.

I sense a much more powerful line of energy descending from the quarters above down into us all. A line so thick, it seems to occupy the entire space, going unnoticed by most if not everyone else. I send Thiia a nudge, direct my awareness and therefore hers towards this line.

Maybe the chargers? she suggests in my mind.

I shake my head and signal the suggestion that this feels like something else, something alive.

The pilot tells us to brace for hyper. It kicks in hard, and we're all glued to the seat.

With the newly designed ship traveling so fast, we have about twenty minutes from Denver to Kansas City, twenty minutes to collect ourselves before battling a sentient storm that has taken nearly ten million lives.

As we descend, screens lower from the windows in front of us so that we see the city we've been tasked to save. Ahead of us, a darkened thunderhead, known to conspiracy theorists as the "apocalypse from outer space," is slowly creeping down towards Kansas City. Its wide billows roll down as purple-black, intercloud lightning bursts within. The city lights reflect off the dark plumes descending through the night sky.

"Hard to even see the damn thing!" A man from a couple seats down says with a thick Southern accent that makes me a bit homesick.

I reply, "As long as we've got a good pilot, all we have to do is shoot and the pilot will aim."

He looks back at me, terrified. "We got a good pilot?"

"Of course," I say. I really have no idea, but surely.

The captain's gruff voice comes through the intercom again. "Divs prepare for charge."

"Kinda early..." someone behind us mumbles.

Carmel yells, "Comps, brace your divs!"

This is not part of the procedure that's been outlined for us, but Thiia and Carmel have talked to every single comp about it, and we're all utilizing this unapproved strategy for the first time.

The charger delivers a powerful but disorienting blow when kicked into attack mode, and using Thiia and Carmel's method, all comps shield their divs by taking part of the blow, part of the pain. We all wind up slightly disoriented, but each divs recovery time is minimized.

The surge from the charger pummels us again and pulls back hard. I feel care surging through all one hundred of us as our comps take part of the surge for us and we pour our concern for them into the space the charger is creating. The fast-moving light-threads brighten between us. All of us can see them now, interconnected stars sitting in our hearts.

Amidst the surge moving between us divs and the charger as the channel is stabilized, I feel the thick line of energy from the upper-level cabin pulling some of the energy off of us, maybe helping stabilize the waves into a steady connection to the charger.

"Team ATL in proximity," the captain says.

The plane veers left hard.

"No time to wait on Nuevo Angeles, folks," Sergeant Dunn says, "We're going in with Atlanta. Let's get that motherfucker."

The crystal rings lining the helmet vibrate as fifty divs begin to send their energy up, into the channel, towards the charger. The thick line to the cabin pulls again, siphoning some of the energy.

A flash of light in my mind unfolds, and I see those beautiful eyes again. I see his strong jawline and the hint of a smile on his lips. The vision is prescient, a new sight that feels like memory. The thick line siphons my delight in the vision, and it's swept away. My mind spins. Thiia stabilizes me but doesn't seem to sense any concern about the thick line drawing energy from us.

Bakkeaux begins to spread over the city. Crackling extensions of purple-black lightning crawl through the swelling plumes as the cloud expands. It reaches down multiple thin vortexes, too many to count. Each mind-warping tendril reaches out for someone's brain, about to distort their minds while it drains their life force.

My heart aches for the people who weren't able to evacuate fast enough.

Another flash unfolds. Thiia seems to notice. She looks over at me but doesn't seem to get a full sense of the vision coming from within me. Celebration. Joy and relief on a global scale. We will succeed. We will banish this monster. Certainty fills me, a crescendo rising. I want every one of these divs and comps to know this sureness.

I reach out to them. Thiia is there, witnessing me. She sees what I want to do, and she shows me how to create my own psybridge, and together, we cast it wide, connecting one hundred people for the first time. One by one, connections to the other divs and comps fall into place. We see each other held within the network. I send them the vision, and we are all elevated, infused with the realization. Collectively, our fears are quelled. Our worries fall away.

This is it.

The vision folds in on itself, disappearing within me. Thiia squeezes my hand to let me know that she sensed it too. She believes. She takes her hand away, but I feel her through the light-threads between our hearts and through our comp-bridge. We are no longer psybridged with the other divs or comps, but we know they felt the vision pouring through us, and as the screens over the windows close, having given us a glimpse of the descending hellion and the city we're here to defend, we feel only confidence.

A pulse comes from the charger, and all divs are forced to drop in. It feels as if the plane itself has vanished, and I begin to fall before Thiia is there to catch me. She secures my position, and I'm fixed. The charger begins pulling from me as the Levels above open up, and a deluge of divination moves into us.

The crystal ring in the helmet sings like an angelic halo. The sound of multiple helmets harmonizing their frequencies fills the cabin. The song rises into an ephemeral haze above us, moving through the cables towards the massive crystal chargers along the wings.

The plane rocks as if it has hit turbulence. Sergeant Dunn's gruff voice blares through the intercom. "Disbursement shields are activated. That bastard can't reach in here!"

Dropped in and charged up, I hear the raging of the plane's engines more clearly, the mechanical turning and positioning of the charger's plates, and underneath it all the humming of the crystals lining the channels, conducting our energies.

When the co-pilot releases the charger's energy, there's another pull that unsettles me. It's stronger than in any test-runs, more forceful than expected. Thiia helps me regain composure.

It's just the pull from the ray, she says, trying to reason for the both of us. *Maybe because we're making direct hits?*

The disbursement shields kick on again, preventing Bakkeaux from reaching its vortexes into the plane, but also, shaking us all inside. All unRisen crew tighten the chinstraps of their crystal-lined helmets.

We make sweep after sweep. The Atlanta V-wing does the same. The chargers wrench our divination away forcefully each time. With each pass, the rays of our energy fly from the chargers into the killer storm's billows.

"Oh my god! It's working!" whispers the scientist next to the sergeant who immediately shushes him. I can actually hear the fear in Dunn's breath. Fear of not just Bakkeaux, but fear that the scientist's enthusiasm will disrupt our meditation, the thing that is defeating the extradimensional monster.

I tune them out and bring my focus back to Thiia, back to her steadiness, guiding me back into my own. The halo lilts. The charger pulls from us again. The strange, thick line reaching into us all siphons away more energy.

The sergeant risks disrupting us. "Good work so far, folks. We've taken out most of those tentacles and crystalized most of its body. But the eye is still there, glowing. We're not sure why. Keep it up. We're gonna pass again."

I can hear it in his voice. He does not understand why it is not working on the eye. The scientist shakes his head, checks his monitors. The communications officer leans toward them. "ATL is falling back. Their disbursement shields are low."

"We're so close, god damnit!" Sergeant Dunn punches the wall and the sound startles some of the divs out of their concentration. He realizes what he's done and looks back at us with defeat. He turns toward the comms officer to say something, but the officer holds a finger aloft, silencing him. There's a message coming through his headset. My sense of hearing is so heightened, I can almost recognize the voice.

"It's um..." the officer points up toward the upper-level cabin. "He wants us to sweep again... from under the eye."

Sergeant Dunn squints his eyes as if questioning the request, then shrugs. "Do it."

While the officer directs the request to the pilot, the captain tells us to get ready to go again.

By the time the plane has circled back, we've all dropped back in, and when the charger tugs at us again, the thick line to the upper cabin is stronger than ever. It tears through my mind, ripping energy out of me. Memories of my crew, my family, moments where my heart has been soothed or lit up are snatched, pried, and peeled out of my being. My breath feels like thin, fibrous filaments, none of them big enough, and I gasp. Thiia's hands are on my shoulders, turning my face toward her. My eyes feel like they'll explode, but instead I lose peripheral vision into shadows. She slaps my cheek, says something, and even the urgent care she is giving me gets ripped away, pulled through the screaming halo. I hear, feel, know the memories of me getting pulled through the space behind me, out of the hearts of my dear friends, Carmel and Mira. I start to question how I can know their memories of me as a bolt of energy before I realize. It's all being pulled through the thick line, to the cabin. I did not know he was even in our camp, much less on board.

The kid. Arun.

The sound of divs screaming and comps crying out fills the cabin, and I see Thiia move her hand back to slap me hard. I'm about to black out when her hand connects. It's like an arrow through my face to my heart. I sit up with a jolt and will all of my energy to again psybridge every other Div on board before they all sink into blackness. A sudden rush reverberates through the psybridge as scores of divs snap awake.

A jolt moves through the atmosphere and rocks the plane in the air. The sky shakes with the wailing of Bakkeaux, and I know Arun has shot a trident into its eye.

Carmel's hands are on my shoulders. "I thought she was gone," she sobs. "You caught her. You caught everybody."

But as soon as the words leave her lips, we can feel that they are not entirely true.

"Medic!" one of the comps is yelling.

"Medic! We need medic too!" Another comp. Then, more.

Only one medic slides down from the cabin upstairs. The other must be tending to Arun.

"What happened?" Mira asks.

I can't tell her what I know just yet. Thiia looks at me with stunned awareness. Carmel will not handle this well when we tell her. For now, I hold my words and let Carmel hold her lover and shed her tears.

"What happened?" someone on the front row asks, looking toward the sergeant, the scientist, who are both looking eagerly towards the comm officer.

The scientist holds out a fist, thumb up.

"We did it!" Sergeant Dunn shouts.

The captain does his best to contain his excitement as he announces over the intercom, "We have destroyed a third of Bakkeaux! Skies over Kansas City are clear!"

Dunn turns to an officer. "Get the teams in Mexico City and New Singapore on the line."

We divinators and accompaniments cannot feel their excitement.

While the scientist and the captain celebrate, we sling off our helmets, and our bodies ache as we move to care for our wounded and dead.

Twenty of us are comatose. Fourteen of us are dead. None of us are okay.

ꝏ

It's a bit too quiet as we drift.

Thiia cues up the music again. "Unaccompanied Cello Suite No. 1 in G Major" undulates through Old Girl.

Franxis' voice comes through Thiia's comm station. "Ah, thank you."

Harjaz's follows. "Do you take requests?"

"Depends on what you want to hear," Thiia replies.

"Not this."

"Then no, we don't take requests."

I check debris projections, weather forecasts on multiple floating screens. The multi-eyed hurricane is moving north through the Atlantic, barely touching its outer bands to the continent's eastern shore. There are no predictions for potential surface to air missiles, rouge wings, or terrorist attacks, so I ask the expert.

"Mira, see any trouble up ahead?"

She says confidently, "The path all the way to ground zero looks pretty uneventful from what I can see. We should still be on guard in case that EDB disrupts prescience around itself. I don't see anything about our encounter."

A kilometer above the Kárman line, Carmel and I tilt the crystal discs forward, increasing our burn as we skirt the gradated beginnings of the Earth's atmosphere. We set Old Girl on her auto-nav route to Amparo-1 in Ecuador and release the piloting discs which float in place. For a moment, I marvel at the wisps of fog held in the crystal piloting discs, and I'm reminded of the crystals we created defeating Bakkeaux. The crystals were shaped from our psychic energy, which encased the cloudy hellion, bit by bit, before they fell out of the sky. It was quite the hailstorm that day in Kansas City. UNAF did their best to retrieve all they could to study them. Once what was captured inside was determined to be inert, they gave some of the crystals to us as trophies. Concerns over crystallized EDB remains have grown over the past few years, and although we don't know why, the UNAF outlawed possession of the crystals and asked us to return our trophies.

"Did you and Mira turn in your rings? I haven't seen you wear them in a long time." They had one of their crystals broken down for engagement rings. Each diamond-like stone has a dark vein of what many called a demon running through it.

"They're not getting our wedding bands. We've got them on us, but the stones are impractical for a warrior's finger." She tugs on a gold chain around her neck and lifts the ring at its end from inside her uniform. The crystal shines in the light from the control panels. "Now, we keep them closer to our hearts."

"Of course, you do." I smile back at her.

"And this way we don't fuck up our rings when we have to crack some heads."

"It's been a long time since you've had to punch anyone."

"Had to, yes. Maybe we can keep it that way, but I've got a feeling this trip will come with a fistfight. You still know what a fistfight is like?"

"You know I do."

She smirks. "I don't mean sparring when I'm taking it easy on you."

"You do not take it easy on me." I snort lightly.

"You sure?" She raises her eyebrows. "I mean a real fight."

"I remember." I nod.

"Good," she says. Seems like there might be more she has to say, but she instead monitors the crystal energy array screen.

"CEA okay?" I ask.

"Yeah, yeah… of course."

"Wanna tell me how we wound up with an extra div for this assignment, cap?"

She sighs. "When I suggested Arun be taken off the mission, the other Sages disagreed, including Arun." I'm not surprised she made her request right in front of him. "The other Sages we left back on Scire are staying behind to monitor and study MaalenKun. We're going to rendezvous with a third ship, The Grail, from a Helixx Corp contingent. They'll be bringing over one of their Elders, so Arun can learn from them, and our extra div from Yerum is bridging with Mira. The whole way. They're syncing prescience and EDB communication skills. He's learning foresight from her." She thumbs back towards Mira.

"Wait. Isn't he at Eight?"

"He'll be Nine soon probably if he can get foresight locked in, but if you ask me, he's still dragging a smidge from lower levels, like maybe Three. He doesn't seem to learn well from Sages. I suspect he's got issues with authority figures."

"That's weird. We're sure he's an Eight?"

"He's at Eight," Mira whispers from behind us. "He's also psybridged, so he can hear everything you're saying."

We both whip our heads around so fast that we almost bump into each other. We mouth the word, "No!"

Mira laughs at us and shrugs. "Maybe."

"That's not a nice joke, my dear," Carmel whispers.

"Like I said, maybe, so..." She closes her eyes again, becoming still, save her breath.

"I might be pissing off more people than I care to today." She faces the windshield, sarcastically adding, "Oh well..." She laughs. "When I couldn't get Arun off the assignment, I asked that he take the other ship. He didn't seem to mind. Honestly, he seemed unfazed by it all. Typical Sage." She pulls up an info screen and passes it over to my side. "I had Mani Ops run checks on internal communications from Amparo-1."

I smirk. "Who'd you not trust to get it right, outdated Scire or shady Helixx Corp?"

"Both. This came in as we were leaving the harbor. They've picked up on something unusual. I've put it through to all the other stations, including Scire. The other ships will be informed. I just have to tell our crew. Starting with you." I look at the profiles of the divs on the info screen. Mostly Level Threes, a Five, a couple of comps, a couple from Ops, one decorated. They all have stern expressions like soldiers.

"This something unusual why you're talking about cracking heads?"

"Indeed, it is. Mani Ops has picked up on conversations within this group. With the rest of the team at Amparo-1, which numbers around a hundred thirty-five, they refer to the EDB as Vasif."

"But amongst themselves?"

"Diosa en flor."

She asks Thiia to silence the music, and when she addresses our new crew, I share the info screen with them.

The assignment feels more dangerous. There is no real way of knowing who in the camp is compromised. At least knowing a small group within the camp has converted to whatever cult is growing around this thing, we will be more prepared.

"This cult better not get in the way." I sigh and rub a hand down my beard. "I've got a date when we get back."

"Ops is still sorting things out with the ground crew at Amparo-1," Thiia updates us. "They know we'll be welcomed, but don't know how warmly."

"We can plan for a chilly reception, but it'll be okay," Mira says. The smile in her voice is assuring.

"Typical ground divs." Captain shakes her head. "Did we get intel on where these particular cultish clowns are?" She motions to the info screen still floating in the cockpit. She's been poring over it since she gave us all a heads up about the potential trouble. Everyone on board is still conferencing through the intercom.

"They're working on it. Mani Ops has hacked in and gotten the comm signatures for all of them, but there's some sort of interference with their stealth-stream. Other stations have tried to boost it, but it borders detection, so they've had to back off. It'll be easier once we're closer, much easier after we've landed and can get a more stable signal for them to cloak theirs with. Then, they can ping all locations to us."

"I'll be taking lead," Captain says. "I want all other comps on stealth comm with Mani. Signal your divs when you know what these clowns are up to."

"Heard that, Captain." Franxis' voice comes through the ship's intercom.

Then Aaliyah: "Heard."

Thiia gives us a thumbs up.

"Div Liam, Div Mira, turn up your prescient talents as much as you can and limit interaction with ground divs so you can focus. We're all staying close, so we'll do the talking. That way you don't have to walk and chew gum at the same time."

"Heard that, Captain." Liam's voice is pleasant. Maybe he couldn't psychically hear us talking shit about him, or maybe he's so close to Sage that that sort of thing just doesn't faze him.

"For the record, I can walk and chew gum," Mira whispers.

"But can he?" I whisper. I've still got my doubts about a Level Eight who is taking pointers from a Level Six. Not that all Sages have a great deal of foresight, but I wonder why he has a hard time learning from the Sages who do.

Thiia smiles at Mira before placing her fingers over her ear to signal an incoming call. She taps her keypad and sends a message screen from Scire Control Ops into the cockpit. "All clear. Contact: Commander Leonardo Awá. Ground in thirty-six." She turns on a holoscreen timer that ticks down our arrival time.

The captain continues. "Like I said, we're staying close the whole time. I know we've never worked together, and mixed crews blended from various stations can feel a little awkward at times, but this is us. I can vouch for every single one of us up here in the front. We've got your back. Anyone want to add anything else?"

"Happy to be here as part of your crew, captain." There's practically a smile on Liam's voice, and I feel a little bad for my shit-talking.

Harjaz calls back, "We've got your backs as well, Mani."

"Same here, captain," Casey says, and I can hear the smile in his voice. I want to see it too.

"See you lovely people when we land." Captain switches off the intercom.

"Hey captain," I say, tapping in a code on the floating keypad. Translucent gold octagons of the plasma shield emerge across the ship to protect us from the heat of reentry. "How would you like to sit next to your wife for the rest of the trip down? You know, since we're clear, and even she says we're good to land."

"Are you asking because you know I'm not about to trade seats with him?"

"Figured you're not about to let anyone from Scire in the cockpit. Franxis can take Mira's meditation cushion."

"I'll let Old Girl's auto pick up your slack for landing." She cocks her eyebrow at me as I unbuckle my harness.

As I climb down from the cockpit, my psychic uplink to the ship fizzles. When I step down, I'm more aware of the shift in gravity. Movement feels momentarily different, a bit sluggish, like my body is somehow heavier. Div abilities make adapting to changes in gravitational pull much quicker, and in just one step, I feel things begin to smooth out. My movements feel more fluid and easeful.

I turn to say something to Mira, but she holds her hand up. "Saw this coming a mile away." She flashes a quick smile and a wink at me before climbing into the cockpit.

"Want me to dial down the comp-bridge?" Thiia asks.

"We've got thirty til ground." I laugh. "Hardly enough time to need that much privacy."

She laughs too, "It is if you want it to be, but okay."

I widen my eyes and cock an eyebrow up. "What I meant was, thirty is not enough time for me to do what I want to do to him."

"All right then." Her eyes sparkle playfully as she smiles, juts her chin towards me, and swivels her seat around to her console.

As I make my way back, I hear Thiia asking Franxis to come up front. In the corridor, Franxis strides sprightly, giving me a knowing smile.

The door to the port side charger chamber is open. Casey leans over the arm of his seat to watch me cross the cabin.

"Hey, handsome," he says. "Wanna be my date for this dance?"

I prop an arm up over the chamber entrance, trying my best to look half as dashing as he does in spite of his scuffed up blue gear. I smile coyly, shake my head. "Sorry. Two left feet... literally. Took me a long time to learn how to walk."

He looks down at my feet, and I hold a hand up to his gorgeous eyes. "Don't look," I say, feigning embarrassment. "I'm very shy about the right left foot."

"They seem all right to me. Sure you don't want to dance?"

"First, we gotta get on the ground."

"Such a limited imagination." He sighs, momentarily turns away, but looks back with a grin.

"We'll dance if that's what you want," I say playfully and honestly.

His smirk grows into a smile that lights up his eyes. "I'm actually a terrible dancer."

We both laugh.

"Can I sit with you? We'll land soon."

"Hoping you would."

I have to lean down and duck under the entrance to the chamber. As I crawl over his long legs, the ship hits a little turbulence. I grip both of my hands on each of his arm rests. He puts his hands on mine. He's looking at the more lifted corner of my mouth again. I know my smile is crooked, but I can't even it out when I'm standing between his legs and holding on so as not to fall on top of him. He looks up at me, grinning as if he wouldn't mind if I fell into his lap. The ship stops shaking, and I can easily move again, but I hesitate as he leans forward. I watch his eyelids begin to close as he brings his lips closer. My heart shakes.

His soft words land on my lips. "Oh, we should wait."

The only sound I can make is a plaintive grunt.

He falls back into his seat laughing. "Now, you're disgruntled? Waiting was your big idea!"

I bite my lip, let him tease me, and take the seat next to him. I buckle in, nodding. "You're right, you're right. It was my idea." I have a hard time finding the words. I want to confess that it's not just that I'm attracted to him, that I've seen his face in my mind many times before, that his eyes… and that I feel like some sort of promise is being fulfilled. But I also don't want to come across too strong. And destiny is a bit much. "Because…" I wave a hand in front of my chest. "Because this feeling…" He stops laughing and looks toward me, eyebrows cocked, exaggerating interest which dials down on the exaggeration as I continue. "This feeling, physical, mental… my breath… and somehow… knowing. The way it all rises and comes together. Does this make sense?"

"Are you saying I move you?" He smiles a little too slyly and quickly reigns it back into a gentle attentive expression.

A rush of heat brightens my cheeks, and I look down at his hand still on mine. "Yeah, I'm moved… and I really want to pay attention to where I'm going. I don't want to go there alone." I smooth my beard and turn to look into his green eyes ringed with grey. "Shit… If this is too much too fast—"

"We're definitely not moving too fast," he says, obviously not realizing that I wasn't referring to physicality. He looks forward toward the wall lined in circuitry and crystal panels. "I'm used to fast... and to very little interest in anything other than fucking." A couple of his fingers move slowly over my thumb, he squeezes my hand before letting it go and returning his hands to his lap. He speaks slower. "I know what you mean. This feels good. There's no rush."

I lean toward him. "I'll say it again, I'm very interested in fucking... but I'm also interested in knowing how you're doing this to me." I make the circular motion again. "So I can move you too."

He leans toward me. Our faces are close. "You don't have to worry about that. I'm just not used to waiting, that's all. I'll stop teasing you about it."

"I think I kinda like the teasing a little." I swoon seeing his rascally grin. "You tell me if I'm being too much. Or not enough."

"Oh, I will," he says, laughing lightly and closing his eyes.

Our lips move closer together, almost touch, when the signal to prep for landing interrupts. The forward moving force of the ship slows and finally halts as the hover engines burn brighter.

We both sigh heavily and rest our foreheads against each other's. I run my fingers through his hair. He groans but keeps a smile on his face, beautiful eyes closed, as he leans into me.

ꝏ

The ship from the Helixx Corp contingent, The Grail, and the second ship from Scire, The Arrow, are already in the landing zone.

Captain rotates Old Girl so that the ship descends facing the group of men behind the heat shields fifty yards away. Commander Leonardo Awá, a hero from the first successful countermeasure against Bakkeaux, and a group of UNAF soldiers, divs, and Ops stand at attention, awaiting our arrival.

Old Girl's cleats touch down gently. "Smoothest Terran landing I've had in three decades," Casey says.

"When was your last trip down?"

"Three decades ago." His grin is mischievous. "Didn't you read my file?"

"Not more than what an FO needs to know. I want to get to know you through you." This makes him smile. "Did you read my file?"

He smirks. "Only had time to skim the basics. I think I learned more on Joynr. That reminds me, I still have to DM you to send nudes."

"Eagerly awaiting your DM."

As steam billows from the cooling vertical thrusters, we watch Commander Awá and several decorated Ops, divs, and comps marching over to the landing dock. "Still running things like we're military here, I guess," Harjaz grumbles over the comm.

"They are military here," Carmel replies with a touch of humor.

The ship's whirring and humming fades as it goes into low energy mode.

We meet the rest of our crew at cargo access. Most of us are a bit tense. A lot of stern faces stare straight ahead.

Thiia turns to the group and quips, "Okay folks, brace yourselves for some un-regulated climate."

With a pop, the seal is broken and as the door opens to the world outside, the humid air rushes in, like a wave moving through the ship's corridors. It hits us all at once and most of us groan, which leads to much-needed, tension-breaking laughter.

Panels on the wall lift and the arms of Old Girl's robotic cargo system begin passing our gear packs through the space. Harjaz appoints himself to distribution. He calls out the names printed on the sides of each pack and hands it back to the group. All the packs from Scire are scratched, dented, or both, and they look much older than our shiny gear from Mani.

"Franxis... Aaliyah... Liam..." Harjaz uses first names until he gets to Mira's, our second officer, and then Carmel's, our captain. "Me..." He sets his battered pack aside.

As the others shoulder their packs, they walk towards the door.

I'm standing close enough to Harjaz that when he has my shiny gear, he hands it to me and lowers his voice, "For you, sexy."

I pause for a moment. "It's First Officer Kenzari—at least while you're on this crew."

"Yes, sir," Harjaz says, and I can feel Casey behind me trying not to laugh.

I pull on the pack and turn down the hall.

"And for you, handsome," Harjaz says as he hands the last pack to Casey.

Casey lowers his voice, but surely, he knows that any div nearby can still hear him. "It's Div Casey Isaac—at least while you're on this crew." More jokes, but this one lands differently, with a bit of a sting.

I subdue my insecurity before I feel him next to me brushing his fingers across my hand once more before we really have to get to work.

"Crew of the Old Girl," I say, my voice louder and stern now, commanding attention. "Pair up, double line, Mani front, Div Ulloah single center, then Scire. Franxis and Div Isaac take the rear and confirm with the UN Ops our request: no checks, no claims, they are not to touch Old Girl. Y'all smile for the nice folks out there." Everyone except Carmel smiles, some exaggerated, some completely fake. "Terrible. Too nice. Won't work." Some of their smiles become genuine. Carmel looks at me like she doesn't know what the fuck I'm doing, but I'm trying to get this crew of temps to start syncing unconsciously while also dispelling some nervousness. I'm trying to bring them together. "Okay, tone it down, relaxed but attentive game faces. Be careful with these folks. We know there are at least eight clowns out there who don't want us coming near this being they've started to worship. There may be more than eight. Regardless, we have a rift to close, and that being has come through a rift which maybe it knew how to close. We are not here to force it to leave, but we will ask it politely. We'll be subtle about it, so we don't stir up the locals. Clear?"

"Heard," they all answer.

"Stay alert. Look out for those compromised clowns."

"Ulloah, Adivar, how far ahead can you see?" Captain Carmel says, stepping next to me to face the group.

Mira replies, "Looks clear and cordial all the way to ground zero. Beyond that, it's shady. Getting darker."

"Same. Also, Captain. And..."

Carmel speaks firmly. "Speak up, Ulloah. What is it?"

Liam seems uncertain. He turns toward our other EDB communications expert. "Mira, do you hear a wordless but strong suggestion?"

She nods her head. "Seems Vasif knows we are coming, Captain. It wants us to refer to its position as the chapel."

Captain Carmel cocks her eyebrow. "Fuck that."

Of the eight individuals we believe to be converts to the cult of *Diosa en flor,* we encounter our first in the group of men with Commander Awá. He marches alongside the commander, a tablet in his hand, surely scanning us.

The commander and ship captains greet each other, and Awá stalls while his team makes sure we are indeed who Ops said would arrive.

I look around at the camp, an eyesore on the edge of the beautiful rainforest. The camp is a converted soy farm that was taken over by the UNAF in order to stop the beef industry's encroachment into the rainforest. Some of the old structures including a barn, a pump house around the well, and a farmhouse which is technically a small mansion still remain, but all have been modified by the UNAF-Div team. Other structures, like the landing dock, barracks, hangar, comms tower, and anti-aircraft rocket cannons were added when the UNAF moved in to monitor and protect the rainforest.

Awá and his soldiers greet the crew from The Arrow, and there is clearly some tension between Awá and Arun. The commander stares at the Sage long enough for it to be concerning. Seems like Awá might want to say something but feels it is not the right time. The Sage stares back at the commander patiently, without expression. My concern that Carmel was right about bringing

Arun planetside grows within me. I'm relieved when Awá nods respectfully, and Arun returns the gesture.

Thiia's voice comes into my mind loud and clear: *Mani has the stealth-signal locked. They've pinged all eight. One is right in front of us obviously. A few are driving the walking cars to us. The others are scattered around.*

I signal back my gratitude.

To our group of party crashers, Awá simply says, "Follow me."

There are seventeen of us, none of whom Awá expected to be stopping by when he got up this morning. Can't say I blame him for being grumpy about having to drop everything and see to a big group, but there is a rift to close.

Awá stands next to the Old Girl crew with his eight men lined up in a similar formation behind him. His voice is gruff, but he tries to make polite conversation. "Any of you ever ridden in a walking car?"

If I answer truthfully that I have ridden in a Walker, we miss an opportunity to let Awá think he's showing us something special. If I lie, right now, and say that I haven't, I'll dampen my Level Five capability to "make truth," which might be essential. I psychically nudge Thiia to reply honestly.

"Can't say that I have, commander." Her melodic and naive tone is entirely performative, but having a pretty girl talk to him seems to disarm his foul mood. "Will the road take us all the way to the site?"

His tone has shifted now, and he seems more cordial. "The road only goes halfway there, but the Walkers will take us all the way to Vasif." He turns to wink at her.

"Are we not hiking?" Franxis asks with a touch of genuine excitement.

Awá chuckles. "Depends on your perspective."

ꝏ

At the other end of the road, we realize what Awá meant about our perspective on hiking. His voice comes from the other walking car to our car's comm. "Trying to get to Vasif on foot would take too long, so we'll hike the rest of the way. Keep your seatbelts buckled."

The carriage of the car rises up as the driver extends the car's jointed, robotic legs. Its wheels lock so we don't roll, and the car steps off of the dirt road and crawls into the dense bush. The carriage stays level as the car navigates the uneven terrain with robotic steps.

Shade from the canopy blocks out much of the sunlight. Branches brush past the carriage as the car walks on. Thiia cannot hide her excitement. Several others seem pretty amazed as well. These walking cars have been around for decades, but they're so specific to certain types of terrain, most people have never even heard of them.

Leaves crunch under the car's wheels as it steps over large roots, rocks, streams, and rare plants and fungi.

Div Argis, one of Awá's men, glimpses Thiia's enthusiasm and decides to play tour guide.

"We don't take the walkers out here too much. Both the UN and the eco-loving tree-huggers hate when we step them into the protected zone, but we're on a somewhat familiar path. The cars know the route. And their systems scan for obstacles. It'll be smooth sailing from here on."

Argis is right about the smooth ride. As the lifted carriage stays level, the robotic legs step their way into the dense vegetation. It's a slower but smoother ride than the bumpy dirt road out of the base.

"Can you tell us why Vasif has chosen this particular site?" Thiia asks, playing the role of inquisitive beauty to get the soldiers to drop their guard.

"No ma'am, no clue. Those who can speak to it say it doesn't answer those questions. Where's it from? Why's it here? But it does have something to say, I think."

"Does it really ask to be worshiped?" I ask. Every head on board turns his way.

"Hard to say. I mean..." He shrugs. "Many believe this is a goddess."

Detecting strong impulses in Argis, I signal to Thiia that he seems suspicious.

"And why is it still here? Why not crystalize it?" Harjaz asks because he obviously has not read the file on Vasif. Aaliyah rolls her eyes, and Harjaz cuts a glance sideways at her.

As Argis speaks casually, I start gleaning from the tangential thoughts arising in his mind. I look for any hint that he is part of the cult. I don't have to look hard to find it. When he speaks of the EDB, there is a connection strong with reverently spoken language, repetition of a name: *Diosa en flor.*

"They tried that when they first found her, but it just regenerated, and a swath of the forest died. Maybe the EDB killed the trees on purpose in response, not sure. I don't think so though. Since then, we've discovered that the EDB has regrown that part of the forest and then some. UN wants to see if we can use it to renew the rainforest. We've lost so much of it, you know."

Heard that? Thiia says, turning back towards me.

I heard it.

I risk revealing my secret div-attainment and send psychic transference to our entire crew: *He called Vasif "her." He's culty, damn it.*

Div. Argis, like our driver, has been compromised. I turn back towards Casey who shrugs his shoulders ever so slightly. Nothing we can do about it but add Argis to the list and keep an eye on them all.

I notice Casey's hands, close to his seatbelt harness release, just in case. I look around at the rest of the crew, and everyone else but Carmel, Mira, and

Liam sit in the same position, ready to sling off their seatbelts and flick their wrists, firing the sonic cannons in their armor's forearms.

Our captain notices what I'm looking at, takes a look at everyone's fists and snickers, then snorts. "If our prescient divs are relaxed, you can too. Ease up, crew."

The mood in the car shifts. We ride in silence, the carriage held level, as the car walks through the protected forest. Rare birds spy on the strange vehicle from a safe distance, but they are the only wildlife we see aside from the small clouds of insects that drift past our windows.

"We're almost there," the driver says, pointing to the floating navigation holoscreen.

"Prepare to be awed," Div Argis says with a wide grin.

What we see is amazing, indeed. If not for the risk, I would get out and walk the rest of the way, steeping in the beauty of the EDB.

"Well, this is the prettiest EDB I've ever seen," Casey says to no one in particular.

The darkness of the forest canopy is swept away by the soft yet strong white light coming from Vasif's large body. The extradimensional being has draped its flowing body of fog across the canopy. It gracefully angles down the trees like thick blankets of incandescent flora made of mist. From one end to the other, its sides pitch up much like the roof of a cathedral. Ephemeral spores of golden light drift in the open space around the being. Beams of sunlight shine through the shifting canopy that is Vasif's mist-like body. Like sunlight in a stained glass window, the beams are tinted by the rainbow colors that drift within the EDB's mostly pale body.

I'm not the only one in awe. Everyone in the carriage cranes their neck up to see the glowing spectacle. The driver sets the carriage down as low as it will go on uneven legs.

"Like all EDBs on record, Vasif is a gaseous colony organism. It's rare that they bring their entire being near the ground," I say.

With a worrying degree of reverence, Argis says, "It's like it wants to be closer to us."

I want to see the look on Casey's face as he takes in the beautiful sight, but he is no longer looking up. He is looking around. The other cars have stopped, and as the crews from the other ships step out, he scans the groups looking for the clowns on our list.

Something within me urges me to break procedure. I speak soft and low. "We're lively, Captain."

Carmel is less subtle. "Power up packs now, crew! All amps online!"

Considering the EDB is not attacking, it's not the standard approach to turn on our amplifiers before we're ready to psybridge with the Sages, but the crew complies without question.

Argis moves a bit too quickly and taps a floating panel to raise all four doors and lower the step ladders. "We're not even to the platform yet," he simpers.

Aaliyah nudges Harjaz ever so slightly. There's something wrong with her old, dented amp pack. A quick obscuration goes up from Aaliyah as Harjaz slaps the pack. I notice a small flash of divination moving from his hand in glowing circuitry through it. She then subtly nods to him that the pack is online.

Harjaz sees me watching them.

"Technical difficulties," he says, casually dismissing my concern.

The two of them are hiding something. I quickly and stealthily glean that Harjaz gave Aaliyah's glitching pack some sort of spark through his divination. Yet, there is no mention of technopathy in Harjaz's file. Like me, Harjaz holds a secret divination skill.

I almost say something to Thiia about the gear checks on Scire missing a faulty pack, but I decide that since the pack is online now, I'd rather not let Harjaz or Aaliyah know that I put much thought into it. Instead, I transfer what I've sensed in a quick flash of light across our comp-bridge. She makes eye contact with me to confirm that she understands.

I look up at the glowing spores wondering if we need to click our helmets up and on. What was enchanting only moments ago now looks like a potential contaminate, but as we move towards the platform, the spores seem to drift reflexively back toward Vasif's glowing mists.

"I can feel it watching us," Carmel mumbles as we fall in line.

"Liam and I can hear chatter about us. I think it's gleaning info from the other crew that haven't powered up their packs."

I'm on my comm link immediately. "Arrow, Grail, amps! Right away!"

I glimpse an almost comical flurry of psychic movement in the formations up ahead as eleven people will their packs online.

"It's going quiet," Mira reports.

"Good call, Oscar," Carmel says as we take the metal stairs to the platform.

Across the metal landing, an enormous, crystal platform is elevated and extends into the awning made by Vasif's shifting mists draped on the trees. The atmosphere grows thicker, even more humid, even more still as we move across the platform to stand underneath the radiant, flowing canopy. A grounding charge comes through the crystal platform, through my feet, vibrating upward while anchoring my energy to the forest floor. When its embedded tech is switched on, we all feel a rush highlighting the divination coursing through us.

Awá and his team stand at the other end of the platform, just off of the crystal on the metal landing. Many of them look disgruntled to only be playing the role of chauffeurs.

As Arun and the Helixx Corp Elder step out further, the EDB's light shines on their faces. The tiny lights from their packs blink in sync. The divs from each crew stand in a semi-circle around the Sages. Our comps stand behind us. As the lights from all of our packs begin to blink in unison, I feel the Sages psybridge cast wide, and I secretly cast mine with it to strengthen the connection. I can feel the other divs linking. Strong vibrations build within me, through my midline, down my limbs and up into my skull. In unison, guided by the movements of the Sages, we rest our right hands in our left and join our thumbs creating a circular shape. The mudra channels a protective, planetary energy through us. We channel that energy through our gear and cast our prismatic shields wide. A protective sphere expands around us, over our comps and almost all the way to the metal platform where Awá and his team watch.

Without words, Thiia signals that Awá's men look put out. Maybe they wanted to be a part of this conversation, but now they are literally blocked.

We watch as the radiance from the EDB shifts and briefly flickers to almost match the rainbow waves slipping around the sphere. We send a friendly call, an offer to link to our mindfield, and Vasif reaches its mind toward us. The psybridge connects and integrates easefully. A fragrant waft of various flowers moves across the psybridge like a welcome offering. I detect tropical flowers and hints of varieties not indigenous to Ecuador like rose, and underneath the floral scent, a trace of something stinky-sweet, like decaying petals. The hint of rose and foreign flowers fades as if they were just memories triggered to heighten my olfactory senses. I notice the strong scent of damp soil. I look out beyond the crystal platform. The EDB slowly transfers a superpositioned vision of its own sight on top of what we're seeing. Around us life begins to glow in vibrant, white light flecked with softly colored tones. Streams of the light move up the trunks of trees as if flowing through now-visible veins through the branches and leaves, coursing through vines, flecking moisture in the air. The sky above us seems infinitely vast. The ground below pulsates deep below the surface. The living glow is soft and pale in rocks and stones along the forest floor. It is fading within a fallen tree and a bed of rotting vegetation, yet bright spots—insects—crawl through the compost. I finally see the animals of the forest, some near, some farther away. The EDB reveals their auras in brilliant, glowing colors pulsing with each heartbeat, each breath.

I look to my crew, to Casey, and we are all bright with the light of life flowing in our veins. It radiates within the massive crystal platform grown with div-tech. It's lovely. I could steep in it longer, but my concern builds over how vulnerable our large group is while awestruck.

The Sages signal us to focus our awareness, and we turn down the brightness of the vision as if we were changing the setting on a holoscreen. Sensing a bit of our delight in the vision, Vasif reaches toward us.

There are five divs at Five or up, one each from The Arrow and The Grail: Liam, Mira, and me. We pour ourselves forward to guard the border. Vasif momentarily pulls back, a vein of grey flickers through the radiance of its body, and its mist-like flora pushes the vein further away from us, pulling it deeper within. It steadies its mind across our psybridge. The glowing spores mostly float in the air around the being, but some begin to bounce off of the shield.

Without speaking, Arun and the Helixx Corp Elder Sage reach out to Vasif. It turns a beacon of its attention towards them. The Sages do this again and again until Vasif has narrowed the beacon to a smaller stream which reaches toward the Sages.

As one of the Sages asks a question, the other "makes truth." It is intended to be covert and gentle manipulation.

Where did you come from? the Elder asks.

Vasif does not reply.

The Elder asks again to hold the being's stream of attention longer. This time, Arun simultaneously pours into the stream. *You will tell us.*

Vasif replies, *Many.*

An image like the flash of a memory flickers through us. A glimpse of another dimension. A green light moves slowly through the being's body, merging of other similar EDBs' bodies and consciousness. The glimpse is too much for our human brains, and we're vexed. The shield shivers, and a few of the glowing spores fall through and drift down toward our bodies.

Liam reaches toward the descending spores, creates tiny shields around each one, and sends them back up and out.

Harm Less, Vasif says towards Liam.

Listen to us, Arun requests.

Vasif's stream slowly turns toward him.

The Elder slips in the same words but as a demand.

Harm Less, Vasif says again, and I'm highly aware of the space between the words. It's not just talking about the spores. Thiia helps me to quell my rising worry that it is talking about the Sages' manipulation of making truth. Perhaps forcing the truth from it is somehow painful, and it is requesting less harm.

Did you come to our world through a rift? The elder asks, and the stream moves toward him.

Arun pours in the demand to know how it came to the Amazon.

Vasif shows us images from multiple directions—all moving too quickly. We see at once, the canopy shifting above, the trees and forest passing us by, even the dirt and leaves of the forest floor. Our minds struggle to process Vasif's path the way it sees—in multiple directions. The view moves back over the village Yahima spoke of—flashes of the Indigenous tribe that was there, stepping forward. We move back into the river. Processing the images of water all around us is much more manageable for our brains. The colors of the water shift, and we see the ocean waters moving quickly before the vision is pulled into the sky. The images are stretched impossibly long, as Vasif must've transformed into misty filaments—slipping by the stations undetected. We see glimpses of stations, the mines of the moon, the asteroid belt, various planets and gasses, comets, and stars. All of it flies by faster and faster. Then, images of open space which are even easier to process.

Our connection to Vasif lags. A heavy, bright, red flash, leaves an afterimage of the forest on our vision.

That wasn't the EDB, Mira announces.

Another heavy pull moves through the psybridge. The blinding flash is coupled with a dulling weight. It's too much. Sages, divs, and comps are all being pulled down. I quickly quell the echoes of awe that kept me from noticing the dullness building before it weighed us down. I try to shake off the weight from the psybridge.

Three of us fall. One of the divs from The Arrow goes down when his knees buckle. He slumps to the crystal platform, and his comp kneels to assist him. We guards are pulled back as the psybridge crackles and misaligns. Vasif does not pull away. When a comp from The Grail falls back against her div, he loses our sync, and the psybridge becomes more unstable. It's when Franxis falls, and Casey spins around to catch them, that the shield breaks like a bubble, bursting in slow motion.

Aaliyah, our crew medic, rushes to Franxis, who seems mostly okay, but groggy.

"Somebody fucking dulled me," Franxis sneers towards Awá's group.

One of the culty clowns, a div, stands with one foot on the edge of the crystal platform, where he must have sent a strong impulse to dull us. Perhaps that's his special attainment, a dulling power channeled through just one foot but strong enough to affect an entire group of divs. Anyone who didn't take a gravity assist pill has been psychically and physically weighed down by this one fucking div.

Carmel speaks quickly and clearly. "Commander Awá, we have reason to believe these four individuals and five more of your team back at camp are a part of the cult causing a ruckus at the gates."

The comp is on her wrist comm before Awá can disable it. "We're found out!" A message for the clowns back at the camp.

Awá unholsters his swift, aims it towards the clowns. "Drop your comms and swifts!" he yells. They all comply.

One of the clowns step forward, lifting his arms toward the light from Vasif behind us. Argis pulls on his collar, telling him to snap out of it. Awá stares at them, brow furrowed, as the puzzle pieces fall into place, and he realizes several of his men are compromised. The dulling div steps forward, eyes staring up at the growing radiance behind me. A chill moves up my spine, and across our psybridge, I feel terror creeping into Thiia. The UNAF Div falls to his knees with wide eyes and a foolish grin.

The light grows brighter and louder, and we turn slowly. Psychically willing our helmets to snap up and on, everyone steps one foot back into a warrior's stance and raises their fists, sonic cannons whining and waiting for a flick of the wrist before releasing their concussive blasts. But no one fires.

Over the end of the platform hangs a luminous humanoid body suspended by glowing vines of light growing out of its crown, funneling from the uppermost reaches of where Vasif's mists hang from the trees. Ephemeral leaves uncurl, expand, and wither along the vines. Luminous, gold spores drift around it as it turns its expressionless head toward Argis and the div who dulled us.

Harm Less.

Casey gets Franxis on their feet and puts his arm around their shoulders to steady them. His stance says he's ready to pick Franxis up and run if it comes to that. Aaliyah glances at the being hanging by vines of light, and actually scoffs in annoyance before turning her attention back to Franxis to check their vitals.

The rest of us look on, entranced. The Elder Sage stumbles back, shaking his head. Arun is one beat behind him. They turn our attention towards the lattice of almost invisible vines moving all around us, creeping toward our minds.

We fall back into our warrior stances and aim our sonic chargers at the EDB.

Its color shifts, and a cry of fear moves through its entire body. A grey vein of light is pushed through its body by shifting leaves. The movement forces the grey vein further back, where it is buried within the white light.

Shield, it calls to us as the leaves push another grey light vein through the headdress of vines moving it further away from us into its body draped over the trees. *Shield!*

"I think it wants us to shield ourselves from it," Mira says.

Yes. The strain in its psychic voice is grating.

"Awá, keep your men off the crystal!" Arun roars. His fury alarms all of us who remember his power. He turns toward the EDB and places one hand over his heart, the other out towards Vasif's hanging body, palm forward, fingers closed, thumb bent in slightly: a mudra for eliminating fear.

We all follow his lead and soon a stronger, more powerful shield expands from within us, synergizing with our gear's shield generation. It expands to protect Awá and his team as they restrain Argis and the other div. The other clowns, the level three and Ops, are entranced by Vasif still.

"We mean you no harm," Arun says to Vasif.

I'm relieved to hear that his voice rings with truth.

The EDB's radiance shifts to a soft, warm glow. The humanoid body reaches forward to touch the shield. Seeing that it is steady, tension is released from within the being's body, and the thin, almost invisible creepers tap and pop against the shield.

"I think it can't control that part of itself," I say, stepping forward to stand with Arun. "It looks like Haddyc energies that Vasif is straining to contain."

"Or get free of," Mira says, her voice full of sympathy.

Yes, it transfers, turning its luminous head towards Mira.

Mira says, "I think communication with us is difficult for it, right now, but I discern an eager willingness to learn and a lot of pattern recognition happening within its mind."

A note of sympathy moves from Mira and echoes in us.

Pass? Vasif asks. *Harm Less.*

Our divs with specialized attainments in EDB communication unpack the words.

"It wants to know if the humanoid body can come into the shield," Liam relays.

"The part it cannot control, the thin fibers which can harm us, will get pulled away," Mira infers. "It will be harmless."

"You believe it?" Carmel asks Mira.

"Yes," Mira says. "This is by far the most peaceful EDB we've ever encountered." She turns to face me, and there is certainty in her eyes.

"Elder?" Arun asks, turning to the grey-haired senior.

The Elder says, "We must keep the Aethonic and Haddyc energies at bay. Maintain the shield. Let it step through."

"You have our permission," Mira says, smiling to the EDB. "Come through."

The misty vines coming down from the draped fog into its crown rustle as they extend, lowering the being's feet through the shield. Grey veins are pulled through the body as it descends through the barrier. The shield pulls away the toxic Aethonic and Haddyc energies which pulse through the viny headdress before they are sent deeper into the drapes of Vasif's larger body hanging from the canopy. Its leaves shuffle over the surface of its misty drapes, concealing the murky grey energies. The feet of Vasif's humanoid body land on the crystal platform. It lifts its hands to its face; its head tilts back. It runs its hands down its neck. The humanoid extension of the EDB glows brighter, and it coos an audible and ecstatic sound of relief.

The being steps toward Mira, and before Carmel can power up her sonics, Mira halts her with a gently lifted hand.

Mira says, "It's okay, honey."

The being transfers something to Mira, but despite our strong connection to the EDB and Mira, we cannot discern what.

Liam asks, "Was that 'your,' possessive, or 'you're,' as in you are?"

"Both," Mira answers, delight building in her. "Vasif said 'Your song,' and 'You're song.'"

The being looks from Mira's chest to Carmel's, then mine, and Thiia's. It coos with delighted curiosity.

"Seems fascinated with our heartstars," I note. "Has Vasif done this before?"

"All of this is shit is new," Awá says. "I've never seen an EDB take a human shape."

Taking control of the conversation, the Elder transfers: *We have come to you to ask something of you.* He pauses as the being tilts its head as if to turn a good ear towards him. Its shoulders and body sway gently like branches in an unseen breeze.

It turns its head down toward a lifted shoulder, a slight flinch. *Harm Less here.*

"Um," Liam says, "We are doing much less harm to… the being within the shield."

"No more forcing it to answer questions," Mira says. "We were causing harm. And it was unnecessary."

Ask, Vasif beckons the Sage. Its voice is far more mellifluous without the strain of holding back the toxic energies.

The Elder speaks slowly as Arun conjures images of what the words mean in his mind. The rest of us do our best to buffer the images, so that we don't accidentally frighten Vasif or lose its trust. "There was another being, like you in that it was not from this world. It was Haddyc. It tried to harm us. It was going to harm the Earth." Vasif's head tilts and weaves as he speaks. "It came through a breach between worlds, a rift, which we must close. But first, we much send that being back through the rift. Can you help us?"

The being pauses, tilts its luminous head as if listening to subtle vibrations, and the golden spores drift around its viny headdress.

Assist, Vasif transfers in the same melodic tone.

The Elder turns toward Mira who unpacks the word. "No, it cannot close the rift… It can however assist in sending the Haddyc back."

Haddyc. Back. It gestures back toward its larger body outside of the shield where it has pushed the grey veins. It swipes its hand as if it's sending something away from itself.

"And it wants to send the Haddyc energy within itself back as well."

Arun nods. "We will figure out a way to assist each other."

Vasif brightens, and again, coos, seeming genuinely delighted.

"What assistance do you need from us to make it happen?" the Elder asks.

Certainty… Key.

Liam deciphers. "I believe it's saying, it can send a part of itself with us for a test, to be sure it will work. So that we're certain."

Mira adds. "And 'key' refers to… an object? I can almost see the shape."

Arun signals us all to buffer as he narrows a channel open to Vasif.

"What is the key?" he asks.

Before he can finish speaking, we feel the image coming into our minds. A golden ring, a festoon floating within it.

Arun sends back the energy of a smile, and Vasif seems pleased.

Relief comes from Casey. Carmel still looks skeptical. Thiia sends a note of elation towards me.

"We have acquired this key from the Haddyc." Underneath Arun's words, there is a sense of delight in knowing the purpose of the object, even as he obscures awareness of the other four ornaments. He lifts his forearm, launching a holoscreen. Blue lights spin up an image of the extradimensional ring. He holds it out to Vasif.

Bring. It reaches out a hand asking for the key.

"The key is not here with us." Arun layers in a feeling of kindness as he says, "It is with friends, closer to the rift." Then, he signals a feeling of that kindness being threatened. "Closer to the Haddyc, MaalenKun." He calls from us what we feel about the fiend.

Vasif picks up on the fears in our minds, recoils, and groans. It shakes its viny headdress as if sending the images through the channels back to wherever it pushes the Haddyc energies within itself. I sense a fierce compassion within the luminous being.

Take, it transfers.

Its arms spread wide, and a flurry of leaves flies forth from the heart of the luminous body.

Jolts of tension and fear fly through us, and Mira, Liam and the Sages moderate them. Arun tries to guide our crew back to calm.

Within the shield, the misty leaves fall and drift toward us. The Sages hold out their gloved hands and allow two misty leaves to land in their palms. Some of the other divs and comps step out of the way so that the leaves miss them. They land on the crystal platform and disappear. Mira holds out a gloved hand and a leaf changes course to fall into it. Same for Liam.

I hold out a hand, and I am surprised to see a leaf spinning through the air, leaving a misty trail as it hurries over to land in my palm.

I look back at our group. Some of the divs from The Arrow have leaves, both the div and comp from The Grail have them. Carmel is, of course, dodging them. Harjaz has one.

Casey's face is now a mix of amazement and hesitation as he looks up from the glowing semi-solid leaf in his gloved palm. Even without sensing it psychically, I know he's thinking of MaalenKun's sting.

"Kneel before *La Diosa!"* Argis shouts, falling to his knees.

"Idiot," Awá mumbles.

The worshipers have lost it. In spite of swifts aimed at their temples, they scramble forward, grasping for the fallen leaves on the crystal platform. All of the fallen leaves evaporate before they can reach them. Tears stream down their faces.

"They don't deserve it!" they cry as Awá jerks them back by their uniforms.

One of Awá's soldiers with his swift trained on the compromised divs is briefly distracted by the commotion, and the clown kneeling near him takes the opportunity. The div snatches the swift away and points it toward the Elder, fires. Mira, already close to the Elder, and surely having seen the shot moments before it happened, takes one small step and the bolt. We hear the charge crackling as her body jerks and loosens. She slumps back and the Elder makes no move to catch her even though she just spared him the stunning electric charge. Arun catches her.

Carmel's raw scream shakes us all as her rage swells. It takes all we have to hold the shield. Carmel runs for Mira, crying out as Mira's eyes roll back.

"She'll be okay," Arun says. "Her healing factors—"

Carmel looks at Arun with furious eyes. She checks that her wife is breathing and looks back at the clown that shot her. She's up and running across the platform. She levels her whining sonics. I'm not fast enough to stop her, but Casey is. He catches her, and she allows him to stop her.

I run to her side.

The clown slides the forend to recharge, and Awá shoots him. The bolt from Awá's swift clasps on, and the clown goes down twitching onto the crystal platform.

"Goddam idiot," Awá mumbles, dragging him off of the platform. The crew of The Arrow steps forward, blasters raised toward Argis and the only other conscious clown.

"Let go, Carmel," I tell her. Her body eases less because I've said to, more because her target is already down. "See to Mira." She pulls away and rushes back over to where Aaliyah is already treating Mira.

Casey looks shaken.

"Are you okay, Casey?" I hold my hands to the sides of his helmet. "Carmel's okay. You did good."

"It's not that..." he says, backing away slowly.

"Casey?" Franxis says from behind him.

"It's..." Casey says. He winces hard enough for me to worry that he's hurt. "The leaf."

"It's okay. I lost mine too." I look around at the other crews, see the cloud-like leaves in several palms. "We have a few to take with us. We'll examine—"

"No, it..." He shakes his head and pulls away.

I reach towards him, anxious for him to look in my eyes. He won't, and my heart sinks.

"Oscar, step back." Franxis pulls my arm away, speaking slowly. "Stay back. It went into him."

As Franxis pulls me away from him slowly, Casey's face drops as if he has been punched in the gut. His eyes flicker and his jaw drops. He activates his combat gear's prismatic shield. A forcefield of rainbow light flickers into a visible barrier around him, sealing in any potential contaminants.

"Fuck!" Harjaz shouts. I turn my head in time to see him activating his own personal shield. Others do the same, sealing themselves off from the rest of us. They didn't just drop their leaves. The leaves went into their bodies.

Franxis and I turn to see Vasif's humanoid body ascending as the vines of its headdress pull it back through the air. It disappears into the larger glowing body of mist. The EDB hangs amongst the trees. Glowing golden spores continue to drift under its cathedral-like awning.

Aside from small noises of frustration and surprise on the crystal platform, the forest seems quiet.

"Franxis, step back," I say. "My arm... feels odd."

I activate my shield. I didn't drop the leaf after all.

ꝏ

excerpt from After Action Report #91759-83
filed by Scire Sages
following encounter with Haddyc, MaalenKun, confined to crystal chamber
restricted access to Central Command, UNAF-Div Command, Helixx Corp CEO Griselda Harris Ferand
4 April, 2138

Extradimensional objects were obtained while defeating the Haddyc known as MaalenKun. These objects were first glimpsed in the EDB's mindfield during the initial encounter. After a successful attempt to communicate with the being, the five objects were drawn from the EDB's mindfield and manifested in our physical realm. This was not our intention upon engaging MaalenKun, yet we seized the opportunity in an attempt to disarm and de-power the being.

Sages from Helixx Corp are meditating on them, but there seems to be a disruptive frequency around them, making it difficult to discern their true purpose.

The objects have the look of gold but emit various vibrational and energetic signatures. Each emits a different unknown quantum signature. Div-tech departments have been unable to determine any molecular make-up of the objects due to the disruptive frequencies.

Extradimensional objects obtained during MaalenKun encounter #5 (4 April):

- ringed festoon
- polyhedron (This object appears differently to various viewers. It has been seen as having as few as six and as many as fourteen sides.)
- orbs (transparent gold orb containing four smaller orbs around a central orb)
- knot, ever moving and shifting (it is unknown what energy source is moving this object)
- chime (much like a tuning fork) with floating teardrop

Div-tech will submit an attachment detailing exact measurements of objects.

- request by Sage Murtagh: removal of objects to a secure location, perhaps a less populated site on Mars.
- query from Elders: Are these objects now the property solely of Helixx Corp? Since the station was under UNAF supervision during the transfer of power, does the UNAF have jurisdiction over these objects? Central, please advise.

CASEY

I'm grateful they don't have div-bars at Amparo-1. Awá said that they haven't had a shipment of div-bars in years. He said that the last time they had an incident, they kept an eye and a swift on the risky div until they knew there was no threat. He laughed at our shocked faces and said they'd forego the swift this time.

I'm sequestered in a tiny room directly across from Oscar's tiny room. Thick duraglass walls border the hallway between us.

Others from The Arrow and The Grail are further down the hall. Harjaz's room is next to Oscar's, Mira's is next to mine, and we can see them across the hall when they step close to the duraglass.

I sit on the edge of the cot, head down, as I have for the last hour or so. I'm worried I'll again be held in quarantine with my only fears and memories.

When I look up, I meet Oscar's eyes as he is patiently watching over me. I'm not alone this time. I give him a soft smile. He smiles gently.

When Carmel comes in, we all approach our glass walls so we can see her.

She stops between our four rooms, switches on the intercom, and says, "Well, Captain Commander N'guwe is both angry and pleased. She chewed us up for not demanding sealed suits from the start, but since that's not regulation for Earth runs, she couldn't really say much. But like I said, N'guwe is pleased. We made contact, and we got more interaction from Vasif than any other teams have in three years. Pretty sure the EDB was charmed by Mira and Liam. Central is discussing options for how to make it happen, but there is hope we can at least send the Haddyc back, if not seal StillRift-2138. And each of you is instrumental in creating that hope. Thank you."

Oscar's mood lifts, and he smiles wider. I try to look less sullen.

"Sages from all over are discussing what to do with the ornament—or key as it may be. They have to determine if there is any risk in moving the key so far away from MaalenKun and the other ornaments, which they don't yet want Vasif to know about. They're not so sure we can trust Vasif, and I've got to say, after this bullshit with those misty leaves getting inside my crew, I'm right there with them."

I step back from the glass and let my head hang.

"Div Isaac," Carmel addresses me, and I look up, not hiding the worry in my eyes. "Don't fret over this. I know you've had a lot of quarantine lately, but it's not uncommon for divs at Level Four to be quarantined after a direct encounter. When you're Level Seven, you won't have to fuss with quarantine anymore. You'll be able to sort any shit those EDBs leave on you. Wallowing in your sorrow will only train your mind to do that every single time, which can keep you from leveling up to Seven. That said, don't bypass that mood. Quarantine sucks. Process, but don't indulge, handsome."

Her endearment is as much for Oscar's benefit as mine. I'm amazed to find the echo of the psybridge cast on the platform still connected to Oscar. Her words lift him, and I feel his confidence. He looks from her to me, and I wonder if he can feel the echo connecting us. He glances away briefly smiling sheepishly, but maybe he's just flirting.

"Just so everyone is up to date: Mira has already recovered from the swift bolt thanks to her rapid healing factor. And all of you can rest easy. From the readings Aaliyah and MedOps took, your energy signatures look healthy, auras are signaling fine, and they find no reason to keep you in quarantine past the standard twenty-four. I am sorry that you'll miss the sunset though. You can take off that combat gear and get comfortable, folks. We'll get your dinner to you soon. Awá said he'll speak to the cook about getting you something plant-based, not sure the cook is used to that though, so it might just be beans and rice."

Harjaz knocks on the glass. "I'm not completely vegan, just when I have to be on the station."

"You know that shit dulls divination. You're eating plant-based while you're on my crew, Div Hassenstein."

Harjaz's face drops and his jaw hangs as he watches Carmel switch the comm over to Mira's room. I do my best to suppress a laugh. Oscar looks over towards me, chuckling as he backs away from the glass wall.

He points to the antique comm on the table next to the bed. He picks his up, taps a few buttons, and the light on the comm in my room blinks.

"I have to agree with the captain," I say. "You are rather handsome."

My smile widens. "I have to agree with her too. But more about not indulging the frustration and disappointment. It's there for sure, and she saw that I was starting to sink in it. She's a good captain."

"She is." He smiles at her as she walks past our rooms and leaves the quarantine ward.

"And we should definitely do as she says." I cradle the comm against my shoulder as I take a few more steps back, out of sight from Harjaz. "And get out of this combat gear." I psychically will the suit to loosen, unfasten the front, and peel the armor away.

"That was an order, right?" He takes a few steps back so Mira cannot see him.

"Definitely sounded like an order." I watch his eyes move over my chest, my uniform pulled down to my waist. When his eyes return to mine, I lift my eyebrows as if to say, your turn.

With an adorable hint of shyness across his face, he wills his suit to ease, slowly opens the front, and slides the sleeves down. As soon as I see his chest, I want him against my body again, his chest hair brushing against my skin. He grins, less timidly, more mischievously as if he's read my mind. And maybe he has.

I set the comm down and will my boots to relax. Slowly I bring the suit down below my waist. I lean back against the wall and kick off the rest of the suit. I watch his eyes move over my tight-fitting tank and briefs, and I see him laugh more than I hear it. I pick up the comm again. "Your turn again."

I glean a hint of his shyness too easily. He's worried someone will walk in, see us stripping for each other, and ruin the moment.

I quip, "We're just following captain's orders."

The corner of his mouth turns up. Moving with less performance than me, he pushes his uniform down and pulls his hairy legs out. When he looks up, I facetiously bite my lip. My playful humor is enough to make him laugh and maybe forget a bit of his shyness.

He squints and tilts his head. "If we go any further, I'm going to be standing here at full attention, and I don't want to surprise whoever is bringing our dinner."

"I'm halfway there now." I laugh hearty and full, grateful for this delightful shift in my mood.

"I can see." He cocks one eyebrow up.

"You're the expert at taking it this far and quelling the desire," I tease. "What do we do now?"

He frowns in jest. "It's not about quelling it, but just letting it be." His hand moves down the side of his beard. He nods towards his cot, in view of only me from across the hall. Mine is the same. "Lay down with me," he says.

When he tells me to lay down with him, I'm happy to, but I wait until he's next to his bed so we can lay down at the same time, together, even though we're in separate rooms divided by two thick walls of duraglass. Through his tank top and briefs, I can see the outline of his body as he lays on his side and props himself up on one elbow. I take in the sight of his hairy legs, curves of his pecs, his little freckles, and spots across his tawny skin.

I'm happy to realize that my bed cannot be seen from the room next to Oscar's where Harjaz is practicing asana. Oscar and I actually have a semblance of privacy which feels tenuous yet thrilling.

"Why couldn't we quarantine in the same room?" I ask.

"Might not be fair. Everyone else doesn't have a quarantine buddy to get almost naked with," he jokes, turning towards me.

"Hey! I'm just following orders."

He laughs and repeats, "Just following orders." His deep voice is soothing in one way and exciting in another.

"She did not tell us to put on the loungewear, just to get out of the combat gear."

"Loungewear? You mean the green sweatpants they put in here?"

"Mm-hmm. You'll look good in mint."

"They'll really bring out the color in your eyes." He says, rolling onto his side and propping himself up on his elbow. "Kinda I wish I were closer, so I could get lost in them."

"I wish you were closer too, so I could do a lot of things." I put my hand over my chest, near my heart, and he does the same.

"That would be nice." His eyes. Thick lashes, dark brown irises. Dreamy gaze.

"So, I want to ask you something." I inhale fully, hoping I won't scare him away.

"And I want you to answer honestly."

"I'll tell you the truth, Casey. Always."

I pause, letting his words in their promising tone land.

"Did you bridge me earlier?"

He grumbles. His eyes wince shut, and he dramatically falls forward, face down on his bed. He brings the comm back to his ear, and his voice is muffled. "Please, don't tell everyone, but yes. That's my special div attainment." He looks up from the bed. "I'm basically a div who can comp anyone Risen. And I use it to strengthen the Sage's psybridge network, but honestly, I can bridge more people than most Sages can. There can be more to it, but that's how I use it in the field."

I try to look casual. "Thought I felt you. Your Mani crew mates know?"

"Of course. We're a tight crew."

"And the Sages?"

"Some."

"Ops?"

"Some," he nods emphatically.

"But not the other divs, other comps?"

"No." He looks away pondering something. He covers his mouth for a moment as if he is hesitant to speak about it. He winds up smoothing the beard on his chin and looks back at me with serious eyes. "It's not in my file. It's kept secret. Mostly for defense against other divs that might go rogue. I felt the dull from that clown building, but it was too late. If I'd noticed it sooner, I could've caught everyone."

"I see."

"I use it during encounters to assist, to protect, to lift what we need, to snuff out what we don't. I don't glean anything that anyone doesn't want me to..." I cannot read his expression. "Are you upset?"

"No." I wonder if I'm excusing it because I'm attracted to him. I probably wouldn't feel the way I do if another div did the same. Regardless, I do feel a little bit awkward about it. "I understand. It's just a bit... you know with Sages and comps we let them in because we know about it, and we've matched with our comps in training."

"I don't feel great about it, Casey," he says, and I can hear honesty in his voice. He shakes his head as he turns back onto his side. "It's my job to give added protection during an action. I would not psybridge anyone without them knowing otherwise."

"I believe you." As I say this, he smiles wanly. "So, are we still psybridged?"

He sighs. "I think maybe my interest in you is making it linger a bit. I have been tuning out while trying to disentangle, but every time I think I'm out, something reconnects. Feels like you're reaching out and pulling me back, but... I apologize."

"It's okay." I add flirtatiously, "Could be fun."

His inhale is sharp, and the exhale deep. He seems very reassured to hear me toy with him. He sighs and says, "I'm glad you're not upset. I was going to tell you tonight..."

"But I got half-naked and distracted you." His crooked smile makes my heart flutter. "It's okay. I trust you, Oscar."

"Can you keep this secret? I also have to let Ops know that you know."

"Sure. Franxis will know, of course."

He nods.

"So..." I watch his eyes move with my hand as I rub my chest, and his smile returns. "If we are psybridged, can you tell what I'm thinking about?" I let my eyes trace the lines of his body and land on the bulge of his briefs.

"I think I already know." He winks playfully. "If you want, I can tune you in more. Or I can work on drawing it back, but you might have to put on some clothes and—"

"I'm not putting on clothes." I sit up on the edge of the bed and he does the same while laughing. I send a signal through Franxis' comp-bridge for them to give me a little more privacy, and immediately, I feel them dialing down. "Tune me in a bit more. Just for now."

"Just for now," Oscar says. He tucks his chin in slightly, and I can almost see the channel opening up around his head as it expands and crosses the distance between us. Surprisingly, I feel what seems to be a channel reaching from my body towards his psybridge. Perhaps it's my eagerness that makes it seem that I'm reaching a psybridge toward him as well. We connect. My body feels cooler. A breezy rush moves throughout my being as the psybridge is integrated all over my body.

He transfers, *I'm going to create a loop. Just signal when you want me to tune out.*

I signal delight… excitement… and I obscure many things I'm not ready for him to know or see. He nods, and I feel assured that he respects those wishes. He's more interested in my delight, my excitement.

Into the comm, he asks, "Can I touch you?"

I nod, even though I feel that he is amused with my puzzlement.

He sets his comm down. His lips part as he runs his hand across his chest, and I feel the fabric of his tank top, his body heat, in my fingertips. The feeling of my chest being rubbed moves through me, and I gasp. I have to breathe deep to refocus on the present moment.

"I can feel you on my fingers. I've never experienced anything like this."

"Oh, we don't have to stop at fingertips."

My mind begins to whirl with the potential, and I can't not make a joke. "Versatile guys must go nuts over this."

Again, he laughs, deep and full. When he looks at me again, I can see in his eyes and sense through the psybridge that he knows that he is a skilled lover. His confidence excites me.

"Yeah," he says. "Yeah."

He touches his lower lip, and I feel the sensation of his finger on my mouth. He lightly bites one of his fingers and moves his tongue across its tip. The salty taste of his fingertip dances on my tongue.

The sensation of his hand tracing a line down my neck emerges as he moves his hand back down to his chest. I signal how turned on I am by his chest hair, and he toys with me. He points towards his chest, eyebrows lifted. *Oh, this?*

I nod, maybe too enthusiastically. He laughs and runs his fingers across the curve of his pecs. I feel his chest in my hands, his hands on my chest. He lightly pinches my nipple, and a pleasant but intensifying charge moves through me as he squeezes a bit harder.

I gasp again, trying not to moan. When I reopen my eyes, his crooked grin shows a hint of playful wickedness, and I'm more turned on than I've been in years.

You okay over there? His turn to return some of the teasing. I can feel him relishing watching me squirm.

You might be getting me too excited considering our privacy is tenuous.

I can see how excited, he teases, glancing down my torso below my waist.

My hand trembles lightly as I pick up the comm, and when he does the same, I tell him, "I sincerely think I cannot handle any more, and this is the first time in my life I've ever decided to ease up when things were getting hot."

He tunes the psybridge back slowly, and I feel it coursing through my body, a lover's embrace, easing and letting go.

"You know me," he says. Bedroom eyes. "Don't mind building anticipation."

A faint call like a gentle knock at the door comes through Franxis' compbridge. I signal back that they can dial me in more. They do, and the familiar comfort washes over me. *Are y'all hungry?*

"Our dinner is coming," I tell him.

"Think those sweatpants are gonna be enough to conceal what's going on down there, or do you need to put your armor back on?"

I take the pillow and place it over my lap. "No one will know a thing."

He pulls the comm away from his face so that his booming laugh doesn't hurt my ear.

A dream of putting in a transfer to Station Mani flashes across my mind. It's followed my sudden doubt that they'd accept me, that he'd want that. And I quell it all before he might notice.

He shakes his head. "We likely won't have another moment alone for a while if we're needed to send back the Haddyc."

"Glad we had this moment." The happiness I feel brings with it release and relief.

Oscar smiles, replies, "More. Soon."

Oscar and I spend most of our waking hours on the antique comms chatting. He's easy to talk to.

"Seems like I'll be moving on from Scire soon," I tell him. "Rumor is very few Queers have received a favorable assessment from Helixx Corp."

His brow wrinkles. "Sorry to hear that. Can't believe Central is letting Helixx get away with that shit."

"Even if I didn't have to worry about being let go for being Queer, it took me over one hundred years just to get to Level Four. I'm sure that if it weren't for my secondary role in div-tech, UNAF would've kicked me off Scire long ago. Now that they've sold it to the world's wealthiest person, the boot feels inevitable."

"I know a lot of folks leaving Scire are seeking reassignment back with the UNAF, transferring to the other stations. Some have gone to Mars or lunar colonies." He shifts to a more promising tone. "Maybe you could apply for Station Mani."

"That would be nice," I admit, forcing my smile, knowing how unlikely that would be.

He maybe senses me forcing my smile and steers the conversation toward something that makes him smile. "Scire has one thing far better than anything on Mani." As he says this, he looks genuinely impressed.

His smile is contagious. I lean forward just a bit. We're both on the floor behind the thick glass walls, so we can sit as close to each other as possible. I'm aware he could have psybridged me for this conversation, but for now, I'm content to share our time this way, just talking face to face.

"Yeah, our div-tech department is way better."

"What? No way. I know every station has this idea that their div-tech is the best, but come on. Mani came up with the personal prismatic shields all divs use."

"Which is pretty good, but Scire already had that tech shielding ships. Mani just miniaturized it."

"Just miniaturized it? Mani made it so we're almost bulletproof in the field."

I smirk and raise my brows. "Almost bulletproof kinda sounds like it's almost awesome. Also, Scire div-tech recently pulled down designs for a hyperspeed engine. Those nerds have been meditating on it for decades, and they think they've finally found the math."

"I heard the news," he half-gripes. "It's exciting."

"I'm helping them with the ship design."

"Seriously?"

"If you'd read my file, you'd know that I spent the past seventy years working with tech on ship design. It's knowledge I can pull down from upper Levels. You're looking at the guy who designed the crux-wing."

He raises his thick eyebrows. "Oh, that's actually really fucking impressive."

I lean forward. "And I did it with Scire tech."

He holds up his hands. "You win for now."

"Right." We both laugh a bit, and I realize I diverted the conversation and put myself on a pedestal. I make a mental note to be more tuned in to him. "Enough about me… What is it that you love about Scire more than Mani?"

He leans back, props up on his arms, takes a deep breath. "The Avifaun Gardens." He shakes his head a bit and slowly blinks. "Beautiful."

I take a moment to look at his face as he soaks in the memory of the beautiful gardens. "It is. Scire designers really nailed it with that one. I mean, I feel a bit sorry for the birds who didn't sign up to be astronauts—" I must've killed his delight; his face is more sober now. "—but having them there for biodiversity actually makes the Ag-Gardens work better too." I shrug. "Also, each species is extinct on earth. There's talk of breeding them and reintroducing them to the planet. Maybe they're happier in a controlled climate. Who knows?"

"It's sweet that you consider the birds that way."

"I mean they seem okay to me, but I'm not a bird scientist."

"Ships are more your thing." He looks genuinely impressed to know this about me. "Makes me happy to hear the birds sing. It's why my crew set up camp in the garden. Reminds me of more peaceful times pre-EDBs, pre-divination." I hear a tiny bit of what sounds like remorse.

"Do you ever regret going div?" I listen actively just as he has, without judgment, without question.

"No." His voice grows more solemn. "But it was very painful those first few years. We were part of the crew that drove Bakkeaux away."

"Denver. I read it in your file." I think of trying to steer the conversation in another direction, but I realize my own pattern of avoidance is resurfacing and getting in the way. "I was there too—Nuevo Angeles, just late for the party."

He smiles but it doesn't shine in his eyes.

I try to bolster him, "Your crew changed everything."

"After the battle, we watched so many comatose crew mates pass away one after the other."

I don't speak. I listen. I can hear how much it hurts him. I sit with him and his pain. My heart hurts for him, and I feel compassion moving both ways through the light-thread connecting our hearts. Something shifts in me. I sense a re-orientation toward more fully processing my own memories, my own hurt. But it scares me.

He shakes his head. "I've spoken enough about me for one day."

I return a smile with understanding in my eyes, hoping to not seem relieved that he doesn't need to talk any more about his pain.

There's a bit of a long pause between us before I change the subject.

"I got a holo-pal. Please, don't tell anyone."

ꝏ

By mid-afternoon, we dress in our combat gear again and walk out of the quarantine ward. Free again.

The air is sweltering, but I'm happy to be outside, touching the Earth. Oscar walks by my side as we approach our crew.

All of us Scire divs have gotten a message from Yahima. She is ten minutes out, coming in cloaked. Awá is not at all happy to have more visitors, and this time with only ten minutes notice via visiting divs that he's already annoyed to have around.

We set out for the landing zone and wait behind the heat shields. Before we see them, we hear the ships. They're just a few meters above the tree line when they uncloak. The surfaces of the ships flicker with reflected sky before the details of the ships emerge. Two crimson clash-wings from Helixx Corp flank a saffron and orange crux-wing, Yahima's personal fighter jet, Lacassine.

"That is a beautiful wing," Carmel says, speaking of Yahima's crux.

"You know Casey helped design the crux," Oscar says half-proud, maybe half-teasing me after I'd bragged too much. "What aspects did you work on exactly?"

"Wasn't all my design. I helped integrate the wing rotators and thrusters for agility, so the ship can shape-shift when in space."

"That's how they move quickly through debris fields, right?" Carmel asks, not taking her eyes off of the ship.

A chance to appear humble. "Well, that's still up to the pilots."

"The crux is the most agile wing in the fleet," Franxis says with a hint of pride.

"Pretty impressive, Div Isaac." Carmel crosses her arms and leans towards me as she peers out at the cross-shaped jet. "Can you get me in one of those for a little spin?"

"I'll see what I can do, but even I don't get to fly them. Only divs Six and up have that privilege." I grin at her.

"I can psybridge my wife. She's a Six. Maybe that works?"

"Do they not have crux-wings on Mani?" Harjaz sarcastically asks.

She raises her eyebrow. "A few, but not that pretty."

Oscar quips, "We can't all fit in that ship, captain."

"Only reason I don't already have one," she nearly sings.

The ship begins to shape-shift for landing. The vertical and horizontal wings rotate around the stationary spherical cockpit. Designed to weave through the incredible field of debris from destroyed satellites and starships that drifts in the Earth's orbit, the four wings rotate and retract. The ship shape-shifts to move quickly through wreckage. In the low but cloudy atmosphere of Earth, the shifting wings look stunning. For landing, the cross becomes an x, and the landing skids extend towards the Earth. The multi-directional thrusters light up along the edges of the wings, and the ship vertically descends with grace. The light of the afternoon sun dances across reflective charger panels, and a rainbow spark runs down the clear quartz blades at the wings' leading edge.

The crimson clash wings settle down vertically on either side of the crux. Their cockpits remain closed, pilots inside. One of the clash wing's cargo opens and a robotic arm lowers towards the ground. It releases a small pod about 40 by 50 centimeters. The pod hatches and its panels shape shift. An antenna extends up, and the light at its end glows red, then yellow, then green.

Yahima stands from her meditative seat in The Lacassine's cockpit. They carry a small, ornate coffer and descend the staircase as it unfolds a few steps ahead of them. Yahima's saffron and orange combat suit stands out as a bright splash of color against the backdrop of green forest. As Yahima reaches the ground, the pod unfolds robotic legs and arms, and a flat display screen where a head would be. Yahima, expression neutral, gazes toward the robot as it steadies itself before they walk towards us.

As we step out to meet them, Thiia whispers, "That's a distans. Someone's on the other end of its signal piloting it from afar."

"Wonder who our special guest is today," Oscar says.

As we get closer to each other, the face on the screen is more and more clear. I recognize it from her book cover.

"Holy shit," I whisper. "It's Griselda fucking Ferrand."

Awá mumbles, "Goddamnit."

ꝏ

Meeting Griselda via the bot is awkward at best. The screen displaying her face remains stationary, but the cameras she sees through move all around. The bot stands in front of me, and I introduce myself. Just like everyone else who got a personal souvenir from our first visit with Vasif, the bot's cameras scan me up and down.

How does it feel to have the world's richest woman undress you with her eyes? Franxis transfers.

I signal back that it feels like I should get paid more.

Awá shakes the bot's hand, and although she operates the robotic arm to comply, Griselda Harris Ferand makes no effort to conceal her snicker from afar. Harjaz and the divs from The Arrow smirk and look away, doing their best not to laugh. Yahima flashes them a potent glance, and they stifle laughter.

Awá leads us all into the EDB research labs. We find Amparo-1's UNAF-Ops team waiting for us. The three scientists seem excited to speak to Dr. Ferand, celebrity scientist and CEO.

"In light of what happened to several divs, we have not opened the strongbox Awá brought back from the site." The clear box sits on the table, the luminous leaf shaped puffs drift around inside. "Scans indicate that these 'leaves' are very different from what went into your bodies. Med-Ops has told us that whatever you picked up on, it's far more benevolent, even if it looked the same. The 'leaves' in the strongbox contain a unique energy signature that they've never encountered."

The other div-tech waves his hand and a holographic screen floats near the table. "Each of these leaves serves as a sort of pocket. It encloses energy and can even conceal the signatures. We noticed the samples shifting that energy around a lot when we scanned them. I think the glowing surface is definitely a living extension of Vasif, but the energy it wraps itself around is not always a part of it, and perhaps not conscious in the same way that Vasif is."

"Those of you who are fresh out of quarantine, have no reason to worry." Yahima says. "We do not believe Vasif left behind much more than a gentle touch of Dymetian energy."

I haven't experienced any phantom pain from the Haddyc sting since the cloud-like leaf went into my body. My arm feels more easeful than it has in weeks.

"You're not the first to have been touched by those leaves," one of the Ops says. "We've had several instances and all those other divs are okay. And before you ask, no, none of the idiots we had to arrest, none of the idiots who got away, reported being touched by the leaves."

I look over at the robot. The screen shows Griselda's face turned to the side, and she appears to be barking orders at someone off camera. She looks calmer and more collected when her face turns forward again. A voice comes from the bot's built-in speakers, "Do you understand how Vasif is sorting and containing this energy?"

"We are not entirely sure. We've been observing this behavior for only a short time and not with this particular strange energy. It does appear that Vasif may be extracting something from it, perhaps, slowly digesting it."

Griselda says, "I'd like all your findings on this. I'll go through the proper channels for the request. Have the data ready for transmission as soon as you get the approval from Central."

Her voice is confident, but cold, addressing the Ops team as if they are robots themselves.

Yahima sets the small coffer down on the table across from the clear strongbox. "May I?"

The Ops scientists nod and step away from the control console as Yahima steps towards them and lifts their hands, and a large holoscreen appears in front of them. With a few quick taps, a shield is projected from the ceiling down around the table to the floor. Another couple of taps, and Yahima holds out their hands, fingers spread wide. A blue grid is traced along the skin of Yahima's beautiful hands. The holoscreen drops away. Yahima lifts their hands gloved in traces of blue light, and as they bring their hands down, two robotic arms descend from the ceiling within the shield's barrier.

Yahima smiles gently as they move the robotic arms down and slide away the coffer's silver metal cover, revealing a clear box. The ornament, the key, the extradimensional ring encircling the festoon, hovers at the center of the box.

The misty leaves glow brighter and crowd to the side of the strongbox nearest the ring.

Yahima speaks with clear commands. "Prescient divs, please, join the Sages.

Focus your divination on the leaves. As the energy from Vasif reacts to the ring, look ahead for the energy of the EDB, see if the ring can indeed be used to unlock the rift so that we might send back the Haddyc. It's not impossible to do so, but we've had difficulties gaining foresight around the rift. You will probably encounter disruptions if you focus on the ring or the rift. Instead, focus on the energy of Vasif that is here, focus on how Vasif might assist us in vanquishing the Haddyc."

Yahima looks to the Elder from Helixx Corp standing amongst the rest of us. He nods. Yahima looks to Arun who also nods. Along with Mira, Liam, and a couple more prescient divs, they stare straight ahead at the fluttering misty leaves.

Yahima moves the robotic arms to the strongbox as one of the leaves bounces eagerly at the seal to the opening. The robotic arms tap in the unlock code and there is a brief hiss as the seal is broken and removed. The leaves pour out of the strongbox and fly towards the ring and land against the outer edge of the clear box.

A growing high-pitched hum comes from the ring.

I hear it too, Franxis transfers. *But only through you.*

The other divs and comps around us shift on their feet, some divs turn their heads toward their comps, and I know they hear it too. The Sages stay steady.

My right hand, where I caught Vasif's leaf, feels cool. The coolness becomes a spaciousness which travels up my arm, vibrating. I sense a white light inside.

It's okay. I've got you, Franxis says.

I signal to Franxis that I think I'm okay, but it's at that moment that Yahima reaches the robotic clamp around the clear box and lifts it away from the ring. The leaves fling themselves onto the festoon at the center of the ring. The hum intensifies. A jolt of pain runs through my arm where the needle from MaalenKun's crown, which once held the ring, was driven deep into my psyche. I wince, and Franxis helps steady me. It's too much. My arm grows hotter, more painful. At the center of the ring radiates a golden light which grows brighter and brighter as the leaves swirl over the festoon. The pain burns hot, and I try to dispel it. As the ring's golden light fills the room, a vision pierces my mind.

Shapes unfold from within the light. I can see only vague suggestions that feel like a memory that hasn't happened yet. A shadow falls, stretching toward me. It lands within me, coiling around intense pain. I'm reaching for the ring, but perhaps that is my memory of being stung by MaalenKun's crown. My mind whirls, and the vision folds in on itself only to unfold into another scene. There are hands all over me. Rays of light are bending, reshaping themselves, creating an opening. Vasif is there. Franxis. Oscar. Others. An emerald light. We're fighting the Shadow. My fears taint the vision, and a gash unfolds across the scene.

The light overtakes the vision again.

The misty leaves of light cling to the key, and the painful heat in my arm dissipates. The echo of my pain fades quickly as the hum of the ring grows softer, then quiet. The golden light fades, and the ring simply floats at the center of the coffer. The pale fog spins at the center of the ring, perhaps sorting the energies it emits.

I stumble and Franxis catches me.

"Div Isaac, are you okay?" Yahima moves forward quickly.

I nod. "I'm okay."

A collective sigh of relief moves through the group. Oscar steps to my side and places a hand on my back.

Yahima looks at me, tilts their head, and smiles gently with their eyes. Joy moves through the light-thread between us. They walk over to the clear coffer and slide the silver cover back into place, concealing the altered extradimensional object. The coffer's lock closes with a snap. They turn to the other Sages, the prescient divs. Each of them assents.

The robot and Griselda's puzzled face turn towards me. Her cameras scan me up and down. The forced concern on her face seems cumbersome, out of place. Her eyes glance away, surely looking at screens of data from the bot's scans.

My brow furrows, and I tilt my head down a bit. I'm ready to tell her to stop leering. I feel Franxis turning towards the bot, ready to have my back.

Arun says with a smile, "Vasif likely will not close the rift, yet it will most likely unlock the barrier that has prevented passage into the rift. This is how we will send the Haddyc away from Earth. We will need to support Vasif as it does the heavy lifting."

A wave of excitement and gratitude lifts us all.

Yahima takes the coffer from the table. "Sages and prescient divs, with me. Everyone else, please, wait for us outside."

The robot moves to follow Yahima as the group begins to move out of the room. The Sages and prescient divs stick close to Yahima and the coffer containing the ring, the key to unlocking the rift and sending MaalenKun out of our world.

"Casey," Oscar whispers as he pulls my hand toward him. "What happened?"

"Oh." I almost laugh thinking it would be easier to have him psybridge me so I could signal the memory to him, but instead, I smile and say, "I think… maybe prescience. But most likely triggered trauma."

Most of the others have left, following the Sages, hoping for some word as to what their foresight revealed. Thiia and Franxis wait just outside the door.

Oscar takes my hand. "You good?"

I flex the fingers of my other hand. The place where the Haddyc stung me feels… freer. The phantom pain is gone.

"Yeah. I am."

ꝏ

Twirling a dry ramón leaf by its stem, I walk back to my crew. Oscar watches me with a sparkle in his eyes. Our crew relaxes in the shade of a tree waiting for the captains from each crew, Awá, and the Sages to return from another hologram meeting with Central. We watch the Griselda bot chatting with a group of UNAF officers.

"Is she taking a tour of the camp?" Harjaz squints and smirks.

"Heard she's interviewing the troops about Vasif," Liam answers.

Now that I'm close enough, Oscar holds my hand, even while Aaliyah examines my arm again.

Aaliyah shoos away his hand and smiles big. "Oscar, I promise you can have him back when I'm done."

"Kinda clingy, Kenzari," Harjaz mumbles. He folds his arms over his chest and looks back at the robot going into the old barn.

Oscar might've been about to say something, but Aaliyah shifts the mood. "I think it's sweet." She scans my arm with her handheld, has me flex my fingers, move my wrist. "I don't see anything odd going on, Casey."

Across the yard, the captains and Sages exit the side door of the farmhouse. We can't hear them, but Yahima motions for Carmel to hang back as the other captains set out to meet with their crews.

"Is she signaling what Yahima's saying?" Franxis asks Mira.

"I hear them both," Mira says.

Yahima tilts their head and looks into Carmel's eyes as they speak. Carmel stares at Yahima.

"Carmel's not happy," Mira says. "Oh… You guys, she's got plenty of reason to not be."

Carmel folds her arms across her chest and says something back to Yahima.

Mira adds, "Guess Liam isn't riding back to Scire with us."

"You mean…?" Oscar asks.

"Yeah. Arun."

I hear Yahima's words faintly as she slowly says, "Carmel, you have got to let it go."

Mira shakes her head and snorts. "He's not the only one hitching a ride with us."

We collectively realize the risk Central has decided we'll take.

Oscar sighs, "Anything unfolding we should worry about, Mira?"

Mira places a hand on his shoulder. "I don't see how, but I think… this is how we send the monster back."

ꝏ

It's dusk by the time the walking cars return, rolling fast. Awá, the Sages, Mira, Liam, The Grail crew, and the robot ride in the first car. The second car, piloted by remote, carries only one passenger. Vasif's radiant light glows brightly from the windows. A trail of glowing spores flows behind the car like magic pixie dust, only far more unsettling. Both cars speed down the dirt road across the camp towards the landing zone where we've been waiting.

"Everybody! Shields up!" Carmel shouts when they're halfway to us.

At first, I think she's overreacting to having Vasif coming toward us. Through Carmel, I glean a signal from her div. Mira is alarmed by her own foresight.

A light flickers at the edge of the forest.

Klaxons throughout the camp sound off, and spotlights illuminate the perimeter. Hundreds of people emerge at the edges of the camp. Despite Awá's notice to the UNAF, they'd never caught the other clowns who had fled the camp. They're back. And they brought their friends. The cult of *Diosa en flor* is no longer held at the gate. With torches and primitive weapons held high, they rush the camp, screaming toward us.

A few meters away, the cars come to a halt, stirring up a plume of dust.

The first bullet bounces off of Awá's car. The walkers are bulletproof, but even with shields up, our gear is not. Mira screams for Carmel to get inside the ship. Carmel runs aboard Old Girl and powers up the systems. Heat builds in the ascenders as the engine roars.

Carmel's voice comes through our comms. "That thing need life support in the cargo bay?"

Yahima's voice comes back. "No!"

"All pilots board!" Awá shouts as he bravely steps out of the bulletproof car. "The rest of us will have to hold them off. This thing's slow as fuck." He opens the door of the second car, and Vasif pours out like a sedate fog.

Awá spins his hand wildly in circles. "Quickly please." He ducks behind the bulletproof car as more bullets whiz around him.

We position ourselves to guard Vasif's path.

"Casey!" Oscar shouts from behind me. He's walking backwards toward Old Girl. "Be careful."

"I will. Go!"

The red clash wings which escorted Yahima's Lacassine are finally hot enough for lift off. The tall vertical ships tilt towards the ground, aiming their huge sonic cannons down. They hover along the edges of the approaching crowd. Some of the fiendish attackers are armed only with sticks and torches. Others aim their guns on the clash wings, but the bullets can't break the wings' powerful shields. The clashes move in closer, sonic cannons whirring. They fire before the charge can build too high. Designed for blasting space debris and EDBs, not human bodies, and the minimized blast is enough to knock dozens of them to the ground. Some of them try to get back up and join the melee. The cannons whirr longer and the pulse hits harder. Limbs are twisted.

Griselda's robot runs from the car and grabs a man who drops his torch. The other mechanical arm winds back, and she punches him with her metal fist. Blood splatters across the screen displaying her face, wild-eyed, sneering.

"Lady! We're not trying to kill them!" Franxis yells at her.

The face on the screen turns towards Franxis before the robot runs into the mob, spinning its arms around like a fan, knocking several people down before the crowd descends on the bot and it disappears in a wave of bodies.

Vasif crawls along the ground toward Old Girl's cargo ramp. When the crowd sees its glowing spores and radiant body of rambling vines and leaves, they begin to shout and cry out.

"La Diosa! La Diosa! Save the Goddess!"

It seems to be moving as fast as it can away from them, and I wonder if it ever actually meant for them to worship it. Perhaps it was telling them to revere the forest, to see the forest as sacred.

"Casey, look out!" Mira screams.

A UNAF-div, one of the clowns, steps around the car, pistol raised toward me. Liam's arms wrap around me. The gun pops. I see the flash, but the bullet gets lodged in my shield right in front of my face. Liam's heart glows. I glance down to see the star at his heart bright with protection on each light-thread. The bullet falls away to the ground, and we both laugh.

"You merged our suits' tech-shield with a divination shield! How?"

"Shielding is my special div-attainment," Liam says.

Oscar is at the ramp to the ship, unable to take himself out of the action and into the safety of the cockpit. I hear him through his hastily connected psybridge. Franxis hears him too, and she amplifies him.

Tell Liam I'm bridging him. Let's try to share that ability throughout the group.

You know how to share attainments? Franxis replies.

Shouldn't be possible, but if the protection is coming through Liam's heartstar, we're all connected to it.

"Go for it!" Mira shouts.

I signal to Oscar that Station Mani still won't get credit for making the shields bulletproof, and a note of amusement rushes back.

"Don't let go yet, Liam," I say. "Pour your divination out towards me. We're going to strengthen all the shields!"

Liam nods and closes his eyes as his heartstar grows wide. I reach with my mind, hoping I can open some channel to push Liam's divination attainment towards Oscar. When I see the channel open, I let go of hope as a confidence in Liam and Oscar rises. The energy of protection shines from Liam and—somehow—through me.

Oscar's psybridge unfurls in a wave, landing smoothly within each of us, bringing assurance and courage even as the frenzied crowd rushes towards us. Divination flows as fast as light from Liam's Level, coursing throughout the psybridge. I siphon the shimmering energy towards me and push it through Oscar's psybridge network, connecting all of us. Immediately, our prismatic shields are enhanced, glowing brighter and stronger as the shield of divination is coupled with the shield generated through our gear.

Liam lets me go and steps back to see the radiance of our prismatic shields growing brighter as he steps back. The man with the gun fires several times. Each bullet is lodged in our shields before it falls to the ground. Mira jumps out of the car, and with a flick of her wrist, releases a sonic blast from her suit's charger. The gunned assailant goes flying.

Awá shoots his swift repeatedly from the window of the second bulletproof car. The electric charges bring down several people before they can make it to the slow moving EDB. Scores of his men from the camp—divs, comps, Ops—are all out in the field, shielded and tackling the cultists, taking them down with swifts and stun-batons.

Vasif is only halfway to the ship. We level our arms, sonic blasters recharging as the remainder of the crowd comes up fast.

Mira backs away from the car as several men step from behind it. Another man slides over the front of the car, and they descend on her. She snaps her head back and her shield slams into a man's face, breaking his nose with a bloody crunch. Three other men rush her. Theyhave her pinned. She gets one arm free and turns her charger up to forty percent. We hear the bones snap as one of the men is thrown back. The remaining men pin her arms down again, and I hear Oscar shouting as he runs toward them.

"Kenzari! We need you ready to fly!" Awá yells from the car.

One of the men attacking Mira lifts a spear high above his head ready to drive it down, and he freezes in place. A flashing rainbow wave of div-shields envelops him. Oscar stops, eyes wide. Arun steps toward the men, both hands shaping a protective mudra. Prismatic shields surround the men holding Mira down. Arun raises his arms and pulls up on the shields. The men lift away from the ground, dropping their weapons, hanging in the air another moment before Arun casts them into the crowd. The div-shields break just before they crash into the oncoming cultists.

Oscar scrambles over to Mira and helps her back onto her feet.

The Arrow, The Grail, and Old Girl are hot and ready for lift off, yet all but the pilots are standing guard over the crawling EDB. Its fog-like body drifts over the ground slowly.

More gunfire. Bullets lodge in our shields and fall to the Earth.

Anxiety builds within me as images from Bakkeaux's first assault flash through my mind. The other divs wince.

Oscar's psybridge, Franxis groans.

The insane faces coming down on us. (The confusion, misdirected rage.) I look for the vortexes coming out of their heads. Franxis moves to obstruct my memories from moving through the psybridge and to protect the rest of the team. Fear couples with the trauma. My Level Four becomes unstable. (Violent shouting, cursing.) Rocks, sticks, and torches bounce off of our shields.

I signal for Franxis.

I can't reach for you without releasing this flood of traumatic memories into the psybridge! It could disrupt everyone's Levels! Franxis' tone changes to a strained, forced calm. *You have to steady your mind, buddy.*

I breathe in, close my eyes, feel the steadiness of the Earth underneath my feet. The Earth's stability feels constant. It flows into me, through me. Steadiness is within me, just as the Earth is in me. Vibrant support moves up from the ground, through my legs and torso to expand around my heartstar.

I look around at the rest of the crew. Oscar's old crew mates love each other so much. Instead of being in the safer position on the ship, Oscar stands and fights alongside us. Franxis, the best friend I've ever had, continues to fight back the crowd while keeping my trauma from impacting others. Our teachers and leaders, the Sages, all the other crews from other ships, other stations, face this danger to protect others. My heartstar turns, radiates, and pulses. The light-threads to these people that I admire, this community of divinators, radiate with interconnection. My heartstar aligns with purpose. Level Four locks into place with a powerful low *AUM.*

The voice of Truth. Four, the level of my Heart, opens fully. My heartstar blazes bright, shining through the light-threads, and we are all illuminated with stability and clear interconnection.

I realize that this connection is something I will feel for the rest of my days, even though I am frightened and intimidated by it.

I open my eyes and exhale as the stealthy Lacassine rises up from behind the other ships. Yahima's eyes meet mine. They sense that I've locked in Four, and they nod approvingly.

Lacassine glides closer to the ground towards the mob. The chargers flash, lighting up the quartz ngars, and with a buzzy shush, a bright blade of light sweeps across the crowd. Yahima dulls scores of our attackers until they fall unconscious.

Only a small crowd of the cultists make it within blast range. We strike a few of them to the dirt, but they keep advancing, picking up the rocks and sticks they'd thrown at us. They inch toward us. A man raises a gun, and Thiia flicks her wrist to send a sonic blast his way. Her blast hits him in the chest, and I hear his ribs snap. His arm whips down, and he pulls the trigger.

The bullet flies into the misty depths of Vasif's body.

The crowd gasps and stops. We all do.

Vasif halts.

The sound of a forest wailing with wild wind swells from within Vasif. Many of the cultists fall to their knees. The howl fades to a low moan which is drowned out by the crying of the cultists. Some of them prostrate themselves on the ground. A collective cry moves through them and most fall back and scramble away.

From within the layers of luminous mist, something presses against the EDB's body. A familiar shape emerges, and my gut hollows. A human face rises, and then, two, three and more faces press against the borders of the being's hazy body. Slowly, the misty flora peels away from broad noses, reddish-brown skin, and dark eyes. Hands reach forth from the luminous body and press against the Earth for support as a tribe emerges.

The missing Waorani step forward and out of Vasif.

One of the women emerges with tears trailing through the red paint around her eyes, down her face. As she steps up from the viny haze, we see the reason for her tears held in her arms. She presses a small, unmoving child to her breast. The child's head lays limp on her shoulder, long hair cascades down her back and over the mother's arm. In the child's back, a bloody bullet hole bleeds down over her other arm.

Aaliyah moves quickly toward the woman, and the woman recoils, eyes wide and furious.

Vasif calls out in Sabela but the translation unfolds in our minds.

Healer.

Aaliyah takes a blood-stop pack from her cargo pocket and injects its sealant into the wound. She measures vitals.

Awá steps forward and radios for medics. More of his men arrive and begin to cuff the quieted cultists one by one.

The Waorani stand firm glaring at all of us.

Yahima runs forward in graceful strides, and their helmet snaps back and folds into its raised collar chamber. Perhaps seeing something familiar in Yahima's Indigenous features, the elder tribesman steps toward Yahima.

Yahima gestures to the woman to turn the child around. A big blue bruise on the child's abdomen darkens, and Yahima touches it lightly. With the other hand, Yahima brushes the child's forehead. Their fingers begin to glow white, and Yahima moves them painlessly through the child's skin. When they draw their glowing fingers out of the child's chest, they hold a bloody bullet. Yahima rubs the bruise with their luminous fingers soothingly, pouring in healing divination. The child gasps and loudly cries. Yahima continues to soothe the child as the big blue bruise fades.

Yahima speaks Sabela but signals the meaning throughout the psybridge so that we understand them. "Please, allow the doctors to care for the child. They can see to it that the child is fully healed."

Without a word, the woman turns away from Yahima. She ignores the stretcher that MedOps has brought and carries her crying child as they lead her towards the medical facility.

The Waorani Elder gestures towards the illuminated mass of vines that is Vasif. "This being has come to help heal the forest. Within her, we taught her of protecting the forest, of living with the forest." He gestures all around him to the cultists, saying, "They have not come to the forest for the sake of the forest." He looks towards the UNAF officers, our ships, us. "Why are you here?"

Yahima gestures towards the sky. "A door hangs open. Another being has come through that door to threaten all life on Earth. This being might banish that threat."

The Waorani Elder stares back at Yahima.

Yahima looks deep into his dark eyes and says with an earnest voice, "If Vasif wants to return to the forest, I will escort it back myself. If it wants to help heal the forest, I will send people here to protect it as it does so."

"Keep your word." The Waorani Elder nods his head once and leads the small tribe toward the medical facility.

We watch him leave as we catch our breath. Even Griselda's bot is still, but on the display, I see her mouthing commands to someone off-screen.

Yahima sighs deeply.

"Perhaps we've been in orbit too long."

Behind us, the cultists sob and beg Vasif for forgiveness as the UNAF troops begin to drag them away.

"Perhaps it would be no different if we had been planet-side all that time. So many of us have become disconnected from the forests, the Earth." Yahima looks toward the Waorani walking away. They move their braid and wrapped hair back over the front of their shoulders. "Even the people."

Yahima turns towards me and Franxis, who stands at my side.

"We must remember that we are interconnected. You see now, Casey. Four is supported by the Earth, connecting all hearts."

"I see."

Franxis and I sit in silence within the charger station in Old Girl's wing. The metal shields are down over the windows, and the engine's roar becomes white noise behind us. The small space is almost a refuge. The silence we hold for each other is palpable. Franxis reaches out their hand and I give mine. They lean their head over onto my shoulder, transferring soothing support mixed with signals of delight.

"You locked in Four without a Sage assist and while steadying yourself," they say. "Good job, buddy."

"I can't say that I locked it in on my own, because really, it was done by realizing the power of interconnection. That's something no one can do alone. Because we need each other for that awareness."

Franxis soothes the echoes of memories in my mind.

I try not to be hard on myself for putting others at risk with my trauma, but my guilt gnaws at me, making me feel weak, and I diminish myself for it, reinforcing the destructive pattern, deepening its grooves.

"Remember when Project Ascension had you hide a lot of those traumatic memories and tendencies in the first couple of decades after Rising."

Franxis sighs. "Worked for a short time, long enough to help banish Bakkeaux and a few other storms. But after that, the obscurations themselves became corrosive."

I glean a bit of their own guilt.

They add, "Sometimes I wonder if that's what kept you from leveling up."

"There were plenty of divs using the same techniques who didn't get held up."

"Yeah, I know… but I still wonder."

"It wasn't you. I promise. You're the best comp." I cannot see into their mind and don't know if their guilt is diminished. I could ask, but I hesitate.

"Even with me sometimes, you hold back." They highlight my heartstar. "You'll get used to feeling this. Take your time."

I think about how I'm working to heal. My impatience with healing makes me feel like a failure. The groove deepens, the pattern strengthens. The cycle is exhausting, even with the extranormal endurance of divination.

Franxis squeezes my hand tighter, guiding me away from that slippery slope where all my pain and trauma seems compressed and coming down on me.

Their voice is soft, calm, but direct. "Touch the experience with compassion."

ꝏ

I'm surprised to see that The Queen is still docked at Scire. I guess Zinwara is still in quarantine, and her crew still refuses to leave without her.

Old Girl sits in a controlled drift several kilometers out from Scire. Yahima's crux-wing drifts not too far to our starboard side. We can see her sitting cross-legged, meditating in the crux's cockpit.

As we incrementally move closer to the station, many checks and scans are made on both Vasif in our cargo and the extradimensional ring with Yahima. We've never had an EDB board a station, and the unRisen maintenance crew and staff are nervous that our visitor will be the first.

Helixx Corp sends us a different plan based on Oscar's original.

We are in route to rendezvous with Ferand's Helixx Corp yacht. The Eminent is as much a tourist ship as it is a science vessel, both luxury cruiser and earnest explorer.

The Sages are being moved around to support the Divs ready to Level up and to protect the extradimensional ornaments.

Thanks to their experience with unpacking Vasif's limited but quickly growing vocabulary, Mira and Liam have been chosen to stay close to the being, which means they'll be close to MaalenKun. They asked the Old Girl crew for volunteers to assist and protect our EDB communications experts. Carmel was first to step up, but they want divs by their sides. Oscar, Harjaz and I each offered, but Central decided that Harjaz was not the right guy for the job.

All precautions are being put into place as quickly as possible, and the time it will take to get all the moving parts in place will give us a sixteen-hour break even after we board the science vessel. According to Arun, the Sages have had to insist to Central that time be allotted for rest. Although we have div-enhanced endurance, we all feel that our minds will benefit from some down time before we put our lives on the line again.

Captain Carmel relays the plan to us, saying, "We'll be taking these baby steps towards the yacht for about one more hour. Got to make sure there are no surprises brought up by changing proximities of MaalenKun's ornaments. All crew, join me in the common space."

I turn to Franxis. They shrug.

All nine of us fill the common space in a tight circle.

Carmel is the last to enter from up front. "I just want to take a moment to say something before we board the yacht and split up to do whatever it is we'll be doing with a sixteen-hour vacation. I can guess what some of you will be doing." She smirks but doesn't look directly at Oscar or me.

I wink at him. Oscar bites his lip, but one corner of his crooked smile curves up.

Mira's grin is cheeky when she interrupts. "I foresee what I will be doing."

Several people laugh, including Carmel.

Harjaz's grin is a bit too naughty. He leers at me and raises his eyebrows. I had almost forgotten that he likes some action after filing his After Action

Reports. I smile enough not to be rude, but Oscar sees me and maybe misinterprets the expression. Oscar looks away before I want him to.

"Yes, she usually knows what my plans will be before I do." Carmel puts an arm around Mira's waist, and Oscar and Thiia's reactions tell me that Carmel's display of affection while on assignment is rare. "She's not always capable of seeing every moment of the future though—"

"Doesn't work like that," Mira retorts.

"Which was evidenced today when several of those whack jobs pinned her down." She turns toward Mira. "Didn't see them coming, huh?"

Mira shakes her head.

"No one saw the danger until it was on top of us. But—and this is why I wanted to call you all together—we all had each other's backs. Thank you for getting yourself and each other—but especially, my wife—out of that mess safe and sound." The air around us feels lighter. "And thank you, Arun."

Arun's posture remains steady and tall, but Carmel's words bring Oscar to full attention.

"Not only did you peel those guys off of her, but you worked with her carefully when things really could have gone sideways in the forest with Vasif. You stepped up and helped lead us all, and now, for the first time since the bastards started vacationing on Earth, we're going to banish a demon."

Arun's smile slowly spreads. I feel he is not keen on her words but appreciates the sentiment, especially considering she has held a hundred-year grudge against him.

"Thank you, captain. It's true what you've said. This will be the first time we have sent an extradimensional being back to where it came from. Thanks to all of you." Arun brings his palms together in front of his heart, looking each of us in the eye before bowing his head. We each return the gesture or nod and smile in his direction.

Carmel sighs and says, "And please, do not tell Ops that Old Girl was on auto while I was out of the cockpit with an EDB on board." There is plenty of laughter as our circle breaks apart and people start to move back to their assigned positions.

Oscar taps Mira's shoulder and says, "Hey, would you mind—?"

"Come on, Franxis!" she interrupts. "Let's let these two have the wing again."

"Actually," Carmel says, looking towards Franxis and then, me. "I'd like to take the wing and a nap with my wife, if you both don't mind going up front."

Oscar looks pleasantly surprised.

"Fine with me," Franxis says.

"Not about to complain." I move aside to let Mira climb into the wing.

As I move past Carmel, she winks at me. "I let you fly my ship, you get me in a crux. That's how this works, right?"

"I'll see what I can do."

She looks genuinely pleased and claps me on the shoulder. "That's what I want to hear, Casey!"

Again, everyone is out of the room before Oscar and me. He tugs on the front of my uniform. "A sixteen-hour vacation."

"Whatever will we do with ourselves?"

"Maybe take one of The Eminent's cruisers out?"

I squint an eye, look at him sideways. "I was thinking we'd just be naked in whatever room—"

He grips the front of my uniform tight. "Oh, we'll be naked." He pulls my body to him, puts his hands around my waist, and my body relaxes into his arms. "Some distance from our comps might be nice. I don't want anyone else hearing you moan."

I'm pretty sure the luxury rooms on Ferand's ship are soundproof enough to buffer moaning, but I don't want to tease him or try to be funny. I just want to give him what he wants, especially if he wants me.

"Come on. I'll introduce you to Old Girl."

"Introducing me to your ship? I feel like this is a big step. I'm not sure I'm ready for this." I hold up my hands and delight in his crooked grin as he brings it closer to my lips.

When the call from Ops comes to move one kilometer closer to the yacht approaching Scire and the rift, Oscar takes the ship out of autopilot and heats up the thrusters. He gestures toward the floating crystal discs in front of me.

"Go ahead. Bring her in one kilometer."

"Yes, sir, FO." I sound a little more sarcastic than I want to.

He laughs politely, "Don't joke about my role in this crew, please. We might not be military, but I'm still in command of this crew, even for those who've almost talked me out of my clothes."

"'Almost' just makes me want to work harder—" I try to keep up the flirty banter as I place my hands on the discs, but the tug from the psychic uplink is the strongest I've ever felt in a ship. A surge of information floods my mind.

"Shit. Wow!"

Old Girl is far more intuitive than I'd expected her to be. The engine's burn is immediately too hot and the ship lurches forward.

"Ease up," Oscar says, laughing. "She's very spry for an old gal."

"Where did you get this interfacing system?" I level out the thrusters, and the burn gets smoother.

"Been trying to tell you: Mani tech is the best." He puts his hands behind his head and leans back.

"You're so handsome, I might stop arguing with you… but they're not the best." He chuckles but shies out of the position. He waves a holoscreen on and the video feed from the cargo bay shows Vasif's glowing body. Its luminescent spores dance around the stationary robotic arms folded to the tracks in the ceiling above it. I get the feeling the EDB is staring into the camera and somehow sees us.

"If we weren't escorting a potential demon banisher, I'd love to see how you could handle this spry old girl."

"Another time then." As soon as I say it, I'm reminded that our time together is limited. "When the Haddyc is gone, do you go back to Mani?"

"The original plan was for us to escort Sage Pyaar to Scire, help study the Haddyc. No station has snared an EDB in over a decade. Vasif has only been on our radar for three. We've got this opportunity to send the Haddyc back… but should we?"

I facetiously say, "Well, you came up with that whole plan…"

I'm happy he chuckles at my sarcasm.

"True, but since MaalenKun presents itself as more than a storm, and Vasif is also capable of the same thing, I personally don't think we should send it back. Perhaps these things are changing, or this is a whole new type of EDB coming our way." He smooths his beard with both hands. "We should be studying it. Also, that might keep me at Scire longer."

"You really love that bird garden, huh?"

He rubs the beard on his chin and smirks. "It's not the big draw anymore."

My heart flutters, and my doubt stirs. "You'd get tired of me before long."

"Maybe…" My heart sinks before he playfully shrugs lifting it, saying, "Only one way to find out."

There is a moment of silence where we stare at each other, sharing the moment. I dream that potential begins to weave together our separate futures into one, and my cynicism shatters the idea. I look away first.

He looks back towards the comm console behind me. "Thiia, do me a favor, hail Ops on The Eminent, put in a request for a private tourist cruiser please. You can let them know that I'd like to borrow it to take Div Isaac on a very romantic date—"

Her laugh is adorable.

"—for our sixteen-hour vacation."

"Those exact words, First Mate?" she asks.

Franxis sends waves of joy across their comp-bridge, and I signal them back.

We are at our next stop. I tilt the discs back towards me, and the main engine cools as the reverse thrusters pulsate. Oscar flips the anchor lever, and the auto-alter thrusters and navigation nozzles keep the ship floating in place.

From Mira's navigation console, Franxis layers implication into her words. "Coordinates matched to request."

Oscar sends a text message to the captain about the updated position. She texts back to wake her up only when necessary. He waves the screen away and asks Franxis to scan the EDB again. Thiia transmits the data to the Helixx Corp Ops at Station Scire and on The Eminent.

Franxis reports, "No trouble from the strange quantum signatures in the leaves that clung to the ring. Glad Yahima has that thing, and not us. In our passenger, the energy levels of each unique signature fluctuate with some variance, but the rare Aphrytian and Dymetian energy seems to work together to keep the Aethonic and Haddyc energies suppressed. No significant changes in Vasif."

"I think you'll find that Vasif is content." Arun says from the door. "Yahima and Ops insisted I return with you guys so that I can maintain a psybridge to the being and keep an eye on it. Is that a deal breaker if I wanted to join you up here?"

"Psybridged to an EDB or not, you're always welcome, Arun," Oscar calls back from the cockpit. I get the sense that he is not speaking for the captain of the ship.

Thiia pulls down one of the panels next to her station and a chair unfolds from the wall. "Strap in. Casey might take the wheels again," Thiia quips.

"Oh, that's what that was," Arun jokes.

"It was barely a bump…" With the ship in auto, I can spin my chair around to face the rest of the group. I cock an eyebrow and pass the blame to the first mate. "If someone would've told me about the interface surge…"

"Just don't wake up the captain next time," Oscar says as he turns his chair, and Thiia laughs.

"Everyone back there is sound asleep." Arun steers the conversation away from their teasing. "Including Vasif—It's resting, at least. Not really sure if we can call it sleeping."

Franxis lowers the floating screens with the scan data. "It's definitely not doing much, which is fine with me."

"Agreed," Arun says. "Very interesting that we've recently seen two EDBs behave in a way that is new to us."

"In what way?" Thiia asks. Surely, she's already gotten a sense of what he's referring to from the conversation Oscar and I just had. I get the feeling she is being polite, bringing Arun into the group dynamic more.

"They have presented themselves in a humanoid shape. First MaalenKun's humanoid body was presented as its storm fell away when it was trapped in the crystal chamber. That seemed less concerning to many of the Sages because it was encountered in the mindfield. Vasif, however, stood on the crystal platform with a humanoid extension of its body while its larger body contained an entire tribe of people living inside it. Perhaps, these beings are trying to be somehow more relatable." He looks toward Oscar but addresses all of us. "It might be best to end the practice of demonizing them. Simply call them EDBs. The word 'demon' can be problematic in this case, just because it brings up so many stories and images. That word has a lot of baggage. For most people, it brings up a lot of fear. For others, they use it, because they hope some magical force will save them from these things. Or perhaps, they demonize these beings in the hopes they can be the hero. Hope and fear are two sides of the same coin. It's a heavy coin to carry. Both fear and hope can cloud our minds. Both can get in the way of perceiving the world clearly. If we are truly on the cusp of a new era, we have to toss that coin aside to see what is coming. It's time we consider giving up both fear and hope for the sake of clarity."

As Arun says this last line, I feel a note of resistance to his sentiment move within both Oscar and Franxis. I do not find the same resistance within myself. I want to toss that coin away, but I'm not quite sure how to let go of it.

"You know, the word daemon was used in ancient Greek mythology to refer to an 'attending spirit—' essentially an inspiring force," Thiia says.

Oscar adds, "Yeah, some people can be inspired to do some fucked up things."

"I remember that inspiration well..." Arun cocks an eyebrow up.

I smile at him with polite solidarity, aware of my own patterns of self-abuse. He looks at me with understanding, but I cannot hold his powerful gaze for long. Oscar nods at him and looks over at me with compassion.

Arun goes on, "There are still plenty of people who demonize us just for identifying as Queer."

"Didn't know you were family," Franxis quips with a sweet smile.

Arun nods. "It's completely ridiculous, but I've been demonized for being asexual, seen as something other than human simply because I have always found sex uninteresting." Arun and Franxis make eye contact, and I feel the bright spark of kinship within them. "Fear keeps so many people from clearly seeing me, us... family."

"But most of the EDBs are dangerous, violent invaders." Oscar puts no forcefulness behind his words.

Arun does the same, as if they are just stating facts. "So are we sometimes."

Oscar snorts very lightly and assents.

Arun inhales deeply. "There is a saying that goes: we don't see the world the way the world is; we see the world the way we are... The way we use our language affects our minds, our perception. If we can keep from demonizing these beings, we might be able to understand how to predict when they come and how to deal with them in a way that minimizes our losses. Perhaps we can better recognize the beings who can truly help us, like our passenger who can regrow the rainforest. Wouldn't that be amazing? The whole planet might breathe easier."

"I'd like more time to study the Haddyc for that very reason." Oscar says.

"Several similar requests, from planetside and from all four stations, have been received by Ops, but Central has determined our course of action. Perhaps, you'll have a chance to study Vasif. Not everyone sees their presence as an opportunity, and we must admit that the Haddyc, MaalenKun, is certainly dangerous. Why did it bring a key with it? Why did it have a weapon like the mirror mask? Beyond that, it was a powerful storm that took out several wings, killing several divs from Station Scire and The Queen before it was contained. People have already lost their lives because it came into the sector. We have a duty to send it back if we can. And it looks like we can." He shrugs, and it's the first time I've seen the gesture from a Sage. "We can perceive the possibility of success."

"What if it just comes back through the rift?" Franxis says.

"We try something else, I guess. I feel Vasif would have mentioned that risk though. We plan on keeping the key. Perhaps without the key, it will not be able to return," Arun says with a smile that does not shine in his eyes. "I have a feeling Scire will remain in place, out of the Earth's orbit, guarding the rift. I'm sure there will be many powerful divs stationed near the rift. What our roles might be in that endeavor are yet to be seen. I am willing to do whatever I can to close that rift, even if it means working with Helixx Corp. I'm not sure about my future with that organization beyond closing the rift. Like many of you, I've heard the rumors of discrimination and while I cannot speak to the organization's intentions in that regard, the dwindling diversity on Station Scire is concerning. Maybe by working with Helixx, they see that we are not so different, that we can accomplish great things together. What that would mean to all the Queer people of the world, especially the younger generations. If they don't see that, we still did our best to protect those we have vowed to protect."

Oscar smirks but speaks kindly. "I would say that I'd hope so… but I'm letting go of hope."

Arun nods and grins, appreciating Oscar's comment. "Remembering our Queer ancestors gives me something greater than hope. I think of all that Queer folx have faced, and we've remained resilient by supporting each other." Arun turns his powerful but sweet gaze on each of us one at a time as he speaks. His words uplift us one by one. "I look at your faces, faces of family, and I see powerful warriors and brilliant individuals coming together. Beyond hope, past fear… I have faith based on our resiliency. It's important for all of us to work together, to support each other, to develop faith in one another, in our family. This faith is not the blind faith so common on Earth. This faith must be experiential. A bright faith."

ꝏ

When Old Girl is mag-locked in the yacht's harbor, we step down the ramp and Carmel halts two technicians walking over.

"No one touches my ship. She's UNAF. Not Helixx. Got it?"

She stares them down until they step back nodding.

Liam trots toward us from The Arrow, dodging several distans bots with cameras and display screens turned towards the ships. The remote tourists piloting the bots to gawk at each ship seem completely unconcerned that they're in the way in the busy hangar.

"Are you fucking kidding me?" Carmel is not trying to be quiet as she glares at the bots. "Did they sell tickets to this event?"

"Looks that way," Liam says. "There are a lot of distans here."

Mira says. "Sorry I didn't warn you. I think my prescience is a bit off since that leaf got in me."

"Mine too," Liam says. "But it is a tourist ship. Maybe it's just bots and not people though."

We all step aside for a group of bots, identical aside from faces of various ages on the display screens. The pilots on the other end of the signal do nothing to make space for us, piloting their bots shoulder to shoulder, and we have to squeeze against fuel tanks and maintenance equipment to let them pass.

One of the bots bumps Aaliyah hard. I think—but can't be sure with the bot's comms on mute—that I saw the pilot utter a racial slur.

"Excuse you!" Franxis yells at the robots, which do not stop or slow down. "Watch where you're going!"

Carmel is right by Aaliyah's side and loudly says, "Fucking entitled assholes."

One of the flat screens on the bots whips around and an older white woman's taut face sneers at us as the bots walk away.

"You okay, Aaliyah?" Harjaz asks, taking her bag.

"Yeah, more annoyed than anything else," she says.

"Mira, Liam, let's go see the Sages about your foresight," Captain says. "On the way, anyone want to co-sign my complaint with Ops about all these tourists?"

"Already on it," Thiia says, looking up from her hand-held. "Shall I add everyone's signatures?"

Every one of us consents, including the Young Sage.

Harjaz tries to politely break away from the group.

Carmel says, "Not so fast, Harjaz. We're still on assignment until we officially disband back on Scire. We'll meet the Sages together, as a team."

ꝏ

We pass the Helixx Corp divs guarding the room with a nod, and the door slides closed behind us. The pontiff suite is huge. Descending the steps down into the room, I feel we are almost bowing before the grandeur of the luxurious space. Rose quartz crystal chandeliers hang from the high ceiling. Antique carpets cover most of the wide floorspace. A small fruit tree grows from the floor at the center of the room, and as we step closer, we see that it is full of rose kumquats, a rare hybrid fruit. The sound of gently running water comes through hidden speakers accompanying the light piano music from the musician at the holographic keyboard across the room.

The Sages are gathered at the floor-to-ceiling reinforced metaglass windows which curve along the sides of the room and meet at the bow of the ship. The rift's dull half-light fluctuates ominously some distance behind the group of saffron and orange uniforms. A team of Helixx Corp div-tech is putting finishing touches on the Haven tech installation. Crystal plinths rise up from an array of connectors and a motherboard. The cables have been patched into the wall units, and I'm almost certain that this is the first time this type of tech has been merged with this much luxury.

On a singed black and polished wooden table across the room sits the coffer with the ring inside. Scanning devices and monitors measure it constantly for any changes. Two stylish crystal ring chandeliers hang over the table, reflected in the ornate coffer's designs.

Several Sages from each station chat and laugh by the large window. There are more Sages present than there are crystal plinths. It's as if they have come together for a little pre-game party to cheer on whomever will be seated on the plinths. Murtagh is there, but only a few Elders are among them. No Helixx Sages from The Eminent are present.

The Sages' excited chatter softens and goes quiet. They all move in near sync as they lift their palms together in front of their hearts and bow gently. We return the graceful gesture with our own.

Arun joins the other Sages as they chat merrily, looking out the windows towards the rift. Some of them study the plinth apparatus. As Pyaar and Yahima step away, I feel as if we've broken up their little saffron party.

Pyaar and Yahima both gesture towards a sitting area with plush couches.

Only Yahima and Arun are still in mission uniforms like our crew, but we've all shed the armor.

Pyaar sits on the sofa and bounces up and down. With a giggle, she proclaims, "Too soft!"

Yahima laughs gently. "After several hours meditating in Lacassine, I'll take it."

"You wanted to speak to us, Captain Kosse?" Pyaar asks.

"Arun told us that the Sages demanded the break for us. We appreciate that. We all need it after Ecuador. I wanted to personally report that Vasif was transferred into the shipping container before we docked. The tugs have already taken it out. Mira communicated the reason we're taking a break. Vasif understands the plan on our end, so we've got one EDB all set." The Sages both smile gently, mostly because Carmel pauses. "Ops tells us for the upcoming action, they're needed for EDB communication and not foresight. They say others will cover foresight. But we're concerned. Both Mira and Liam's prescience has been off since our first encounter with Vasif. Pyaar, I'm sure you've read the AAR's or at least heard… Both Mira and Liam were touched by Vasif's falling leaves. Mira's went inside of her, but MedOps on the ground says she's okay."

"And what does Mira say?" Pyaar turns toward Mira. "Are you okay?"

"Normally, I would've been able to predict that we'd have so many distanses on board The Eminent, but I feel like I can only see a few minutes ahead of me."

"Same," Liam says. "And those few minutes are too fuzzy to be reliable."

"It's not uncommon to have an ability fade a bit when integrating a new energy. I've seen this happen with divs who pull down or access a new Level. I suppose it stands to reason that integrating an energy from an EDB could do the same." She smiles at them with compassion, signaling for them to not worry. "If you feel it would be of benefit, I would be happy to sit with you and assist you, but I do feel you will be able to sort this out on your own in time."

"The assist might be a good idea," Mira says. She looks worried, less sure of herself. "I feel like I won't have enough time to do it before we take action."

"I'll work on my own," Liam says, and I get a brief, sinking feeling in my gut.

Pyaar smiles. "Liam, you should find plenty of time to meditate before we call on you again. Thank you for being a part of this team. Were you able to observe and learn from Mira on this assignment?"

He bows his head towards Mira. "I learned a lot."

Mira places a hand over her heart and smiles humbly at him.

"Mira," Yahima says, tilting their head slightly. "It might serve you better in the long run to retune your prescience divination yourself. Perhaps you and Liam could meditate together?"

Carmel looks momentarily surprised to have Yahima push back on Mira's request for the Sage assist.

Mira replies, "I would like to spend my time resting and relaxing with my wife before we're needed again to send the Haddyc back. I think I'll take Pyaar up on the Sage assist after the assignment if other prescient Sages foresee it going well."

"I'll be happy to assist you anytime," Pyaar answers. "However, all of our prescient Sages are having a bit of trouble seeing much of what happens with the rift. They've instead focused on the EDBs, and while they can't quite see how, they do feel this plan will send the Haddyc back."

Mira and Yahima smile politely at each other.

A Helixx Corp room attendant brings over a tray of cool peppermint-lemon iced teas in ornate glasses. Surprise moves through those of us from Scire who haven't had ice in our drinks for ages. The tea is perfectly flavored and refreshing. The mood of our meeting shifts, and we all relax more.

"Div Isaac." Yahima's voice sounds sweeter than usual. "Do you remember what I requested you bring back for me? Before I got called to Ecuador myself?"

"Yes," I say, opening my side bag and bringing out the small case. "I brought you a leaf."

Some of the others visibly tense up immediately.

"From a tree, you guys."

I remove the slender, dry ramón tree leaf from the case. Yahima holds out their hand, and I gently place the dry leaf on their palm. Yahima extends the leaf toward Pyaar, who frowns down at it.

"A leaf?" Pyaar frowns at me, then Yahima.

Yahima seems amused with her. "I got one for myself, but it's much more curled. I think this one will work better."

I have no idea why she requested a leaf, so when the others look at me, I shrug.

"I have a hobby." Yahima says and waves the comment away. "But for now... look." Yahima takes the leaf by the stem and holds it out toward us. "Do you see the cloud in the leaf?"

Liam smiles. He must know this one. The rest of us shake our heads no.

"Give it a little spin," Pyaar says. "Maybe it's on the other side."

Yahima turns the leaf around. Oscar's brow is momentarily furrowed, and I watch as it relaxes, and a brightness comes into his eyes. He's figured it out, I guess.

"I don't get it." Carmel bluntly states.

Yahima says, "Comps, if you get it before your divs, no transferring. Let them figure it out."

I study the apex, the margins, thinking maybe the light coming through the leaf is creating the subtle shape of a cloud. I wonder if Yahima had some sort of foresight about the very shape of the leaf I would return to them, and

I let the thought go, thinking that what Yahima is asking us to see is much simpler. I look again at the blade, the veins, the midrib.

"Where is the cloud?" asks Yahima, turning the dry leaf. "Don't rely on your eyes alone to see."

"Oh..." Aaliyah's got it now. "Nice."

"It's harder to see because it's so dry," Yahima says. "But the cloud is here. The leaf was once vibrant and green—"

Now I see the cloud.

"—nourished by the rains which came from..." They hold out their other hand.

"The cloud," Franxis says.

"And when I'm back on Scire—" Yahima pauses, holding the dry leaf between their palms over the small case. They crush the dry leaf and hundreds of tiny pieces cascade into the case. "I'll put the leaf back together again. Like a puzzle."

Pyaar snorts, "You must've attained superhuman patience."

"Also tiny tweezers and a magnifying glass. We need the right tools to put things back together, but even then, we'll always remember that they were broken. And that's okay. The cloud is in the broken leaf as well."

"Thank you for remembering, Casey." Yahima closes the case and the smile on their face lifts my mood. They obviously wanted to share this teaching with me, and I'm happy they got to share it with the whole crew. "I won't keep you any longer. Go. Be sure to get at least a little rest." This might be the cheekiest I'll ever get from Yahima, and they turn away before I can blush.

Oscar notices my cheeks blushing, and one corner of his mouth creeps up slowly.

ꝏ

To save some time, Oscar is in his own room to clean up, and I'm in mine. The ultralight shower sizzles away the layer of sweat and dirt from our skirmish in Ecuador. I feel fresher when I step out, and I'm happy to find that even this basic room on the yacht is stocked with everything I need to shave, brush my teeth, freshen my breath, and get ready for our "romantic date."

Again, I wonder why we didn't request one of the deluxe suites here on the yacht, but I'm also happy to have time alone with Oscar with a bit of literal space between us and this whole operation.

In the mirror, I notice myself smiling.

There's a knock at the door, and I think Oscar must be finished because he didn't need time to shave. Also, knocking on the door is so quaint.

When I open the door, I find Harjaz, and nearly lose the towel around my waist. I quickly pull it tighter, and stammer back a step. He smirks as he takes a step into the room, and I put a hand up against his chest.

"Woah! Harjaz, I was not expecting you."

"You know how I get. I know how you get." He bites his lower lip, and I wonder if I found that sexy last time we hooked up. "I don't want to waste time on Joynr looking for someone else. We both know what we like, so... let's do what we like."

He tries to step further into the room, but I push my hand against his firm chest, shaking my head.

"Yeah, so..."

A part of me doesn't want to hurt his feelings, another part of me doesn't want to ruin my chances of hooking up with him ever again. After all, Oscar will go back to Mani, or he'll get tired of me, or there's a hundred other excuses.

"You're a really good fuck—"

"Then let's fuck." He puts his hand on mine still pressed against his firm chest, but I keep him at arm's length.

"It's just... I want something else." I take my hand away.

"A not good fuck?" He smirks, looks at me as if he's hoping I'm joking. His persistence would be a turn on if I hadn't already said no in several ways.

"No... more than sex, I think." I realize what I've said after I've said it, but it's the truth.

Eyes wide, Harjaz steps back quickly. "Oh, I don't think I'm, you know, emotionally in a place where—"

I wince. "No, no... I don't want more from you. That's not what I meant."

He sighs, looking relieved. "Oh, oh, shit. You're expecting someone else. Fuck! I'm so sorry. I'll get out of here."

We both laugh.

"No hard feelings?" I ask, wondering why I really care.

"No, none at all." He steps back towards the door, looking over my half naked body with a devilish grin. As he turns and leaves, he says, "Have fun, Casey,"

I'm standing there at the open doorway somewhat amused, going over what I said. "More than sex." There is a sweet longing, not for someone to take away loneliness, not for someone to distract me from my hurt, but just a sweet longing for someone in particular, because I want to be with him.

There's another quaint knock, and I look up to see Oscar. He leans against the doorframe, strokes his beard, and stares at the towel around my waist.

"Hey," he says.

"Hey, handsome," I adjust the towel, trying to conceal the fact that I'm immediately getting excited. "We're not going to make it to the cruiser if you keep looking at me like that."

He laughs as he steps into the room. His hands are cool against the sides of my body as he pulls me closer. Again, he does not kiss me even though he's near enough for his words to fall on my lips.

"We've waited this long, what's a little while longer?" His warm breath and cool hands on me send a chill up my back.

He lets me go and leans against the wall and watches me as I drop the towel.

"Must I get dressed again?"

ꝏ

Oscar seems excited. He holds my hand as we walk, and I realize that until he took my hand, I don't remember the last time that I've held hands with another man in public.

We pass several of the tourist distans bots, and more than one of the remote bot pilots tries to stop us with questions about their bot or the ship. We wave them away without explanation.

"It's the uniforms. We all look like we're here just for them." I roll my eyes.

"Could these rich folks not afford to get online with the ship's system?"

"I'm sure they could, but they'd rather have someone else figure it out for them. They get something out of having another person to do it for them."

The cruiser harbor is mostly free of the annoying bots. I get the feeling the yacht is only renting them out to the sentries at a very hefty price. That minimizes how many rich folks are risking our necks by flying their bots closer to the rift. Of course, there are a few.

Ops has the sleek crimson cruiser ready for us.

"Need to run your own system checks?" I half-tease.

"Old Girl deserves the respect, but this cruiser doesn't even have a name."

The small cruiser is a two-seater with one chair in front and an elevated chair behind it so that both passengers can have full views right and left out of the panoramic cockpit window. In the back, there are more windows for viewing the cosmos, consoles for guided tours, and thankfully, a large enough bed, because of course there is. We're not the first to request a cruiser for a romantic jaunt. After all, The Eminent is not just a science vessel, but an exploration ship open to tourists.

As soon as we're out of the harbor's plasma-grid airlocks, the yacht's generated gravity loses its hold on us. I tighten the straps on my harness and grip the armrests.

Oscar pilots the cruiser away from the yacht, away from the rift, away from the extradimensional beings which await. He steers closer to the moon, where the lights of the mines glitter across on the cratered surface. Behind the moon, the sun peeks over the bright blue edge of the Earth.

"You want me to psybridge now, Casey?" Oscar's voice is deep but soft.

I almost tell him that bridging me is just one of the things I want him to do to me. But I'm getting tired of so many jokes, trying to buffer my emotions with humor.

I answer, "Yes," and I open to my desire.

The psybridge opens up from him, reaching towards me, and enveloping me like a tender embrace. Our obscurations float between us, and I feel him move right past them without interest. Then, they fall from my view. His adoration of the edge of Earth's blue glow washes through me, and I sense what he feels when he steeps in its beauty: awe. I've ignored the beauty so available to me for so long that a wave of self-loathing swells in me. He places his hands on my shoulders. Together, we subdue the disruptive wave, and I feel receptive again.

He breathes on my neck, sending chills up my spine, my arms. He shudders receiving the synced sensations through our psybridge, and his breath quivers. His arms reach around the seat, and he unfastens the straps holding me to the chair. My body drifts up.

"Closer," he says near my ear, and I hear in his voice that he is letting go of his resistance, urging me to satisfy the longing he has allowed to build over the short time we've been together. He's done maintaining just enough space between us to build a pleasant anticipation.

The hair of his beard brushes my neck as he pulls my weightless body against his. His hand slides apart the front of my uniform and he reaches inside. His fingers slide over my chest as he kisses my neck. Through the psybridge, I feel what he is feeling, the delight in my taste, the feeling of my body in his arms, the release of no longer waiting and the ecstasy of not rushing. He keeps his mind focused on me, transforming my pleasure into our pleasure. It's almost too much.

"Doing okay?" he asks, a bit louder than his previous words. He can feel what I'm feeling, including the delight. He knows I am more than okay, but it helps me further integrate the connection to hear him ask.

"Yes. Consider my consent fully ongoing, handsome."

His light laughter is full of delight.

The psybridge opens wider, and I feel a rush in his body meet his self-control. Excitement begins to overtake his restraint.

I reach behind me, grab hold of his waist, and pull him towards me. His body presses against me through our uniforms, and he chuckles when he senses my thrill to feel him against me.

He pulls my uniform back over my shoulders, and I spin slowly in the air as I pull the arms out of each sleeve. I press my feet against the back of the chair, and kick to push our floating bodies to the back of the small ship. As we sail through the air, my hands slide into his uniform, and I pry it open to reveal his hairy chest.

He chuckles. "Nice move."

I cannot look at his crooked smile any longer. I need his lips on mine, and he senses that need. When he gives me his mouth, our sensations loop: his, mine, rushing, coupling experience. My lips move down his neck and his breath quickens. I sense his urgency rise like a wave as he pulls the uniform down below his waist. He kicks his own boots off, tugs my uniform down. I slip out of the boots and kick both of the uniforms aside. They float away.

Our naked bodies press against each other, his chest hair rubs against me, and I delight in him sensing how much his body thrills me. Having my mind exposed feels more thrilling than I thought it would. The vulnerability I feel is respected as he skillfully syncs his pleasure in my body. His sensations become my sensations. His enjoyment becomes my enjoyment. Both his touch and pleasure in touching move through me as his body and breath warms my skin.

He skillfully turns our entangled bodies around, and I feel his synced delight in my enjoyment of our bodies moving together mid-air. He kisses gently down my torso. I know he can feel my anticipation building. He syncs it with his, loops it back to me, and it builds. My back arches and I gasp ever so slightly when his lips reach the erogenous spot below my navel. He breathes against it just once as he psychically signals that he cannot wait any longer.

My entire body begins to float up, the physical pleasure moving through my body slides against his enjoyment of my thrusting, my moaning, my taste. Desire and gratification couple and loop back. When it's almost too much, he draws back the psybridge a bit. When I begin to pleasantly ache for it, he brings it in stronger. He rubs his beard against my inner thighs and laughs playfully as I twitch. I run my fingers into his hair and feel the sensation in my own scalp.

When he pauses, I look down at him wondering if he's just catching his breath. His eyes glow with happiness. I soften into the warmth of his eyes, feel him captivated by the color of my own, and he brings his face closer to mine.

Our hands find each other, and we share each sensation.

The rush of my feeling, his feeling, the release of anticipation moves through me with force, my head arches back, and I moan. His lips are on my neck, my face, easing the tension as he gently turns my face back toward his. Our eyes meet and he begins stroking slowly, rhythmically. I cannot look away. I'm captivated by the smile growing on his face coupled with the sense of his enjoyment in my body, in his body.

As he presses against me, moving with me, I feel gratitude to feel weightless, touching only his body, only each other, and he laughs playfully. I realize that he can hear my wordless thoughts, and I shift it into thankfulness for his touch. His crooked grin becomes naughtier, and he brings his chest to mine, presses his weight into me, and we keep our eyes open to each other, holding onto each other and nothing else.

His pleasure is mine, mine his.

ꝏ

His body presses against me. I cherish our closeness as he pulls me toward him for another kiss. His lips linger close, I feel his breath on my neck. I stroke his beard soothingly.

I think to myself that I could bury myself in his beard and live there close to his mouth listening to his breath, and I would sleep in his beard and grow old there and die a happy man.

Oscar chuckles, rubs his beard against my neck, and I realize he heard my ridiculous thoughts. I laugh at myself, the things I intentionally didn't say aloud because they would reveal too much. I guess it didn't matter after all. He must be quite adept at reading a psybridged mind.

As we are cleaning up with the convenient supply of wipes and towels stocked by the bed that was obviously designed for these types of adventures, he asks, "Have you ever cum in zero grav?"

The question seems so naughty, so crude coming from him.

With all seriousness, I say, "Against regulation."

He laughs loud and full, and I love the sound of it bouncing around in the small ship. I can't stop laughing or holding him close with my arms and my legs.

"So," he looks into my eyes. "That was Harjaz leaving your room before I got there?"

I almost shy away but feel respected as he waits for me to verbalize an answer. He could easily find it through our psybridge. Instead, the connection relays how these words make us feel.

"Yeah, he came by. We sometimes hook up after assignments." No need to hide. "We both like sex after the thrill of victory, I guess."

He seems mostly amused but I'm also aware of some obscurations, boundaries. He seems to drift a bit. I don't pull on the psybridge to reveal his thoughts.

"Yeah, me too," he says. "Although, it's been a long time since I've hooked up with anyone."

"Really? Because you're very good at it," I say.

He acts shy, smooths his beard, and turns away.

"That whole 'Div that can comp' thing is fucking amazing."

He blushes.

I add, "You can loop me again sometime, handsome."

He wraps an arm around me and traces his fingers along my shoulder, down my spine.

It's his turn to be confessional. "I think I've been wanting something more than just a hookup." One corner of his mouth smiles, the other seems hesitant. "No pressure, though. This can be whatever you want it to be."

His warm eyes draw me in, and through the now spacious psybridge, I feel that I'm closer than I've ever been to a lover's sincerity.

(Usain.)

(Abandonment.)

I need to change the subject.

"Always loved a prominent proboscis." I hear myself confessing, breaking the relative silence save for the low hum of the gravity generator. I inch closer while his laughter fills the small shuttle. "Can I touch it?" I ask in a sultry voice.

He feigns modesty. "This is an honorable nose, sir."

"Please. I really want to touch your… nose," I drop the sultry voice, "but if you find my advances offensive, please, forgive me."

He laughs more, and this is the first time I hear his deep belly laugh, and I think I'm not even being that funny, but he wants this. He wants this playfulness, this delight in each other. And I want it too.

"If you must." He inches closer.

For comedic or dramatic effect, I slowly reach my hand towards his nose, extending my index finger, and the awareness this requires makes the impression of the moment stronger.

"But I must warn you," he says, and I freeze, inches away from his face. "I already like your touch very much."

I trace my finger down the bridge of his nose. Twice. "One more for luck." I whisper, and he holds my hand and guides my finger down the length of his nose and then to his lips. He kisses my hand twice, slowly, lips a bit more parted the second time.

"One more for luck," he whispers, and after a quick kiss, he guides my hand to the back of his head where I bury my fingers in his dark curls.

I slowly, deliberately close the space between us, so I can press my body against his. I bring my lips close enough to his, so he feels the words, my breath landing on them.

"What are you doing to me?"

Oscar is naked at the window, looking out towards the sun disappearing behind the planet's edge.

I walk to him and trace my hand down the length of his arm, kiss his shoulder, stand just behind him. He takes my hand and wraps my arm around himself and takes a small step back. Again, our bodies press against each other. I bask in his body heat.

For a moment, we watch the sun's rays color shades of pink and orange in the massive clouds of the Earth's atmosphere. Having spent the majority of the last seventy years orbiting the Earth, seeing sunrises and sunsets every couple of hours, I'm surprised to see the colors differently. Through the psybridge, I sense his appreciation of the beauty, the uniqueness of each sunrise, each sunset.

"Could steep in that view all day," he says.

"If only we had all day..."

"Goes by so fast. Like those colors." He points toward the quickly fading hues sweeping across the clouds.

I hold him close as we look out towards the darkening skies. In the northern curve of the atmosphere, bright green bands appear, growing and spreading into massive radiant swirls. The auroras seem to appear, dance with each other, and fade.

"What do you feel when you're steeping?"

"Awe," he answers. "I feel like so much awe is available in this beautiful scene, and I don't want to miss the opportunity to let my mind be still and just observe, in awe."

"I think that awe that is accessible our bodies close together..." I can't stop myself from saying words that I know will draw him in. "Our breath syncing..." He softens into me, physically, mentally. "Our energy dancing closer to each other." I sense his heart flutter, and part of my old pattern to shy away from intimacy falls.

I observe my internal landscape, wondering if through his psychic abilities he is disarming my pattern to turn away. I feel him there, offering me the space to steep in the beauty of the moment, what we're seeing, what we're feeling, letting what we've just said resonate and become part of what draws us closer.

"Sixteen hours isn't long enough."

"Only six left now," he replies, voice low and soft.

"Counting down?"

"Savoring every moment."

His body eases in my embrace. He tilts his head back, turns his face towards mine. My defenses melt; my hesitation dissipates.

(It's going to be O.K.)

I lean towards his lips whisper, "We're just getting started."

ꝏ

excerpt from decrypted message to Captain Griselda Harris Ferand from Helixx Corp Div-tech Lead Operative, Dawson Craig

23 March, 2138. 23:16 (Greenwich standard)

"The prescience restrictors throughout The Eminent have been tested multiple times as requested. All are functioning and reliable, capable of being dialed up or down to dampen or disable the prescient divination of most divs. However, the current generation of restrictors might not be able to fully disrupt divs or Sages who are highly skilled at prescience. They might catch glimpses, but they won't fully see your future actions. Our department continues their work on the next generation of div-disruptors."

ꝏ

OSCAR 4

When I wake up, he's already awake. I had toned the psybridge down, so we would not accidentally merge our dreams.

I didn't sense him watching me sleep.

He smirks. "Two days."

I laugh. "That was long enough to build anticipation."

His grey-ringed citrine eyes are bright and refreshed. He cradles my chin with his hand and pulls my blushing face towards him. He kisses me sweetly, smooths my beard, and gazes into my eyes.

Between our hearts, a light-thread shimmers bright with rainbow light.

"It's time?" I'm not sure how long I slept.

"It is," He says softly. "Did you sleep okay?"

I stretch and yawn, and he rubs my chest.

"You wore me out," I grumble.

His mischievous glimmer resurfaces. "Did my best. Only because I knew you needed some sleep."

"So kind of you."

"Just doing my part. Got to have you rested and ready…" he trails off there. We already know the plan. It's incredibly risky.

I groan and trace my fingers down the arm he has wrapped around me. "You want me to tune out the psybridge?"

"Just keep it going. I think we'll need it in a couple of hours for the ass-kicking anyway."

Another gentle kiss, held long to wake ourselves, to seal in closeness.

Casey is quiet, but I sense a small whirlwind in his mind as he pilots the cruiser back to the yacht. Where there was clarity hours ago, he's back to running through old patterns, deep grooves in his psyche. I wouldn't dare disrupt or change his mind. That's not how I want him.

Before we're even out of the ship, I'm on my comm. I message our crew to say that we've returned.

He walks a step ahead of me in the hallway with his head a bit down. I quicken my pace, and he looks at me like he was lost in thought when I speak. I sense him pulling away, physically, mentally.

"What?" he asks.

"I asked if I could hold your hand."

He smiles, but it does not extend to his eyes. "Of course," he says, taking my hand, interlacing his fingers in mine. A few steps later as we pass a group of distans bots, he unweaves his fingers and instead cups my palm. A camera on one of the bots scans us up and down, and I ignore it.

At his room, I ask if I can come inside.

"You're so old fashioned," he says, standing in the entrance.

My concern gleans a memory from him. I glimpse a past lover tethered to the sense that he thinks of himself as… I almost can't make it out. As I realize that he thinks of himself as dangerous, he becomes aware of what I'm sensing and pulls back from the bridge with a psychic snap that jars both of us.

"That was an accident," I whisper.

He looks pained, but nods. "I know."

We both need to get into our freshly cleaned and repaired combat gear. But neither of us moves.

I try not to come across as clingy. I lean against the doorframe, doing my best to look sexy, but knowing that I just look awkward. "Are you okay? Is this weird now because we're on an assignment together?"

"No, it's fine. I'm fine." A bit of pattern recognition rushes through the bridge, and I intercept it without trying to. He's told himself this so many times. He seems uncomfortable to know that an obscuration is falling away naturally. I can see hints of his self-loathing. He's accustomed to a pattern of his issues resurfacing after hooking up with someone, a sign that he has a pattern of avoiding his issues through sex. I let it all land free of my judgment, and signal to him that none of it discourages me.

"Casey…" I tug on the front of his uniform, and he pulls me into the room. The door slides closed behind me. "Casey."

He simultaneously pulls me toward him and grows tense in my presence. He shakes his head a bit. I strengthen the care in the light-thread between our hearts.

He sighs heavily. "I'm a mess, you know."

"Everything is a mess." I wait for him to look into my eyes again. "I feel moved by you. I want to see where we can take this."

He laughs again, but his defenses are back up. Obscurations are strong.

"Okay," he smiles but again, not in his eyes. "Ready for date night? Thought we'd go to that rip in our reality."

"That place is so hard to get into!" He's kind enough to laugh. "How'd you score a reservation?"

"I have connections." His laughter gets his shoulders to release some tension.

"Are you sure you're—?"

"Yeah," he sighs. He wraps his arms around me and hugs me tight with his head tucked into the nape of my neck. He breathes against me, and I'm reminded of steeping in the viridescent aurora borealis. He's right—there's just as much awe in my lover's breath. I want to hold him longer, but our comms chime.

Messages from Ops.

Emergency lights throughout the yacht blink three times every thirty seconds. More divs and comps from all four stations and planetside hurry through the hallways and onto the decks.

Casey and I are the only ones on the deck in combat gear. I try to give him a tight hug, but the armor makes it somewhat awkward, and we both wind up laughing. I hear excited laughter from other divs watching us. He holds the sides of my helmet, and I hold his. The crystal charger over his third-eye reflects the half-glow of the rift in the distance.

We gaze out at the deep space V-wings filled with divs and their comps preparing to boost each other to new levels as we sync our power, turn our heartstars, and with Vasif's help, banish MaalenKun.

"Gentlemen." Someone slaps my armor, and I turn to find Mira, smile beaming. "Nice of you to come back from your vacation. Were you two far enough away to keep your moaning out of Thiia and Franxis' minds?"

Almost, Thiia says through our comp-bridge, and I'm almost mortified before I realize she is joking. I signal back that it's nothing to joke about, and she says, playful and sincere, *Aw, I'm so happy that you're so happy though.*

"Couldn't let you go out to the rift alone," I tell Mira.

"Alone? What about me?" Liam asks from behind Casey.

"No one's doing this alone," Casey says, clapping Liam's shoulder.

I see a spark of purpose in Casey, a stability that comes to him through this role. He seems more vibrant and alive, even as we prepare to do something incredibly dangerous.

The crystal chamber looms into view from underneath the yacht. The tugs attached to its glistening surface burn bright. It's pushed further out before the tug engines dim and the auto-thrusters control the drift.

"The Sages have their psybridge connected?" Liam winks at me, letting me know that he sensed my secret attainment when I psybridged our crew to share his shielding attainment.

Liam turns on his armor-shield as he generates the div-shield. His two shields merge seamlessly, doubling protection. I reach out and connect the four of us as we turn on our own armor-shields. Liam extends his special divination attainment toward us, but it curves back through Casey before rushing through the psybridge. With the psychically and technologically generated shields integrated for all four of us, I don't question the flow of divination. Sharing abilities is said to be nearly impossible. It's working and I can study how when we've got more time.

A rainbow wave passes over the border of Casey's shield.

"You guys have surfed before, right?" Casey asks.

"My first time," I admit as we step toward the plasma-grid airlock. "Should I have mentioned that before?"

"Too late now," Mira nearly sings.

We step through the plasma-grid, across the narrow platform, and closer to the edge. On the platform, the yacht's gravity generation has less of a grip on us. A thrilling rush moves through me, and I'm the first to run to the edge and kick off. The thrusters all over the suit whistle as they send me away from The Eminent. My heads up display pings their suits sailing through space behind me. I will the landing target onto the crystal chamber and thrusters align.

"Old Girl, are you still with us?"

"You know I am. Rest of our Ecuador crew is on board. Thiia and Franxis are ready in the chargers. We'll be with you the whole way."

It's good to hear Carmel's voice. Old Girl floats a short distance out from the DSVs.

"Ready, grav-gen, divs," says an unfamiliar voice from the Helixx Corp Ops stationed on the yacht.

I send the psychic signal through the suit and the gravity-generation icon flashes ready at the upper periphery of the heads-up display.

"Ready," I say.

One by one, the others call back the same.

The thrusters woosh one last time before my boots connect with the surface of the crystal chamber. The "ready" icon changes to "grav," and the boots generate enough to stabilize me on the floating crystal. I turn to see Casey land with ease, Mira runs two steps before sticking. Liam comes in too fast. He hits the crystal and stumbles forward. Mira catches him. The crystal bobs and weaves ever so slightly as the tugs auto correct. I look at Casey with his feet apart, knees bent, arms out.

"Surfing," he laughs.

There's a resounding thud from inside the crystal chamber as the storm awakens. The crystal tilts from a hit within, and the tugs' auto thrusters burn hotter to re-stabilize its position, aiming us towards the rift.

"Don't lose that shield, Liam." I tell him as I watch the dark cloud creeping through the crystal under our feet.

"I got you," he calls back as he and Mira move into their first position towards the rear end of the crystal. "I got all of you."

"I like this guy," Casey says, jerking a thumb towards Liam. "You know he made my shield actually bulletproof?"

I cannot help but adore him for bringing humor into this while referencing another highly stressful moment. His quip releases a small amount of my tension.

The shipping container moves out from a small highliner. Its tugs guide it closer to us. Several Helixx Corp drones buzz alongside the container.

"Did Vasif give any clue as to what it's going to do to MaalenKun?" Casey asks.

"It said one word," Liam answers.

Mira wryly adds. "Eat.'"

"Reminds me, I'm hungry." Casey jokes back. "You guys want to get a bite later?"

The storm inside thunders and the crystal lurches again.

"Guess the Haddyc doesn't like your jokes," I say. "I'm a fan though."

He turns back to me and quips, "You might be a bit biased."

The shipping container moves behind the crystal, and the front panel swings open to slide down its topside. Yahima is inside, prismatic shield strong. A shape-shifting tangle of ephemeral vines and leaves moving within fog glows next to Yahima.

The kinetic, psychic reach of the Sages amplified in the pontiff suite and the Haven on nearby Scrie, moves around us. We receive their connection and integrate their psybridge as I simultaneously unfurl my psybridge.

"Old Girl," I say, looking towards my ship in position nearby. "Anchor us."

We feel an increase in stability from Carmel, Thiia, and Franxis almost instantly, and we reach up towards our Levels to call divination down.

Power courses down from my Level, and I sense someone other than Thiia helping me unfurl my psybridge. I kneel down to feel more grounded, and the grav-gen in my kneepad powers up. My secret psybridge reaches the Sages, and it unfurls across space, along the edges of the Sage's psybridge, reaching from the amps on the yacht to the clash- and crux-wings along the planned route. The interconnection resonates loudly as several hundred divs tune in from nearby deep space V-wings. It's so much to hold. I'm amazed to find that my psybridge doesn't feel stretched thin, pushed to my limit as I reach it further and for more people than ever before. I feel the support of the Sages but sense that more than anyone else, it's Casey who is somehow assisting me in moving the psybridge.

The shipping container moves even closer, and Vasif's golden, glowing spores rush to the crystal edge as the body of misty flora creeps forward. The luminous being's tangle of vines twist. It pushes around Yahima's shield, and Vasif's human-like shape emerges briefly. Its jaw opens as it roars, the sound of massive tree trunks splitting. Some of the vines shoot toward the chamber before Vasif flings itself onto the crystal. Immediately, Vasif sends up sharp extensions before slamming them down repeatedly into the crystal surface.

Yahima holds the coffer to their breast and takes their position at the edge of the container. The plan is for Yahima to jump, but it doesn't look like their jump would clear Vasif's unpredictable needle-like extensions springing up and jabbing down with enough force to crack the crystal.

Hairline cracks break into split extensions and spread through the surface of the crystal.

"That's not a part of the plan," Casey says, looking down at the cracks growing under our feet.

The storm inside slams the side of the chamber, and the crystal lurches again.

A large crack spiderwebs out across the surface under Mira and Liam's feet. They step back closer to Casey and me.

"Tell Vasif this is not a good idea," I nearly plead.

"I am," Liam groans.

Mira shakes her head. "It's not responding with words. Just fury."

"For us?"

"The Haddyc," they reply in unison.

I am concerned about the worry in their voices. I almost quell my worries thinking they'd have their prescience turned up if they felt threatened, but I remember that their prescience is off. And I can't quell my fears.

The storm slams into the front of the crystal, and the giant gem lurches forward away from Yahima, away from the coffer, the ring, the key.

I radio Ops. "We've got to spin the crystal! Vasif is going to break through this end! Aim the breaking end at the rift."

Vasif's assault is relentless. Shards of the broken crystal drift away into space as the EDB chisels away at the shimmering surface. The tugs fire up and the crystal swerves away from the shipping container. One of the cracks spreads toward a tug, and the two forces meet each other. A large sliver of crystal breaks away, taking the tug with it. The crystal chamber lists quick and hard. We're thrown down to our knees, but grav-gen in our armor keeps us from sliding off. The other tugs fire sequentially in an attempt to direct the end of the crystal that Vasif is destroying towards the rift. The crystal rocks side to side. More cracks spread, and I radio to Ops to shut the tugs down.

I help Casey onto his feet, and we walk to the end of the crystal nearest Yahima. The distance between us grows. Yahima holds tight the precious cargo in their arms. The glow of the rift dances along the ornate silver cover of the coffer.

Casey urges Yahima, "You can make it. We'll catch you."

In spite of the listing crystal, Yahima does not hesitate. They hold the coffer tight and leap. The intuitive thrusters in Yahima's gear fire up and guide them toward us. Our shields merge as the Sage floats into our arms. I feel Yahima's grav boots kick in, and their feet are planted firmly.

Yahima signals gratitude to us while taking command of the team. Their voice is oddly calm. "Everyone, second positions."

Mira and Liam step away from Vasif and move to the center of the crystal. Casey kneels down and sits on the heels of his boots, facing the cracking end of the chamber. Yahima stands behind Casey ready to open the coffer. I stand behind Yahima with my arms raised to pull in from the psybridge.

I realize that without assistance nearby from Casey, I would not be able to maintain the psybridge alone. I send him waves of gratitude and he nods at me. No one has to do this all on their own. It occurs to me, then to both of us. His special divination, his unique attainment, is empathic. He gleans from other divs that he syncs and replicates their capabilities. This is a new skill he is tapping into. He smiles with a hint of surprise and amazement before a hint of fear shows in his eyes. We both know the ability he is beginning to unlock through Four is incredibly rare and powerful. I nod at him, signaling my confidence in his abilities.

"Ready, Div Kenzari, Div Isaac," Murtagh speaks and transfers her message to ensure we are tuned into each other in body and mind. *"Prepare for mass heartstar turning."*

Murtagh stands in the pontiff suite at the metaglass bow of the yacht. She lifts her hands to the heartstar shining brightly in her chest. Casey does the same. Through the psybridge Murtagh's voice is mighty as she addresses hundreds of divs ready to level up. *Everyone, steady.*

Murtagh and Casey turn hundreds of heartstars, locating within each the light-thread connecting each Div to MaalenKun's energy. The sound of a bass drum echoes throughout our connections, and a low steady *AUM* builds as glowing mandalas expand and turn around Casey's mudras. Hundreds of light-threads pour through the psybridge, glistening through space, and funnel through the mandalas. The array reaches into the crystal chamber and pins MaalenKun down just as Vasif breaks through, tearing away an entire end of the crystal before flowing inside and descending onto the immobilized Haddyc.

Now! I shout through the psybridge.

All the divs, all the Sages create space with and through their light-threads.

Casey channels it into the trapped storm being enveloped by Vasif's radiance. Vasif expands like rolling fog descending onto the darkened storm cloud. The force pushes against the Haddyc's body within Vasif. As planned, the force steers the crystal closer to the rift.

Vasif roars like breaking timber as MaalenKun screams the sounds of bending metal. With fast moving vines, Vasif pulls MaalenKun into its body. A flash of purple-black lightning is quickly disarmed within Vasif's expanding luminous body. The dingy cloud that is MaalenKun explodes into sprays of grey light and ash which slam against the interior of the crystal chamber and knock us onto our knees. The violent bursts of grey give way to explosions of white light before the explosions become invisible light, seen only psychically. As Vasif's luminous body rips apart the Haddyc's storm, sounds of metal bending and breaking reverberate through the crystal's cracked surface.

The cracks grow and spread as the crystal chamber moves toward the rift.

Yahima looks back toward Mira and Liam. "Signal Vasif!"

"Hurry!" Mira urges. "Vasif is struggling!"

Yahima slides the ornate cover away from the coffer and hands it back to me.

The misty leaves which merged with the golden festoon within the ring shine brightly as they peel away. The leaves stretch long and thin. They become a film of glowing colors which psychically reaches towards Vasif. The EDB has shifted its shape as well. It has become a luminous whirling pale mist stretching toward the rift. A flash emerges from within the ring and a high-pitched peal pours from it. The rift crackles before a low hum reverberates from it. It is unlocked. The Helixx Corp drones zoom forward into the rift. Their flashing lights drift into the half-lit interior and disappear. Hundreds of divs work to immobilize and dull MaalenKun, and Vasif consumes the Haddyc. Vasif stretches itself into the dull half-light of the rift and expels the shredded body of MaalenKun and all of the Haddyc energy it had consumed and contained back into the rift, out of our world. The dim shreds pass into the half-glow, inert and quiet.

Through the psybridge, the sounds of hundreds of divs reaching new Levels builds. An ebullient music of their emotion swells and cascades around us. Joy bubbles forth from within and rolls like a wave through us, uplifting us all.

The unstable crystal shatters!

Vasif begins to drift. Luminous thin mists stretch from its body, and it clings to the open space around it.

From within the rift, a bolt of purple-black lightning rushes out, sizzling the space around it. As it moves past us, several of our gear functions are affected. I try to call Ops through the comm but hear only my voice reverberating in the helmet. My HUD flickers and faintly indicates that all of our thrusters are offline, but I swear I hear their quiet whistle through a looped sensation.

Casey drifts into the rift first. Yahima slings the coffer containing the ring back, away from the rift, as they sail into the half-light. Through our psybridge, I hear Liam and Mira and Carmel screaming as the two prescient divinators who could not see this coming disappear into the rift. They all drop away from my psybridge.

The music of the levels becomes discordant. Joy is torn away. A mass of nimbuses grind against each other as they fall out of sync. There are so many. Even the Sages cannot hold them in place.

Vasif catches the coffer and begins to shapeshift into its more human-like body. I drop the ornate coffer cover, and it floats toward Vasif. Misty vines wrap around the cover and the clear box containing the ring.

Behind me, a bright, fiery light grows, and then another one as the purple-black lightning breaks the shields and pierces the wings. The psybridge is filled with wailing moments before the low boom of exploding deep space V's reaches me. It all fades into muffled distortions as I drift helplessly amidst broken crystal and empty space.

My thrusters come back online, and I right myself.

Realizing my intentions, Thiia cries out.

Without pause, I fly into the rift.

ꝏ

The space within the rift feels different, textured, thicker in places. As I drift slowly, I feel pressure increase and ease. At times it feels as if I'm moving through turbulent waters. I bump into invisible pockets that jostle my body and mind.

I pass through the fog within the rift. It half-glows here and there. In other places, it is dense with shadows. I cannot tell what the source of the dim illumination is, only that it fades and brightens slowly in the distance.

My breath is rapid, and I struggle to slow it down.

Wisps of a thick smoke-like substance waft around me as the thrusters propel me forward. I can barely see my hands in front of my face. I veer through a dim expanse. The push of the thrusters and the parting of the haze are the only indications of movement. I finally feel the terror already filling me. It's too much to extinguish, so I scream.

The comm begins to crackle. Mira's voice. I cannot make out any of the words.

"Mira, can you hear me?" The HUD flickers but gives no coordinates for the others. "Anyone?"

Static.

A low rumble of thunder shakes me as I drift.

I cannot find them on the psybridge, but it remains. The psychic network feels empty.

In the semi-lit haze ahead looms a large structure. And another. The presence of a third behind me sends an unfriendly chill up my back. They are colossal and alive! They surround me. I cannot tell if they are coming closer to me or if I am drifting towards them. Part stone and crystal, part metal and tech, their bodies crack and groan as they move. The eldritch machinery merges with the stone in shifting shadows. Grey light and a light-refusing, viscous substance seep through the spaces where the tech and stone merge, slipping through the stone's porous surface. My mind grasps to perceive the strange machinery. Hardened light shapes phosphorescent facets akin to cables, gears, cords, vents, and circuitry. The technology slips into and out of my perception as if my awareness is reshaping it before my eyes. Refracted light and dense shadows pass over each part. The tech is somehow the most difficult aspect of the being to perceive clearly. Like branches of giant trees, several stone arms reach through the half-light and thick clouds around it, breaking and resealing with terrible noise. Behind the slowly moving arms glows an orange cluster of lights set into a curved grid of eldritch tech: a face of lights.

I breathe deeply, trying to silence my mind.

Below me are two small figures. My HUD finally pings them. The small locator points lock onto the two figures, and another circle flickers as the scanner picks up another crewmate buried in shadow. Above me, a face of lights flickers like fire and turns down toward me.

Yahima's saffron combat gear stands out amidst the dim haze. Liam and Mira are with her. I cannot see Casey. I want to call to them, but as I open my mouth, they lift their hands. They move towards me, eyes wide. Mira shakes her head no.

Through a faint psybridge, she signals to me to not speak a word—to not think a word.

A low rumble of complaint bears down on us as one of the titans turns its fiery lights of a face towards us. The haze ebbs around it, and I see it more clearly. Giant coils grind along its body of stones which snap and break before the cracks in the stone and crystal seal themselves again. The grey light and the strange light-refusing substance runs along the surface in streams and rivers. It slowly extends its eldritch arm and reaches toward us with a massive hand of reshaping stone and metal claws.

Our shields flash bright rainbow waves as Liam pours his divination through them. The eldritch hand slams into our shields, sending us drifting through the dismal cloud. Liam vanishes into shadow. Yahima's silhouette passes over a half-glow before it dims, and she's gone. I reach for Mira, but the blur overcomes her frantic, silent face and outstretched hands. Their HUD locator points blink off as all three of them disappear into the gloom.

Something pulls at me. I panic and push away. It tightens around my waist, pulling me backwards. I fight against it, but it pins my arms to my sides. A misty white tendril bearing one cloud-leaf moves across the helmet shield, and I gasp. A note of kind relief moves through me. Vasif.

I'm pulled out of the glow of the half-light, out of the rift. The high-pitched peal of the extradimensional ring fills my mind.

Through her comp-bridge, Thiia sends me the sensation of a full embrace.

Captain Arianne Holt comes through static on the comm mid-sentence. "—you hear me? Kenzari, can you hear me?"

"I hear you." I wince. A migraine is building quickly.

I sense Thiia shaping a mudra for healing and her energy pours towards me.

There are clash wings and crux wings surrounding Vasif. The extradimensional being releases me from its vines. Like anchors, stretched pellicles of its form extend back from its humanoid body fixed seemingly to open space. I drift further back. Vasif directs the vines extending from the crown of its head back into the rift.

"Kenzari, get the ring! The EDB has the ring!" Captain Holt shouts.

In its arms, Vasif holds the coffer. The part of it that extends from within the ring maintains its connection to the rift.

"It needs the ring to keep the rift unlocked."

"Get the ring, Kenzari!"

"Not yet!" Carmel and I both shout.

The vines pull back and Liam and Yahima drift out of the rift towards us. I engage my thrusters, fly to them, and catch them both.

"My head," Yahima says, wincing.

"It gets worse." My head feels like it's going to implode. I realize that the lights of Liam's gear are off. "Liam? Buddy?" I turn him towards me and find a crack in his helmet. A sticky light-refracting substance crawls over his face. "Liam!"

The viscous gel begins to move towards me.

Yahima pulls my hands away and sends Liam's body drifting.

Ops is in our ears. "Medics are on their way."

"He's gone," Yahima calls back to Ops. "Send a containment unit. Confirmed extradimensional substance in Div Ulloha's suit."

The lights from the cruxes and clashes shine on us, on Vasif.

"Yahima! Get the key back from the EDB!" Captain Holt shouts.

Yahima raises their voice. "No! It needs to keep the rift open to find the others!"

"We've been waiting hours!" Holt shouts. "If it didn't have the rift unlocked, we would've crystalized it by now."

"Don't you dare!" Yahima's voice is firm. They spin toward the cruxes and clash wings. "Stand down, divs!"

They lower their lights, perhaps their crosshairs. The shards of the broken crystal drift all around us, tapping against our armor.

"Oh my god…" I watch Liam's frozen body floating further away. A containment drone flies out to intercept it.

The fear that Casey has met the same fate catches my breath. I search for him through the psybridge. I cannot find him. Panic builds in me.

I turn to see the wreckage of V-wings.

Yahima follows my gaze, mutters, "Hours…"

Teams from medical ships search for survivors. Rescue shuttles buzz about with their lights flashing. Larger mining and cargo ships have come over from the moon to stabilize the larger pieces. One bit of fuselage might have survivors on board. Dozens of bodies float amidst the ruins.

My own sense of panic is amplified as I touch the fears spreading through the psybridge.

"Oscar!" Carmel's voice is fraught. "Where is she?"

"Oscar, did you find Casey?" Franxis is less frantic than Carmel, but I can hear the tension in their voice.

I don't know how to answer.

I feel our comps' heartaches merge with my own. I cannot quell our worries.

Yahima maneuvers toward Vasif. The EDB seems to ignore Yahima, but continues turning its head side to side, sweeping its crown of vines around in the rift. It stops moving and the vines begin to pull back.

Mira.

I move toward her and see that Carmel has left Old Girl. Carmel catches her wife in her arms and pulls her close. I can see their tear-streaked faces, but I can't hear what they are saying. It looks like Mira is laughing through tears while calling Carmel crazy for having been moments away from diving into the rift after her. They hold each other in their arms as their thrusters take them both towards the safety of Old Girl.

Vasif reaches its vines back into the rift. Yahima waits next to it patiently, peering into the rift as well. The high-pitched peal of the ring continues.

My stomach feels hollow.

Oscar. Thiia's voice is soothing. *We lost you for almost two hours… but Vasif shows no signs of giving up.*

She's right. The luminous EDB looks determined.

Honor flies from my heart. Shining with rainbow glimmers, the light-thread shines through the space between Vasif and me. As the light-thread moves into Vasif's chest, the light of its body pulses brighter. Its mouth opens as if it gasps. More of the vines extend from its crown and towards the rift. I move closer to Vasif.

Yahima sees it too. They connect their heart, their light-threads. Another pulse of light moves through the being, and it reaches more of itself into the danger to search for Casey.

More light-threads come. First from Franxis then the rest of our crew on Old Girl, then the cruxes and clash wings, the other surviving ships, the yacht, and Scire. Receiving the energy, Vasif's vines grow vast and strong. I see Murtagh at the glass bow of the yacht. She turns the heartstars of everyone connected through our psybridge. Vasif channels all of our care to search for him. The vines reach over me, past me, into the rift as the peal of the ring grows louder. The vines shift and move about as the energy of our hearts uplifts the being. Channeling all of our gratitude and heart, Vasif uses our energy like searchlights glowing from the misty vines. The vines halt suddenly, pulling back. Vasif withdraws as the light of a heartstar pierces the half-glow. Dark smoke-like bands swirl around Casey as Vasif pulls him closer.

Within the rift, something dark lumbers through the haze. The lights of the titan's face emerge through the half-glow. A bolt of purple-black lightning is cast out of the opening.

One of the lunar mining ships stabilizing a wrecked DSV is hit. The explosion shakes us and propels us away. The ship breaks apart, falling into the refuse of other destroyed ships.

Vasif recoils all of its vines. It pulls its leaves back into the extradimensional ring, and the peal fades. Yahima slides the ornate cover over the coffer. The light of the golden ring is concealed.

Casey floats away from the breach and toward me. The fire from the mining ship reflects across his helmet. The lights of his suit flicker. The half-light of the rift and light from the wings sparkle in the cascade of broken crystal all around him.

I see the pain on his face. The lights of his gear go dark. His thrusters must be offline. His heartstar begins to dull and weaken.

Franxis' transference is a scream: *Hurry!*

I rush to him and pull him further away from the rift.

The titan peers out of the rift at us. It rumbles before fading back into the haze. The sounds of its body, breaking and sealing stone, grinding metal, fade.

Something is off. I turn Casey to see his face. He's turning blue. Then, I hear it. A sharp hiss. His gear is leaking. His armor has been broken.

"Why did no one see this coming?" I'm furious. Every time I quell my anger it comes back. "You all knew Mira's and Liam's foresight was unclear!"

From my quarantine room, I gaze at their images spun up onto the curved glass of the hologram receiver. The holograms of all four station captain commanders, the UNAF Div division Lead, others I don't recognize, and Griselda Harris Ferand peer down at me. Several physically present Elders behind a sealed wall of duraglass stare at me.

The UNAF has stuck us in quarantine rooms onboard an unfamiliar ship, leaving me feeling vulnerable and defensive on top of my fury.

Mani's Captain Commander, Areta Maarama, looks at me with concern and a bit of dread in her eyes. Her hologram flickers slightly. Her thick Māori accent is a welcome balm. "Divinator Kenzari, I understand your frustration. You know as well as anyone else that we haven't been able to predict much of anything that might happen around the rift. No one could see this coming."

"Lives were lost!"

N'guwe inhales deeply and lifts her chest. Her medals reflect a bit of the light. "Yes, eighty-seven lives to be precise. Those ships were lined up according to the plan you and your team came up with—" Her words hollow me. "—A plan many Sages and I, even Central, approved. Every single Div that we lost was needed." Her voice cracks, and she bows her head. "I knew some of those divs personally since before their Rising." The hologram of Captain Commander Gala N'guwe looks down at me. "This is a time to mourn our losses and tend to our wounded. It is not a time for blame."

Maarama says softly, "Kenzari, Central thinks it's best that everyone who went into the rift or came near you afterwards stay onboard The Eminent for a bit. It's temporary. Just to put some time between. They'll be able to observe you in case any problems arise due to you having gone into the rift."

My shoulders slump, my face turns down.

Behind the glass wall, an Elder from Mani whom I've seen and never spoken with steps forward. She says, "I will remain aboard The Eminent until you are out of quarantine, Div Kenzari. Like most Elders, I am mostly free of identity, yet I have chosen to be called Black Elder to honor my ancestors. Please, call on me at any time. I am here for you and your crew." Her eyes are full of compassion. "I understand your anger. You must find a more productive use for it. This is no one's fault, Oscar Kenzari. Not yours or anyone else's."

Pyaar looks through the duraglass wall that separates us. I feel her wrap me in her compassion, shining care through our light-thread. I recall our century-old conversation from the temple the day we met. I remember the cracked cup.

Akhilandeshwari, the broken goddess. How can I save the people I love in a world that is always broken?

Across the hall, Mira and Carmel dance close to music I cannot hear. They're probably not even playing music, just holding each other, and swaying to their own rhythm. Over Mira's shoulder, Carmel sees me gazing at them. She smiles and gives a gentle wave. It pulls on my heart strings, and I smile and wave back gently. She nods, signaling an invitation. I tune in and see their heartstars shine brightly. All of the light-threads coming from them radiate brightly when they're together. Through their love for each other, a supportive, healing light is carried on throughout each light-thread. It crosses the space between us, glimmering, and lands in me, relieving tension.

When I go see Casey, I stand behind the glass looking in from the hallway. His body is still. Machines beep and display his vitals. There are several monitoring discs stuck on his arms and neck. The div-bar in his left temple reflects the lights overhead. His skin is paler, and dark circles cover his closed eyelids. His healing factors keep his body and breath going, but he is in so much pain that he's shut down. He has not woken up since he came back from the rift.

"He looks worse than yesterday," Franxis says, stepping next to me.

I reach for their hand, and even though we are still new to each other, they take it, accepting my care. "Are the Sages helping heal him?"

Our Black Elder stands at the head of his bed with hands hovering alongside Casey's temples. Arun stands to Casey's right, Murtagh to his left. They join hands. Their heartstars begin to glow brighter. Murtagh turns them, and I feel my own heartstar move. I look up to see the Sages looking towards us. Their minds reach out inviting us to join them. They disable my div-bar and Franxis' psy-barrier. Relief accompanies divination as it rushes in cool streams throughout my being.

A mandala of light glows around Casey and the Sages. Light-threads pour into him. Rainbows slide along the light from every direction. The thread between Casey and me pulls at my heart. I tighten my grip on Franxis' hand, but they vanish from my grip. My body feels lighter, even as I slump down to the floor. The light is so bright.

When it fades, I'm standing with the Sages in a darkened space.

"Tell no one that we brought you here," our Black Elder tells us gently. Her voice echoes through Casey's dreamscape. "Franxis is anchoring him, but a comp cannot enter a mindfield the way divs and Sages can. We think you might give Casey enough assurance to pull away from the force that holds him. Please, call to him."

Arun gives me a look of gentle assurance.

I gaze into the darkness around us. "Casey, can you hear me?"

Nothing.

"Casey… closer."

The emptiness around us begins to shift. Shadows become more gradient and amorphous shapes begin to rise from them. Everything moves with the sounds of low, stuttering thunder, rippling thuds.

"Casey is pulling away obscurations to bring us into his mind more fully," Arun says. "He may show you things he will never speak of. It might be hard not to turn away, Oscar."

I think of Casey's eyes, his humor, his delight. How he makes me feel. I steady myself in what I appreciate in him.

The Sages work to integrate the psybridge into Casey's dreamscape.

The shadows around us shift. Shapes are more fully realized, although a sticky, light-refusing substance clings to and pulls at almost everything. South Los Angeles emerges in chaos. Buildings have toppled. Several fires burn, sending thick smoke into the sky. We hear the river and someone moving through it before we can see either. Then, the river is there before us—as if it always was there. Casey stumbles out of the water. Several bands of the light-refusing substance stick to him as he pushes forward, breaking through webs of the stuff. He collapses onto sand which hardens into concrete as the flowing river behind him becomes the asphalt street. Another building falls behind him. More stuttering thunder.

The Sages say nothing as he crawls closer.

"Casey," I whisper. I cannot tell if he can see me. He holds his bleeding shoulder. Blood runs down his neck.

He turns towards me and seems surprised to see me standing in his way. "Oscar!"

His smile is brilliant. The blood is gone from his neck, but he still holds the gushing wound on his shoulder.

"Casey." I want to reach out to him, check his injury.

"It's not my blood," he says. He takes his bloody hands away from his healed shoulder. "I'm so sorry."

"What happened, Casey?"

His heartbreak spins the world around us.

The Sages and I are folded into the space around Casey. He's struggling to pilot a SkyDrive. The rotors are locked to another SkyDrive and the vehicles are sure to crash soon. But Casey is more afraid of the man in the passenger seat. He has a knife in his hand and a vortex in his head. The man strikes at Casey, and I try to block the attack. The knife passes through my arm and cuts across Casey's shoulder. He strikes again and again, and each time there is nothing I can do.

Everything around Casey becomes leaden and heavy. His guilt becomes an obscuration that seeps out of him, unlike the conscious obscurations we create in our psybridges.

I do the only thing I can. I reach for Casey through our light-thread. I send him the sense of being held. I feel him leaning into the sensation. He moves toward me. I hold him until he can feel supported, until he can overcome his self-condemnation.

The obscuration grows thin and fades.

Casey's voice comes to us from somewhere else. "I had been telling myself that it was an accident, that in the chaos I panicked or slipped."

He tries to defend himself and is cut again.

"I know what happened with Usain."

Casey looks at Usain and choses.

"It wasn't an accident."

He breaks the security seal and pulls the lever.

"I meant to eject his seat."

Usain's seat is flung from the SkyDrive. His head hits the bridge, and the dreamscape spirals again.

The Sages and I are tossed back into the shadowy dreamscape amongst the ruins of South Los Angeles.

Casey sits facing a large pile of rubble. "I'm so sorry."

"Casey," I plead. "It's not your fault."

With more of the eldritch substance clinging to them, bodies emerge from the rubble of the city. Light bounces off the stretching tacky substance. Vortices fly up from their heads and disappear into the black sky. Stars emerge. The crowd mills about, draws closer. Their clothing is indistinct. Their faces are hidden. They grasp at each other, almost fighting but evading each other sleepily. Things shift, and we're no longer in South Los Angeles. I don't know where we are, maybe a climate refugee camp. The crowd surrounds us, bumping into us. The Sages link arms. Murtagh grabs my hand, and I reach for Casey, who seems ten years younger.

"It's hard to carry when it's all I hold," he says as several gnarled hands grip his shirt.

I cry out, "Casey, you don't have to carry it any longer!"

He's pulled into the crowd and disappears again.

More rippling thuds and the crowd is swallowed by darkness. We stand there looking for Casey. I turn around more than once before the headlights of the truck appear. The truck rolls to a stop in the distance. The light-refusing substance crawls up the tires, and sensing Casey inside, I want to run to him.

As we get closer to the truck, I hear a struggle inside. I open the driver's side door to find a man punching a young kid, barely a teenager: Casey. The man's fist comes down on his head repeatedly. Young Casey tries to duck. The man slams his head into the dash, grabs him by the throat, and growls, "You don't belong..."

An urge to stop the man rushes through me.

"It's no use," our Black Elder says. "This is his memory. We cannot change it."

The beating goes on as young Casey cries.

Arun comes to my side. "Casey is finding his way to us by showing us his past."

When I turn back, the truck is gone. The space is empty again. I turn to find Casey with the Sages.

"Oscar." He sounds defeated.

"Casey." I hold him close to me, and even in his dream, I can smell his skin. He loses his balance, and I move to catch him. He waves me away, stumbles to the side.

When I look at him, it's as if the space around us is turning slowly. Vignettes of his life, each sticky with the light-refusing stuff, fade in and out far away. More beatings from that man who I discern is Casey's father. His father kicking him out. Learning to survive on the streets. Substance abuse to the point of passing out face down on the hard cement. Group therapy, walking away angry. Several arguments with different men, different lovers. Trying to avoid himself through sex with strangers whose names and faces will never be recalled. Bakkeaux reaching a tendril into his partner's mind. His partner attacking him with a knife. How he survived. Feeling guilty for it. Struggling to level up, the pressure he put on himself. A few memories free of the light-refusing substance: meeting Franxis. Moments of joy with Franxis, bonding over his surname change to "Isaac," Franxis dropping their surname altogether. Stepping onto Station Scire for the first time. Sliding doors open and I see myself presenting to station commanders and divs. I turn towards him and feel his heart skip a beat. I'm there, one of his happy memories.

I realize. "This extradimensional energy is bringing all the hurt up, isn't it?"

"Guess I don't have to tell you about all of this now," he quips.

I hold him closer. "None of this could make me want you less."

The memories spin around us, and the light-refusing stuff stretches from so many of them, from the darkness around us, and from the spaces between us. It crawls over him, clinging to his skin like clear tar. I make to pull away the tacky bands, and our Black Elder stops me.

"We must not touch it!"

His memories and visions spin and morph around us. The tone of their presence shifts, and an unearthly wailing comes from all around us. Bending metal, the screams of a Haddyc, pierce the chaos.

Murtagh gasps. "These are no longer memories. He's losing hold of himself."

"No," he mumbles. "No."

An image of Franxis manifests before me. They turn towards me and set brassy-pink eyes on me. The hair on my arms stands on end as pellicles of the sticky stuff creep over Franxis and pull them into the void.

The moon is on fire.

Rolling mammatus clouds of shadow and light-refusing void sweep over us, and I feel the Earth beneath me grow cold with the loss of sunlight.

Casey's carousel of visions fades, and we are left in near darkness.

"No," Casey mumbles. We turn in the direction of his gaze, and see only void, incomprehensible emptiness.

Something ominous lurks in the space beyond our sight. We hear it, a nearly imperceptible but threatening tremor moving through the space around us, never settling.

"That's it," Casey says. He seems to drift toward the sound as it moves.

"Where is it coming from?" Arun asks.

"It's several places at once, then on the move." Our Black Elder steps closer and takes my hand, then nods at Casey's hand. I take it. He pulls back from the sound. Murtagh takes Casey's other hand, and Arun completes the circle.

The threat bears down on us, its clattering sound rattling the space around us. Pressure drums in our ears.

Casey's in pain. He grips my hand tight.

Murtagh leans toward him and shouts over the noise, "Casey, we're with you!"

Casey tries to look up, but the sticky substance pulls his head down. Murtagh turns our heartstars and the nimbuses above us push through the roaring vibrations to come together. Divination washes over us. The light of a mandala emerges above us, and light-threads shining with compassion pour down from above. We begin our attempt to force the strange energy into integration, where our divination will subdue it within Casey.

Casey shakes his head.

"I don't deserve this help," he whispers. A flash of him defending his life during the First Assault comes and goes. The guilt he feels over having to kill his lover weighs him down. A realization illuminates an old pattern. A struggle to prove his father wrong, to be worthy, to belong, reveals itself. The obscuration that held it in his subconscious begins to loosen.

Our nimbuses tremble and briefly slip out of alignment. I stand before Casey, but the substance keeps him from looking toward me. The sages form a protective circle around us. The threat grows louder, and Casey's tears become rivers. He shakes his head slowly, and the threat pulses side to side with heavier force with each turn of his head. The space beneath us pulls harder, and we fight against Casey's reactive dulling.

"He's trying to dull himself!" Arun shouts as his knees buckle. "He doesn't mean to hurt us!"

"Casey!" I want to hold his face. His body is so tense, wound tight. I cannot turn his face towards me. His face turns bit by bit, and I force myself to make joyful, happy sounds through my fears. He blinks hard several times, struggling to direct his gaze. His ringed green eyes roll forward, and they slowly become discs of brassy green, like an animal's eyes caught in headlights. But I know that he sees me.

"Oscar," he says. "I can't."

"I know it seems that way." As I watch the sticky substance drop away from Casey, my tears fall with them.

He cries out as the injury within his right arm glows bright and hot. I signal to him the image of Vasif's leaf, and the energy glows white and soothing in his left arm.

I add, "We're here. We got you."

His eyes roll back, and he refocuses on mine. He sobs. I want to shout over the pressure and noise, but I know he can hear the love in my voice if I just lean in. I pour out from my heartstar to his. "Whatever this is... whatever it brings up... none of that changes who you are or how much we care about you." His eyes roll back, and his head pulls back again. I feel I don't know the right words. I fear I'm going to lose him.

I look past the remaining bands of strange, viscous stuff crawling around his face. I look into his green, grey-ringed eyes which I glimpsed so long ago.

"I saw your eyes gazing into me when I became Risen, Casey. I saw you. For so long, I knew you would be my future. Now that you're in my present, I can't lose you to your past. You're still a part of my future."

Tension seizes Casey.

"You have so much love coming to you to help you with all this. All of it, Casey. You're not alone in this. You have Franxis, you have a crew now." I hold his face with both of my hands so that he sees me. "You have me."

Casey's nimbus pulls down from above, integrating with my own. Casey's heart draws me in, and I rise to hold close to Six. The surge from leveling up opens me to even higher Levels, and I strain to pull down.

"Casey Isaac," a voice, soft and melodic, reverberates through the dreamspace. "I AM aware of your pain. Come to me, Casey Isaac. Meet me where I AM."

Casey vaguely recognizes the voice. "What—?"

An explosion of rainbow light rushes from our nimbuses towards us. The last of strange substance is flung away from Casey. It unravels in the light with high-pitched shrieks, but several bands slither between the lights, disappearing into his dreamscape.

The noise is gone.

There is light in his beautiful eyes again.

He kisses me. And we wake up from his dream.

I lift myself up from the hallway floor and peer through the window.

Slowly, he blinks open his eyes. The Sages help him sit up. Arun smiles as he opens the door for me. I make it in before MedOps. A nurse tries to pull me away, but I hold Casey tight. The Sages guide the nurse and doctors away. For a few moments, they watch me hold him. His chest rises and falls against mine, and I steep in the movement of his breath. He puts his arms around me and returns the feeling of being held.

He whispers, "I got you."

ꝏ

(Decrypted) message sealed under authorization: Acolyte 003
permanent delete engaged upon opening comm; file will self-corrupt in 00:00:20
7 April, 2138 9:36 (Greenwich standard)

"control of spacial thrusters acquired through stealth signal. all targets steered into StillRift-2138 as planned. unplanned: div oscar kenzari regained control of his thrusters and followed targets into the rift. message will permanently delete in ten—"

ꝏ

CASEY

"Were you watching me sleep again?" Oscar reaches towards me and yawns deeply as I scoot closer to him. He wraps his arms around me and pulls me against his chest as he rolls onto his back. "I can't decide if that's really sweet or kinda weird."

"It's both." I drape a leg over his and run my hand down his muscular arm.

He chuckles sleepily. "Why are you so awake?"

"I'm not quarantined alone this time." I kiss his shoulder. "That's all."

"Oh, so nothing to do with last night?"

"That too..."

He yawns deeply again. "What day are we on now?"

"Counting the three days we were apart, it's day seven."

"Did you sleep okay?"

I sigh. "In spite of your best efforts to wear me out, I did not."

He turns toward me, rubs his hand on my back. "Did you dream of the voice again?"

"No. Just nightmares." I smile, trying to force away the memory of the dream where a sentient cloud was destroying me from the inside.

His eyes convey worry. "Want to tell me about them?"

"You can't save me from all the nightmares." When I kiss him, I press my body tighter against him. "I'm fine now. I woke up next to you. I'm happy."

He straddles me and says, "Bet I can make you even happier."

"Ops has brought in several Counselors to help everyone process the collective trauma that rippled through the psybridge." Franxis leans forward on their elbows. "I can set up a session if either of you need it."

"I'm mostly okay," Oscar says reverently. "Still a bit upset that no prescient Sages could see it coming, but even Arun and Yahima have been feeling off lately. Who knows what effect the rift is having on all of us." He shrugs. "And I can deal with how I feel about my plan succeeding in one respect, failing in another. If I need more help, I'll reach out. Thank you, Franxis."

Thiia gives Oscar a gentle smile.

All three look to me. I sigh. "I'm sad about Liam. That psybridge-ripping trauma wave skipped over me because I was in the rift. But I've had a lot of old stuff coming up. Something still feels off."

Franxis nods sympathetically and says, "I'll talk to Ops, get you a sesh with counseling."

"Helixx Corp has some of the best div-medical in the sector," Thiia says. "Have you talked to them about it?"

"They tell me what the Sages usually tell us: I'm not the first div to struggle to integrate a difficult, extradimensional energy—just the first with this unique signature. They say it'll probably get integrated soon." I sigh. "In the meantime, I feel more tired than I have in a hundred years. My dreams are fucking weird." I hesitate to continue. "There's also this occasional buzzing on the periphery of my perception. It's almost… language, but as if it can't quite make it through. Like some feedback that doesn't integrate."

"That's concerning." Thiia says. She looks at both Oscar and me. "Did they let your scientist boyfriend look at your charts?"

"Yeah," I answer with a half frown.

"Other than the unclassified energy signature, nothing seems abnormal from what they showed me." Oscar shrugs but signals something more to Thiia.

Their quick signals to each other take longer for me to decipher. Something about my charts feels incomplete, but we can't be sure of it.

"I'm happy you two are together, at least." Franxis looks both amused and bewildered. I can read them well enough to not need a signal. Franxis thinks it's strange for Oscar to be in my room while this unknown energy moves within me.

All I have to do is look into Franxis' eyes for them to know I picked up on their bewilderment. With a smile, I honestly say, "Me too."

A touch of worry rises within me. I don't want to continue sitting here signaling that the Helixx MedOps are withholding info about what's going on inside of me. I'm ready to change the subject.

"How is life out there?"

Thiia perks up. "Well, Yahima's still planning to keep their promise to the Waorani and get Vasif back to the Amazon. Yahima plans to walk right out of here and take the EDB back to Ecuador."

Oscar says, "Might not be that easy. I expect that even after the rest of us are out of quarantine, Central might want us all to stay on The Eminent a bit longer. Just to make sure we didn't bring anything back from the rift. Especially Vasif."

"Where is Vasif?" I ask.

Thiia raises her brows and says, "The science crew has set up a quarantine unit for the EDB. They've let me visit—behind glass, of course." Thiia shrugs. "I've kinda developed an affinity for Vasif now that it saved two of my best mates. Is that odd?"

Oscar gushes adoration for her. "Makes sense to me. I have my suspicions about the intel we had before going to Ecuador."

"Hmmm... wonder where that intel came from?" Franxis glances all around to suggest The Eminent, Helixx Corp, Griselda Harris Ferand.

As if on cue, the hallway doors slide open, and a rolling projector bot leads Dr. Lee Wallace towards us. The hologram lights spin up above the bot to display the visage of Griselda Harris Ferand. Unlike every other hologram I've seen, Ferand's comes through without the standard blue lines that run through projections. I get the sense that she has highly advanced tech and isn't concerned with the mandates on technology imposed by the UN.

I have the sinking feeling they were listening to us. However, they are all smiles.

"The comps!" Griselda's voice comes from the bot. She seems pleased to have placed why she knows Thiia and Franxis' faces, but she obviously does not know their names, nor does she care to look them up or ask. "Divs Isaac and Kenzari, I haven't seen you face to face since Ecuador, but I've been keeping an eye on you."

Is this face to face? I ask Oscar over the psybridge.

He replies, *She obviously doesn't remember me yelling at them a week ago.*

"I have a gift for you, Div Isaac—Can I call you, Casey?" she asks.

"Uh, sure."

Dr Wallace opens a small container and retrieves its contents. He holds out a cobalto crystal merged with tech. He inserts the data crystal into the panel by the door, and it begins to glow as the room's systems integrate the information.

The holographic image of a tabby cat appears nearby. The image walks closer to Oscar, tilts its head, and twitches its tail. "Hello, I'm Lilly."

"Lilly!" I force enough enthusiasm to hide my skepticism.

Random, Oscar transfers.

A gift of something I already owned. She took Lilly from my quarters on Scire.

"I thought maybe Lilly would make you feel more at home here." Her forced smile is awkward.

Maybe sensing my bewilderment and wanting to help Ferand save face, Dr. Wallace asks, "How are you two feeling today?" He doesn't wait for an answer. "Is it okay if your comps see your charts?" Again, he doesn't wait for our answer. He taps the panel by the door and several holoscreens float up onto the glass wall.

Lilly looks up at me and squints. I smile back.

Ferand says, "The doctor tells me that you're integrating the novel energy."

She's lying, Oscar immediately transfers.

"I still feel off," I reply to Ferand. Wondering how Oscar would know if Ferand was telling the truth, I transfer back, *How?*

Five, he transfers. *Sort of a lie-detector. I hear it in her tone.*

"I feel tired," I tell the doctor. "And I'm having terrible nightmares. Lots more chatter in my head than usual."

"Perhaps recent events have brought up some of your old trauma?" Ferand's face conveys an almost convincing concern. "The Sages told me you took quite a big step forward with some assisted healing. And that was with the help of Div Kenzari." Her holographic face turns toward Oscar briefly.

"That's true. How much of my file have you seen, Dr. Ferand?"

"Oh, you can call me captain when I'm on this ship, or—you know what..." she shrugs and winks. "Just Griselda. I'm also Helixx Corp's head scientist... I've read a good deal about you, Casey. You are, after all, under my care here on The Eminent."

"Are you actually on the ship?" Franxis asks, looking the hologram up and down.

"Good question. Yes! I am. I do a lot around here, mostly by hologram. I'm actually en route to the EDB science deck. I'll be joining the team today to study Vasif."

"Is Vasif going back to the Amazon? We brought Vasif up here to help with the Haddyc, and it did that and more. Does it understand what's going on?" Oscar asks.

"Good question. We hope to get a clear answer today. We've been trying to communicate but the being has grown less responsive over the past couple of days. I was coming here with Dr. Wallace to ask your crewmate—" She checks her notes. "—Div Adivar to join us. I believe she already has a rapport with the being. Kenzari, your secondary role is EDB physiology, correct? Would you like to join us? You'll have to suit up and shield."

He looks excited, so I don't mention that Ferand didn't answer his first question. I let it go.

"Yes! Please, have them drop the suit to the closet. I'll be ready in five after they do!"

"Wonderful!" Griselda's holographic image turns to someone in the room where she is. She holds a finger up towards them. "I have to go. It was nice to see all of you. Kenzari, I will see you soon."

The hologram flickers off and the bot rolls back through the hallway and out of the door. Dr. Wallace looks back toward the holoscreens. Franxis steps closer to him, asks him to show them the div energy matrix. He acts happy to oblige.

"Hey," Oscar says to me, visibly enlivened. "Are you cool with me going?"

I wish I had the energy to be as excited, but I feel lethargic. "Of course! I think it will make a difference to Vasif."

Oscar says, "I'm sure Vasif will be happy to see Mira."

A thud in the closet means they've dropped Oscar's gear.

"Go," I say, and he kisses me quickly. As he is walking away, I notice a spring in his step.

I shade the glass wall and take the meditation cushion out of the closet. I open the window to see the shifting half-light of the open rift in the distance. A couple of transports veer towards Earth. Most of the Sages, divs, and Ops brought on board The Eminent go back to their posts today. Each station and numerous divisions planetside will receive divs who leveled up or locked in because of Oscar's plan. Each station will also be coping with the losses of team members. The trawlers and scrappers are still picking large pieces of the DSVs out of the debris field.

The memory of Liam wrapping his arms around me, increasing my shield just in time surfaces. Even as the bullets lodged in the shield, we were giddy. We knew each other for a day and a half, and he still took a risk for me. He must've been confident, or brave, or foolish.

Div-tech from all four stations and Helixx have already come together to take the obsidian data cubes from Liam's gear and decipher how he merged the tech with his divination shields. All of the shields in our combat gear will be bulletproof now, thanks to Liam.

A faint glow builds in my heart. My sadness over his death begins to shift into honor for him. It dims almost as quickly as it surfaced.

Maybe I'm just tired, I think.

I bring to mind his face, the moment when he sent his divination through Oscar's psybridge, and we shared his shield ability to us all. Perhaps my empathic power was key, but we did that together. The light in my heart brightens, but something else moves within me.

Across the light of honor, a shadow falls.

Liam saved my life. What he did will wind up saving many more lives, but I can't find it in me to honor my own contributions. It feels out of place to think that I am not a part of protecting others in a similar way, yet this thought arises.

("You don't belong...")

The shadow snags my self-loathing, doubt, fear. It pulls up heavy insecurity. I try to quell it, but it clings to my awareness.

I let the meditation cushion fall to the floor with a soft thud. Whether or not I should even try to sit and focus, I don't know.

Tension builds deep in my shoulders and up the back of my neck.

I'm being watched.

I tell myself not to worry. It's probably just the medical scanners monitoring me.

I position myself on the cushion, lengthen my spine, and try to soften around the mental tension. I let the tension and my tiredness be. I curl my middle fingers in, touching the bases of my thumbs as I connect tips of my thumbs, index, and ring fingers, a mudra for the heart. Being careful not to feel sorry for myself, I watch the heavy emotions.

The shadow moves. There is no pattern for this movement within me. It's the unnamed energy from the rift and within it, the shadow. It falls on my heartstar, and an echo of loneliness gets amplified.

I focus on my breath, refocus my heart. I tell myself what the Sages and MedOps have been telling me. I'm integrating difficult energy.

It moves again as if it is dodging my awareness. The heat of the Haddyc sting flares again. I thought it was gone. The space within me where Vasif's leaf landed feels cold and unnatural.

The shadow moves, and a new worry begins to build. I try not to feed the worry, I try to quell it, but I feel it expanding. The extradimensional energy that has invaded my being is something to worry about, something to fear. It is alive.

It hisses in my mind, **You...**

I open my eyes as mistrust of what is within me creeps into my mind. I try to extinguish it. The shadow disappears behind the light. Deep breaths.

Hey buddy, Franxis transfers, tuning their comp-bridge in further. *Kinda lost you for a moment. What was all that?*

When Oscar gets back to the room, he comes in slowly. I'm still on the meditation cushion. I have no idea how much time has passed, but it feels like hours. My legs are stiff as I stand up, but my healing factors assuage the soreness quickly.

"Any progress?" Oscar wills his gear to fall away piece by piece as he moves towards me. When he finally has me in his arms, I'm delighted that he's wearing only his briefs.

"I don't think this energy is going to be easy to integrate." His excitement over his own day makes it easier to obscure that I've been lost in my worries and fears for hours. "Did the science deck have tech as good as Mani? I know you're partial."

"They've got some cool shit." His eyes sparkle with the aftereffect of enchantment. "They're using a type of pin-point sonar micro resonance imaging to literally map all the shifting energy within Vasif."

"You're such a cute nerd."

His tawny cheeks brighten. At this point, he's used to my teasing, I think, but I catch a note of insecurity coming across the psybridge. I catch a glimpse of an obscuration getting ready to fall as Six begins to shine through more and more of his insecurities. I know this is happening for his own benefit, but as I witness it, I am reminded of him in the dreamscape, accepting so much of what leaves me feeling insecure.

I pull him closer to me. "For the record, I love nerdiness. I mean it as a compliment."

He wraps his arms around me. "And I like your playful teasing. I know you only do it with the people you really care about."

"Oh, you think I care about you?" I meant to be sarcastic, but my words sound colder than I intended. I open my mouth to say something, but the shadow moves, and I lose my words.

He gives me an exaggerated stink-eye, but he holds me tight. "I do. And I want you to know that I care about you."

"I do, I do." I relax my hold on him a bit, but he still looks puzzled. "That came out wrong. I'm just feeling off… maybe you can use that sonar resonance probe thing on me?"

He chuckles as my lips graze his neck, and he tightens his arms around me. "It's a scanner, not a probe."

"Your other probe, maybe?" My joke gets him to laugh lightly, even though I'm sure he saw it coming.

He brings his bearded cheek to mine, and I wind up pulling away.

The Shadow scrapes against old wounds, and its words rise like a phantom thought, ***Never belong, never have it. No love.***

A distorted echo stirs up self-depreciation, doubt, and fear.

You are mine.

He gives me space. "You okay, Casey?"

A strong signal says he means that I just pushed and pulled away several times. His concern seems validated. That's not what I meant to do, but it's an old pattern. I have been trying not to replay it, trying to allow myself to be with him, to be myself with him.

I must look so dramatic.

Did you hear that? I transfer.

In here? he asks back.

Yeah.

I hear you, me… us. He smiles, signaling care.

I sigh. "I'm tired from trying to integrate that strange energy."

He takes my hand and leads me over to the window. At the edge of the planet, the lights of the megacities below us have begun to pierce through the Earth's late afternoon sky. As the clouds drift, they reflect the day's last light. He stands behind me and holds me to his chest with his cheek on my shoulder.

"Are you having a lot of memories come up after our dreamy rendezvous?" His beard gently brushes the back of my neck.

I run my hands across his arms as he holds me. "I maybe should be half-naked too."

He smiles gently at my touch, but still cocks his head to the side, patiently waiting for me to answer.

"Yes," I tell him. "But it's not like before when things would come up. I feel like the energy I picked up on is amplifying things."

"Want me to call the doc? Or a Counselor?"

"No." I snort. "I'm sure MedOps are already scanning, watching."

"Is that bothering you?"

I shrug because it doesn't really matter. "I don't want to wait to be with you… so, I'm ok with them watching." I graze my fingers across his nipple, and he grabs my hand with a good-natured grumble. "Does it bother you?"

He wrinkles his nose. "I'm not crazy about the idea that they might be scanning us right now. Or listening." His smile is momentarily mischievous. "It only bothers me that it's not my choice as to who gets to watch and when they get to watch."

I look over my shoulder and arch an eyebrow. "You didn't seem to mind this morning."

"I forgot," he whispers and smooths his beard. When he looks at me, his inner eyebrows lift, and he bites his lip. Signals of shyness, embarrassment, and insecurity transfer. "You distracted me."

A glow from forgetting to be insecure brightens within him, and for a moment, I forget my own worries. I half-smile and nod understanding.

"Look," he says, gazing over my shoulder, out the window.

Below us, the viridescent northern lights dance on the Earth's atmosphere. He is intentionally silent in speech and mind, steeping in beauty. I look at him more than I look at the flickering green lights. After a few moments, I can sense his joy building.

I unwrap his arms from my torso and guide him in front of me.

"So you can see better." I wrap my arms around him, and he pulls them tighter to his body.

"It never gets old to me," he says, soft and low.

I look out at the green lights and try to see them as if I haven't seen them thousands of times. I remember the feeling I had the first time I did see them.

Back when I was a commercial V-wing pilot, I picked up a route when another pilot was sick, just so I could fly to Alaska and look up at them. I almost open my mouth to tell Oscar about it. The shadow stretches towards me.

Your story is meaningless.

I glance at Oscar, see the awe in his eyes, and it seems like a bad time for a personal story. I want to let him steep. I don't need to interrupt him and pull his attention towards me again.

A thought turns over in my mind. It twists. It seems that Oscar just doesn't want to hear that voice in my head. I soothe but cannot fully quell the fear that he would ignore it.

He looks over at me, sees that I'm not looking at the lights but down and away. I smile at him and return my gaze out the window until he does as well. When he is again staring into the play of lights, I gaze at him.

I steep in his beauty, and the shadow slips away.

He maybe senses that I'm steeped in the sight of him. He chuckles and holds out a hand to me.

"Closer," he says softly. "Come take in the beauty of the world."

The viridescent lights below us swirl and spread across a patch of Earth's sky.

I take his hand and stand behind him with my head on his shoulder. He doesn't need to say anything, and I almost don't need him to.

I'm done with watching the glowing lights. I step back, but only so I can see him better.

I trace a line from one dark spot on his shoulder to another on his neck, another half-way down his back, another near his waist. He glances over his shoulder towards me.

He snorts and says, "Blotches and blemishes. Used to make me so self-conscious."

His body becomes ever so slightly more tense, but he allows me to continue mapping his beauty marks.

"A map of stars," I say.

His body eases, and he turns toward me.

"The constellation of you."

ꝏ

I cannot bear to watch him being precious with the damaged equipment anymore.

"One of the things that we Capricorns struggle with the most is watching someone do something in an inefficient way."

"Oh, wow…" On his belly, he slides back pulling his head out of an open panel in Old Girl's cockpit. With raised eyebrows, he props himself up onto his elbows. He's already a bit frustrated after struggling to retrieve a damaged crystal piloting disc lodged in its housing unit. He tries to set the crystal x-ray diffractor down on the hovering tool tray, and the extra gravity meant to keep the tools in place snatches it out of his hand. "Are you struggling right now, babe?" he asks.

I tilt my head enough to be adequately adorable and reply, "I am."

"You want to do this?" He says with frustration creeping into his voice.

Through our steady psybridge, I simultaneously bring Oscar's awareness to his abrasive tone of voice. We both are getting the hang of observing each other's minds while giving each other emotional space. He dials the psybridge down now, and I get that he's steeped in his frustration. "I was only trying to make you smile, babe. Wasn't trying to be a smartass."

He dials the connection back open just a bit.

So needy so clingy, the Shadow hisses.

It makes a move to claw into my insecurity, and I apply the only strategy I know to occasionally work. I quell everything it might creep into by not taking Oscar's tone personally. It flails as it grasps and misses, fading back into obscurity. It is subdued, but I still worry.

"Shadow?" Oscar asks, voice free of frustration, eyes full of concern.

I sigh and nod. "I fear I'm the one who has being trained and subdued, but I manage to ignore that fear most of the time. I think it knows that its effect on me is only mild annoyance, and I worry that it is beginning to want more."

"I still think you should talk to counseling about it."

"They'll tell me the same thing Med Ops has told me for the past month."

"We can request a counselor from Scire if UNAF demands we remain in the Helixx Corp network. Maybe your old counselor."

"She's not there. Helixx gave the boot to all wheelchair users."

"Someone else then."

I quell my father's voice before the reminder that the UNAF has left us in limbo triggers my abandonment trauma. I force a stoic smile.

His crooked smile leaves me feeling grateful that I have him and our crew still on board the Eminent. Sensing my need to, he changes the subject.

"Old Girl needs a ship-tech expert."

"Good thing I'm here," I reply sweetly, picking up a disc pick.

I lean down into the open panel next to him.

"This interface dash is... oof! So many sloppy patches. Okay. Let's do it together. She likes you better anyway."

I pass him the drive re-router.

He chuckles as we both crawl on the floor to peer into the open panel. Hairline cracks spread through the amethyst interface dashboard, the converter bears a few burn marks, and the cracked piloting disc is decades old. I was not expecting it to look this rough.

"I can't even make jokes," I say as I reach in with the retuning forks. I flip the switch and the tool sings its healing song into the crystal. Some of the cracks fuse, but the scars remain.

"Good. I don't think I can handle any jokes about her. This makes me want to cry." Oscar sighs.

Weak fool clinging, it says, returning unexpectedly.

I suppress the critique.

"We might not show the signs of aging, but everything else does," I say. "Can you re-route that blown converter to shields?"

"Think so." He reaches in and begins working around the singed converter. A touch of gratitude comes across the psybridge. I realize he had overlooked the converter before.

There is one new panel of tech that seems out of place. "What's that? Did Helixx install that?"

"What!?" He realizes what I'm talking about, and an obscuration goes up with a lot of delight, concealing a thought. "Oh, that. I put that in. It's a surprise." The corner of his mouth glides up, and I don't pry. He sighs as he resets the channels between the crystal and tech. "Maybe we should overhaul the entire shield-gen?"

"GHF is pretty forthcoming with the gifts."

"No thank you. Helixx is not allowed to meddle with her."

I chuckle. "But you're okay with them meddling with me?"

He laughs. "MedOps is different. They'll figure out what's going on soon, babe."

He shines compassion through the light-thread between us. Our light-thread is growing brighter. It could become a potent light-line soon.

A flicker of joy rises. I'm grateful to feel it free of the Shadow's attempts at disruption, and I immediately lose it when I realize that I'm thinking of the Shadow and not feeling the joy. Even without its voice, the moment of emotion is tainted by its influence by the pattern it's created.

I shrug it off, pressing forward.

"That piloting disc is really jammed," I add.

With one hand, I unbox the spare. The smooth ametrine encasing the tech is mostly purple amethyst with a streak of citrine running through its center. My other hand holds a reinforced steel pick.

"You want me to spare you the pain?"

"No," he says quickly. "My ship, my responsibility."

As I hand him the pick, he sighs and leans down into the open panel. With only a touch of his divination strength flowing through his arm, he jabs the pointed end of the pick into the jammed piloting disc, cracking it into pieces. With a crystal magnet, he pulls the remains of the disc out, reverently handing me each large piece.

"Hold on to those," he says.

I hand him the new disc that will be used to guide his crew, and he slips it into place. A pleasant chime signals the acceptance and integration of the tech.

"Thanks for believing me about the Shadow. I'm grateful for you, Franxis, our crew. The Sages listen—Arun and Yahima, more than the others, but so many of the Sages from Helixx are just neutral. Something's not right about this energy in me. Sometimes, I think our crew are the only ones who listen."

Oscar stops working and waits to speak until I make eye contact. "I want you to know that even without our psybridge, I can hear you. You have every right to insist when the doctors tell you they don't see anything concerning. And I've got your back. Always. The whole crew—we got you." He turns his gaze back to the shield generator. "It scares me a bit that whatever the energy is, it's still not integrated." He looks back at me. "And I can feel that you get scared too."

A weight drops from me.

He doesn't need me to say anything.

The light-thread between us shines brighter than the shadow could ever conceal.

ꝏ

The training facility on The Eminent is by far the poshest gym I've ever been to. Other divs work out on sleek machines with holoscreens displaying their personal data and vitals. Incredibly fast divs test their speed on in-floor treadmills where the sight of their legs gets lost in motion blurs. Another div is pushing massive kettlebells with his mind. Every time one of them tips over and rolls, an assistant sets it back upright and the div strains his face to slide it forward again. Another div skips in and plucks the huge weight from the floor with one finger. She smirks and hurls it towards them. The assistant ducks just in time, and the other div catches the kettlebell. He looks at her with a furrowed brow, but they all laugh.

I pass a glass window open to a shooting gallery, but instead of guns, swifts, or sonic cannons, the divs fire from their bare hands. A small stream of blue lightning, a whip of highly focused air, a blade of white light. All three pierce their targets at the center. I've only heard of divs with such physical capabilities. One of the gifted divs, the lightning thrower, looks over her shoulder and snickers at me.

I take a deep breath. The whole place smells like eucalyptus. Everyone has the same matching sleek grey training gear with red trim, including me, thanks to Griselda.

As I walk through the facility, I want to be a part of their club. The Shadow pulls at and amplifies my insecurities.

Don't even want slow learners on their clunky station.

It snuffs out my brief dreams.

Sliding doors which seal off the pool area open as I step to them. The absurdity and impracticality of a swimming pool on a spaceship hits me, and I wonder about the tech required to ensure that the water stays in the pool in low gravity situations. I shake my head at the willful ignorance of Helixx Corp. The extra gravity generator ring underneath the pool whirs loudly as it holds the water within the pool boundaries. Its low hum becomes soothing background noise.

Above us, lighting panels mimic a sunny day with a fake blue sky and warm artificial sun rays shining down. I think to myself that the artificial sun feels good on my pale skin. I wish I were here to relax and soak it up.

A div dives into the long pool and swims across its length back and forth three times without coming up for air. I stop and count for three minutes, and he's still going when I hear someone call my name.

I turn to see three figures—one Griselda's hologram. One of them wears the red and orange uniform of the Helixx Corp Sages. The other div turns slowly, and I realize who I am looking at when I see the sun-like light sparkling along the crystals growing out of her face.

"Zinwara! Are you joining the crew here?"

"Ah! Casey!" Griselda gestures towards Zinwara. "This is your gift!"

Zinwara does a double take, looks slightly offended, more baffled.

"Did I say something wrong?" Griselda asks, feigning innocence.

Zinwara seems to be at a loss for words.

I speak slowly but wonder if I'm using the right words. "Yeah, Dr. Ferand. I don't think it's cool to refer to anyone who's Black as someone's 'gift.'"

"You know, because slavery," Zinwara adds quickly. There is a note of humor in her voice, but I wonder if she feels offended still.

"Ohnonono!" Ferand looks visibly shaken. "Oh! I didn't think of that. That was so long ago. That's not what I meant. I'm so sorry. I meant that my gift is bringing over a friend from Station Scire. It was not my intention to offend you, Div Osei."

Griselda grimaces and holds her hands up, fingers splayed, anxiously awaiting forgiveness.

Zinwara says nothing.

The Sage smirks and glares at Zinwara's stoic expression.

Ferand looks momentarily miffed that she isn't immediately given what she feels she deserves. She begins looking toward floating screens that are not in the projection.

"I will give you two some time to catch up, while I try to recover from embarrassment," she says.

Zinwara smiles politely, and I follow her lead. The hologram blinks off, and the Sage gestures towards some lounge chairs by the pool. There are several chairs, but the Sage does not join us. We leave him standing in his red and orange robes under the fake blue sky, and we sit.

I gesture towards the div swimming back and forth under the surface. "He still hasn't come up."

"They tell me he can hold his breath for nearly twelve minutes." Zinwara looks unimpressed.

"That's amazing, I guess."

"But a pool? In space? How stupid."

I'm obviously far more excited about the facility than she is.

"Did you see the divs in the firing range?"

She smirks. "Yeah, everyone's been brought out to show off for us like they do for the wealthy wannabes that vacation on this ridiculous ship." She shakes her head slowly at the production and sighs deeply. "I know we don't know each other too well. Not well enough for me to be brought here so you have another friend on board... but I do want to thank you. It was kind of you to write to me while I was in quarantine. I didn't get to see anyone for a long time. Mourned the loss of my crewmates, my captain, alone. Really missed my comp. Your handwritten letters were like medicine. Thank you, Casey."

Her beautiful smile extends to her dark eyes.

I try to meet her eyes but end up glancing toward the spectrolite crystals growing out of her skin. The reports being made about Zinwara's condition have labeled the crystal growth zin-spectrolite. The facets growing out of the healed skin around them hold iridescent streaks within them. If not for the fact that they are growing out of someone's body like some strange parasite, they would be lovely to behold.

I feel gratitude for Franxis for having encouraged me to write those letters. The Shadow stirs, and I turn my attention away from it.

"Haven't seen you since you surprised us during that MaalenKun encounter."

"Oh, yeah. Good times." Her sarcasm makes me laugh out loud. "I really hope all of you Scire divs are not upset with your Sages. I knew they were bridging me, but we had to keep it secret. We didn't want to freak anyone out."

"And yet that happened anyway. I'm just glad we could recover quickly. Otherwise, things could've gone wrong." I quell my annoyance with our Sages' tendency to keep things from us. "How are you now?"

"Fine other than the gnawing concern that comes after meeting casual racism from a very powerful woman."

"That was awkward," I grumble.

Zinwara sucks on her teeth and shakes her head. "Super geniuses with poor social skills."

"Even more awkward than when she gifted me the AI from my room on Scire... but at least that wasn't racist."

"She just went in your room and got your personal AI?" Zinwara raises her eyebrows.

"Technically, she owns the room, or Helixx does anyway. But, yeah."

"People that own so much forget that they don't own everything. Part of the reason I don't work for the UNAF anymore. And to answer your question from earlier, no, I'm not joining this crew. No way could I work for that woman."

I pause for a moment. "Think she really meant that as racist?" I ask.

"I don't think she meant to sound racist. It just happened to come out. She wouldn't be so obvious, I'm sure. Not until she gets what she wants from me, but... Behaviors reveal beliefs and all." She folds her arms across her chest, and I take it as a cue that I'm not the person she wants to talk with about it. She glances over at me and gives me a kind smile. "You're wondering why I'm here though. Why subject myself to more of Helixx Corp?"

"And where The Queen and your crew are..."

"The Queen's still docked nearby on Scire. My stubborn crewmates won't leave without me. They wanted to come here, but Helixx wouldn't allow it unless they paid the standard vacation fees." She smirks; I groan. "I demanded my comp come with me, of course, but I came without the rest because I need to be here to get what I want. My div-attainment is a lodestar. It's not always 100% accurate, but it often shows me where to go to get what I want. It tells me to be here."

"Sounds awesome."

"It's not always," she quips with a firm voice. She softens the blunt response with an ironic smile. "It's what caused me to slip back to Three. After MaalenKun, I sort of wanted to get away from all this. If I ever question whether or not I really want to be a div, I can slip back, lose power. It takes a lot of training to really understand how to use my desire and keep the lodestar pointing me in the right direction. I have to be sure of what I want and not waver, because the lodestar will guide me that way if I'm even toying with a little desire."

"But that's got to make dating easier."

She laughs, "Well, turns out both my crush and my ex are on board."

"Crush? Hmmm... Aaliyah?" I smile, thinking that they would make a cute couple.

"Yeah, but it's complicated." She laughs lightly at her own thoughts but smirks and shakes her head as if telling herself to quell those thoughts.

"Complicated because… Harjaz is your ex?"

"Like I said: complicated." She smirks but not playfully. "I guess technically I'm crushing on them both."

"So, polyamory is why your lodestar told you to get on board a potentially racist trillionaire's extravagant space vessel?"

She laughs lightly. "Maybe. Though, I feel like it has more to do with my strong urge to get rid of the massive, alien crystals growing out of my body." She shrugs. "I don't know how just yet, but my lodestar tells me Helixx Corp can help with that."

"How do you feel?"

She holds her palm up and poses as if she were a sarcastic fashion model, but next to the shockingly large crystal formation growing out of her face, it looks absurd. "All things considered… fabulous."

The zin-spectrolite crystals stem up from her shoulder, her face, and the side of her shaved head. Streaks of gold amidst the light blue to violet ombre crystals glisten in the sun-like.

I don't feel her glean, but I sense that she knows I'm curious.

"Please, don't be shy with me." She still has the sparkle of a smile in her eyes.

"Does it hurt?"

She nods, "I can manage. It itches sometimes, which is a very strange sensation. I'm scared it's growing, but they tell me it's not." She shrugs. "Mostly, it's just weird. I can feel into the crystal. Like if you touch it—but don't, please—I could feel your energy vibrating through the crystal. We think it's kinda synced with my subtle body. And… I hear it. Or something through it. It's like the lodestar in some way. It's like it wants to find something. Weird, I know." She holds her hand out towards me and laughs, and I realize this is her bit. "It's not contagious though. Scire scientists even tried cutting some lab-grown skin with samples they took, but it didn't have the same effect as when MaalenKun attacked us. Mostly, it's just disappointing. Like now, instead of my breasts, people just look at this thing. I'm like, hello, my tits are down here."

I throw my head back and laugh harder than I've laughed in years.

The Helixx Corp Sage glares at us. Zinwara chuckles with me as I collect myself.

Her mood seems to have shifted. "And, at least, the thing's not heavy. Or I'd have neck issues for sure."

"Really?"

"Yeah, it's light as air as far as I can tell. All the tiny samples taken seem to be almost weightless, too. It's like the crystal doesn't obey the same laws of physics or something."

"Oscar will find all of this very interesting."

"The Level Five from Mani." She smirks. "He's so handsome. Are y'all a thing?"

"Uh... yeah." The Shadow creeps up, but the glow in my heart overtakes it. "I think I might have it pretty bad for him."

Something flashes in her eyes as if she has accidentally transferred something from me. She raises her eyebrows, and her smile brightens her cheeks.

"That's nice, but..." she says. "Helixx obviously has their own reason for keeping you here. Think this might be your new gig?"

I laugh lightly and shake my head. "I'm not like the divs on this ship. Pretty sure my comp and I are done with Helixx anyway. When Central says we're free to go, we're gone."

Somberly, she says, "We lost a few mates and our captain out in the wings when MaalenKun showed up. We could use you on The Queen if you want to go indie. We don't have a swimming pool, but..." We both laugh. "We get by all right. I'll admit it's nice to not have to answer to Central." She smiles and playfully says, "And maybe you could finish the designs on those pod ships so people stop asking about the empty ports."

I appreciate the light teasing. Feels like we're becoming friends. "Scire might have that hyperspeed CEA finished by the time you guys leave. Maybe you can retrofit The Queen before you go."

She laughs, "Our secret reason for sticking around."

I smile back and nod, "I'll see what Franxis thinks. Your offer is the best we've gotten yet."

"It's the only offer, isn't it?"

"Yep." I nod emphatically.

She smiles wide, and we turn our faces up towards the warm sun-like.

I add, "In the meantime, we're here."

"Indeed. Helixx was nice enough to make me this custom gear, but I wish it was in my ship's colors." She nods down at a perfectly tailored opening in her uniform for the crystals growing out of her shoulder. "I've also been doing some training with their Sages. I lost Four for a bit, but I've got it back. Helixx Sages helped me level back up, and they locked it in pretty easily." She glances over at the Sage. "This guy's supposed to take me to some field and give me pointers on how to teleport."

"He can teleport? That's amazing!"

"There's more to it than that, but yes. Anyway, since you're one of the few people I've met on this fancy ship, I'd love your company. From what they tell me, you have a strong empathic power, can sync another div's abilities, so they want you to psybridge with us—"

"I'm not trying to teleport!" I shake my head emphatically. "I've got to get more practice at drawing attainments from others before anything so risky."

"They just want you to observe, maybe help support."

"Well, in that case, I'm in."

The grassy field of verdant grasses and occasional clusters of exotic flora is covered in an arched ceiling of metaglass. Stars shine above us. In the distance, several wings stand guard between our world and whatever lurks in the half-glow of the rift.

As our small transport rolls across the green toward another car, we see three more figures. Our comps stand next to another Helixx Sage and wave to us.

A hint of a smile emerges, and my mood lifts when I see Franxis.

We get closer, and I notice that Ehsan has an atypical limb. His left arm extends 15 centimeters below his elbow, and he has a custom uniform with a short sleeve that stops above his elbow. I'm reminded of when I was five years old, and I asked my mother's father if his hand had been cut off or if he had been born that way. I don't remember his answer, but I remember my father scolding me for asking.

When we get closer, I notice a few unusual tech implants in his forearm next to a tattoo of swirling script that reads: "Hold fast."

Ehsan's unified eyebrow lifts and his painted neon blue lips make an exaggerated smirk when he makes eye contact with his div. Zinwara returns her own knowing smirk, and I'm sure the two are gossiping through their psybridge. Ehsan's uniform in The Queen's colors reminds me that the two of them are independent, not beholden to Helixx, the UNAF, or Central. They're friendly, but not committed to me or my crew.

The moment I see them, Franxis rolls their eyes at the long, grassy field that has been brought to space. In an incredulous tone, they transfer, *Rich people…*

"Is this field only used for teleportation training?" Zinwara asks the Sages.

The Helixx Sage who escorted us in snorts and replies, "Of course not. It's such a rare ability. This is a hunting range."

"People come to space to hunt animals?" I make no attempt to hide my disdain.

"Sometimes. Reduced gravity gives tourists the ability to leap far and fast with each step, and we put custom grav boots on game so they move a bit slower than they would planetside. It gives the hunter quite a thrill to chase down deer."

"Disgusting," Zinwara asserts to the Sage's face, and I can literally feel my respect for her expanding.

"That was years ago." The other Helixx Sage, who looks so much like our escort, says as he waves a hand dismissively. "Now, this space is primarily used to hunt EDB."

"What?" Zinwara and Ehsan both sound surprised.

With eyes wide, Franxis quickly turns towards me and transfers, *We have to find new jobs immediately. I can't work for idiots.*

"Well, we've only had a few guests choose the experience. It is rather pricey. But there was no real danger. A div was standing by in case the hunter's charger cannons failed, and the EDBs were mostly benign anyway."

I signal concern for Vasif to Franxis, and they agree. They immediately open a holoscreen and begin texting a message to Oscar on the EDB science deck with Vasif.

The other Sage adds, "We have a more affordable experience coming soon. Our scientists have been working on manufacturing a synthetic EDB. Essentially, it will be a cloud much like many conscious EDBs, and we will be able to control it from nanotech within the cloud. Hunters will have a similar experience to crystalizing an EDB, comparable to what our divs in the field achieve. I believe Div Kenzari is assisting our scientists with this project today."

Franxis blows right past the mention of Oscar. "So then, you've got handheld chargers? Why hasn't that tech been shared with the UN-divs on the ground or the stations? I'd think Scire would have that tech, since it's a Helixx Corp property now."

Ehsan nods in agreement.

"Ah! Well, I'm just a Sage here." He feigns humility. "I don't know much about tech distribution."

As he makes his point, I realize why the two Helixx Sages look so much alike. "Are you two twins?"

They flash identical smiles.

"We are," our escort says.

"Fraternal," the other says. "My name is Sigrund, my brother's name is Runar. And we know your names. We know a lot about all of you." His tone is polite, but a chill still runs through me. Franxis signals that they share the same feeling. "Let's get down to business, shall we?"

Runar waves his arm, and I notice a light flash from the tech in his gauntlet. A grey case nearby hovers closer to us. Its locks spin and unfasten. Runar places his palm on top of the case, and the seal breaks with a hiss of air.

The grin on Runar's face reminds me of when I used to take the first hit after days of craving anything that would get me high. It's been decades since

I've even thought of that feeling, but the memory rushes back to me now. This is their drug.

Sigrund lifts the lid of the case. Inside, nestled in custom-shaped memory foam is a single large crystal shard. Within the smoky quartz runs a vein of iridescent blue-pearl. Whatever the EDB was before it was crystalized, it was also beautiful. Sigrund traces his fingers across the length of the shard. Runar's breath quivers ever so slightly.

"What is it?" Zinwara asks.

"This, Div Osei, is how we train you."

"Divs, prepare to psybridge." Sigrund is also eager, but he hides it well enough behind an order to commence training. "Comps, you should stabilize your divs."

"Hold up. First, tell me what the plan is." Zinwara points toward the crystal. "Second, you tell me where you got this thing and what that EDB did."

"Third, slow your roll a bit." Ehsan adds. "We're not moving fast with this. We are in no rush."

The twin Sages seem surprised to hear a lithe and effeminate guy with a nasal voice demanding such a clear boundary.

Sigrund gives Runar a scolding look.

"Of course, of course," they both say.

Sigrund tries to recover by answering. "In our explorations, we have encountered many extradimensional beings. Near Ceres, we encountered an EDB capable of teleportation. We believe it came from a rift far away, much like the infamous Bakkeaux."

"What was it doing on Ceres?" Franxis asks, and I hear the skepticism in their voice.

Sigrund begins to shrug his shoulders, but Runar interjects. "We had reason to believe it would target the Earth. Perhaps the same way MaalenKun did, using an asteroid from the belt in some way."

"When we saw that it could teleport, we sent out wings to hunt it down," Sigrund adds. "This shard will give my brother and me access to that EDB's power."

"When we leveled up to Four long ago, we discovered that we could channel energy contained in crystals," Runar nearly brags. "We experimented first with all the crystals used in div-tech. I'm sure you're familiar with their qualities of bringing focus, clarity, protection. Master-Doctor Ferand recruited us, gave us the opportunity to broaden our horizons. Helixx Corp trained us to draw the power of crystalized EDBs from the remnants of battles waged by you divinators. With some crystals we're even able to use an EDB's ability against the Risen even if that EDB could not."

"Why would you?" Franxis blurts.

"For defense training, of course." Runar shrugs.

Sigrund looks down at the crystal in the case and then at Zinwara. "And we believe that with Div Isaac's empathic abilities, we will be able to share at least the knowledge of teleportation with you, Div Osei." He does his best to look patient. "We do not expect you to test any abilities until you feel prepared. But we all know teleportation is within the realm of possibility, because you've already achieved it."

Zinwara raises her eyebrows, "So we just psybridge while you two transfer some knowledge, correct?"

"Of course, of course." The Helixx Sages hold out their hands, gesturing for us to stand in front of them.

Zinwara steps forward, and I follow. "Do we need comps to buffer?"

"Couldn't hurt," Runar says as he reaches a hand towards the crystal.

Franxis opens their comp-bridge wide and steady, but I detect their reservations.

I wish Mira were here to tell us what's coming next, they transfer.

I quash the urge to comment on the Sages. I don't want them finding an echo of it when they psybridge us. I try to signal to Franxis that I want to trust them, but the Shadow twists around the signal. It shows me that I don't trust the Helixx Sages. I try to quell it, but it lingers in the periphery of my mind.

Your signal has static. Franxis' transference is full of worry, but I've already begun opening to the Sage's psybridge.

It rushes into us hard, nearly bowling us over. Franxis falls silent in their effort to stabilize me. It's the most forceful sync I have ever experienced.

Zinwara raises her voice. "Ease up!"

The force dials down.

I apologize. Sigrund looks almost sincere. *I think I'm more accustomed to our divs on The Eminent. We have a different training here. Quicker sync, I guess.*

Zinwara holds her hand out to me, and I take it. I recall the feeling of helping Oscar strengthen his psybridge. I draw my empathic attainment forth. A hint of sweetness emerges, and I know it's from Oscar. The delight, the joy in connecting is key. The divination moves from within me to Zinwara, Franxis, and Ehsan. They correlate it easily. The Sages seem to fumble with its sweetness for a moment before finally integrating it into their own.

Both Sages place their hands onto the crystal. Runar briefly closes his eyes as if he is savoring the sensation. Their fingers splay wide, and their third eyes begin to fill with vibrating, blue-pearl light.

Runar transfers, *We begin now.*

A vortex flies forth violently from Runar's third eye and into the crystals growing out of Zinwara's body. The force shakes her. She looks towards me, and through the rippling vortex, flashing with light, I see that her eyes are wide with shock. She squeezes my hand and closes her eyes.

I gaze at the light-thread between the Helixx Sages' third eyes, and I begin to coordinate the energy within myself. My empathic abilities seem to be getting more easeful and fluid. I draw the brunt of the force away from Zinwara. The vortex pummels energy into me, but Zinwara is steadier. She trembles but receives the force with greater clarity. Ehsan works to help anchor her. I realize that the Helixx Sages wanted me here to serve as another buffer, siphoning off their aggressive force.

I shine my heartstar to strengthen the light-thread of connection between me and Zinwara. I reach out to her to offer support from me, from Franxis, to sync with the support from Ehsan. The vortex enters us all. The comps grab our hands, and our bodies shake.

As his eyes roll back in his head, Runar bears the vortex down on us.

He transfers coldly, *This will be easier, if you kneel.*

The crystalized EDB's prowess hits us like rapid tidal waves. Between the waves, we can sense each other losing stability. The Sages alone are steady in all this. As the waves rock us, our knees buckle. The information in the waves of light crackles around Zinwara.

We stumble to our knees, holding tight to each other.

Zinwara strains to say, "Lodestar is telling me to open our eyes to their eyes!"

I focus my empathic energy towards my third eye. I feel the energy turning as if it is moving the skin of my forehead. It opens, spilling out bright blue light.

I direct my mystic gaze to the shining third eyes of the Helixx Sages. The fast threads between them begin to shine into the vortex. The pearl light aligns, touching Zinwara's crystals and shimmering across their surfaces. Zinwara opens herself to it. The light enters into the zin-spectrolite and the beautiful array of colors within them begins to shift and radiate. The rivulets of pearl light move through the formations and deeper into Zinwara. Her head snaps back and her eyes roll back. A sound of uncontainable pleasure and pain escapes her mouth. She centers herself, faces forward, and opens her fiery eyes to look at Sigrund.

Runar's eyes roll forward, and he blinks hard several times as we siphon his proficiency of how to sort the extradimensional knowledge. A flash of anger spreads across his face.

Sigrund snaps, *That's enough, Runar!*

Runar continues to bear the vortex down on us, bashing us with its waves.

"Slow it down!" Zinwara shouts.

Begrudgingly, Runar dials down the force of the vortex, and the pulses become lengthened but bearable thrusts.

Zinwara bows her head.

I open my empathic connection to Zinwara, and she signals for me to notice her heart. Inside, she is weeping with compassion. The EDB was a gentle being. Its knowledge echoes in her, creating beautiful iridescent flashes that merge with the contours of her mind.

I open myself to compassion for the being, and a flash of its fate plays out before me. The Helixx team came down on it, and it didn't fight back. It was so gentle. They immediately crystalized it and killed it.

There's a sense of unfolding around Zinwara. Prescience. One of the pulses moves through the psybridge and into me. It unfolds into a quick flash of multiple colors of light moving in me, but they pass quickly.

The Shadow peers into me. My spine goes cold. The Shadow stalks forward like a predator. I am being hunted. I try to brighten my heartstar, try to refocus my gaze, but the Shadow has hooked my awareness. I signal to Franxis, but Franxis cannot sense it. I try to signal the others, but the signal is lost.

I force my voice out in a strained cry. Franxis moves closer as Zinwara and Ehsan turn towards me.

The twin Sages seem to be deaf to my cries. The Shadow grows harder, and I feel it pulling at my subtle body, snagging mind and breath in searing pain as it bounds towards the radiating Haddyc wound.

I overhear Sigrund again.

Div Isaac's eyes...

Both Sages step closer, their own eyes wide. Again, Runar looks too eager, too greedy.

Franxis, still bearing a good share of the vortex thrashing, turns to me and with their free hand, grabs me and turns my face to meet theirs. As Franxis' eyes go wide, they intentionally transfer a flash of their vision to me. Fear grips my throat. My eyes grow dim and distant. The grey and green colors of my irises merge with my pupils into a reflection of brassy yellow, like an animal caught in headlights. The vision of my own eyes changing alarms me, yet I see through them just fine.

The Shadow crouches as if to pounce, and hisses, ***Your body... your mind... your power—***

I pull the psybridge back and I push Zinwara away.

—are mine!

The Shadow pounces on the pearl light with rows of jagged teeth and begins tearing into it. Only Franxis remains psybridged to me. Part of me is desperate for Franxis to at least catch a glimpse of the Shadow, but they don't see it. Franxis moves to stabilize me, mentally and physically, reaching their mind toward my nimbus, their arms toward my body. I waver and Franxis catches me. Their concern is interrupted by shock and horror.

In a bloody flash, something cuts its way out of my arm, my uniform.

A light-refusing void, like clear liquid-glass, surges up from the gash in my arm. Inside the void, distorting everything we can see through it, the Shadow swirls. The substance shapes itself into sharp, jagged extensions, like claws ripping through the world around me. It undulates in jagged and irregular outcrops sharp enough to literally cut through open space.

The vibrations coming from it jerk my arm upwards. The void severs the light-threads between the twin Sages' third eyes and Zinwara. As the connection breaks, everyone winces from the flash of heat stinging our foreheads. The vortex sputters out, and Sigrund is knocked back onto the ground. Ehsan pulls Zinwara away as she scrambles back. Franxis wraps their arms around me tight, but I push away, trying to keep them safe. The pulsing void slings my arm across the space. The sharp edges of the flickering void cut through the air towards the twins, and Sigrund knocks over the hovering case. The crystal falls to the ground, and Runar fumbles after it. The void yanks my arm toward the crystal, towards Runar. It feels as if it is going to dislocate my shoulder. It pulls my arm back towards Zinwara, toward her zin-spectrolite crystals.

A flash of blue-pearl light envelopes me. My entire being feels impossibly spacious before it is pulled back into a familiar solidity. A glimpse of Zinwara, her crystals glowing with shifting reflective colors, moves away quickly as she lets me go. The light of the blue-pearl flash is suddenly replaced with the field around us, stars above us.

After the teleportation jump, the force of her shove propels me further away. I hit the grass, trying to hold my arm away from me. I can't find my footing. I roll. I feel the void and the smokey Shadow within retreat into the phantom pain of the Haddyc sting. The wound is not healed the way I thought it was. Instead, the wound is a home for some horror.

"Stay down, Casey," Zinwara commands firmly.

"Wasn't supposed to teleport today," I groan before the feeling of defeat overtakes me. I hold my arm and focus my divination on the cut. It begins to heal immediately. I look back at the others. They are fifty yards away, except for Franxis who is running towards us.

"Thank you, Zinwara." I mumble. "Keep them away. I-I'm sorry..."

"It's going to be okay, Casey." Zinwara urges. "Just stay there until we figure this out."

The flicker on my periphery returns. It's the same as when I had the div-bar removed, and I remember seeing it when Oscar was in my dream. Maybe my brain is not integrating info from my peripheral vision. Maybe it's nothing. I have no mental energy to wonder what the flicker is, why it returns.

I fall back against the grass, panting. I hear Zinwara telling Franxis to stay back until they know it's safe. Through our connection, Franxis wraps me in their care, and I feel them signaling the sensation of being held. My fear makes it harder to receive Franxis' care, but it also leaves me with certainty.

I am certain now that the Shadow is dangerous. And I'm not alone in that knowledge.

ꝏ

decrypted message sent to Griselda Harris Ferand from Helixx Sage Sigrund
15 April, 2031

Those bleeding-heart divs will surely get word back to Div Kenzari that the nanotech is to replace EDBs on the Hunting Field. I feel we do not need to worry that he will suspect anything.

You will be pleased to know that during Div Osei's first teleportation training, the unintegrated extradimensional energy inside of Div Isaac emerged. They are indeed the Unlit, as you theorized. Div Isaac was injured as the Unlit emerged from his body in a large wave which he was unable to restrain. It appears to have its own consciousness. The Unlit seemed poised to attack the crystal from the vault (containing remnants of EDB9175-04; prowess—teleportation) or perhaps, the void would have attacked Runar. The moment was interrupted when Div Osei teleported Div Isaac further away. Clearly, the transfer of teleportation knowledge was integrated within Osei and—we suspect—the zin-spectrolite crystals.

Success all around. I suggest continued training sessions with both before harvest.

ꝏ

OSCAR

I hover over the holoscreen displaying results from the last scan.

"Well…?" Mira asks.

I look up and smile.

Mira's shoulders ease with relief.

"For the record please, Div Kenzari," one of Helixx's scientists prompts.

"The Haddyc energy that was within Vasif can no longer be found. Appears Vasif shed the toxic energy it had been working to restrain into StillRift-2138, along with MaalenKun. We no longer need worry about that lattice of almost invisible vines that came from Vasif in Ecuador."

A ripple of disturbance moves through the network of psybridges I hold. A strong disruption moves from Casey toward us. My first thought is that Casey has put up an obscuration. I immediately feel insecure and clingy. Then, I sense the movement of something.

A Shadow.

A voice rolls from Vasif's chest through the shifting mists of its neck and is funneled out of its face. Its multi-layered voice doesn't settle into one chord. Instead, its voice is slightly buzzy, organic but almost robotic, clearly not human.

"Danger. Casey."

It's the first time the EDB has said any of our names, and it carries with it the weight of worry.

My heart pounds.

"We need to go," Mira says through the psybridge to Vasif and out loud to the crew of Helixx Corp scientists observing us.

From the viewing room above the lab floor, our comps signal that they'll meet us at the door.

"Get location on Div Isaac," I bark at the young man closest to an array of holoscreens.

He looks baffled. A Helixx Corp lab technician shouts at him to snap out of it, and he springs into action. The young man swipes away one of the holoscreens and lifts another as Mira and I pull back the psybridge from Vasif.

"He's at the Hunting Field," the young man says.

"Hunting field?" Mira questions.

"Where?" I snap at the technician.

"Nine decks to the top, lower level, stern," one of the scientists says to us as we're on our way out the sliding doors.

I try to reach Casey through our psybridge. The Shadow is gone. I turn up the power of our connection. What I hear is breaking up, but it sounds like him, just stuttering in and out. I try to reach him on the comm in my gear. Nothing.

Franxis' slightly shaky voice comes through Thiia's handheld as Thiia and Carmel trot towards us. "I don't know what happened, but he's hurt. The thing he kept telling us was... It came out..."

"We're on our way." I manage to get the words out without choking on them, but my throat is tight.

"Stay safe, Franxis." Carmel says.

We run through the spacious hallways past the crew and tourist-bots who stare at us blankly. I want them all to run towards him. I want everyone to stop what they are doing and see to his safety and care. I want to see at least some sign that someone on the crew of this luxury yacht gives a damn.

The door to the hyperloop ahead opens for a group of tourist bots.

"There's an emergency! We need that car!" Thiia shouts.

The robots rush to get on board, and they seal the door behind themselves as we reach them. I slam my fist on the window.

"Selfish pricks!" Carmel scorns.

The digital screens turn sour faces toward us, and their car zooms away down the track.

"Another car is coming, Oscar," Thiia says as Carmel pushes the call button. A steady stream of patience, centering calm, moves from her to me.

I do my best to integrate Thiia's grounding assistance. I run my hand over my beard.

"They've cleared the field, except for Casey. MedOps is sending in drones," a face on Thiia's hand-held reports.

My heart is beating fast. I move to unsnap some of the combat gear we've been testing.

"Keep it." Carmel nods towards my gear, and my stomach drops.

"What are his injuries?" Mira asks the face on the screen.

The Ops officer turns to a screen out of projection, "Large gash in his left arm—"

"Haddyc injury," Carmel mumbles.

Ops casually says, “Possibly EDB related, but no EDBs were released in the field today.”

“What the fuck?” Carmel says as another car slides to a stop. The channel doors slide open, and we board the car. “They really hunt EDBs?”

“Yeah,” I sigh. “We found out on the floor today. The synthezoids I’ve been working on are supposed to replace the actual EDBs in training, but I take it they’ve let tourists crystallize the real thing.”

“Unbelievable,” Thiia says shaking her head. “Actually, no, that’s believable unfortunately.”

I stroke my beard again, leaning forward in my seat. Thiia puts her hand on my shoulder, and I feel her energy grounding me.

We ride in silence as the car zips through the network of channels throughout the massive yacht. Soon, it drops us off on the top deck. An escort waits for us at the channel door, he waves away a tourist bot who is asking for a ride and calls us over. We step on board, and the car hovers across the sunstar deck, past the observatory, past the sardonyx cannons, and alongside an empty banquet room.

“Get Harjaz and Aaliyah to the field,” Carmel whispers. “I want our own medic on this.”

“Helixx might not let a comp with a secondary medic role do anything, but I’ll get them in route.” Mira taps a message into the comm, and it chimes.

“Is that them, already?” Carmel asks.

“MedOps. They’ve got a drone nearby, but Casey’s quiet.”

The metaglass dome bubble covering the open top deck arches up in the distance. Inside is a long stretch of grass, a field. Another small hovering car with a red cross and flashing red and white lights moves through the opening, and I feel a mix of relief that they have medics on the way and anger that they’re not there already. A group of people are milling about, looking off in the distance. We cannot see what they are looking at with the med-cars in the way, but we know it’s Casey.

When we get out of the escort car and join them, my heart sinks. He’s so far away, at least a hectometer out. The open space around him makes him look smaller. He lies on the grass unmoving. A solitary drone hovers near him.

Franxis emerges from the crowd and embraces me first. Their face is streaked with tears, and their hair is disheveled. As we hold each other, I feel a quivering within them.

“We’re going to take care of him,” I say.

“They won’t let me go near him, but they said since you were in quarantine with him before… it doesn’t make sense.” They look both confused to be held back and relieved that I can go to him.

“He’s going to be okay.”

“I’m glad you’ve got gear on. Go.”

Their words are like ice-water in my spine.

As Carmel and Mira move to speak with the medical team, I notice security amongst the group. They are taller than average divs, heavily armored in bright red, with stun-batons hanging from their belts. There are more of the Red Guard than there are doctors. A man from the medical crew stands in front of a holoscreen, displaying the image from the drone. Casey is on his side, holding his bloody left arm. He is curled into a fetal position with his head tucked in as if he is trying to protect his heart.

A beautiful woman with a crystal formation growing out of her face and shoulders waves at me. Zinwara Osei.

"Oscar?" she asks as she approaches.

I nod.

"Red Guard wants us far away, or I'd still be out there." She looks from Casey towards me. "What do you need right now, Oscar?"

"I need to be closer to him."

"I'll walk with you."

We're only a few steps out when the Guard shouts at us to come back. "We're sealing off the area, everyone out."

Zinwara looks at me, and I tell her, "It's okay."

She steps back without me.

I turn up my shield generator. A flicker of prismatic light slides around me.

"I'm going to him," I tell the guard.

The guard sneers and steps toward me, but another guard grabs him by the arm. He has a finger against his earpiece.

"Let him go." They both turn back toward the crowd. "Everyone else, clear the field."

My crew looks back at me. Carmel and Mira have been talking to the doctors. They signal that his physical injury appears to have already healed.

"Franxis—" At the sound of their name, they step forward as if they are eager to come with me. A guardsman holds up one hand in front of them, his other hand hovers over the shock baton in his holster. "—it's okay." I transfer the rest: *They'll probably want you to unbridge with him, but I can bring you in.*

Do it. Franxis replies. *I'm with you. Both.*

Our psybridge is set before Franxis stops talking.

Ahead of me, Casey lies in the middle of open space, and I'm struck by how alone he appears. I try to shine my care through the light-thread between us. I try to find him in our psybridge. I sense only that he is there. No movement, no return.

As I cross the field, I try to imagine what Casey is going through. He's been hurt so much. A memory of our encounter in his dreamscape surfaces, and my heart aches for him. He's been hurting for so long. Seeing his body curled on the ground ahead of me, I realize what he feels, that there's not much more, if any, that he can take.

My eyes stay on him as I walk closer. About ten paces away, he senses me approaching. I feel both relief and shame wash through him. He doesn't quell the emotions. I don't think he can. But he psychically reaches for me.

My heart swells. The light-thread becomes a line, conveying tenderness more fully.

His transference is faint, weak. *Hey, handsome.*

Hey, beautiful.

A bit of tempered delight comes back.

He signals for me to stay back but doesn't say why. He moves uncomfortably, adjusts, and resettles into the same fetal position. He keeps his head tucked and face covered. He snorts, and I can hear a joke coming.

"Hello, dear," he says, sounding almost like a polite stay-at-home partner but for a bit of exhausted cracking in his voice. "How was work today?"

"Oh, very interesting." With an almost genuine chuckle, I kneel down. "My co-worker Vasif asked about you."

"That's your friend from Ecuador?"

"Well, not originally." Our light laughter feels more genuine now, and I see that he's lifting my spirits as best as he can.

"What did y'all do today?"

"Helixx has been working on a synthetic cloud to mimic the EDBs. They brought me in to help integrate the gasses with the crystalized EDB remains in their nano-drones and test it with our Ecuadorian friend. Mostly, they just wanted to know what Vasif thought of it, but you know, Vasif doesn't talk to them so much."

"Tell Vasif hi for me when you go in tomorrow."

"I was thinking maybe we'd just spend the day at home tomorrow."

He sniffles. I can sense his tears without looking at his face. "Sounds nice. I would like to do that. I might be busy though."

"Oh? What do you have going on?"

A bittersweet sound is carried on his sigh. "Well.... it's just—" He holds up his arm. A long pink line of injury is healing quickly. "I got hurt at work today... and the company I'm working for has, you know, policies about this kind of injury. I might have to quarantine alone this time... just to keep you safe."

The drone quietly sweeps around us.

I inch a bit closer to him, and he springs halfway out of the fetal position. "Oscar, you should stay back!"

"I want to see your face." I whisper. "Please, just look up, Casey."

His groan turns into words. "I don't want you to be afraid."

"I promise I won't—"

But when he looks up, I realize that I cannot keep that promise. I can only do my best to not let my fear show.

The color has mostly drained from his face. His eyelids are red and raw as if he's been rubbing them for days, and his beautiful eyes are changed. The green and grey colors of his irises are gone. Shining back at me is a disc of brassy yellow light.

"You said you wouldn't be afraid."

"Can't hide it, can I?" I open to him further, drop any obscurations. As he does the same, my heart aches. I don't know how to help him, and it pains me.

Tightness in my chest begins to draw the line between him and me. I shine my heartstar to transform it into compassion, strengthening our light-line. His pain, or at least some of it, becomes mine—ours.

Our highlighted interconnection opens my Levels above, and a flare pours down from Six and into Five where most of it lands and integrates to move me closer to Six. It rains down on me. My third eye begins to radiate. Slowly, my perception begins to take in Casey's aura. Murky shades of anxiety, gradients of grey depression emanate around him. Only a few spots of pink and purple can move through the muddled glow.

I see him more clearly, even as he looks away and sinks his head back to the ground. I notice his breath moving his body. An echo of him holding me, encouraging me to steep in the beauty of our breath moves between us. A note of joy rises as we remember the moment together.

Even now our breath is syncing, finding harmony.

A movement of light pink glow emerges in his aura. He returns his gaze to me, unguarded. But a flood of his memories overtakes him with insecurity. His pink glow sinks behind the gloom again.

I want him to use his empathic power, to see my aura, see it bright with the love I feel for him. But I don't want to ask anything of him at the moment.

His cloudy aura shifts, his pink glow moves closer to the surface. "I feel your aura more than I see it."

I extend my hand to him. The shimmer of the shield passes over my hand, but he rests his hand on it and smiles at me weakly. I call forth all of my ability to speak with the power of Five and make true. "You're going to be okay, Casey. We got you."

I feel the words land within him and again, I see the Shadow. It shrieks and moves to hide deeper within him. His pink glow transmutes to a warmer orange, but again the gloom takes it over. The sunset colors lie behind the woe.

Over his shoulder, I notice three figures moving closer to us. I can see only one of their auras. The central figure with a familiar stride is surrounded by a bright red and yellow glow. I see no similar glow around the other two. I blink and the ability is gone, but I keep my eyes on them until they come into focus.

Two Helixx MedOps walk side by side with a hovering container floating in front of them. They're the two whose auras I could not see. The third person is Aaliyah. All three of them wear combat gear, prismatic shields up. The Helixx medical team stops ten yards away, but without pause, Aaliyah marches toward us.

I hear a light chime in my helmet as they patch in their comms.

"Hey, our orders—" one of the MedOps calls to her.

Aaliyah doesn't bother to look back. "You thought I'd follow orders?" She waves at us but speaks to them. "Just send the tech along. Don't make him walk to it."

Casey's body grows tense, his mind taut as Aaliyah comes to his side. He starts to tell her that it's risky to be so close.

"I'm not scared of you, Casey." The hovering case moves in closer. "And before you start, I'm not scared of whatever it is that hurt you either. I just want to make sure you're okay, and if you're not, I'm gonna help you get better. Got it?"

"Okay," he says.

The surveillance drone hovers closer to us.

Aaliyah pops open the hovering container. Inside is Casey's old, Scire-issued combat gear. "We're gonna get this shield around you, so we can get you to med bay." Her words are careful, her voice is casual. She doesn't mention quarantine. "Guess you two are psybridged, and maybe Franxis is still dialed in?"

Casey shakes his head yes. He's keeping his eyes low. He doesn't want Aaliyah to see the change in them.

"Okay," Aaliyah says as she takes the tech out of the container. She passes it to me, so Casey doesn't have to look up. "Considering what happened and that we don't know what this thing can do, we're gonna need everyone to unbridge from Casey." She looks in my eyes and a spark of transference rushes into my mind and unfolds. *They're listening.* She nudges my attention to the nearby drone. *Just dial down very low, but do not disconnect from him.*

I do what she says while transferring to Casey: *I'm still with you.*

As I tone down the psybridge to a thin but consistent connection, I hear his reply.

Always.

I sit on the edge of the bed after a night of studying data on the extradimensional substance within my lover. I am typically up at this time every cycle, but this morning, I haven't slept. This is the time of the morning cycle when I usually stretch and meditate. Today, those practices seem like a waste of time. I know my mind will not focus if I am in here alone—if I don't know how Casey is doing.

When I turn the lights up, a pleasant chime rings to indicate a waiting message. I walk to the panel at the desk and tap the message icon. A scanned, hand-written note from Casey says only: "Stop worrying. Go to work. Get your mind on something else. xo"

I wonder if my worrying and restlessness could be felt through the faint psybridge left in place. I can barely feel him through our connection, but maybe he can feel my worry. When I focus on him, there are shadows that make it difficult to tell if he's sleeping or awake, but I can feel that he's there.

The light-line between us glimmers with compassion, and I notice it moving in both directions. Even in all of his fear and distress, he is sending care to me, because he knows I'm worried.

I swipe away his message. I'll do as he says and go to work, try to put my mind on something else, but first I want to see him. My fingers move slower and slower as I punch in the number for the nurse's station in the quarantine ward, but I stop short of putting the call through. Maybe, it's best to give him space, but my heart is aching. My finger lingers over the delete button before I hold it down to clear the number off the comm.

I lean back in the chair, and run both hands down the sides of my beard.

We know that Casey is being watched, but we don't know to what extent Helixx's MedOps are monitoring him. The information being shared with me is basic, far too basic considering Casey has within his being an unknown substance which may or may not have its own consciousness. I am absolutely certain that things are being kept from me, but I have no idea why. I pull up his file to see if the video feed from last night has been made available to me. It is, and I press play and speed through the silent footage.

Casey sits on the floor, hunched forward, apparently speaking to the holographic cat in next to him. There is no audio file attached, and I wonder if it exists at all. Casey works on a holographic model as he speaks to Lilly. Using his aerospace design skills, he creates what appears to be a drone. He's possibly pulling down designs for advanced tech from his divination.

I speed up the video looking for any significant change in behavior, but Casey and the holographic cat sit that way for four hours. When, I finally notice a change, I stop the fast-play and skip back. The holograms blink off, Casey stands up, and turns his gaze toward the camera. His face is pallid, and his eyes are still brassy yellow, reflecting a bit of the light.

Feels like he's looking at me. Into me. But it's not him.

My spine is ice.

I watch the video as Casey moves over to the bed and curls up into a fetal position, pulling the weighted blanket over himself. The lights dim, but I get the sense he isn't sleeping, just lying still. I speed up the video, but it only shows Casey lying as still as a stone save for his breath until the end of the 24-hour cycle. At that point the video abruptly ends. There is no video for today's cycle available.

He feels me watching last night's security feed. He senses my troubled mind. A flash moves through our psybridge, and transference lands in my mind.

Give me some space, Oscar.

I feel as if I've been punched in the stomach. My heart drops.

Through what remains of our toned-down psychic connection, I sense that he does not want to strengthen it. I tell myself that may be because he is worried that thing might move through our psybridge toward me or that he does not want MedOps to know that we are psybridged. My heart hurts with feelings of rejection. My mind spins with inadequacy.

I'm being pushed away. It is difficult to accept that's what he needs, and he needs me to give it to him.

ꝏ

After a few stretches, I start moving my body to burn off some anxious energy. After working up enough of a sweat, I jump in the ultra-light shower. Thanks to div-endurance, my eyes in the mirror look unaffected by a night without sleep. What I do see is the troubled look in my eyes. I smile like everything's fine, try to hide the worry, but I can tell that I'm faking, and it feels dishonest. I can still see the sadness. I smooth my freshly trimmed beard with my hands. The sensation soothes and centers me. My mind feels clear. There's no real benefit to me or anyone else if I try to seem less bothered than I am.

When the door chimes, I know that Mira and probably Carmel and Thiia are on the other side. I'm grateful to know that my crew is always there to prop me up, or let me break down, whatever I need. When I open the door, I'm surprised to see my Old Girl crew, but also Franxis, Aaliyah, Harjaz, Yahima, Pyaar, and Arun as well.

"Yeah, we all love you this much, man." Carmel smirks.

"And Casey too," Arun says.

I'm surprised to feel so much support, and I catch a glimpse of the feelings of unworthiness that Casey sometimes feels. I don't even have to counter the glimpse of feeling. I know it's not real. It fades quickly.

When I step out into the hall, all but the Sages wrap me in a group hug that brings all of us, including the Sages, some much needed laughter. I notice a small package in Yahima's hands, but don't think much of it.

Harjaz says, "I seriously don't have any idea what you might be going through, but I imagine it's not easy. How are you holding up?"

I sigh more because I'm surprised to hear these words coming from Harjaz, even though I've been cold to him, jealous of him. I shake my head slowly and reply, "I'm worried. Didn't really sleep."

Franxis raises their eyebrows, eyes full of sympathy. "Me either." They reach out to me, and I move in for another hug.

Harjaz nods and claps a firm hand on my shoulder. He pats my back. "I'm going to meet with Zinwara today. She and I used to date, decades ago. I think we're on good terms now." Behind Harjaz, Aaliyah rolls her eyes. "I'll see what she has to say about what went down yesterday on the field. I'll get back to you and Carmel about it."

"Let's walk," I say to the large group crowding the hallway. I want to get everyone out in the main corridor to put some space between us and any passing bots or crew. Once we're out in the larger space, I look back over my shoulder to everyone and say, "There's a lot going through my mind." Every single one of them opens to receive my psybridge. I no longer have to be concerned with eavesdroppers. Just in case we're under surveillance, I add, "I'm so worried. I don't think I can eat breakfast."

If we're being scanned for psychic activity, they won't know what we're saying, but they'll still know we were talking about something, Thiia transfers.

I can shield us from any potential scanners, Pyaar says. *As long as we keep the chatter to a minimum.*

Please, feel free to say whatever you need to here, Oscar. Yahima's transference is like song.

Yesterday, I accessed something from Six. I saw Aaliyah's aura, but I couldn't see auras of The Eminent crew members who were walking alongside her. Is that unusual? I ask.

A gist of correlation moves from Arun to Yahima.

Mira replies before anyone else–at a locked in Six, she has the most insight other than the Sages. *I only get random glimpses of auras. I seem to have reached Six and gotten little of that skill in favor of prescience.*

Well, I've noticed, Arun says.

Yahima admits, *Sight for auras does not come to me, either. Arun came to me early in our time here on The Eminent with the same concern. I believe it might be suppressed as a defense strategy by the tech in their uniforms.*

"Can you believe they have a hunting field for EDBs?" Harjaz verbalizes this just in case we're being monitored. A big group of seemingly silent psychics would look suspicious.

Yahima decodes the reminder from Harjaz. *The crew has dealt with many EDBs, and even had some encounters onboard the ship. I feel that the aura concealers are always on because of that. The Eminent has been traveling as far as Jupiter to observe and study EDBs. They've captured several which were later used in developing the new forearm charger cannons and Scire's crystal chamber trap.*

Franxis snorts a reply to both Harjaz and Yahima. "Yeah, one of the Helixx Sages told us that they've let tourists crystalize them."

Several of us notice Yahima quelling disgust. Yahima signals a polite concession. *I am disappointed to hear that. Developing tech, training divs is one thing. A tourist attraction is another.*

Thiia offers, "But they aren't going to do that for tourists anymore when the synthezoid clouds are ready. They'll look and crystalize the same."

Franxis adds, "So the rich wannabes can have their fun and take home a nice crystal souvenir that looks like a dead EDB."

Yahima is noticeably neutral.

"Those synths are almost ready, I think. Mira and I will work on them again with Vasif today," I say before falling back into transference. *Are we all sure that it's a good idea to be working with these people?*

"Good" is subjective, Arun replies. *The question is whether or not our values and goals line up with theirs in the work we're doing together.*

"I'm going to be joining Medical Operations for Casey's examinations. They've been on it all night. When I checked in this morning, they were 93% sure whatever is in him is not necessarily an EDB. If it was, we'd need your expertise, Oscar."

Ferand seems genuinely regretful that Central has forbid those of us who went into the void to return to our stations. She has welcomed those of us who had the option to return to Scire but chose to stay to keep our crew together, Yahima says.

Franxis transfers, *If by welcoming us, you mean, she's convinced Central to keep us here, then yes.*

She seems sincerely concerned about what is happening to Casey.

We all are, Franxis snaps back before rescinding their anger.

Yahima signals openness, a willingness to hear Franxis no matter the tone.

Franxis signals a humble apology and is quiet for a moment. "I'll go with you Aaliyah. I want to be there for support."

"I'll be speaking to Ferand about our extradimensional friend today, so I'll be on the science deck. Please, send this to Casey for me, Franxis." Yahima hands a package to Franxis.

"Of course," Franxis says. The two of them hang back from the rest of the group, and I take it as the cue to withdraw the psybridge. I tone everyone's connection to it down quickly, but as I'm tuning out, I hear Franxis confess that they don't entirely trust Griselda Harris Ferand.

"One car for the EDB science deck." Thiia taps the panel at the hyper loop door. "One for Medical." The first car is already lined up. The doors open with a hiss and my old Mani crew steps inside. I hold the door for Yahima. The second car silently slides in behind ours. I notice the tourist bots beginning to gather behind my expanded crew. Right away, their faces look anxious, impatient. Even when piloting a drone bot from the comfort of their earthly mansions, they are not accustomed to waiting.

"What about you, Arun? What are you working on today?"

He winks at me. "A surprise."

ꝏ

The entire EDB research deck looks different after hearing that extradimensional beings have been used as a tourist attraction for "hunting." The containment units seem much more malevolent. As we approach the big, duraglass box containing the luminous, misty being who saved us, I feel more determined to get the synthezoids operational and to get our friend away from Helixx Corp.

Mira heads over to the containment unit right away. Yahima peels away to speak with the twin Helixx Sages. A group of EDB scientists, Ferand's acolyte, and the holographic projection of Griselda Harris Ferand approach.

"Div Kenzari, good morning," Ferand says. "I am happy you could make it today. I want to assure you that we are taking care of Div Isaac. I checked in with the doctors this morning, and he is resting comfortably."

"Thank you." I feel relief to hear it, but I'm reminded of the sting of being pushed away.

"As for our work on the nanotech, we took your notes and refined the application last night. We've modified the quantity of the synthezoid cirrostratus to maintain the particle spacing in proportion to the vessel's shape so that the conduction is circuitous. Per your suggestion, that degree will factor into the magnitude of the nanodrone's stimulation of the crystallized EDB remains. I think you were right. We've likely been giving the crystals too much power and not enough space. We'll need to get that right if we're to use the nanotech to close StillRift-2138. You'll also be happy to know that our work here today may be of benefit to Casey. I'll explain later." The hologram begins to turn away, but she addresses me as she rotates toward Yahima and the Helixx Sage. "I'll see you when you're suited up."

In the locker room, I ponder how what we're testing could help Casey. I quickly pull on the new combat gear. With a quick psychic nudge, the armor panels hug in snug to my body. The in-suit climate controls kick in immediately. It is, by far, the most comfortable combat gear I've ever worn. As I hold my palm towards me, I will the system check screen on. A projector in the armor panel on my chest blinks a holoscreen open in front of me. Vitals scans are functioning.

I scroll the holoscreen past the more immediate gear info and notice that the uplink to Ops is disabled. It seems like an error but inconsequential. I decide not to say anything about it to Ops. I don't want to get the technician who set up the gear for me reprimanded.

When I walk back out into the lab, I notice another door across the big room. Red Guard in combat gear stand at either side of the door. They are taller, broader, imposing. Members of the troop we encountered on the field yesterday. Their gear is similar to what I'm wearing with both chargers and sonics; their holsters also hold stun batons and swifts, weapons used to disarm humans. One of them stares at me as I walk across the room, and I am reminded that I am not fully a part of this team but a guest they are keeping an eye on. I'm aware that Yahima and my Station Mani crew are the only outsiders admitted to these experiments. It seems highly unusual to me, but Griselda Harris Ferand is an unusual person.

Mira is suited up and standing in front of the clear cube containing our extradimensional friend. She has new combat gear on as well.

I transfer, *My uplink to Ops is disabled. Helixx won't be able to tap into the suit until I relinquish control.*

Mira replies, *That's weird, considering it's their gear and we're not their employees. It's too late for me to check mine now. Might tip them off if I scroll through the systems screen with everyone looking at us.*

It occurs to me that I might be making a big deal out of nothing. I'm distracting myself from the feeling of rejection and helplessness with minutiae, approaching paranoia. I mentally shake it off and signal to Thiia for assistance to focus on the work we are doing in the lab today. Above us in the observation room, Thiia and Carmel look down towards us. I feel Thiia's comp-bridge strengthen, and I open to harmonize with her keen sense of presence and focus. My awkward feelings get quelled while maintaining concern for Casey, and my focus gets tuned in to the room as Thiia helps me gently calm my fears.

"Ready positions," the acolyte calls across the room.

"One moment." I hold up a hand towards the acolyte, who looks miffed that I'm not following her orders. "We have something to take care of first. It's important."

The acolyte begrudgingly assents, looking to the time display. The scientists look worried to have this interruption.

The light coming from the extradimensional being's body spreads over our faces as the tangle of misty vines rolls closer to us.

"We might as well psybridge now," I say.

Yahima opens their Sage psybridge to Mira and me, and I feel even more focused as they tune the connection. Our nimbuses expand and sync above us, and Yahima offers the psybridge to the EDB. The being integrates the connection seamlessly. As our minds tune in to each other, a humanoid body emerges from the larger body of luminous mist. Misty vines ramble around the incandescent figure.

A signal of concern about the Helixx Sages moves from the being to us. Their interest is beginning to creep out the EDB. Yahima assures us that the Helixx Sage poses no threat, and I have to work to subdue my suspicions. I sense Mira doing the same.

"We want to thank you again for your assistance and patience," Yahima says. "Today, I will arrange transport back to the rainforest. I fully intend to escort you myself."

A note of gratitude moves from the luminous being to Yahima. Warm notes of friendship and care follow, and I feel the weight of trapping this being in this glass box, on this ship, far away from the rainforest.

The being's transference is clearer than ever. *Happy. Soon.*

Mira says, "We want to talk to you about what we've been taught to call you and what you might want to call yourself."

I add, "The name Vasif comes from the word 'invasive,' and was meant to imply intruder. After getting to know you, we want to change that."

Without words, Mira asks for the being's name.

Many.

We're all more accustomed to unpacking the being's statements. Many names have been given, and many names are accepted.

Again, without words, Mira transfers the name and implications that Central has assigned to the being.

The EDB winces and pulls back.

We offer apologies, and the being moves toward us again.

"We just want to get it right," I try to explain. "We want to call you by a name you appreciate."

We feel the being searching through our language comprehension, all the connections different words make. She moves through our minds, gently probing, lifting words to our awareness. The combination of syllables creates a discordant music like individual musicians warming up before a symphony. Words begin to lift or fall away, as the being chooses words we've associated with the rainforest. Words in multiple languages rise and fall, and like an orchestra playing its first notes, one sound emerges clearly from the cacophony.

Vinea.

We pause to let the name land within us.

"Vinea," Mira nearly sings.

"A lovely name," Yahima says. "One more question about how we might speak about you: which pronouns do you use?"

Vinea tilts the head on its shoulders as if pondering the question.

Yahima gestures towards me and Mira, "Oscar uses he and him. Mira uses she and her. I use they and theirs. Do you—?"

She, Vinea interrupts.

We delight in her enthusiasm. I get the sense that she chose the pronoun and even the shape of her humanoid form because she admires Mira the most out of all of us.

"Thank you, Vinea." I pause for a few moments and notice that Vinea's body is brighter, more of the glowing spores lift from her radiance and dance in the air around her body. "Today, we will be testing something, and we want to stay connected to you, to observe what you feel about the test. Are you okay with that?"

Vinea signals assent.

Mira places her hand on the glass, and Vinea places a glowing palm on the other side. Vinea's golden spores drift toward their almost touching hands. Vinea brightens, and Mira smiles. We feel their connection strengthening, bonding. The light-thread from Mira's heart to Vinea glimmers with kindness, and kindness is returned.

Delight comes from Thiia as we witness Mira and Vinea's friendship budding. I look up towards our comps in the observation room just in time to see Carmel turning away, mildly annoyed.

The acolyte sees my head turning as the opportunity to urge us again. "Ready positions, please."

"One thing," Mira says as she steps across the grid at the center of the room. "Let the record show the name change of this extradimensional being. She has chosen the name Vinea."

Yahima and the twin Helixx Sages move behind a safety glass wall close to Vinea. One of the twins seems to have a hard time peeling his eyes away from the glowing being behind the glass.

As planned, Mira and I take our places at opposing sides of the grid. Two Helixx Corp divs, also in combat gear, step onto the grid at the other sides. I look up at the towering lab grown crystals behind each of us. They begin to glow crimson, and the grid over the floor emanates a more subtle glow. Two crossing lines of crimson crystal meet at the center of the square, but the x remains dark. A group of scientists behind safety glass walls directs a floating chest to the center of the grid.

The acolyte steps from behind the safety glass and stands at attention in front of the door flanked by the Red Guard. When it slides open, the mood of the room immediately shifts as all Helixx personnel give their full attention to Griselda Harris Ferand, in the flesh. Two more divs in combat gear strapping two swifts each walk alongside her. The cut of her attire is similar to what all Sages wear, but the entire outfit is bright red. On both of her arms, tech gauntlets blink with various lights. Unlike in her hologram projections, her hair is tied back in a tight bun. A small piece of tech is plugged into each of her temples. The lights of her implants blink with every step she takes.

All those div-tech treatments keep her looking much younger than she actually is, Thiia transfers. *And no one knows her age because she scrubbed the entire internet of her birthdate.*

Thiia's humorous tone lifts my spirits a bit, and I have to hide a smirk.

The acolyte bows her head, and Ferand smiles awkwardly.

Ferand steps toward the grid with the acolyte. The bodyguards keep to their sides. She holds her hands, fingers interlaced, in front of her. "This is a special occasion. I had to come see it for myself! Mani, Scire, Helixx Corp… even an extradimensional being working together."

I want to roll my eyes.

Scire is owned by Helixx, and it's not like Vinea has much choice here, Mira transfers.

"It's nice to meet you all…" For a moment, I think she is talking to Mira, Yahima, and me, but she actually turns toward members of her own crew, her own science team. "In person." She pauses for laughter, and some of the scientists force out a light chuckle. "My father inherited an innovative shipping company and started building rockets for NASA in the early days. With his investments, he expanded the company into genetic research, bioengineering, robotics, and more. He positioned Helixx Corp to be capable of answering the UN's call to study the 'space-cloud' that came to be known as Bakkeaux. We were the first to recognize that dangerous being's sentience and the first to determine its otherworldly origins. I know that my father is here with us today, as we continue his work, expanding his legacy to merge with our own—"

Give me a fucking break, Carmel transfers.

"—as we continue to study these magnificent beings, identifying those from which we can gain, and those from which we must defend ourselves. Today, we take a confident step in a new direction." Her tone changes, and I realize that she is not being entirely honest with her words. I tell myself that it's because not everyone in the room is a Helixx employee. "We are building a tool, or a weapon, depending on the application. It will be equipped with intelligence that will be able to seek out those virulent EDBs and contain them. In addition, we believe the technology will help us explore the interior of Rift-2138, looking for a solution to closing it permanently." She turns her lipstick smile back towards her adoring acolyte and nods.

The acolyte speaks with almost the same air of grandeur. "Div Kenzari, as per your recommendation, we strengthened the zirconium dioxide micro containers while keeping them permeable enough to transmit the atomic deposition of the crystalized EDB particles. The micro containers have been coupled to the redesigned nanotech, and our tests run last night shortly before midnight—"

I note that this was around the time Casey went to bed after he was done talking to his AI.

"And yes, we've been working on this around the clock." Ferand interjects. "Along with other projects." She winks an eye at me a bit too playfully to indicate that one of her other projects is watching over my lover in his strange condition.

I have to remind myself of what Ferand said via hologram earlier. What we are working on may very well help Casey.

The acolyte smiles and forces a light laugh towards Ferand. "During the auspicious first hour of the new cycle, our team observed successful neural network synchronization between the nanobots in flight up to point-two centimeter apart. We are here today to push that further and to refine the control syncing of the synthezoid cirrostratus during integration while attempting psybridge integration to the synth AI." Her voice deepens a bit, and I realize that she is speaking more for the recording of the experiment than for the people present. "For this experiment, Divs Alister and Wan of The Eminent will attempt a psybridge with the synth-AI brain-computer interface. They will be assisted by Helixx Sages Sigrund and Runar. Divs Kenzari and Adivar of Station Mani will psybridge with the extradimensional being formerly known as Vasif. This being is from today referred to as Vinea. They will be assisted by Sage Yahima of Station Scire."

"Shall we begin?" Ferand holds out her hands in what appears to be a welcoming gesture. A spacious elliptical tube of metaglass rises up from the floor around her. It extends slowly up to the ceiling, a protective shield all around her. As it rises, she playfully taps her fingernails against its sides, and flashes an unintentionally pompous smile at us guests. Holoscreens emerge on the glass and encircle her. With her eye movements, she scrolls them around until she finds the one that she wants. She taps a few buttons and holds out her arms. A red grid of light traces over each of her hands. "Acknowledge when psybridged to divs."

"Acknowledge: Helixx Sages psybridged." Alister and Wan say.

"Acknowledged: Sage psybridged, EDB psybridged," Mira and I answer.

The acolyte joins the scientists behind the safety glass. "Dr. Ferand, the nanotech is in your hands."

"Opening the case." Ferand moves her light-grid traced hands back, and the lid slides aside, the seams of the case part, and the container unfolds to expose a cube. The red, orange, and yellow gradient of condensed nanotech appears dull and stagnant.

"Powering up."

Ferand's hands move forward as if she is pushing energy into the cube, and its dull colors begin to brighten.

"Syncing cells."

Her hands move left and right, and each nanobot glows brighter as a wave of movement passes over the surface of the cube and back again.

"Deploying." Ferand's eyes are hyper-focused. The top layers of the cube expand as the billions of nanobots whirl into the air. "Releasing cirrostratus." Ferand sweeps her hands apart and the bots release their gaseous conductors. The metallic smell of ozone spreads across the grid with the synthezoid cloud.

"Testing movement." Her hands move around as if she is slowly conducting a choir. The cloud moves in accordance with the patterns she creates. The red, orange, and yellow gradients shift around in the cloud.

"Dawn of a new era!" Ferand exclaims as she pulls one hand far away. The sunrise colors part as one plume separates and moves away from the cloud. Ferand moves her hand to control the separated plume while keeping the larger body stationary. She brings her hands closer together, and the nanotech re-integrate into one cloud.

"Now, the real test." She sweeps her gaze across the holoscreens, and they scroll to a panel displaying two fluctuating patterns. "On my mark." The lights of the implants in her temples flicker, and the fluctuation of one of the patterns is altered. With each flash from her implant, it moves closer in sync with the other pattern displayed. Brain computer interfacing is syncing her mind to the AI. Aspects of the tech must be similar to the tourists' distans bots, allowing a user to pilot tech from a distance, but I have never heard of someone doing so by plugging the tech directly into their brain, controlling it with their mind. The fluctuating patterns move closer to the same rhythm before finally syncing perfectly.

"Ready, my divs..." Ferand very calmly says, "Now." She closes her eyes. Her chin juts up and wrinkles deepen around her tightly closed eyes, her brow momentarily furrows, and her lips tighten. Then, she softens. Her eyes open, and I can see it before they say it.

"Acknowledge: synth-AI psybridged to Dr. Ferand." Alister and Wan say. There is a strain in their voices as they work to integrate the fluctuating patterns of the artificial intelligence connecting Ferand's mind through their psybridge.

Dark spots move through the cloud among the hues, and bright beams of sunrise colors pierce through as the crystalized extradimensional energy is reinvigorated. The cloud begins to pull in on itself.

Ferand has her fists together in front of her heart. "This is divination," she says. "This is shaping the future."

Vinea signals disturbance. Mira tries to soothe the being, thinking Vinea does not understand the experiment. Vinea cannot be consoled but makes no move to upset anything.

"The EDB's energetic patterns are fluctuating wildly," Ferand says without looking Vinea's way. "Div Adivar, please, assure our guest that we have this under control, and while you're at it, ask about the state of the crystalized EDB's."

I sense glimmers of Mira speaking into a cascade of shifting lights which decode our language into something Vinea quickly understands. Without sending an array of coded language back for translation, Vinea speaks out loud.

"No... lifespark."

Layered within her response, I sense a questioning. I watch Mira unpacking the response, untangling words from tone, decrypting something that appears to be hidden for us, but not meant for Ferand.

The crystalized EDB remains are suspended in a reanimated half-life. Not dead, but not conscious. Ferand's consciousness channeled through Divs Alister and Wan brushes against the crystalized EDB's locked potential without noticing their altered state.

Mira quells a question about why we are being secretive about the realization. Before I can signal that we will talk about it later, a purple-black crackle of lightning emerges from the crystalized EDB in the nanotech and whips across the synthezoid cloud. Ferand cries out. She quickly steadies herself and waves away her concerned acolyte.

I can no longer sense if Ferand is in control of the nanotech, and I tell myself that my fear, stirred up by Vinea's secret message, has clouded my perception. Ferand moves her hands together, appearing to regain control of the cloud of small drones.

An orb forming at the center of the cirrostratus grows more and more dense as hundreds of thousands of the small dark nanobots converge at its center. A plume of gas spreads out from the sides of the orb. As the smell of sulfur reaches me, I realize that the tech has formed the shape of an eye. A rumble like low thunder comes through and shakes it.

Vinea fears that the crystalized EDB remains within the tech are being revived. I feel it too. It feels as if something within the strange combination of tech and crystalized EDB peers out at us. Each of us question if our fears are trying to get the best of us.

Mira and I simultaneously will the charger cannons on, and their high-pitched whine builds. I obscure my growing worry that Yahima trusts Ferand too much. Yahima respectfully lets the obscuration settle between us.

Steady, divs, Yahima transfers.

Another thin crackle of purple-black lightning crawls over the orb, and my mind flashes back to this morning while watching the surveillance video from Casey's room. Something looked through him, into me. He hadn't been working on just any drone. It was the nanotech.

Both Wan and Alister strain. Their shoulders round forward, chins tuck, knees bend. Their eyes close, but their faces remain otherwise neutral behind the shield of their helmets. I psychically reach towards them both and find a heavy obscuration around them. The Helixx Sages are blocking something from us, preventing us from bridging to them or receiving any transference.

I let a signal of suggestion fly fast past Yahima to Vinea. Vinea moves closer to the glass, looking towards the Helixx Sages. It's enough to distract one of them. He turns his head towards Vinea, and we glean his greedy desire rushing his mind. An obscuration around Wan slips and Mira reaches for the signal released.

Wan is pleading for help.

"Stop!" Yahima, Mira, and I shout. "Something's wrong!"

Ferand brings her palms down, and the gasses pull back into the nanotech as it lands, reshaping itself into a cube. Its sunset colors dull to darker shades. Wan and Alister fall to their knees. Wan pinches the bridge of her nose as Alister holds his head in tight hands.

"MedOps!" Ferand shouts, and the scientists scramble to make the call for the medics they should've had in the room from the start. Ferand spins the ring of holoscreens to a display of Wan and Alister's vitals. "Administering sedatives from gear tech!" The two divs slump down to the floor, and the lights of the grid dim. At the grid's corners, the red glow of the towering crystals fades.

Medics rush into the room with hovering gurneys. They quickly lift Wan and Alister and strap them to the gurneys before rushing away. The Helixx Sages and Griselda Harris Ferand follow them out of the lab. For the recording, the acolyte declares the experiment a success without mentioning Wan and Alister's conditions.

Carmel doesn't trust these people, Mira transfers to only me.

I have my own suspicions, but as I see Yahima dealing with their own, I quell them. I want to believe that no one suspected divs Alister and Wan could get hurt. I want to believe Ferand can help Casey.

Yahima tunes out their psybridge, and I immediately check my connection to Casey. It's more open than I had left it. A shadowy figure stands there, watching. I can't help but lock my awareness onto it.

Thiia, do you see this?

See what?

Mira's hand lands on my shoulder, breaking my awareness away. The figure is gone when I look back.

I transfer to Thiia, *It's not there anymore.*

I didn't see anything, Thiia says. *But something feels off.*

Thiia announces through our comms, "Carmel is going to check on Casey and the others. She wants to get eyes on them."

After hearing our code for speaking to them in person, not through potentially bugged comms, Mira and I exchange a glance.

"Okay, we'll catch up with her later," Mira says. "We need to make sure Vinea's okay."

The glowing EDB seems brighter now that the creepy Sages have left. Mira places a hand on the duraglass, and Vinea gently meets it with a tangle of vines that shift into the shape of a hand.

Vinea, Mira transfers. *Any insights on what just happened?*

A tangle of words in multiple languages comes back, but we all recognize the cacophony. Confusion. Uncertainty. A few words drift out of the confusion, moving towards us.

Bring back. Take? Vinea grumbles audibly.

That's okay, Mira transfers to Vinea. *It's okay to not know.* Mira begins unpacking the statement. *Vinea's not sure what happened,* she transfers to avoid Helixx Corp interception. *She is turning over a lot in her mind. Sorting a lot. She is concerned that the crystalized EDBs are re… ignited? Awakened? She thinks there could be a way that the EDB remains drained the other divs. She's not sure if what was taken was taken intentionally or by accident, but she says it took their energy… not sure if she means divination or life-force.*

I transfer, *Why just the divs? The twins were okay.*

More time. Vinea says. It's clear she wants more time to think about what she observed. She takes her hand away from the glass, and she points a glowing finger toward the case of nanotech being taken away by div-tech. *Casey. Open.*

The nanotech? I ask. *You think it can help with Casey?*

Vinea points at the cube of nanotech but says nothing. I turn to Mira who squints at the cube.

"Not exactly. The tech is near Casey…" she sighs. "My foresight is still off. I'm barely getting glimpses. Can't make anything out."

Gate, Vinea says.

What do you mean? I ask. *The rift?*

Casey.

Mira seems frustrated with her own inability to piece together a vision of the future, and Vinea seems taxed with our language barriers. I tell myself that the nanotech is going to help Casey. I want to believe that is what Mira sees, what Vinea means.

I tell myself that I'll put it all in my report on the experiment: the fear that something watches us from within the re-activated crystals, that I worry secrets are being kept from us, that the tech shows potential to free Casey of the Unlit. I'm unsure how, but I want to believe that Ferand could use the tech to close the rift.

Mira and I both quell our worries for now, so that our suspicion doesn't stir up any fear that can cloud our judgment.

"Vinea will be okay. We should let her rest." Yahima says. "We don't have to worry about Alister and Wan. Helixx has some of the best doctors in the sector." Yahima says this as if they are trying to make true or as if they are trying to convince us, themself included. Their holoscreen comm dings, and they quickly scan the message. Their face is neutral, but a touch of bewilderment comes through their voice. "You can take the combat gear off. We've been invited to tea."

"You sure Carmel doesn't want to be here for this?" Thiia laughs, holding her hands open towards the buffet of tiny sandwiches, crudites, dips, dumplings, and sweets.

Mira drops her voice to a whisper, "She's not a fan of Ferand."

Thiia whispers back, "Girl, neither am I, but these tiny pies are cute."

"We are guests here," Yahima reminds them in a hushed but firm tone.

We wait, standing around the gilded antique furniture. It appears to be from the early twentieth century and absurdly out of place bolted into the floor of a giant space vessel. After about ten minutes of waiting, Ferand's acolyte enters the room.

"Welcome. Please, have a seat. Dr. Ferand will be with you shortly." She does not pause for a reply. She returns her gaze to the holoscreen floating in front of her and types as she speaks. "Please, don't worry about our divs. I assure you they are fine." She gestures to the buffet and whispers conspiratorially, "All of this was planned before today's little accident, so just roll with it." With a wink, she quickly turns and exits.

I am annoyed to be invited to meet with Ferand but kept waiting. My worry for Casey leaves me feeling anxious. It's difficult to be present with the feeling while remaining unattached and unclouded by it.

The plush sofas are comfortable. As we settle in, the color of the taupe wall in front of the sitting area dissolves to reveal the floor to ceiling view of the Earth's curve. Station Scire floats a few kilometers out, guarding the rift. Station Mani is close to orbiting out of sight around the planet's edge.

"Oh! Hi, home." Thiia says waving toward the station. "I miss you."

"How much longer do you think they'll ask us to stay here?" Mira asks Yahima.

"Everyone who didn't go directly into the rift is already free to return to the stations, but of course, with what's happening with Casey, we don't know about the rest of us." Yahima tilts their head. "Everyone else has chosen to stay together, since the crew might be going back to Ecuador when we escort Vinea back."

"I love that name," Thiia says. I sense Thiia's memories of choosing her own name, and how liberating it was to settle on Thiia. "Glad you thought to ask about pronouns, Yahima."

"I was afraid we'd have to explain what pronouns are," Mira smiles. "But you handled it perfectly."

Yahima smiles politely.

I say, "Our intel about Vinea was all wrong, we were wrong. Not so long ago, we thought the divs in Ecuador were compromised for not referring to Vinea as 'it' but as 'she.'"

"But we were right about Argis!" Mira asserts. "Even the benevolent EDBs can bring out the worst in some people."

"How can we be sure we're not compromised?" Yahima asks, and for a brief moment the question gives us pause. Playfulness shining in their eyes, Yahima tilts their head a bit quicker than usual and smirks. "We're not, but it's a good question, don't you think?"

"I know we're not compromised, because how we feel about Vinea is not head-filled." I reply. "It's far more heart-felt."

Yahima nods and their grin widens. "Bright faith."

"I'm just so happy to be done with calling her an 'it.' That hasn't felt right since she saved my best friend." Thiia looks at me and my heart swells. "All of you, really. I think we're friends with Vinea now—except Carmel."

"Why do you say that?" Yahima asks playfully.

"She says that persistent radiance gives her a migraine," Thiia says, leading us all into laughter. "But really, she's jealous that Vinea's getting lots of Mira's time and attention, I'm sure."

Mira sighs and slumps into the plush rounded arm of the sofa. "I've noticed, but I appreciate Vinea. Like Yahima, I want to get her back to Ecuador, for the sake of the rainforest, but also, to get Vinea off this ship." She doesn't whisper this last bit, and I can tell she's tired of hiding her suspicions. She doesn't like when we don't talk about what we're feeling.

"Mira, I don't believe Dr. Ferand means any harm to Vinea." Yahima speaks slowly and clearly.

Mira replies slowly and clearly. "It's not just Ferand. Those twins that call themselves Sages creep me out."

"Dr. Ferand would not allow any trouble to come to Vinea. I can assure you."

Mira frowns. "Vinea is alone in a solitary confinement unit. She's used to living amongst the rainforest amidst all the plants and animals, with an entire tribe living inside of her. Vinea is getting lonely. This place is maybe not so great for her mental health."

"I will speak to Dr. Ferand about this while we have tea. I'm happy you're here to give her your insight." With a smile, Yahima puts Mira at ease. "I agree with Thiia about Vinea becoming a friend… and I fully intend to keep my word to the Waorani Elder."

The acolyte comes back into the room. With one hand she types on the holoscreen, with the other she holds up a finger to the hologram of a uniformed Guard projected from her gear. "One minute," she tells the hologram. She steps closer to the sitting area. "Dr. Ferand will be with you shortly. She does not consume food, so all of these treats are for you. And yes, we remembered. It's one hundred percent plant-based. Please, enjoy."

Thiia is the first to stand up, "Great! I'm tired of just looking at it." Her humor is the mood booster we all need.

The acolyte's laugh is cute and girly. "I highly recommend the little squash and cumin pies."

"Little pies?" The holographic guard folds his arms.

The acolyte turns back to the projection and holds her finger up to it again. She resumes typing on the holoscreen before she exits.

"Ferand doesn't eat?" I mumble towards Yahima as I place a couple of the squash pies on my plate. I offer them one. "Tiny pie?"

Yahima smiles and holds out their plate. "Yes, thank you. Maybe you'll get a chance to ask Dr. Ferand about her diet yourself…" Yahima pauses. "Though I've seen her drink a shake."

Coming together to share food is comforting as always. The mood of our small group begins to lift, but I feel the others rise past me. The weight of worry over Casey keeps me from feeling jovial.

Thiia rubs my back and says, "We'll get word soon."

I signal that it's not just that, it's that I'm feeling shut out.

I know, she transfers, sending strong support.

We sit on the fancy antique furniture, eating the delicious food and drinking most of the soothing tea as we watch the world turn. Station Mani will disappear to the other side of the planet soon. I'm aware of time slowly slipping away, and almost ready to excuse myself and leave when Ferand finally arrives.

Two armored bodyguards enter but stop to flank the door. The acolyte follows Dr. Ferand without any projections around her. Both women walk quickly over to the sitting area. Ferand's smile is forced; the acolyte's is unrestrained. The acolyte seems ecstatic to be in Ferand's presence, and I wonder how often they actually meet face to face.

"Hello, my new friends—" Ferand says, and I see why Carmel skipped this. Ferand's tone is sweet but saccharine, fake. "I trust you are enjoying the food. We bring up Chef Marcel du Coste—world-famous—whenever we're in the Earth's orbit. I hear he's the best, but he's not accustomed to cooking without butter. How is everything?" She keeps talking as Thiia and Mira try to compliment the chef. "My assistant Vy Anh will be joining us. And you've probably noticed how connected and busy she is. I am ten times busier. I regret that I do not have a lot of time, and I may have to leave immediately if something urgent comes up." She laughs awkwardly. "As you know, I've got a lot of projects happening, and I am always on call. This is my life." She shrugs and the lights of her implants flicker. "I would like to express gratitude to your crew for being so patient with both Helixx Corp and the UN. You were the first human beings to explore a portal into another world."

Explore? Thiia transfers. *Is she delusional?*

"Of course, we had to keep you quarantined for a bit. And Central wanted you here a bit longer just to make sure there's nothing to worry about. We are delighted to have you on board The Eminent." She pauses and her head slightly turns toward the acolyte.

The acolyte delivers her line almost on cue. "It's as if you've become honorary crew members."

Ferand continues, "Now: Divinator Isaac. I know you are all very concerned, as am I. However, our handlers are the best there are. Even the UNAF doesn't have the level of expertise they do. They are highly skilled at coaching divs with incursive abilities." I open my mouth to speak, but she beats me to it. "I know. This isn't a div ability. Or is it? We believe the novel energetic signature Div Isaac picked up in StillRift-2138 and is working to integrate might trigger a latent div ability." But it's more than that, I want to say. "Perhaps, he is uncomfortable with such an aggressive power because of his past, but we believe in time, with the right coaching, which we can provide, he will be able to utilize the ability for the good of all." I want that to be true, but my gut tells me otherwise. "We have our div-tech department working on something that will help stabilize him. Please, do not worry—"

I interrupt and speak as quickly as she does. "If you have tech to disable the energy, even a little bit, you must have an idea of what it is."

She pauses, as if she is nearly unable to grasp that she has been interrupted. It takes her a moment to pick up on the social cue to elaborate on what she knows about the novel energetic signature. "We've had theories about it for a long time. We believe it to be the primordial energy of reality. We call it Unlit. I've been searching for it for a long time, because of a dream I had as a child… I've told very few people this secret, but our paths seem to be intertwined, our stars crossed, if you will…" Vy Anh the acolyte closes her eyes and slightly nods her head with honor. "In my dream, a great being beckoned to me. I walked very far across an ocean of fluid void that refused the light. I called that substance Unlit. When I reached that being, its many arms stretched out like the branches of a mighty oak. It was made of machines and stone and light and

Unlit." Chills move up my spine as Ferand describes the Titans in the rift. I notice Mira's body becoming tense. "This being said to me 'Close the door.' Since it opened, I have felt that Rift-2138 is that door. Vasif—" The lights of her implant flicker. "Excuse me—Vinea was able to unlock the rift and send the dangerous MaalenKun back through, yet the rift remains. The passage is locked for now, but we have no reason to believe that we hold the only key. Another savage maelstrom could come through at any moment. We are monitoring it closely of course, but—" She waves her hand dramatically. "What I'm saying is, I can get rid of it. I can permanently close the rift."

The acolyte slowly nods her head as if closing the rift is her only desire, and surely her boss is the messiah.

"But in order to do so I must access extradimensional consciousness." Ferand says. "I must become what I know I am destined to become." She turns to Thiia. "Like you, Ms. Bacelar, I am also trans."

Thiia moderates her discomfort with having someone else casually speak of her gender experience. She receives my signal of support. Defensiveness and anger for being put on the spot hang nearby, but she lets them drift away. Her tone is flat as she asks, "What does being trans have to do with closing the rift?"

We listen closely, ready to back up Thiia if she needs it.

"Well, perhaps some of you read in my autobiography," she pauses, but finds no glimmer of recognition in our faces. "I am trans-human."

"That's not the same," Thiia responds quickly, meeting Ferand's gaze.

"No?" Ferand asks. She tries to smile naively through her words. "Forgive me if I've misspoken, I spend so much time interacting through holograms and screens—"

"You see, you being trans-human is about you becoming more than what you are now, right?"

"Yes, that's correct. I will move my consciousness to AI or another enhanced technological embodiment—"

"My experience is about being who I already am."

The silence is awkward for Ferand and the acolyte alone. The acolyte looks shocked.

Thiia sips her tea.

Mira, Yahima, and I signal support and a sense of cherishing to Thiia. She signals back that she feels seen and held.

Ferand nods her head slowly. "I see. Yes. Different then." She smiles awkwardly and continues. "I have been looking for the final pieces of the puzzle to create my superior form, and I believe all the pieces have recently come within my reach. The novel energetic signature within Div Isaac is the Unlit. I am working on a way to remove it—healing Casey—and using the Unlit to move my consciousness, my life force, to a new body of my own design." The acolyte closes her eyes and tilts her head back, savoring the words. "If it works, I will be able to close the rift. If it does not work..." She shrugs, a corner of her mouth pulled down. The acolyte shakes her head slowly. "Well, I've accomplished so much. I've spent a lot on div tech to keep my life going, but I understand it can only take me so far. I'm confident our plan will work. I will rid our world of this threat from a near-immortal body of my own making."

Thiia lifts her teacup towards Ferand and says, "To being your true self and saving the world." She doesn't sound entirely convinced of Ferand's plan. There's a note of hesitation and resistance in her voice, but her words also carry a tone of genuine, but strategic kindness to create connection. The language she chooses hints at celebration, but more than anything else, her words carry compassion.

Following Thiia's lead, we all raise our teacups. Vy Anh fumbles to quickly pour herself a cup to join in the salute. As she lifts it, Ferand snatches it from her, and the acolyte's face falls. Griselda Harris Ferand's chest swells as she raises her cup. We all drink. Ferand returns the cup to Vy Anh, who holds it in both hands like a treasure. She slowly touches the lipstick left on the rim.

Ferand's gauntlets chime and a holoscreen appears with a message only Ferand can see. "Ah! The interruption I predicted." She scrolls through the message as her implants flash. "You'll be happy to know that divs Wan and Alister are recovering nicely from that minor energy drain." Vy Anh clears her throat, and Ferand glances toward her. "I'm grateful I got to say all I had to say, but please, excuse me, I must take this in private."

Ferand stands, and we all hop to our feet. She opens her mouth to say goodbye, but Yahima raises their voice. "Dr. Ferand, I will be taking Vinea back to Ecuador soon. You are aware of my requests for a cargo unit for my crux, Lacassine."

"Oh... yes, I will have to clear that with Central and the UN. After all, Vasif was partially within the rift, and has the ability to conceal energy—even entire beings within itself."

Yahima shifts their tone to make truth. "Her name is Vinea, and we will be going soon."

Ferand forces herself to smile politely and assents. The lights of her implants flicker wildly.

Back in the hyperloop car, which is surely being surveilled, I think of bridging everyone but decide that I don't care if Ferand hears me.

"Yahima, Mira, your foresight skills are the strongest of anyone I know. Does Ferand help Casey?" I smooth my beard, trying to soothe my mind. "Does she get the Unlit—whatever it is—out of him?"

Mira reaches across the empty seat between us and takes my hand. She closes her eyes for a moment and focuses. I look across the car to Yahima who smiles patiently, holding their words until Mira answers first.

Mira looks up and says, "I can glimpse some new device that removes it, but I can't see how. Sorry I can't tell you more. My foresight's still spotty."

Yahima tilts their head and says, "I cannot see how, but I see Casey free of the Unlit."

"What about the rift?" Thiia asks. "Do you see her closing it?"

Yahima answers, but so quickly I wonder if they do so because they know we are being spied on. "I cannot conceive how, which suggests perhaps Dr. Ferand is successful in embodying a new type of life form, something my mind cannot perceive through prescience. I feel her presence near the rift as I feel it close. When the rift is gone, I feel her presence move elsewhere."

Mira nods in agreement. "Very much the same. Just a sense of Ferand working to close the rift, sensing the rift gone, and then relief. That's all I get when I try to see how."

"That's a good thing, right?" Thiia asks. "It's honestly hard for me to wrap my head around how she possibly could become fully trans-human, but I'm not a scientist even if I can read one's mind."

Mira laughs lightly and squeezes my hand. "What's your expert opinion, Oscar?"

"EDB physiology is an entirely different field." I shrug my shoulders. "I don't know if it's possible for her to migrate her consciousness. A hundred and eight years ago, I would've said it wasn't possible, but that was before anyone went div, before we could access the knowledge that goes into div-tech. For the past month, we've been working on syncing crystalized remains of EDBs to nanotech, and today, we had success with integrating Ferand's mind through AI..." I widen my eyes for emphasis. "That's different from moving a living human consciousness out of an organic body and into tech, but who knows... maybe it's not that far off."

Yahima looks back up at Thiia. "Perhaps Dr. Ferand's plan will work."

The hyperloop car approaches the medical deck, and jolly chimes ring throughout the car. The car comes to a stop, and we unbuckle our seatbelts, except for Yahima.

"I'm going to the ship harbor to secure a cargo unit for my crux-wing," Yahima says.

As the others exit, Yahima places a gentle hand radiating with power on my arm. "Oscar, I..." Yahima ponders her words. "I adore seeing you and Casey together. I feel the relationship will be life-enhancing for you both, and therefore, for all."

I am not sure what to say, so I simply nod and say, "Thank you."

Yahima's hand stays still on my arm. There seems to be something else

Yahima is about to say, but impatient tourist bots board the car. Yahima smiles and lets their hand fall back into their lap.

The doors close behind me, and muffled chimes sound as the car slowly pulls away before whisking through the hyperloop channel. Thiia is smiling after Yahima's sweet words. Mira is already on her comm with Carmel.

We walk down the long, spacious corridor side by side. Thiia holds my hand. My feet feel heavy.

The memory of the Shadow looking back at me from across my psybridge to Casey comes to the forefront of my mind. I let the memory drift away. I check the psybridge. It seems tuned up more than when I had seen the Shadow there. I signal gently to Casey that I want to check on him in person.

His call back is an adorable, delightful feeling. Tension melts from my shoulders to sense that he not only wants to see me but that he actually feels delight.

Mira turns off her comm, and says, "Carmel wants us to brace ourselves." The words seem wrong, contradictory from what I'm feeling. "Casey is okay, but—" Mira waves her hand over her left arm. "The Unlit is... outside his body."

ꝏ

At the nurse's station, we meet Carmel, Franxis, and Aaliyah. Several Red Guard mill about the hallway leading to Casey's room. Franxis looks frustrated, but Aaliyah comforts them.

"Helixx is refusing to let Franxis get close to Casey again," Aaliyah says.

"I'm so sorry, Franxis," I say. "We'll figure something out."

"Oscar, that thing is coming out again. The comms systems are down, and we can't hear what Casey is saying. It might not be a good idea for anyone else to go in, but I want you to suit up and get in there. Help him get that thing under control again."

I look up and meet Franxis' eyes. I have to help them.

"Captain," I say. "I heard what you said, but I recommend we send in his best friend as well."

Franxis immediately steps forward. "Let me in there."

Dr. Wallace tries to interrupt, "I don't know—"

"If you can send in Oscar, you can send me in too!" Franxis argues.

"We have no idea what that thing is, but we know it's incredibly dangerous," Wallace snaps. "We can't send in a whole party!"

"I want gear for Comp Franxis, immediately," Carmel tells the technician.

The technician makes a move to retrieve more gear but hesitates. He stares back at Dr. Wallace until the doctor rolls his eyes and assents. He quickly retrieves a gear set from a hidden panel behind the nurse's station. He hands it to Franxis, and Mira helps Franxis into it quickly.

"Is he in pain?" I start pulling my gear on as soon as the technician hands it to me. "It hurt him last time." Thiia helps me get the armor pulled on, and I will the suit to run its system checks. Again, Helixx Corp is locked out, but I don't think much of it.

"Well, the wound is open." Carmel places a hand on my shoulder. "If you have to, crystalize the thing. Just be careful not to hit Casey with your sonics."

The rest of our crew stands at the duraglass along with several of the Helixx Corp Red Guard and Dr. Wallace, the only Medical Operative present for whatever reason. With a furrowed brow and narrowed eyes, the doctor observes Casey, but does nothing to help him. A tiny drone near the doctor turns a camera into the room, surely relaying the scene to Ferand, who hasn't bothered to show up in person or on hologram.

As soon as the door opens, we hear the fierce pulsing of the void.

"It was violent on the field," Franxis says, stepping into the room first. "Be careful, Oscar."

The door slides closed behind us. Making little sound, we step carefully over the trail of blood. Dark splatters across the floor lead to the sitting area by the window. Beyond the window in the distance is the rift, and several wings guarding it. Lilly's holographic cat sits in front of a projected chess board. Several of the pieces have fallen over on the board, and several lie to the side. Across from Lilly, Casey sits on the floor with his left arm propped on the meditation cushion. His shoulders slump forward, and his head hangs low. The meditation cushion is soaked with a big crimson stain. A concerning amount of blood pools on the floor to his left. Shifting extensions of the Unlit protrude from his arm and hang over him. The jagged void violently flickers between permeable energy and a hardened physicality. Through the light-refracting void of the Unlit, I see Casey's distorted image. A smoke-like shadow moves within the void, drifting between us.

Lilly's projection turns its head towards me. "Hello, Oscar, Franxis," she calmly says. "I called the doctors when I saw him bleeding, but they only came to the window."

Casey jerks his head up towards Lilly. "What?" He sees us. "Oh… hey, you two." His eyelids are ringed with red, his eyes are brassy discs reflecting the light, and yet I see genuine delight there. My heart simultaneously aches and swoons. He looks toward Franxis, "Hey, buddy."

"Hey, buddy," Franxis replies.

"Hey, handsome," I say.

We power up our shields, and shimmers of prismatic light flash around us as Franxis and I power up our shields.

"Oh, right," Casey says. He looks as if he is high on something, happy but disconnected. "This…" He lifts his arm, and the void pulses aggressively. Franxis leans away from him. Casey winces and brings his arm back down at his side. He turns his face away and lowers his gaze. "The Shadow kept bringing up so many painful things. Even when I slept, it—my dreams were… gory, horrifying… confusing."

"Okay," I say as I kneel a few steps away from Lilly. I find myself watching his body language not out of concern, but out of fear, ready to respond if the shifting void pulls him across the space between us. I quiet the fear, and shine care for Casey through the light-line between our radiant hearts.

"What about now?" Franxis asks. "Do you still hear it?"

Heavy tears roll down his cheeks, and he looks out the window toward the glowing rift. He nods his head slowly and says, "Yeah…" Then, I see it. He feels ashamed. "It says it can take all the pain, the trauma, and do away with it. It said that the world would be free of the pain I carry and cause. It pulled on memories, and… I didn't want to fight it. I wanted to let it take them. But then, it started pulling me too. Like with the mirror mask, I felt myself slipping away, slipping into the void. Felt like it was taking me… out of the world. It told me to let go, let it reshape me. But I didn't want to lose you two." His voice cracks into a cry, and my heart aches. "But when I tried to pull away from it, it had me. The Shadow hooked into my feelings. Inadequacy, failure. It twisted everything into anger… and I wanted to hurt myself. So, I just let it out… to see if it would ease up. And it did. It hurts physically, but it's not pulling at my mind. I feel more like me in my head. But I still hear it."

"It's okay, buddy." Franxis says.

"No," he says. He shakes his head back and forth, looking toward us, but as he fixes his gaze on me, it's as if he sees through me. Chills run up my spine. "No, it's not. It tells me—" he looks towards Lilly's holographic image. "To kill the cat." He shrugs. "But I know that's not real."

"Not even a real cat," I say, hoping to sound concerned and not just stating the obvious.

"How does my mind not know that? Why can't my mind accept that?" He hangs his head down and cries harder. "These are not my thoughts. I don't want to hurt anyone… so I have to stay away from everyone else."

I speak too quickly, "No, Casey."

"It's ok. It's what I'm used to."

Franxis forces a light laugh and feigns offence, "What about me, buddy?"

Casey ignores them. The Unlit grows more pointed and menacing. "And Oscar… I can't."

"Casey…"

"Please, don't."

I open my mouth, but Franxis halts me with a raised hand. "Casey, you're scaring me as much as this weird Unlit shit. This isn't the man I know you to be. It's this stuff. It's amplifying your insecurity, your fears."

"That's all that I've got."

"No, it's not, Casey," Franxis says, voice steady. "Look inside. Go beyond the voice, the pain, the fear. What's inside of you... so much of it is good. It's what I love about you. I want more of that. There's a whole crew of folks who want more of that. What is it that you want?"

Casey turns away from us, shakes his head, and sighs heavily. "I... want to belong. I thought I had that being a div, having a purpose. I need you more than you need me. I know that. It all feels lost now."

"Let us help you," I say. "You're not lost. We see you."

I inch closer, and the Unlit jerks towards me, pulsing menacingly.

A voice comes over the comm in the helmet. "Oscar! Do not get any closer." Carmel shakes her head firmly. Her face is stern, but her eyes are sympathetic.

Franxis looks pale.

Thiia signals to me to change the subject, suggesting the game.

"Didn't know you played chess." I force a note of happiness in my voice, and it feels like the wrong words. "We'll play a game soon, okay?" I feel like I'm fumbling. I don't want to just distract him. I want to comfort him. "We'll figure out—"

"Lilly was winning. I was just trying to turn down the noise."

I want to hold him. I reach through the psybridge out to our crew, excluding Casey. They integrate quickly but steadily, and I signal for them to shine their support, care, and love towards Casey. Their glimmering light-threads, along with the light-lines of my own heart, land within his heartstar. He begins to sob.

"It's okay, buddy," Franxis soothes.

"I know... I know..." he says. He gasps, jerks his head up to look across the room at an empty corner. It sounds as if he is speaking to someone else. "I'm sorry."

The Unlit expands, stretching up and towards us like a cobra.

"It's not you, Casey," I tell him.

I hear a high-pitched whirr as Franxis' charger cannon comes online. I will mine to power up. "It's going to be okay. Hold out your arm, Casey."

He shakes his head as jagged extensions of the deadly void creep toward us.

Franxis raises their charger cannons. "You can do it, buddy. We got you."

He winces and turns his head to the side as if he is about to shake it no, but he quells his fears. He lifts the belligerent vacuity. The Unlit pulses loudly, morphing into more threatening, barbed outcrops.

With a flick of our wrists, bright light beams of divination unload from the chargers, and Casey struggles to hold his arm steady as the Unlit fights against the divination. A spray of murky blue-black crystals falls onto the saturated meditation cushion, to the floor, and into the pool of blood. Casey cries out in pain as much of the Unlit, un-captured by the crystals, claws its way back into his body. He holds his arm close to his chest, heaving breath. When he looks at us, the reflective brassy-yellow glow fades from his eyes.

He looks back at me, sees the concern on my face, and weeps.

Level Six, so close now, shines down insight. I know the Unlit is not going to emerge again anytime soon. I power down the chargers, the shield, and retract the helmet. I scramble across the floor to Casey, and he leans into me as I reach toward him.

"I'm so sorry," I say.

"Thank you." He pulls me tight. His voice is so much clearer, steadier. "You did the right thing. We can study what we crystalized. Learn how to beat the bastard."

Franxis kneels, unshielded, next to me, and together, we hold him.

An array of lights spins across the curved glass and the image of the quarantine examination room emerges before me. Casey is lying down in an advanced resonance scanner. The doctors along with Franxis and Aaliyah stand to the side in shielded gear.

Another hologram in the room turns towards my projection. "How are you holding up, Div Kenzari?"

"You can call me Oscar." I turn my head and the image rotates towards Griselda Harris Ferand's projection. Her expression again looks overacted, forced, but perhaps she's trying to ensure that the sentiment comes through her projected image. "It hurts to see him like this, but..." I recall Yahima and Mira's felt-glimpses of our future. "I'm not worried. The Eminent has some of the best MedOps in our sector, some of the best tech. If anyone can help him, you can."

"We have the best EDB scientists too," she assures me. "We're analyzing the crystalized Unlit you and Franxis obtained from Div Isaac. Seems we can crystallize the stuff when it is not completely merged with vital tissue. As you know, we couldn't kill MaalenKun. We think this stuff was within an organic body, keeping it alive. We still don't really know if Vinea killed that hellion. We just know she shredded it, sent it back into the rift. Regardless, we'll soon be able to better identify the remaining Unlit's shifting energy spectrum within Div Isaac. We don't understand how it hides from us, but soon it won't be able to. We will remove it from your partner fully."

"You're the lead scientist here. What do you think it is? Is there a..." I almost refer to the potential EDB as a demon, and I remember Arun's words about how we shape our perception. The thought of a malevolent being living within him disturbs me.

"I think what is inside of him is exactly what we've been looking for, for a very long time." Dr. Ferand waves her hand across something off projection, and a holoscreen emerges at my side. The icon on the screen says that the file is sealed. "This is the first time I've shared this information with anyone who is not employed by Helixx Corp, but you deserve to know what we believe might be infecting your partner. The world will know soon enough." She taps the screen on her end, and the file is unsealed.

There is so much information that it feels almost overwhelming even to my brain that is accustomed to the scientific jargon. The concern I have for Casey is beginning to shift into worry, as I read the words. "Unlit light... primordial plasma... energetic building blocks of extradimensional beings... programed consciousness..." My mind spins to the After Action Reports from the MaalenKun encounters. Its words: "Ave eversor."

I shake my head, smooth my beard. "You think this thing in Casey is something that propels the EDBs to try to destroy humanity?"

"Or it's something that is used like a tool to program the EDBs. Some of the aggressive EDBs, at least." She waves her hand, and the file flips several pages to a display of fluctuating energy patterns. "This is a common pattern we have observed in many of the more violent EDBs." Her words land in me and my chest tightens. "And some of the not so violent ones as well. We have not observed this pattern within Vinea even after monitoring her for over a month. She's good at hiding energies, though. And she did consume parts of MaalenKun, a being that had inside of it a great deal of the Unlit. In most of the crystalized remains we've studied, the energy pattern is degraded or inert. It seems to fade to nothing shortly after we observe it."

"What about the crystals we got from Casey?"

"It's not fading as quickly. We're able to study it briefly." She almost sounds enthusiastic. "We do feel that we will be able to disarm the remainder within Casey until we know that we can remove it." She waves her hand again, and the file scrolls through several pages. "This company that I inherited from my father was recruited to escort UN scientists to space to study Bakkeaux. Since then, we have been studying extradimensional beings. Helixx scientists were the first to realize that the space-cloud was indeed a conscious being. Our studies of Bakkeaux were interrupted by the UNAF's new div forces. I know you were a part of that effort from the beginning, but there's a lot that's been kept from you." There is a touch of bitterness in her voice, but she changes her tone. "I completely understand why our work was interrupted. You had to banish the beast. Bakkeaux was problematic to say the least..." She glances at other holo-screens. "But imagine if we could have captured Bakkeaux and studied it. We might have—no, would have been able to glean insights about how it worked." She speaks of it as if it were a machine that could be disassembled. "We would have been able to know of what it was made and from where it came. That could have told us where in the universe the part of it that escaped went. We could have taken the fight to it and any others by now."

"Why send MaalenKun back through the rift then? Helixx Corp owns Scire. Surely you could've convinced Central to get a sample from within that monster."

She tilts her head and looks at another holoscreen off projection. "We've known for a long time that if we just crystalized an EDB, the chance to get a viable sample would be lost. The tech we developed to trap an EDB storm in a crystal chamber was developed so that we could contain an EDB. We thought that we could then make an extraction. We tried with MaalenKun. Our efforts were unsuccessful. As you know, the divination energy of the crystal chamber weakened the being so much that it was left running on mostly inertia, mostly reactive, not entirely conscious anymore. A semi-living being. What we wanted, the Unlit, was already degraded, and we were unable to kill the Haddyc. We tried to crystalize it fully. It broke free every time. We hid the reports from you divs, but Ops knew. When you suggested sending the Haddyc back through the rift, we decided to implement your plan. Your strategy to rid ourselves of the monster was our opportunity to send in drones." She hangs her head, and it looks like the most genuine gesture I've seen from her. "We knew there would be risks. But we had no idea."

I turn my gaze towards Casey, still lying in the resonance scanner. "And you think if we extract this stuff from Casey, you'll finally have that sample?" I turn back to her to see that she too is looking towards Casey.

"Or enough of a sample that tells us what exactly to look for within the rift." Her hologram turns back towards me. "To be honest, we do not know if we will be able to extract the Unlit without great risk to Casey's wellbeing. And even if we can remove it, we do not know if the extraction will give us a viable sample. My strategy now is to study the crystals obtained from Casey. I am going to tell my team to move forward with the plans to unlock the rift and look for a source there using whatever they might gleam from the samples we have." She swipes at several holoscreens, sending the orders to proceed with rift exploration. I hear in her voice that she's not lying, but there is much she is not telling me. "As for Casey, we have a plan."

ꝏ

excerpt from decrypted note to Dr. Griselda Harris Ferand from Helixx Corp Div-tech Lead Operative, Dawson Craig
15 May, 2138 23:53 (Greenwich standard)

We have just intercepted designs pulled down by Isaac. The "medicine" MedOps gave him had him up half of the night, talking to his stupid hologram cat, scribbling down designs that our div-tech departments have been trying to channel for months. His mind was in such a trance, I'd be surprised if he even remembers what he actually did last night. I think he's somehow broken through, spoken with the Excellence. Perhaps the Excellence was sending the designs to us through him, giving us another piece of the puzzle.

We were already so close, only slight adjustments needed to be made. The nanotech update will be online in time for harvest.

CASEY

"Feels like the plan is not working. This custom circlet with citrine and black tourmaline crystals is supposed to disarm the Shadow. At most, the new piece of div-tech just dampens the effect the Shadow has on me. It works somewhat, but it doesn't disarm the threat completely." I say all of this as I watch the sinuous Shadow drift in the air in front of me. "I'm still having my thoughts interrupted by its voice, it still unearths old traumatic memories, my nightmares are still horrifying and frequent."

I glance over at him. He's watching the Shadow too.

"I've worked on the pod-ship designs, and even though I know my work is solid, the voice tells me otherwise. It tells me I'm unworthy. Unworthy to have divination abilities, unworthy of the care being given to me, unworthy of Oscar's love. I tell myself that it isn't true."

Some strange combination of otherworldly syllables drifts up from within the Shadow. ***You killed your lover.***

"That's not untrue," Usain says.

You don't deserve love.

I sigh. "Even now, the Shadow competes with my voice. Even in my sleep."

I turn towards Usain, and I'm so accustomed to seeing his smashed and bloody face, his bent neck, that the sight does not surprise me. Through broken, bruised lips, he says, "It has you."

Something is wrong. I am close to waking consciousness, moving from deep sleep quickly. I need to wake my body up. I'm almost there when I feel the sharp sting on my skin. I open my eyes and see the first or second sparks fly from the circlet. Another short circuit. The scent of my singed hair fills my nostrils, and I bolt upright, slinging the circlet from my head. It falls to the floor, and the citrine crystal comes unfastened from the device.

I want to make a joke about the div-tech on The Eminent being worse than Mani's, but not only is it not true, but a psychic flare rips through my brain loud enough to cause ringing in my ears. The Shadow crawls out of its hiding places, realizing the change within me without the circlet. It stretches itself up and causes sharp jolts of pain throughout my body as it snags its way up my nervous system.

I force myself to reach for the circlet. My arm and then my torso hit the floor, and my head falls forward in defeat. I pull my legs down and drag myself towards the broken tech. The Shadow is just about to rear its ugly head, speak from its foul mouth, when I grip the overheated tech in one hand. In the other hand, I grasp the citrine crystal that was knocked loose. I hold the black tourmaline and citrine to my temples, and I fold into myself. The Shadow begins to retreat, slipping painlessly back into its hiding place. I realize its withdrawal has less to do with the crystals and more to do with the light-line from my heart, strong with compassion flowing into me.

I look up to see Oscar shirtless in the well-lit hallway, looking into the darkened room.

"Lights," I groan. They slowly brighten to illuminate the room.

Oscar taps the panel by the door to turn on the intercom. "You okay, Casey?"

There's a look of deep concern on his face, but I can't take my eyes off his beautiful body, the constellation of beauty marks on his skin. He stands with one hand on his hip and one on the door frame, still near the comm panel. His muscles are more defined after weeks of working out in The Eminent's luxurious training facility, but I'm pleased to see he still has a bit of a rounded belly. I want his arms around me, I want him closer, unshielded as he presses his body into me.

I shrug and force a fake laugh. "Shorted out the latest Shadow suppressor in less time than the last." I let the broken circlet fall to the floor. "Either the div-tech here sucks, or the Shadow is getting stronger. Good thing we've got an upgrade coming tomorrow." I get up and move closer to the duraglass wall. Oscar is one of the few people who do not shy away or even tense up when I come closer to them. I glance down at the light-line between our hearts flowing strong with compassion. My words come out as more of a whisper than I intend. "Thank you."

Oscar's hip juts out more, and he cocks his head to the side, grin crooked. He shakes his head gently. "You don't have to thank me. Just doing what comes naturally."

When he looks into my eyes, I feel the pattern of shying away from his gaze that I got so accustomed to in the past three weeks. When the Unlit makes my eyes terrifying, he still looks into them, into me, makes me feel seen. It's only now, after several variations of the Shadow suppressors, that I know my eyes are almost back to normal and I can comfortably meet his gaze.

"I got word from Mani tech about new mission gear they're making for you." The corner of his mouth turns up. "I told them what was going on, that we'd need gear that could be resealed if there was a tear, gear that anyone on your team could control if you ever couldn't get your shields up on your own. Helixx Corp wants to keep working on a permanent solution, but when we get out of here, when you come to Mani, you'll have that gear if you need it."

"I'd like that." The thought of joining Oscar and his crew on Mani seems unlikely, but I smile at the thought, at his wishful sweetness. "I'm so ready for this to be over."

"I know, Casey." He smooths his beard and stands a bit more upright. "I know." His voice is assuring. "Tomorrow's procedure might not be a way to remove the Unlit…" He tries to use his abilities to make true, but it's hard to make either of us believe it. "But we think the implant based on the circlet tech, integrating citrine, black tourmaline, will take away the Shadow's influence on your mind."

"The implant…" My brow furrows. "Like Ferand's, it will plug directly into my brain… that's frightening."

"They're safe. They've been using them since the 1960's, and div-tech has led to even greater advancements. Don't worry."

I hang my head. "It sounds like the Unlit isn't coming out anytime soon."

Oscar sighs, nods slowly. "We've got a lot of people on this, Casey. We think that your empathic divination might be the very thing that is keeping it from killing you, but it's also what makes your mind especially susceptible to the Unlit. This thing has been able to find places within your physical and subtle being to hide, and it's not until it moves that you become acutely aware of it. Our current plan to remove the Unlit will only work if we get the nanotech small enough to go inside your body. It's difficult getting it that small, and on top of that it has to carry a nano-chamber made from divination crystals to trap the Unlit. We are basically developing a microscopic version of the crystal chamber used to trap MaalenKun, but we don't have a way for Sages and divs to aim it. We have to program the tech and pilot it from the lab. It's incredibly intricate and complex, and if we don't get it right, you could die."

I hear what he's not saying, accidentally transferring his fears. If the nanotech malfunctions in my body, it could, instead of removing the Unlit, rip my body apart from inside. Even div-enhanced healing wouldn't bring me back from wounds like that. But I'm growing accustomed to risk.

I nod slowly. "I know, Oscar. Thank you. I know it's not easy. If you think the implant will work, I'm all for it."

My body aches. He notices.

"Do you want me to call the doctors?" he asks.

I nod towards Lilly's holographic cat. "All they do is watch. Guess there's nothing else they can do." I hold up the citrine crystal. "Do you want this? It's not doing me any good."

"You keep it," He says. "It matches your eyes."

I close my hand around the green crystal, feel its density in my fist, and lean against the glass.

"Oscar, I don't really know how else to say this, but I'm really amazed you haven't bailed on me."

He smiles gently and bows his head humbly, waiting for me to continue.

"We've only known each other a few months now, and most of that time, I've been..." I accidentally glean him dwelling on the vision he had of me, the one that convinced him that I was his future. He doesn't mention it now so as not to put pressure or expectations upon me. I half-laugh into a smile. "I don't know if I would've done the same for anybody. I think I might've run away from this if I could've. You've shown me how to be steady. I'm almost surprised every day when you come back from the lab." Tears swell in the corners of my eyes, and through our psychic connection, I feel him holding me in his heart. "We've barely been able to touch each other."

He smiles wide. "You know I like to build anticipation. Just imagine what it will be like when we can touch each other again." His crooked grin melts my insecurity. "Besides, we don't have to touch to feel."

The psybridge opens wider as he syncs our sensations. Oscar raises his hand to his mouth as if he is about to blow me a kiss, but he holds it there. I feel the touch of his lips on my own fingers, and I raise that hand to my mouth and send the kiss back to his lips. A spark flies through me as if he had his lips against mine.

As we agreed weeks ago, to be safe, we only sync sensations briefly. I cannot risk the Unlit harming him by harming me. Oscar dials the sync down, and we both place our kissed palms on opposite sides of the glass.

And for the first time, I tell him.

"I love you."

Franxis and Oscar, both in mission gear with shields up, sit nearby. Our psybridge network bolsters our meditation practices. Together, we do our best to not get swept up in our fears or hopes. We try to let each emotion arise, abide, and subside without grasping any of them. When any of us get hooked by an emotion, we all work to disentangle and detach from it, free ourselves, so we can be present and clear with what is.

Their support flows through the ever-present connections through our heartstars. The light-threads from the rest of our crew to my heart shine bright with compassion. Emerald colored glimmers of care move in both directions along the light-line between Oscar and me. Through the challenges we've faced, we've bonded, learned to rely on each other. We've cultivated a bright faith.

When the timer's chime goes off, the sound ushers in a welcome new day. As planned, we are quiet as we get up from our seats and head toward the door. Oscar and Franxis both reduce their psybridge connections.

Lilly's projection is sitting by the door. Big cat eyes look up towards me, and I smile back as she says, "See you soon, Casey."

"I'm grateful for your companionship, Lilly. You let me win at chess, and you helped me get the ship designs I've been working on to tech at Scire. You also helped me become more aware of the support I have."

"That's what friends are for," she says.

I snap my helmet up and activate the shield. A wave of colors sweeps around me.

"Ready?" Oscar's voice, low and soft comes through the comm.

"I'm so ready."

Franxis smiles, "Me too, buddy." They take my hands.

ꝏ

At the surgical unit, a holographic projection greets us at the door. The projection greets us and gives instructions that we've heard more than once already. When it blinks off, the door slides open, and I proceed into the small waiting area alone.

The connections from their hearts to mine flash bright as Franxis says, "See you soon, Casey."

The light-line shines bright as Oscar blows me a kiss and winks. His crooked smile makes my heart flutter. He doesn't say anything, and I don't need him to.

I wave to them both as the door slides closed behind me and locks with a soft thud. I switch the shield off and peel myself out of the gear. Ultra-light beams trace all over my body, and quantum signature scanners hum.

I put on surgical scrubs and slippers and look into the monitor and say, "Ready."

The door opposite my entrance slides open. A pleasant chime accompanies the word "proceed" on the wall monitor. And I step into the surgery room.

I look up to see several doctors and nurses behind the glass dome, including Dr. Ferand in the flesh. There are several tourist bots in a small section cordoned off from the rest of the group. The bots seem more interested in looking at Ferand than anything else. Between the medical team and bots is my chosen family. Oscar and Franxis sit up front with Yahima and Arun. Behind them on a raised level are Mira, Carmel, Harjaz, Ehsan, and Zinwara.

Aaliyah waves to me from the group of medical personnel. "Good morning, Casey," she says through the intercom. I'm happy to see her confident smile. "How are you feeling?"

"I feel ready."

Her grin widens. "So are we."

I hear both her meanings: the div-med team is ready for the procedure, and my crew is ready to have me back.

I climb onto the monumental surgical chair and lean back into it. The headrest reshapes, cups the back of my skull, and wraps gently around the sides of my head, covering my ears. The chair tips back. Muffled sounds of the hydraulics and motors in the chair drown out all other sounds, and when they stop, for a few moments, I hear only my breath.

My thoughts turn to the images of the implant Lilly showed me last night. I realize that I haven't even seen it in person, and I begin to feel a bit nervous for the first time today. I feel my heart rate elevating.

An unfamiliar voice of some Helixx Corp medical professional comes through the chair's built-in comm. "No need to be nervous, Div Isaac. We've done many of these procedures in this same facility."

This must be part of the deluxe tourist package, I think to myself.

"We'll give you a little something to calm your nerves first."

I don't have time to say I don't really need it before there is a prick in my left deltoid as a needle quickly injects the sedative. Seconds later, I feel floaty. It's as if the chair underneath me has somehow vanished and left me drifting in space.

I look up to see Oscar leaning forward, a hand smoothing his beard.

The unfamiliar voice says, "We'll start the anesthesia now. Count backwards from ten, please."

I make it to only nine before I'm under.

I smell burning hair, and I realize two things: that the laser is singeing away a permanent bald spot in the exact size of the implant base, and that I am not fully under. But I can't move. I can't signal to Franxis or Oscar. I try to through the light-threads, the light-line to Oscar. Care comes back from both Franxis and Oscar, but they do not sense that something is off. I hear the muffled sound of the bone saw, and I brace myself for the pain. As if my body has slipped out from under me, I fall through some space. I fall deeper, under.

Your bridge is shielded from the pain, a voice transfers. *Do not worry about your comp or your lover.* The same resonant voice from my dreamscape rendezvous with Oscar. *I AM holding you.*

And with that, I am unafraid.

I'm in a mindfield or a dreamscape, but I feel alone. I'm not entirely unconscious, but my body is immobile. Far, far above me is a small disc of light. When I look up toward it, I can hear the bone saw. An intense pain cuts into me, my ears ring. I wince, turning away from the light, and it's gone. I don't dare to look directly at it again, but I watch it in my periphery as the disc of light gets smaller and smaller, and I wonder if the doctors have increased the anesthetic. I realize the disc is moving further and further away, and I'm drifting into some unknown place.

My passive body moves aimlessly adrift. I close my eyes to try and find my center. There is neither down nor up, neither left nor right. I feel a bit of motion sickness and realize I'm spinning. Flailing. My awareness keeps rushing to the edges of my body, my feet, my fingertips. I'm trying to find anything to hold on to, anything steady. Nothing. I stop reaching, withdraw, and I notice the glow of my heartstar. Its light moves me in towards my core. The flailing stops. Steadiness.

A terrifying realization moves through me. The nothingness all around me is not just emptiness, it is the Unlit itself. I am within the part of my consciousness consumed by the Unlit. Fear rushes through me, and I turn towards my shining heartstar. The temporary terror passes.

I notice a change in the light beams coming from within me, and I look down to see a growing cumulus cloud spreading as the light rays dance through it. The cloud within the leaf. The extradimensional energies within me move through the cloud as the light of kindness and compassion begins to guide them. The phantom pain of MaalenKun's sting glows hot in my arm, dulls and breaks apart, and is swept into the cloud. My heartstar turns, its rays extending, forcing the Haddyc energy into disintegration, and I realize that the Haddyc energy is where the Shadow has been hiding. The Unlit, the void, moves around me, and I do not fear. I simply hold my radiant heart.

A misty, light-filled leaf floats down before me. As the Unlit continues to shift and swirl, becoming more permeable, a figure emerges from the space behind the shadowy veil. Vinea's luminous body moves through the dim void, wafts towards me in graceful undulations. As I am being psybridged to Vinea's mindfield, her light becomes a beacon.

Vinea spreads her lustrous, flowing mists and ushers the Unlit deeper into the space held by the Aphrytian energy left in me when Vinea's leaf touched me. The benevolent energy in my right arm grows spacious and cool, drawing the Unlit into a calm place. The swirling shadows around me pour into the benevolent space, and several more figures emerge in Vinea's mindfield. Sages. Elders. I recognize only Pyaar, Murtagh, and our Black Elder. There are at least a dozen other Sages psybridged.

The voice. The I AM. It has to be one of the Sages.

I realize that nearly all of them are reaching from far away. Even with the amplification of Havens, their effort to reach me must be great. Pyaar is the only Sage present that I know to be still on board The Eminent. I begin to ask why Yahima and Arun are not here in the mindfield, and Pyaar raises one finger to her lips.

This is being done in secret, Pyaar says. *I'm disrupting any surveillance systems around where I meditate. No one from Helixx Corp, and no one we suspect is being monitored by Helixx Corp, has participated in this Sage assist. Your implant surgery presented the perfect opportunity to contain the Unlit where there will be less risk when having it removed.*

Our Black Elder speaks next. *Before you ask, Div Isaac... yes, the implant is necessary. While the Unlit is contained within the Aphrytian energy Vinea gifted you, the implant will not render the Unilt entirely inactive. The citrine and black tourmaline charges synced in your nervous system will help prevent the Unlit from breaking the confines of the benevolent boundary. You will still need to learn to maintain that boundary by controlling yourself. Your anger, fear, and self-pity will only make the Unlit stronger. Your grace, kindness, and compassion will strengthen the binds containing the Unlit.*

I send the Sages my gratitude.

Murtagh says, *There is still work to be done, Div Isaac. Though the implants should silence its voice, the Shadow remains within the Unlit. You will have to contend with the effects of the trauma the Unlit leaves in its wake. This will not be easy, but your faith in yourself will unlock more awareness of who you are and the power you hold.*

I bow my head. Disappointment cannot touch me after knowing the Unlit is contained. The Shadow remains, but the light of my heartstar shines brighter. I look around me to see that the mindfield is more luminous. The glowing particles that accompany Vinea whirl around the Sages. Vinea spreads her luminous body throughout the space, and as her light moves all around us, the Sages vanish in her glow.

The sharp whine of some gadget coming online comes and goes near my ears. I feel the heaviness and density of my body as my awareness moves back into it. I blink my eyes, but the lights are too bright. Through tears in the corners of my eyes, I see the anesthesia mask being pulled away by robotic arms. The pads holding my head release and slowly move away.

Aaliyah's voice comes through the comm "Casey, you'll be groggy for a little while longer. Implants are online. Just relax. We're going to start scans for the Unlit."

The faces above me come into view. I look for Oscar's handsome face first. He smiles down on me, and our heartsongs harmonize along the connection between our hearts. Franxis places a hand on Oscar's shoulder, and they both breathe a deep sigh of relief. The others look happy as well as they look from Aaliyah, who is speaking to them, back to me. Yahima nods once slowly, their smile is sly, and I know that she senses the assist from the Sages and Vinea.

I breathe deep, and I relax.

I sit in meditation. With the new implants dampening the effects of the Shadow, my mind is at peace.

I feel the Shadow move the Unlit within Vinea's benevolent energy, the container for the deadly force within me. Its voice is muted. My peace of mind feels protected.

I open my eyes to the vast, star-studded space outside the window and allow myself to feel hopeful for a moment. Thinking of the effort of my crew, Vinea, and the Sages, I set aside hope and its attachment to fear. I inhale deeply, freely, and embrace confidence that feels like faith in my little community. Without hope and fear, and with awareness of their dedication, my faith is luminous. Bright faith.

Lilly blinks on near the window, and struts closer to where I am sitting. "I noticed the new implants' sudden increase in activity, Casey." Her tone has shifted to concern.

She's learned so much about human suffering from me, I joke to myself. I smile before answering. "Yeah… It's okay."

Lilly's pupils widen as her tail swishes, and I'm reminded of the original Lilly.

"May I ask of what are thinking, Casey?"

"Time before divination. Feels so far away from me now," I say. "You remind me of the home I was making before Bakkeaux ripped it apart."

"And now, you're creating a new home with Oscar, Franxis, and your friends."

I sigh, "We need a real home. One that isn't *The Eminent.*"

"When you go, will you take me with you?"

"Wouldn't be the same without you, Lilly."

The holographic cat slow-blinks at me. "That makes me happy."

The Shadow within me winces and grows still as if we have struck it back with the power of our gratitude. A lightness moves through me for a few moments. I try not to cling to the ease, but let it come and go.

Lilly's holographic projection follows me as I make my way to the bathroom, and I smile at the memory of Lilly the cat invading the bathroom with no regard for my privacy. I realize that the AI has most likely been studying the internet for cat behaviors specifically to remind me of the original Lilly.

As I shower, shave, and clean my teeth, I notice that my mood is lifted even more. I look in the mirror and catch myself smiling.

The headache is nearly gone as my healing factors shorten my post-skull drilling recovery time. The swoop at the front of my hair falls over the left implant partially, while the right implant is more prominent. Each implant contains both a citrine and black tourmaline crystal which sparkle among the lights. Oscar is right--the citrine matches my eyes. When I stare at my reflection, I'm relieved to find my familiar insecurities are no longer intensified by the Unlit.

I look down at my right arm. I feel the chamber of benevolent energy containing the Unlit. Similar to the phantom pain, it is a ghostly sensation: painless, but occupying space. At times, it feels cool, like placid waters. I wonder if, like the phantom pain, there will be times when I forget about it.

I signal Franxis with an inquiry about any disruptions they might sense.

None, they transfer. *From your post-surgery scans, MedOps and Dr. Ferand have confirmed that the Unlit has moved into the Aphrytian energy and stays unmoving in my right arm. MedOps has deemed the implants more successful than they had expected. Only you, me, Oscar know that it's really Vinea's energy, and not the shadow-suppressing implants, that have trapped the Unlit. Obscurations around that knowledge are reinforced to prevent anyone from gleaning it. Don't want Ferand to think that Vinea could be used to contain the Unlit.*

I signal relief, happiness, and gratitude to Franxis.

They signal back the same before their presence again fades in the curves of my mind.

The implants, my gratitude, how I feel for Oscar, all seems to be enough to suppress the Shadow. I know it's there. I know it can still hurt me and even others, but for once, I feel more powerful than the Shadow.

ꝏ

A silhouette moves into the hallway behind the shaded duraglass wall. I tap the panel by the door to dissolve the opaque shade, and I'm surprised to see Yahima in their saffron and orange mission gear.

They tilt their head and smile. "I thought I'd get you to walk with me if that's okay."

"Of course."

I move quickly to put on the gear, which Oscar designed just for me. "If there happens to be any trouble from you know what, just activate my shields to keep it contained."

Yahima raises their eyebrows facetiously. "Think there might be trouble?"

I meet their eyes and answer truthfully, "No."

Yahima signals back through the hallway entrance to the nursing station, and the nurses open the door. Yahima steps through the doorway with their helmet retracted and shields down. The look on their face says that they notice the tension in my body right away.

My mind reacts with a fearful thought to activate my shield, to create a protective barrier for Yahima in case the Unlit should tear its way out of me.

Yahima smiles gently, and my body relaxes a bit. "I don't think the shield will be necessary, but I can always snap yours up quickly and lock your gear if it becomes so."

"You are prescient, right, Yahima?" I half-joke.

"I have prescient skills, but the Unlit, like the rift, is proving difficult to predict. I have more confidence in you, Casey."

I cock an eyebrow. "Okay." I almost make a joke about Yahima walking next to me at their own risk, but I drop it. "It is nice to not have to feel so guarded."

Even though I've been training myself not to look for the Shadow, my awareness sweeps through me with a quick scan. The Shadow is, of course, contained.

I pick up the going away gift that I wrapped for Yahima. I'm sure they can see from the size of the gift what it is, but I thought the white tissue wrapping was a nice way of honoring how Vinea wrapped up the Unlit inside of me, making it so I can be with Yahima and my crew again.

"Okay. Let's go." Yahima gestures toward the door.

We walk together, slowly, mindful of each step. Yahima seems to be giving me space to absorb the moment. They stay by my side as I take in the feeling of walking out of quarantine with no shield up, no worries. We pass Helixx Corp Ops in the halls, and I watch each of them, wondering if they'll be afraid to see me, but they move along as if I am anyone else that they're too busy for. We take our time walking to the hyperloop.

After some time, Yahima says, "It must have been very challenging being separated from others for so long."

"Other than Franxis—and maybe Harjaz, a little—I haven't known you or our blended crew for very long. But I've missed everyone."

Yahima gives me a cheeky grin. "We don't have to know someone for very long to love them."

I smile and nod. "Beginning to see that."

"You and Oscar seem to be getting along just fine. It's beautiful to see you two caring for each other." She nods towards my heart, and I am reminded of its glow, how Oscar has lit my heart up. "I know your relationship is not without its challenges right now."

I smile and nod. "'Challenges' puts it mildly. I still fear the Shadow. It said it wanted to reshape me. That scares me because I know it can." Yahima gazes back at me, actively listening. "When I saw my face in the mirror mask of dis-existence, I felt it pulling at everything that makes me who I am. It was like that with the Shadow sometimes. It pulled at memories, but also pieces of me, parts of me that grow out of those memories. When I lost control and the Unlit came out, the day Oscar and Franxis crystalized it, it was trying to pull me into its void. It was trying to erase me." I gaze back at Yahima. "I almost let it."

"An erased mind has no history propelling it towards living peace, only a numb presence with an inability to perceive allies. A mind that has processed pain through compassion moves closer to living peace." Yahima pauses. "You said you heard a voice when Oscar and the Sages entered your dreamspace."

"We all heard it."

"Who do you think it was?"

"Perhaps it was just a dream?"

Yahima tilts their head and makes a stink eye at me.

I chuckle. "Right." I shrug. "I don't know. I've thought about it. Meditated on it. I don't know. Maybe some div or Sage somewhere out there knows how to get this Unlit out of me, and they were telling me to find them."

"All of the UNAF and Helixx Corp are looking for a solution, Casey."

"I don't have as much confidence in either. Feels like our old bosses have surrendered us to Helixx. It's like the old days of Project Ascension when they'd lock away folks with troublesome powers. Like they did to Arun."

"We both remember well what the UNAF was like when it was more militaristic. Those early days of adjusting to new-found power while trying to force thousands of super-powered people into the mold of a new military force—all while dealing with extradimensional threats."

Our hyperloop car slides to a graceful stop, and the door opens. Yahima gestures for me to enter first, and then sits across from me.

"I remember. We moved fast."

"Maybe too fast in some areas." Their smile fades a bit. "It was common for Sages to push aside attachments to trauma and other issues that prohibited the flow of divination. That way, divs could be more open to higher levels. We—Sages and Ops—found early on that many aspects of how things were being run would only lead to rigidity, possibly causing our greatest warriors to become less flexible, more likely to break. We stripped away most militaristic elements of the operation and discovered that when divinators and accompaniments were genuinely happy, they were more skilled at defeating EDBs and far more likely to Level up." Yahima's smile brightens again. "We realized that when anyone is not only allowed but encouraged to be free and to love, they tap into an invaluable power. It just so happens that power enhances divination." A soft ding announces that we've almost reached our destination. "I could say more, but what I want to say to you now is that I'm happy to see that you and Oscar love each other… and that your whole crew has become so close. It's a power the world needs."

"We feel like you're a part of our family too, Yahima."

Yahima closes their eyes slowly, as if savoring the sentiment. They meet my eyes. "I feel that, and I am very grateful. The love you have, the love you share, and the love that you are… is how you will defeat the Shadow." They smile gently, see me holding back tears, and shift their direction slightly. "When Helixx Corp purchased Station Scire, I was not surprised. As the station grew older and the three newer stations went online, many of the Sages felt that the operation would be sold. We didn't need foresight to realize that there were few people on Earth with a fortune big enough to afford a space station, and only one with enough interest. The transition from UNAF to Helixx Corp has been slow. It's taking months, but I feel it will actually be of benefit to everyone onboard Scire. I cannot foretell exactly, but I feel that under Ferand's guidance, there will be even more freedom for divs and comps, maybe more happiness."

"More tourists too," I quip.

Yahima laughs and nods. "Well, probably so."

Yahima seems so hopeful that I don't mention that Helixx Corp seems to be dismissing a lot of our fellow Queers. I decide not to mention that Franxis and I will probably be leaving Scire soon regardless.

Our hyperloop car comes to a stop, and the door opens to the small ship hangar.

"Are you ready to leave The Eminent?" I ask.

"Yes!"

"I'll miss you."

"That's very sweet. It's past time I keep my promise to return Vinea to the rainforest. I've been in contact with Commander Awá, and he has restructured his team to better protect Vinea. We've got a div skilled at EDB communication who'll be transferring there to live close to Vinea. Ops on the ground will be giving folks regular psychological examinations to ensure that we don't have any more cults forming within their ranks."

"I'm happy Vinea will be back where she wants to be."

"Part of Vinea will always be with you, you know." She glances toward my right arm, where Vinea's misty leaf entered my body. "When we tested the leaves' attraction to the ring in Ecuador, I believe the benevolent energy from Vinea within you eased the phantom pain from MaalenKun's sting, did it not?"

"At the time, I thought it took away the Haddyc energy completely." I shake my head slowly. "The Shadow is subdued for now." I hang my head and sigh before looking up and forcing a smile. "But it's still there, I'm afraid. Maybe I'll always be a little broken."

Yahima places an armored, gloved hand on my shoulder. I'm aware that I haven't been close to actual human contact in weeks, and I blink back joyful tears.

They gesture toward the gift, clearly aware that it is the reassembled leaf she gave to me. "The cloud is in the leaf, and it's okay to feel broken."

ꝏ

"They're waiting for us," Oscar says from the harbor door. He sees me grinning, happy to be out of quarantine, and moves in for a hug. Even after having his arms around me all night, I feel ecstatic joy when he pulls me close again. He whispers in my ear, "And if they weren't waiting, we'd still be in bed."

I lean into him, enjoying the light touch of his breath on my skin. He holds my chin with one of his strong hands. He kisses me softly and when he pulls away, I steal a few more quick kisses.

He laughs lightly, and his eyes move toward the implants. "They look badass," he says.

"Damn right." I try my best to look tough, and we both laugh. "I'm just glad they're working."

"Me too."

I feel him sending notes of gratitude for the Sages and Vinea through his light-threads to their hearts, wherever they are.

Yahima clears their throat with an exaggerated emphasis. We look up to see them gently smiling, waiting for our public display of affection to conclude.

"Good morning, Sage Yahima," Oscar says.

"Hello, Div Kenzari." Yahima's smile broadens.

There are many more clash-wings than crux-wings in the dock, which surprises me because Helixx Corp certainly has the money for a fleet of the nimble ships. Yahima's bright saffron and orange Lacassine stands out amongst the crimson ships. Several uniformed harbor technicians offer to help with system checks, but Harjaz and Zinwara wave them away. Thiia is on a holoscreen testing the comm system with Scire. Aaliyah and Ehsan are nearby, peering at data on a holo. Franxis waves from the cockpit where Carmel is helping them integrate the navigation system for Vinea's armored cargo container. Carmel winks at me; she's obviously excited to be in the cockpit of a crux. Arun, Yahima, Pyaar, and Mira gaze into the big, clear duraglass cube containing Vinea. Her glowing spores seem brighter today. Her humanoid form rises from a floating, shifting tangle of ephemeral flora-shaped mist.

As we approach the hovering cube, Vinea turns towards us. Her featureless face radiates the energy of happiness. I place my right hand to the glass, and a misty palm meets it from the other side. Her energy containing the Unlit within me feels pleasantly vibrant.

Everyone gathers around Vinea.

I bow my head to Vinea and say, "Thank you."

The vibrant sensation in my arm radiates reassurance. Her cloudy hand pats the glass playfully. I recall the trepidation I felt on our way from Scire to Ecuador, all the presumptions we brought with us, all the fear and frustration I felt when that glowing leaf moved into my body. We were so wrong about this extradimensional being.

I look into her featureless face and say, "Next time we see you, we won't have this barrier between us."

Vinea brightens and coos. *Go StarTemple. End Unlit.*

Hope nearly chokes me. I mentally grasp for the meaning of her words.

Mira steps closer. "StarTemple… How do we get to the StarTemple, Vinea?"

Music light gate, Vinea replies. *StarTemple.*

Mira smiles gently at Vinea. "She says StarTemple, but I get the sense that she refers to our heartstars. Perhaps the music of our heartsongs is the gate for our compassion. I think she means that our care for Casey is what will save him."

Vinea coos.

As my hope is dashed, so is my fear. Bright faith in the people Vinea is telling me to open my heart to radiates. I smile at her, and she brightens.

While everyone else is paying attention to the beautifully glowing EDB, I sense Yahima turn their attention towards me. Maybe they predicted that I have something to say before they go.

I hold out the gift to them, and they tilt their head with a smile. They already know what it is. I nod, and they take the gift.

Yahima unwraps the clear cuboid encasing the reassembled ramón leaf. I see the object as more beautiful back in their skilled hands. Yahima turns the cuboid so that the light moves along the leaf's broken pieces, reunited with thin lines of gold. Where it was broken is clearly defined, unhidden.

"Thank you again for the gift, Yahima. It's been a sweet reminder of so many things."

"What does it remind you of?" Yahima tilts their head, and their smile remains joyful.

"Brokenness can be healed and beautiful… and it's okay for the cracks to show." The rest of our crew turns towards us. "Also, the rain cloud—what nourished us, what still nourishes us—is always there, even when we don't see it right away." I laugh lightly, "I'm surprised it took you only a few weeks to piece those tiny bits back together."

Yahima humbly replies, "I've had a lot of practice."

"Yahima," I speak softly, sweetly, with a touch of humor. "Thank you for being a part of my cloud."

Yahima's smile brightens their lovely face as they accept the return of their gift. "Likewise, Casey." They look at the offering in their hands and ponder something. "You know, my ancestors held a tradition around gifts. After some time, a gift was returned to whomever first offered it to show that the joy is not in the object, but in giving."

I smile, having heard of the tradition, knowing it would be meaningful. "I didn't design much storage in the crux, but there's a little room. Hold onto it for us all."

"I'm honored, Casey."

"Lacassine is all set, Yahima," Carmel says. "You'll find the cargo's nav screen when you power up. It'll be by your side all the way down. Any problems, and you can uncouple. The tugs have a homing signal to the UNAF's Amparo-1."

"Commander Awá's expecting you this time," Thiia says, tucking the tablet under her arm. "Sounds like he's in a good mood today, but that might change before you get there."

Yahima laughs. They look each of us in the eyes as they speak. "It has been an honor to work alongside this crew for the past couple of months. Seeing you come together, face the loss of a friend with dignity, support an injured mate, and bond as a chosen family has been refreshing and healing. My only regret is that we've kept Vinea here too long. Far longer than I wanted to." They look towards Vinea with eyes full of sympathy before turning back to our group. "Zinwara and Ehsan, I suggest you use this time to get close to these folks while you can." Zinwara and Ehsan both assent. "They are truly remarkable individuals." Yahima places their fist across their heart, and we return the gesture. Their words ring with truth as they say, "I will see you all again soon."

Yahima steps toward the cockpit, and most of the crew begins to disperse. Oscar and Mira approach Vinea. They place their palms against the side of the glass, and as she did with me, Vinea meets both of their hands with her own ephemeral palms.

"I'll miss working with you, Vinea, but I'm happy to see you go. This is not the right place for you, and I'm sorry it took so long to get you out of here after you came here to help us." Oscar sniffs and lets his emotions swell. "Thank you for saving us from the rift." He shakes his head. "I don't know what else to say but thank you."

Friends, Vinea transfers to the whole crew.

Everyone else stops moving away and turns to look towards the glowing being.

Friends.

Oscar and Mira both nod their tear-streaked faces, placing their other hands alongside the floating cube and beginning to push it towards the armored container. I notice Mira's hand beginning to glow, and Vinea responds by brightening the glow of her accompanying hand. Mira's arm subtly glows brighter from the benevolent energy retained from Vinea's leaf. Their friendship does not need to voice the word goodbye.

I glance over at Carmel, and accidentally glean a grain of her salty jealousy moderated by a touch of respect for the being that saved her wife from the rift.

Mira and Oscar push the hovering cube into the container. Mira waves her luminous hand as if she is unaware that it is glowing brighter. Oscar taps a panel on the side of the container, and the door slides down, sealing luminous Vinea inside. The brightly lit harbor is considerably dimmer.

Oscar and I both get messages on our comms to join the tech crew working on the nanobots. Oscar messages them back that we will meet them this afternoon, and they reply with apologies, which seems strange at first. Then everyone, including Zinwara, Ehsan, and the Sages, gets a message from Vy Anh. Griselda Harris Ferand would like for us to dine in the yacht's elegant restaurant.

Our large group takes a couple of hyperloop cars to the top deck. I gaze up at the starlit space behind the curved metaglass roof. Franxis walks alongside me with an arm around my shoulders. On my other side, Oscar holds my hand, our fingers interlaced. I feel confident in the safety measures built into my new gear. Tiny vibrations move through my implants, and when I rest my awareness on it, I find the Unlit dormant and contained. I'm overjoyed to feel confident enough to receive affection from my two favorite people.

Since the only tourists we've seen have been bots, we're surprised to see a bustling crowd of actual humans under the grand chandeliers. The tables are crowded with mostly white folks of various ages.

Amongst them are a few uniformed Sages and divs, but their uniforms are not Helixx Corp or like any I've ever seen. They are private contractors working for the rich folks capable of affording a luxurious yet dangerous rift-side holiday on The Eminent.

Pyaar approaches the host station. A droid and two human *maître d'*s turn towards her. The two humans, wearing familiar but different circlets, meet her with tight smiles.

"Did the circlet look like retro futuristic fashion on me or is it just that way for these unRisen folks?" I mumble.

"Could you imagine risking your neck to work on this ship, looking for EDBs for rich folks' amusement?" Franxis whispers.

"Amusement *and* science," Thiia whispers sarcastically.

Oscar mumbles, "I'm sure Ferand's making a fortune selling tickets to her rift-closing extravaganza, but this is also about showing off in front of her rich friends."

"If these idiots thought about what might come out of that rift, they wouldn't think this was so much fun," grumbles Carmel, obviously disgusted by the tourists' willful ignorance.

Mira squeezes Carmel's hand and nudges her shoulder. "Babe, I would think Ferand has some of the most prescient divs on board. Would she have all these people here if there was a high risk?"

Carmel shakes her head. "Wouldn't put it past her."

Behind us, Harjaz laughs, and I'm happy to see him once again connecting with his old friend, Ehsan, and his old flame, Zinwara. Even Aaliyah, normally the most stoic amongst us, seems jolly. She smiles playfully, obviously glad to be on the receiving end of Zinwara's attention.

One of the circlet-wearing *maître d*'s steps around the host station. His voice is strained and carries a touch of snobbery. "Guests of Dr. Ferand are always welcome, but you are a bit early. Please, give us a moment. We are finishing up preparations in a private suite."

"Thank you," Pyaar says. When he walks away, she mumbles to us, "I'm not sure if he's being polite or rude, unless I read his mind."

Zinwara cocks an eyebrow and asks, "Did you read his mind?"

"No." Pyaar lifts her eyebrows. She transfers to the entire group, *I'm surprised to find that something's blocking me out.*

The *maître d* returns, forces a smile, and says, "Follow me, please."

As we walk through the elegant restaurant, I notice that nearly all of the guests are wearing either circlets or have implants. There are only a few among them who have no visible tech on their heads—all Risen, a Sage, a few divs and comps. Many of the diners glance toward our large party and look away. Some of them do not hesitate to stare directly at us.

A white man with skin stretched tight from repeated facelifts cranes his neck to get a look at us.

Zinwara speaks across another table towards him. "You act like you've never seen a person with such lovely jewels."

The man jerks his head back so quickly that his circlet skews.

"They wish they had this bling," Ehsan chuckles.

"They don't want to pay the price I paid," Zinwara mumbles.

There is a quick, almost unnoticeable flash of the lights in their circlets and implants.

I saw it too, Franxis transfers. *But not in yours.*

Both the staring and the quick looks all stop, and the diners return to their hushed conversations and gourmet food.

The door to the private suite slides open. Standing in the cultured diamond archway is the acolyte, Vy Anh. She looks up from her comm device and smiles almost genuinely.

"Welcome, guests," Vy Anh says, gesturing towards the dining table.

The long table is set for twelve. An ostentatious chandelier hangs from the clear ceiling, starry space beyond it. At the center of the table is a lovely arrangement of flowers, but Pyaar asks the host to take them away so we can all see each other. He moves quickly as the acolyte stares daggers at him. The elaborate curved back chairs are gilded antiques bolted into the floor for space travel, but on sliding tracks so diners can move towards and away from the table easily. We all sit, fully aware that the room is being surveilled.

Before he leaves, the *maître d* tells us that the chef is preparing a special twelve course plant-based meal for us, and the first course will be out shortly.

"Too many courses," Pyaar says, waving her hands. "Too much coming and going. Please, give us more privacy, fewer courses."

The *maître d* looks personally offended as he steps out of the private suite.

Vy Anh turns back toward the table and forces a grin. "Dr. Ferand will join you soon." The door slides closed quietly behind Vy Anh as she leaves.

They're surely turning up the volume on the hidden mics now, Arun transfers to the group, and Carmel snickers.

Pyaar waves her hands as if shooing away flies. "I've already disabled them. Disrupting frequencies around tech—even hidden tech—is easy. I'll show you how, Arun."

Arun smiles at Pyaar. "I'd love to learn that trick."

"Me too," Zinwara says. "Feel like I've had eyes and ears on me since I've gotten here."

Pyaar tilts her head side to side. "I'm sorry to hear that, but this skill is Sage level." With a wink, she tells Zinwara, "I'm happy to show you when you reach Nine."

"Well, I'm back at a steady Four. Only five more to go." She smirks playfully.

"This is the first time we've all been together since we came onto this ship months ago," Carmel says. She nods at Oscar, and he sends the signal to everyone requesting psybridge reception. When everyone is connected, Carmel continues, "Thank you for disrupting the mics, Pyaar. I feel it's best to say this privately. Today, I want to talk about how and when we are getting off of this ship, but I'm sure Ferand will interrupt us soon enough."

Ehsan shifts forward in his seat. Others look a bit uncomfortable but not surprised.

Carmel sighs. "I feel like our home station of Mani has surrendered us to not just Helixx Corp but Ferand. Those of you from Station Scire might feel that way too, even though Ferand recently purchased your home station and technically you work for her. Seems like Ferand will be making her attempt to close the rift very soon." Carmel's jaw tightens. "It troubles me that we heard about that from Mani, through a stealth signal sent to Old Girl*'s* comm. Had I not been on our ship to run some checks, I might not have gotten that message." She shrugs her shoulders, tilts her head, and announces, "I don't trust Ferand."

A pleasant chime comes from the opening door and the *maître d* steps through the gemstone archway. He is followed by three circlet-wearing servers carrying water vessels. Harjaz stares at the waiters intensely, making no qualms about his invasive gaze. The waiter filling his water glass seems to mistake his look for flirting, avoiding eye contact but grinning mischievously. When Harjaz says "Thank you," in a deep slow voice, the waiter finally looks at him, and Harjaz surprises him by reaching out and touching his arm. An almost imperceptible flash of divination moves through Harjaz's fingertips, brightening the waiter's circlet with rainbow circuitry. Harjaz's eyes go slightly wider. The waiter nods and shies away.

Harjaz transfers quickly, *The circlets block psychic interception, not EDBs. I also gleaned that the ship itself blocks EDB interference in the unRisen.*

Must be very advanced tech if it's blocking out higher-level Sages, Franxis transfers.

That EDB-blocking tech would be very useful in shelters on Earth. Why is Helixx Corp not making it available to everyone? Thiia asks.

Pyaar patiently transfers, *Please, remember, we are most likely being monitored for general psychic activity, and it becomes more difficult for me to cloak it all when there is so much chatter.*

The *maître d* announces, "Our sommelier has paired each course with a taste of wines from the Ferand estates in both California and Spain."

"We're working, not drinking," Carmel asserts.

The *maître d* opens his mouth to say something, but quickly reshapes it to an exasperated smile. He nods and turns toward the acolyte.

Vy Anh steps forward, tense hands clasped in front of her. "Dear friends, please, allow us to wine and dine you per Dr. Ferand's request. She would like so much to offer you this fine meal in gratitude and celebration before our historic work commences."

"Vy Anh, is it?" Carmel says. "We don't typically drink because that can dampen divination—surely you know that. If Ferand wants us to show up full force, she'll understand."

Vy Anh bows her head. "Of course..." She looks up, and Arun signals the look of her aura to all of us. A bit of disappointment in herself waves around her like a dark cloud. Her implant flashes quickly and the dark wave disappears. The light in her eyes grows momentarily dull.

"One small drink would be okay, Captain," Arun says, and Vy Anh brightens. "I prefer to make a toast with something a little more potent than water."

Carmel looks as if she might refuse, but she doesn't.

Vy Anh looks visibly pleased. "Dr. Ferand will be joining you for the second of four courses." As she turns to leave, she ushers in a couple of waiters with bottles of wine.

Franxis sends a quick signal that turning away Ferand's generosity might offend the ship captain. She pauses and adds that we are still guests.

Pyaar signals agreement and encourages everyone to be gracious.

Carmel's jaw tightens again until Pyaar signals that it was wise to set a boundary, but also wise of Arun to accept a small amount of what was offered.

Twelve waiters enter and place a small bowl of chilled soup in front of each of us. The head waiter presents the dish, saying, "Chilled beet, cucumber and dill soup topped with oat buttermilk and a fine pistachio sift, all grown in our lunar greenhouses." He pauses, flashes a thin smile, and turns to leave.

As others begin to eat, Carmel hesitates.

"Never been a fan of cold soups," she says.

"Can we take a moment to welcome Zinwara and Ehsan into the fold?" Thiia says, raising her voice jubilantly to shift the mood.

Ehsan wipes his mouth, blinks his painted eyelids, and flits his painted nails. His movements are loose and free. He tilts his head toward Thiia and gives her a friendly wink.

Zinwara seems far more confident than she did just a couple of weeks ago. I sense that not only has she let go of feeling self-conscious about the large crystals growing out of her face and shoulder, but she has embraced their beauty. She smiles as she looks around. "I have to say that being on this ship has not been one hundred percent perfect, but I'm back steady at Four because of the training I've received here." Everyone but Carmel smiles back at her as she speaks. "I've gotten more skilled at teleportation—"

"Bamfing!" Ehsan says with a dramatic wave of his hand.

"Bamfing?" One of Pyaar's eyebrows creeps up.

"Comic book reference." She cuts a playful side-eye towards a giggling Ehsan.

I speak quickly with humor. "So, you can bamf with best of 'em?" I flash her a flirtatious smile and lean forward, resting my elbows on the table with a fist under my chin. Thiia laughs.

"Yes, I can," Zinwara says teasingly. "And I'm getting better at teleporting too." Perhaps involuntarily, she glances towards Aaliyah, whose cheeks brighten.

Harjaz laughs fully, and even the Sages crack genuine smiles. Carmel remains stoic until Mira nudges her with an elbow. She forces a smile, which after another polite nudge from her wife, becomes half sincere.

"I'm looking forward to introducing you all to the rest of the crew of The Queen," Zinwara says. "We lost some good folks when MaalenKun came through the rift, but we're a tight group. Like you all."

"To your crew and mine," Carmel says and lifts her glass of wine. "And we'll have a proper toast with more than half a glass of fun when we're off this ship."

We all lift our glasses and salute each other.

"And welcome back, Casey," Franxis says. There are several pleasant echoes of their sentiment through our psybridge. "Really missed you, buddy."

I almost make a joke about wishing we had more wine but decide to instead just receive the sweet vibes. "To us all," I say.

Everyone lifts their glasses a little higher before taking a sip.

"Captain, I have to say..." Oscar says. "I don't quite *mistrust* Dr. Ferand."

Carmel folds her arms. She gazes toward Oscar and tilts her head.

"I feel Dr. Ferand is socially awkward, perhaps a bit disconnected—certainly not accustomed to folks who don't cater to her every whim. She is driven by her goals but also—"

"Entitlement?" Carmel interrupts, overstepping a boundary, ignoring a commitment to remain open to her crew.

Oscar smiles patiently and signals understanding with his warm eyes. He bats his dark eyelashes and shines our recently expanded light-thread brighter for Carmel to see. With the Sage psybridge, everyone can catch sight of the shimmering, bold line from his heart to mine. Accustomed to seeing thin threads between hearts, everyone momentarily pauses in a moment of awe. Awe shifts into joy and delight throughout the psybridge.

A corner of Carmel's mouth turns up as the smile extends to her eyes, and her jaw relaxes. Carmel sees her friend, the div she accompanies, expressing his love openly. Her happiness disarms her own resistance. She unfolds her arms and highlights the light-line from her heart to her wife's. More joy and celebration echoes within us. The other corner of her mouth slides up into a full smile, and she assents silently through our psychic connection, sending along delight, gratitude, and a quiet apology.

Oscar directs a note of forgiveness toward her and continues, "I was going to say that Ferand is driven by her goals, but also… some of our goals are shared. We all want to help Zinwara deal with the zin-spectrolite, to get the Unlit out of Casey. We all want to close the rift. Who cares if Ferand has to put her consciousness into a computer or something? If she can close the rift, I'll help."

Agreement is signaled by everyone else in the group. I am the last to signal agreement before Carmel looks around, meeting our gazes, and sighs before picking up her spoon and tasting the soup with a look of gracious acceptance.

"Still not a fan of cold soups, but… the taste is okay." She signals her acquiescence.

I'm not the only one to hold back laughter.

"So does everyone really believe Ferand can be the first trans-human to…" Ehsan waves his hand, adding, "...transcend humanness?"

"Helixx Corp has been working on this for years, of course." I wipe my mouth, feeling grateful I've finished the last of the delicious soup before I'm about to spill a bunch of knowledge all over the table. I try to keep it simple for everyone—myself included. "Since they realized divs could pull down advanced scientific knowledge, Helixx Corp has sought out the most talented div-tech scientists. Unrestrained by laws she might encounter planetside and endlessly funded by investments in multiple industries, she has—according to her autobiography—come closer than anyone else ever has. Although she has not shared the strategies with the rest of the world, she has achieved a negligible senescence, drastically slowing her aging. Also, several of her organs, including her eyes, are bio-engineered or tech-enhanced. Her book is five years old, and she felt she was on the cusp of full body transcendence then."

Others are finishing their soups, and the second course, along with Griselda Harris Ferand herself, will soon be with us.

"The advanced data integration techniques of polychain-plus—a Helixx breakthrough—make our most advanced AI possible, and more expansive tech can be integrated into our nervous systems with brain computer interfacing." I tap a finger to my implant to emphasize the point. "By many accounts, we've already reached transhumanism in a way, with cybernetic limbs, bone and organ replacements, but... Ferand is aiming higher. She seeks to leave her aging, susceptible human body behind completely. How she will do that, I don't know. Maybe we can ask her ourselves."

The chime announces the arrival of twelve table bussers who move quickly to clear the dishes from our first course.

Vy Anh, the acolyte, marches in with the *maître d*, followed by twelve waiters carrying covered dishes. When all the dishes are placed in front of us, the covers are simultaneously removed. I sense Carmel suppressing an eye-roll at the performance followed by Mira suppressing a laugh. The *maître d* announces the dish again: a savory croissant stuffed with pumpkin and shitake-enoki mushrooms—a special fusion created by Helixx Eats—with walnut crumble and peppered air.

"Air?" Thiia whispers across the table towards me.

I glance towards her plate. "Those grey bubbles."

She looks back and forth from the murky suds to me, and I can't quell the laughter before it escapes, shaking my shoulders. Thiia looks at me with adoration as I stifle the laughter and look back towards the *maître d* and the acolyte.

"Dr. Ferand will be on projection soon," Vy Anh addresses the table as the *maître d* exits. As the door opens for him, I notice that the volume of chatter in the restaurant has died down somewhat. Vy Anh looks to her comm, saying, "Here she is now." She swipes her finger across the comm towards the table, but nothing happens. She looks confused as she swipes again.

Oops! Pyaar transfers. *Dropping comm disruption signals, everyone.*

The projector spins its blue beams down from the chandelier. Griselda Harris Ferand's visage emerges from the blue light. The projection casts her from the waist up, so it almost looks as if she is merging with the table. "Welcome guests, it's lovely to see you all. I would be with you myself, but as many of you know, food is not my thing." She pauses for non-existent laughter. "Instead of eating, I've been making some preparations. With the recent developments in our nanotech thanks to Div Kenzari and de-powering the Unlit within Div Isaac—" she says our names with enthusiasm. "—we feel we are only hours away from closing the rift. Our target time is midnight."

Oscar leans his elbows onto the table and peers into the hologram. "Dr. Ferand, has there been a breakthrough I'm unaware of? When I left the team last night, we had still not found a way of getting the nanotech small enough to go in and extract the Unlit."

"There have been a few modifications to our strategy." Ferand says. "We no longer need to go in to extract *all* of the Unlit."

Oscar shakes his head and smooths his beard with both hands, "But we need to get it out of him. We don't know—"

"It's okay, Oscar." I speak confidently. "The implants are working." I signal to Oscar that the benevolent energy from Vinea is keeping the Unlit contained, and I feel confident that it is not a threat. "We work on closing the rift first, and then, we work on getting the rest of the Unlit out."

Ferand looks at me as if I've saved the day or at least her presentation. "Yes! We'll keep working to get the remainder out. You have my word."

I feel Carmel moderating her mistrust and frustration.

Carmel asks, "Dr. Ferand, how are you going to remove just part of it? It's incredibly ungovernable stuff."

"Oh! We do not agree…" The hologram turns toward Carmel. "In fact, we think it is highly governable. It's just that the governing body which programmed it had only malice and ill will for humankind. I, on the other hand, will give it new programming. I have a team of divs overseen by my acolyte—" Vy Anh rocks forward on her feet, eyes sparkling. "—who have been studying and learning from Vasif—"

"Her name is Vinea," Thiia interjects quickly but firmly.

"—Yes! Vinea. Thank you. Forgive my blunders. I'm incredibly excited." Her apology and excuse are both weakly performed, and she rushes on. "After studying Vinea, our team is now capable of understanding how to use the nanotechnology to sort quantum signatures the same way Vinea did. In our previous test, we were close to having a vessel that could hold my consciousness. My mind was kicked out of the nanotech because the energy signatures of the crystalized EDBs shifted into an unpredicted pattern. We have studied Vinea, learned from her, and now feel confident that we can hold the EDB crystal's energy in a set pattern." She holds her arms out. "We will be able to reprogram the Unlit with my own consciousness."

"What happens to the reprogrammed Unlit?" Oscar sits back in his chair and reaches for my hand under the table. I squeeze his hand gently. "Are you—?"

Ferand waves both hands into an x and apart. "I will be leaving this body. My consciousness will be moved into the Unlit." She sighs, tilts her head back, and waves a hand toward her glistening eye. "To put it simply, the Unlit is capable of containing living data, intelligence. I will occupy the Unlit within crystals faceted to nanotech. Similar to the tech you and Div Mira Adivar helped me test. The updated nanotech is already synced to my mind." She taps her implant with a long, painted nail. "I have been controlling it successfully for weeks through a neural uplink. Whereas before the crystal chambers contained only the remains of EDBs in order to access their energetic signatures, the updated design will also contain me... in the Unlit."

"We obtained samples from the Unlit when it was crystallized in Casey's quarantine room," Oscar says. His face is relaxed but neutral. "We weren't able to keep the Unlit viable."

"Because of the *type* of crystals," she replies. "We've found a solution."

"That's where I come in." Zinwara says, turning toward Oscar and me. "I've already given them samples. It appears that my zin-spectrolite crystals can house the Unlit. They'll remove the majority of this." She gestures toward the beautiful crystals growing from her skin. "Everything that isn't bonded with my body tissues."

Ferand looks longingly at the crystals on Zinwara's face for a moment before her expression shifts into forced veneration. "Yes, with the zin-spectrolite crystals, we will be able to keep consciousness within the nanotech. We have successfully tested the crystals already given to us with a small sample of the Unlit."

Mira's hand flies up to her mouth. "Liam?"

The hologram sighs deeply. "We did not realize that your crew had bonded with Div Liam Ulloah, or we would have been more forthcoming with the information. After his death, Central wanted us to study what had killed him. We found within him the Unlit. It was mostly unviable, but a small, weak portion was collected and stored. It degraded quickly, but recently I realized that the vibrational frequencies of Zinwara's crystals complimented the shifting quantum signatures of the Unlit. We tested them multiple times to great success."

I feel as if there is something Ferand is not telling us, and I sense I'm not the only one.

Ferand continues, "The crystals housed the small portion of Unlit while keeping it active. Because the unique crystals have grown from a human body, and the Unlit has been somewhat filtered through a human being, the two can couple and correlate. The crystals will be reshaped to fit into the nanobots, the Unlit inside will contain my consciousness. And I will be in my new form."

"What about the rift though?" Thiia asks.

Ferand looks as if she is waking from a dream for a moment before she smiles. "With the Unlit, I will be able to access the power of the ring—just as the monster MaalenKun did. And I will use the ring to seal the rip in our reality."

"How do you know you'll be able to use the ring?" I ask.

"It has been foretold." The holographic face turns toward Mira and Pyaar, and they both bow their heads slowly.

Franxis transfers to me alone, *I want to say there are holes in this, but maybe it's just all over my head.*

I signal back that we're not being told everything.

And you're okay with this? they ask.

"To closing the rift," I say, raising my glass, and the rest of our group, including the reluctant Carmel, lift their glasses as well.

Griselda Harris Ferand smiles a little too wide, but at this point, I feel like I'm getting used to her awkwardness. She claps her hands together, and says, "There is more to come, but for now, enjoy your lovely meal. And thank you all. I truly couldn't do this without you." With that, the blue rays spin her image apart.

Oscar pulls on my hand. "I'm sorry, Casey. We'll figure out a way to get the remainder of the Unlit out."

"It's okay," I tell him, and I open fully through our psychic connection to show him that I feel confident that Ferand's crazy plan will actually work. "If we have the chance to close the rift, we have to do it."

I wonder to myself how Ferand's team of scientists plan on getting a portion of the Unlit out, and my comm vibrates in my pocket. There's a message from Ferand saying that she did not want to mention the procedure in front of everyone, but Vy Anh will give me details after our meal. She ends the note with more gratitude.

"It's going to be okay," I tell Oscar. I lean over the space between us, and he meets me halfway with a sweet kiss.

As he pulls away, he smooths his beard, and I finally realize that the move is a nervous habit.

ꝏ

After our third course (tiny eggplants stuffed with shaved and charred Brussels, umami rice, and hybridized herbs with cashew creme) and dessert (baked apples and pears grown into shapes of roses with a pecan creme filling), we all praise the chef and leave the table.

"I can't imagine why Ferand would have wanted me to eat eight more courses with wine before going back into surgery tonight," I groan. "I'm too full after four!"

"That feeling is called crapulence."

I laugh. "That's not a real word."

"It is," he insists, taking my hand and pulling me closer. "One of the most appropriate sounding English words of them all."

As almost everyone leaves ahead of us, I laugh loudly and glean a bit of our comps' delight in our play and affection.

As we step away from the long table and out of our private suite, I admit, "That was the best food I've had in probably… ever."

"Not hard to beat the food on Scire though," Carmel quips as she and Mira walk ahead.

Vy Anh speaks first to Carmel and Mira about their roles for the operation. Predictably, Carmel looks less than happy, but Mira seems agreeable. With a swipe of her finger, Vy Anh sends details about the assignment from her thin tablet to Mira's comm. Carmel nods to the four of us before they join the rest of the group and make their way back to the hyperloop.

The acolyte gestures for us to walk with her, and Oscar, Franxis, Thiia and I follow her through the nearly empty restaurant. Her heels click on the marble floors. All of the diners are gone, and only a few workers and small robots are cleaning the large space.

"They come and go so fast," Vy Anh says. "They're all here for the big event." It's unclear whether she means the closing of the rift or Ferand's occupation of a new body. "And you're a big part of that event, Div Isaac. We'll send details to prep you."

"How exactly are you planning on getting the Unlit out of him?" Franxis asks before Oscar can ask the same.

Vy Anh's heels stop clicking, and she turns toward us. "Please, don't let it frighten you, but we're going to open Div Isaac's arm up and provoke the Unlit. We'll need Casey aware, no anesthesia, so he can consciously uncouple from the Unlit."

I was expecting this, but Oscar reflexively squeezes my hand as his other hand smooths his beard. Franxis' mouth hangs open, and Vy Anh tilts her head, eyebrows raised, waiting for one of us to speak.

"Provoke it?" Thiia places one hand on Oscar's tense arm.

Oscar shakes his head. "But we know it's dangerous."

"Yes. Well, it was. Now that it is de-powered by the implants, it isn't. Because the Unlit is triggered by sound and movement, we will be able to control its direction and keep it disabled by altering its sound using the same frequencies emitted by Div Isaac's implants." Her gaze drifts as she pictures the scene. "It will be reprogrammed with Master-Doctor Ferand's consciousness shortly after." She blinks slowly as the lights of her implants flash. "We're taking all necessary steps to reduce risk. This is Dr. Ferand's new body we're talking about. We are sure it will be a success."

After speaking of my body as if it is but a step in the method of her boss' reinvention, Vy Anh simply turns away. She takes several steps before realizing we've stopped in our tracks. She turns back toward us, sighs, and rolls her eyes. "Div Kenzari, you're at Five, you can hear whether or not I'm telling the truth?"

Oscar strokes his beard. "Your voice is clear."

The acolyte raises her eyebrows. "My only goal is to assist Dr. Ferand in transcending the confines of her human body and occupying an infallible body of her own creation." Her implants flash again. "It will work, and from her new form, she will be able to close the rift. I assure you."

ꝏ

excerpt from decrypted note to Dr. Griselda Harris Ferand from Helixx Corp Div-tech Lead Operative, Dawson Craig
10 June, 2138 16:32 (Greenwich standard)
permanent delete engaged upon opening comm; file will self-corrupt in 00:00:10

Div Casey Isaac's implants are indeed subduing the Unlit within him. MedOps has also detected the same Aphrytian energy signature fluctuations as observed in Vasif. We have a team working on a disruptor/emulator that will be able to nullify the Aphrytian energy and redirect the Unlit.

Don't expect the Mani crew to approach the rift in a Helixx Corp ship. Prescient disruptors installed on Old Girl (Mani registered ship).

Ready the Ascendant.

ꝏ

OSCAR

After he leads me into the room, Casey turns and pulls my hands away from my beard. He puts his arms around me, pulls me closer. Our heads rest on each other's shoulders, and I'm exactly where I want to be.

"It's going to be fine," he says, but I can hear the touch of concern in his voice. I see only a small amount of worry in him, but he's holding onto it tightly. I sigh wondering if I'm projecting my fears. He believes those words even if we are both a bit worried.

He runs his hand through the back of my curly locks and smooths my beard before turning my face up towards his. When he kisses me, he immediately loops through our psybridge all of the sensations that he feels back into me. Our pulses quicken. Chills run up our spines and down our arms. I meet his rising desire with open reception. We have not had sex since before the incident on the field, before the Unlit breached.

"You sure?"

"Last night, after the implant surgery, I just wanted to be held," he says. I catch glimpses of the taxing concern he had, that the Unlit would emerge in our sleep and hurt me. He shakes his head, fully aware of what I'm glimpsing. "Now that I'm absolutely certain there's nothing to worry about, that it can't hurt us now..." He swallows hard. "I'm sorry I pulled away. For a long time, I couldn't forgive myself for what happened with Usain. So I couldn't see myself as worthy of this type of connection. I didn't think I deserved love."

"You are loved, Casey."

"I know." His aura brightens. Sunrise colors wrap around him. "I see that. Through you."

My crooked grin grows. "I want you closer."

My own desire rushes through me, looping back as it couples with Casey's. We both will our uniforms loose and peel them off each other. Every touch, every brush of his fingers against my skin, sends strong currents of pleasure through both of us as we sync our sensations. I open my mouth to ask if it's too much for him, because for a moment it seems like too much for me. He subdues the concern within me and presses his naked body into mine.

I reach for divination, pulling down traces of my attainment from Six. I move it towards him, so that his empathic power enables him to see my aura as well. Shifting and flowing shades of red and orange through tones of pink and purple brighten all around us. We're wrapped in the flowing radiance of dawn. The red glows brighter and permeates the other colors. He kisses me with his eyes open, taking in the shifting colors.

He pulls me toward the bed, and I let him guide me down onto the plush surface. I slide back further onto the mattress and watch his mischievous grin as he kneels on the bed and just looks at me. His hands stroke the length of my hairy legs. I put my hands behind my head and try to look sexy, but I have to bite my lip to keep from laughing at myself. Waves of orange glow surge through my aura. As his hands move up my torso and brush the hair of my chest, he shows me a radiant desire within him. His aura surges bright red. He directs my awareness deeper into him to show me his appreciation of what he sees as sexy—me, my body, my aura, my heart. He traces his finger across the constellation of beauty marks on my skin. I feel the tactile sensation of his aura. It slips over my skin like a stream of heat, radiating and spreading. The light touch of colors brushes over erogenous zones that I'd yet to find in my one-hundred and forty years, and my breath quickens. As my aura moves against his body, he loops the sensations back to me, and I thrill in his excitement.

He moves closer, positioning himself between my legs, and I bite my lip harder. I show him within me the building desire as I keep my hands behind my head, willing myself to just be open, to let him feel me, let him increase my arousal with each touch. He braces himself over me, gazing into me with his beautiful eyes. Through the glow of his aura, even the lights and crystals of his new implants look magical and sexy. He grins at me for thinking so about the tech.

I brighten the light-line between our hearts with delight in every aspect of him. He responds with his own delight and presses his body down onto mine.

Our auras brush against each other. Vibrant, feathery at times, they move past the boundaries of our skin. Warm waves of light move through us, into us, a rush of passionate energy. Our auras begin to merge, the colors flowing into and out of each other. As our bodies move, the unified aura becomes magnetic, connecting us deeper into each other.

Our light-line hums loudly. We are both surprised but pleased to sense the vibration intensify, expanding into a steadier light-line. Our light-line shines brightly through the merging colors of our auras as purple and pink filter the warmer colors. Our heartsongs harmonize.

We move each other as if we've both been on a sex-fast, building up anticipation, and now in the pulsing colors of our auras, in the song of the light-line, with each thrust and moan, pleasure races up our midlines and fills the spaces within and around us. I'm steeped so deep in the shared pleasure that I lose my hesitation to see beauty in myself. Casey lights up his heart with revelry, and I steep in the beauty of his delight in me. I almost feel selfish or egotistical, but those labels fall away. I'm left with only the life-enhancing energy looped between us. I steep in his beauty and show it to him. Even as the wave of synchronized sensations strengthen and our emotional intelligence integrates, he keeps a steady rhythm.

The sensory loop expands with such a powerful force that the borders between his and my pleasure vanish into a fierce and vivid expansiveness which uplifts us as one. The following tremors, heavy breathing, gentle laughter, and soothing touches bring us back to ourselves, wrapped in each other.

We lay in the glow of our integrated auras, and I relish in his charms. There are no words to say, so we feel. Obscurations fall away, and we relax in being seen and cherished. He loops the feeling back around to me while strengthening it with his own bliss for being received into my welcoming heart.

Time is lost. Nothing looms. There is only us, moving each other, being moved by each other's love, and being moved by loving.

ꝏ

Lilly wakes us with a friendly voice. "Your escort will be here momentarily... you two might want to put on some clothes."

"Thanks, Lilly." He groans as he rolls over to face me. He pulls my arms tighter around his naked body and strokes my beard smooth. It feels so much more soothing when he does it for me. He knows from our psychic connection that I spent the past hour watching him sleep in my arms. He strokes my beard again. "I think we better dial down the psybridge before they put me on the table. I don't want you to pick up on the anesthesia-free cut they'll be making."

I squint my eyes and my brow wrinkles. He kisses my forehead until my face relaxes again. "I think we should just shield the pain. I want to be with you as much as I can."

"Okay," he says.

We're dressed by the time there is a ring at the door. Two tall, broad figures clad in armor are silhouetted by the opaque glass wall.

Lilly's holographic cat projection perches near the door. It turns its head and the eyes it does not see with look big and affable. Lilly's image brings up a welcome affectionate feeling within both of us. "Bye, Casey. Bye, Oscar," The AI says as we pass the hologram. We both echo our goodbyes.

When the door slides open, we see two heavily armored Helixx Corp Div Guards with dual swifts in their holsters. I feel a shock of surprise move through Casey before he quells it and says hello to the escorts.

"This way," one of them says, gesturing down the hall towards the nurse's station.

At the nurse's station, we find another armed Div Guard. Her red armor glares in the bright overhead lights. Thiia and Franxis stand on either side of the guard with their arms crossed.

"They say it's additional security with all the tourists on board," Thiia says.

Franxis extends a welcome connection for my psybridge and signals their discomfort about the Guards. Casey wraps Franxis in a tight hug and tells them not to worry. Franxis' smile is slight when he lets go. Franxis squeezes his shoulder, and we step toward the quarantine ward exit.

"Not that way," one of the Guards says. "Lab Hebe is this way."

Another guard holds up a holoscreen, taps a few buttons, and Vy Anh's face appears on the screen. "We've got all four of 'em," he says.

"Bring them in," Vy Anh chirps pleasantly before the holoscreen blinks off.

The back wall pops and hisses as a wide, secret door slides open. A hyperloop car awaits inside. Its door lifts. I wonder how often Helixx Corp secretly moves people from quarantine to its labs. We step into the car and take our seats. The Guards say nothing to us as lights of the hyperloop tunnels flash around us. In minutes, after a few smooth weaves through the network of channels, we lose track of the direction in which we are headed.

Casey highlights every one of our worries and silently asks us to overcome them all. I see within him the desire to not only be free of even a fraction of the Unlit but also to close the rift. He feels a sense of purpose that I will not discourage. I silently begin to empathize and remind myself that our aim to close the rift is aligned with Ferand's, no matter her method. I tell myself that if Casey can go under the knife, take the bigger risk, then I can try to trust Ferand. But trying is not doing.

Thiia sends me support, signals that she feels very much the same.

I reach out to Carmel and Mira. They sync my psybridge with ease, as we've done thousands of times. Both of them signal how strong the psybridge is with Casey's empathic enhancements. Casey grins and bows his head. A note of gratitude rises within me for the clear connection to my friends, my family.

They're prepping Old Girl to take her out to the rift along with a group of crimson wings from the Helixx Corp fleet. Mira and several other divs with EDB communication and manipulation skills are being sent closer to the rift. They'll rendezvous with divs in crux-wings and clash-wings to guard the extradimensional breach. Station Scire is already positioned nearby. Nothing will come through the rift without meeting resistance.

Carmel transfers, *Oscar, I'm only doing this to protect your birdies in Scire's gardens.*

All four of us in the hyperloop car chuckle, psychically receiving the secret joke. All three guards stare back at us with cold expressions.

Not to save the planet? I reply, and Thiia leans her shoulder into mine.

Franxis senses the running joke. They transfer, *Still got a few birds planetside too.*

Well, I guess it's worth saving, Carmel says.

Mira signals laughter and adoration for Franxis getting in on the joke. Mira adds, *Take care of our guy and our guy's guy.*

Franxis replies, *Always.*

Our comps look at us with extreme adoration.

Casey takes my hand, and I notice one of the Guards look away with disgust. I interlace my fingers in Casey's and stare towards the guard, but he doesn't look back at us. Thiia leans her head on my shoulder, bringing my attention back to the psychic group hug.

Without words, Thiia signals a strong sense of love, home, family. Casey shines his heartstar, lighting up the threads and lines of light between all of us. With the upsurge from the light of our heartstars, I reach out further. Soon, I find Arun and Pyaar. They begin moving along the length of the ship towards the signals of our heartstars. They integrate the strength of their Sage psybridge, but I cannot see them. There is only a small impression of their presence. Arun signals not to focus on that. Pyaar signals for me to reach out to the others.

It is unclear just where they are because I don't know them as well, but soon Harjaz, Aaliyah, Zinwara, and Ehsan are connected as well. I'm focused so intensely on stabilizing the connection that it feels as if they are very close. When the hyperloop car slows, I realize that they are awaiting our arrival.

Our four friends move towards us across Laboratory Hebe.

Two of the red armored guards step out first and flank the door. The third, the one who looked away from Casey and me with disgust, says in a gruff voice, "Out."

We step out of the car and onto the floor of the laboratory. The wall closes behind us, seals.

We have no idea where another exit is.

My stomach quivers. Harjaz puts his hands on my shoulders and transfers. *We need you to keep that psybridge steady for us all, first mate.* He looks me in the eyes. "You got this, Kenzari," he says.

My shoulders soften under his strong hands and with appreciation for him. "Call me Oscar, please."

He squeezes my shoulders and nods. "Okay, handsome."

Aaliyah rolls her eyes, but she also can't help but smile, adoring Harjaz's predictable flirtations.

As the others hug each other, encourage each other, and try to settle each other's nerves, I look around the space.

Nearby are two operating tables. Four short, tech-embedded crystal platforms rise up from the floor, one at the head and foot of each operating table. A wider, fifth platform sits further back. Over the right side of one of the tables is a menacing looking robotic arm with an assortment of surgical instruments floating in what I assume is a sanitizing gel.

Further out in the space is the cube of nanotech, humming with low activity. The crystalized remains of EDBs sparkle within the cube of tiny bots. The dimmed sunset colors of fading orange and deepening purple shift as I stare at it, wondering if Griselda Harris Ferand is synced to it, possibly watching us.

Casey takes my hand again, and I notice the chatter from the group dying down as they too begin to see the oddness of the laboratory.

Unconcerned with the Red Guard, Casey quips, "They should fire the interior designer."

Ehsan laughs out loud. "Money obviously doesn't buy taste."

Near the center of the room is a pillar of red garnet two and a half meters tall. A black veil hangs over the top and drapes down the sides.

"The draped column is a bit much," Zinwara quips.

"Who decorates a laboratory like this?" Harjaz says.

Thiia and I walk along the wall for a good look at a series of ten photo-realistic portraits.

"These are her ancestors?" Thiia asks.

I reply, "There's a strong resemblance."

I look down the line of paintings wondering how each previous relative contributed to the fortune, if any of them could have imagined their descendant slipping out of the genetics that they bestowed on her to occupy a body built of technology, to become fully transhuman.

Across the room is a huge, circular window thirty meters in diameter reinforced with thin beams overlaid in an almost spider-web pattern. As if it is all caught in the web, the glowing rift hangs out in the short distance, the fleet of wings heads into position, and Scire floats near the glowing breach. I spot Old Girl amongst the ships.

Vy Anh stands near the window, looking at a holographic projection of a uniformed Helixx Corp officer. Vy Anh is far enough away for the audio to be faint. With a little tuning of vibrations, I tap into div-enhanced hearing.

"Twenty-four ships, light-wings, A-wings, clash-wings are Helixx. Then, there's the old clunker registered to Mani. Those two would not go out in a Helixx ship."

I almost smile imagining Carmel insisting that they would be taking Old Girl, or they wouldn't be going out at all.

"As predicted," Vy Anh says. "We have Red Guard on that ship?"

"Affirmative."

Vy Anh swipes impatiently at the hologram and the uniformed officer is replaced by a nervous looking Helixx Corp technician. "Bring their gear." She swipes through the projection before the technician can respond. His image is replaced by a woman who looks just like Vy Anh. "Ready the Crimson Chain." Again, she swipes, and the face is replaced by another possible mirror image. "Ready the Ascendant."

"Supremacy is near," Vy Anh's identical face in the hologram replies.

"As are our special guests." The blue light rays spin apart, and the hologram vanishes into the comm device on Vy Anh's wrist. Her heels clack across the floor. As she steps into the light closer to us, her grin appears almost cordial but too forced to be friendly. "Welcome to Dr. Ferand's personal research facility, Laboratory Hebe."

I notice a change in her tone from when we saw her earlier at the restaurant, and I realize that was a different Vy Anh.

"This is quite the set up," I say, tuning in Five and listening for any variations from truth.

"I would've gone with a sheer veil," Ehsan cracks, jerking a thumb toward the red garnet pillar, the red drape, and Casey laughs.

She shrugs, almost laughs, and manages to smile more genuinely. She whispers conspiratorially, "Her tastes can be... eccentric."

The joke relaxes us and our willingness to cooperate in closing the rift takes precedence.

A small group wearing Helixx uniforms for MedOps, div-tech, and various science departments enter following the technician from the hologram projection. The technician wheels in a cart carrying six neatly arranged sets of mission gear. The armor is shiny like the Red Guard's but neutral grey. Vy Anh dismisses the technician, and his small, wiry frame jumps at the sound of her voice before he hurries away.

"Our latest design," Vy Anh says. "Although we are confident in our low-risk strategy, we thought you would feel more comfortable and capable with the best in personal shielding technology, Helixx Corp's latest mission gear. You'll need to change out of those old uniforms and don the Helixx uniforms for the psychic uplinks to work. Please…" She gestures toward the cart, the gear designed for combat.

I am the only one who hesitates, the only one who feels less than certain.

No, just the only one who's showing it, Thiia transfers as the group, save Casey and Zinwara, take the gear from the cart.

As we begin peeling off our uniforms down to our underwear, Vy Anh leads Casey and Zinwara towards the operating tables and the group gathered around them. Casey looks back at me and winks as I try to smooth my beard. A team of div-tech power up the robotic arm for surgery while a group of MedOps with floating holoscreens approach Casey and Zinwara.

A flicker of light moves too close to Thiia's presence in our psybridge, and I realize it was an offensive transference aimed at her.

Thiia's voice comes strong, halting everyone in the room. "You got a problem with my body?" Thiia glares at the same guard who looked away in disgust when Casey and I held hands. She boldly stands in only her black tank bra and tight briefs as she confronts the fully armored Red Guard. With her hands on her hips, she cocks an eyebrow and stares down the guard.

New to the group, Ehsan and Zinwara move to raise their voices at the guard, but I psychically reach toward them, and ask them to let Thiia stand strong and lead us. Half of us remain exposed in our form fitting black underwear, half of us have old uniforms or new gear up to our waists. All of us stand next to Thiia, signaling our support.

The Red Guard snickers and mumbles something as he looks away.

We keep our eyes on the guard even as we hear Vy Anh's impractical footwear clicking toward us.

"Is there a problem?" Vy Anh says loudly toward the Red Guard.

"Yeah," Thiia says. She juts her chin toward the guard. "Can we get this homophobic, transphobic jerk out of here?"

The guard looks back toward Thiia with undisguised disdain.

Vy Anh raises her comm and with a few flickers of light from her implants, a man in a red Ops uniform appears in the projection. "Send in the rest of our Red Guard with a replacement for 103. Take him offline."

The offending guard's arms immediately jerk straight as his armor locks them in place at his sides. He winces, and I seize the opportunity to glean a flickering thought from him. The flash of thought lands and begins to unfold in the psybridge between us all. It's unclear just what it contains, but we are all accustomed to catching forced transference that takes a few moments to disclose itself. The thought which he was trying to conceal begins to unweave slowly.

I'll watch it and signal what it reveals, Aaliyah transfers. *Everyone else, heads up.*

As the guard with locked arms turns and marches out of the room, eleven more Red Guards trot in to take his place and position themselves in a semi-circle curving in towards the operating tables. The technician glances over his small shoulders at us as he wheels the empty cart back out of the door which closes and seals behind him.

Vy Anh looks at us with performative solidarity. "So hard to find good help," she jokes before she returns to the medical group.

Casey grins and playfully leers at me, reminding me that I'm half-naked. I want to be near him for whatever MedOps is saying, and I quickly finish getting into the gear. The others make their way over to the operating tables shortly after me.

The guard's thought is still unfolding slowly, Aaliyah transfers.

Maybe it's nothing, Harjaz replies.

I only catch the last of what MedOps has to say, which is basically how they want us to position ourselves.

Casey nods and I turn to him to ask him for more info. He places his hands on my armored shoulders and reminds me once again: *We need you to keep that psybridge steady for us all, Oscar.*

Our light-line hums the song only we can hear between our hearts. He pulls me closer and kisses me. As he lets me go, he looks toward the rift with a sense of purpose in his beautiful eyes. I try not to cling to him and relax my hold around his waist. As he slides himself onto the table and lays down, I look out the window towards the glowing rift.

Old Girl is the last ship to move into position around the rift. Carmel signals that Mira sees no threat ahead. Mira sends waves of care towards me, and I find some comfort in knowing that at least one prescient div and her comp feel confident.

I reach out for Arun and Pyaar, and although I feel the connections are still strong, I cannot see or hear them. I tell myself not to think much of it. They're probably deep in meditation.

Franxis gazes at me from the foot of Casey's bed. I look over my shoulder to see Thiia in position next to Aaliyah on a raised platform of tech-imbedded quartz. Harjaz stands at the head of Zinwara's bed, and Ehsan holds her hand as Zinwara slides onto the other table. She and Casey look over at each other. They signal to each other support, shining into their light-thread. The bulky crystals growing from her body reflect the lights being turned up around the tables. A team of MedOps and scientists stretch large belts across both of their bodies, binding them to the hard surfaces of the tables. Another technician with a holoscreen turns on the gravity restraints, and my heart aches as their faces wince slightly.

A ripple of shock moves from Aaliyah as the homophobic Red Guard's intercepted thought unfolds fully, and I turn back towards her.

Oh no… no no no… Aaliyah panics. *It's all been an act to get us to trust them! To get us in this gear, in this position!*

My helmet snaps up quickly and jerks my head forward, straining my neck. The operating table's gravity restraints increase, pinning Casey and Zinwara to the tables as they cry out. My armor surges and goes stiff. I cannot move. Franxis' eyes go wide. I psychically reach for my crew. Our armor is locked. We cannot move. We're trapped.

ꝏ

My stomach sinks. I didn't hear the deception in anyone's voice. How could we be on board this ship for months and not realize?

I didn't see any of this, Mira transfers, her voice heavy with failure. Mira signals that the Red Guard on board Old Girl have leveled sonic cannons on them. She reaches towards us and realizes that we cannot move in the locked gear. *I thought it was because we'd gone into the rift. They must be using prescience disruptors on us.*

Griselda Harris Ferand steps to the top of the arched line made by the Red Guard. She stands before the draped pillar in a crimson caftan which dramatically hangs off her outstretched arms. Her implants glow a steady, bright red, casting shadows on both sides of her face.

"Let them go!" Casey shouts at her. "Let my friends go!"

"You know I won't do that, Casey Isaac. Before we begin, I want you to know this has nothing to do with discrimination. Only strategy. Our Sages unfolded a vision of the future where you triggered the end of the world. You had to be stopped." Ferand looks at Casey, then Zinwara, then all of us with mock pity. "You need not fight a fight you cannot win. Surrender. For the Supremacy is near."

The ceiling of the room slides open as the walls lower, leaving the portraits on thin wire stands. In the seats of the amphitheater rising behind the descending walls are hundreds of crimson robes, implants and circlets glowing red, casting harsh shadows over each face.

"What is this!?" Zinwara struggles against the restraints. Ehsan futilely fights against his locked gear until Harjaz signals for him to save his energy.

"This is the way back to universal order, Zinwara Osei." Ferand holds her arms out toward the amphitheater of red robes. Hundreds of faces turn to again stare at Zinwara as they did when we walked past them in Ferand's luxurious restaurant. Ferand steps closer to Zinwara. "For generations, the Crimson Chain has been guiding a lineage towards a power promised to us. It is the power to right the world, to bring back natural order, to restore rule to the true conquerors." Ferand looks at each of us as if we are naïve children. "The strong are meant to rule. The weak are meant to dwindle and die. You might think that being poor or disenfranchised, as you call it, doesn't mean that a person is weak, but in a world ruled by money, it means nothing else. Even your supernormal powers of divination are nothing without the financial backing and governmental influence that brings you together, gives you training, positions you to guard the worthy, the true conquerors." She raises her arms to again gesture towards the crowd. "Why, Zinwara, I'm happy you asked... This is a time of harvest, a gathering of exquisite fruits that combined will yield a new body, a body from which I will access the power of fallen storms. I will close the rift and open a doorway into immortality... for the worthy." She slowly shakes her head at Zinwara. "You didn't want to admit it, but you have known all along that I have more power than all of you combined. Your lodestar, your desires, your actions have led you here... where your neck is under my boot." She turns away, crimson caftan flowing around her.

Every arm of every individual in the rising tiers around us extends toward Ferand, and she turns towards all of them with her arms high and wide.

Ferand raises her voice and shouts, "Ave eversor!"

A loud chorus responds, "Ave eversor! Ave eversor!"

As the words MaalenKun spoke fill the air, we tremble in our locked gear.

Carmel's voice comes through in quivers, *Oscar! Why is the psybridge shaking?*

My throat tightens. It feels as if words have left me until I hear his voice. Casey looks up at me from the restraints.

We were wrong to trust them, he transfers apologetically.

I'm so sorry, Casey.

We try to quell the barrage of our anger and disappointment so we can hold our connections strong.

The robotic arm jerks and veers closer to Casey's body. A scalpel-laser emerges from the cluster of sharp tools. The blade of light traces the incision line. Around the scalpel-laser projector, several hooked wires extend and snake towards Casey.

He transfers again, *Hold onto us, Oscar.*

I pull down from Six, so close now, and my sight becomes layered. Mira's head turns to look over her shoulder, and she looks into me. She realizes what is unfolding within me and signals an awareness of multilayered vision acceptance. Hebe lab, the cabin of Old Girl, and the mindfield where we connect our psyches all become super-positioned in my awareness. This is what foresight is like for her. No wonder she often closes her eyes when looking ahead. In the mindfield, she reaches toward me with support, highlighting the skill to smoothly move my awareness simultaneously through the planes of sight.

The rest of our crew comes into my awareness in the mindfield. We are positioned much as we are in the laboratory. Our heartstars glow brighter, and the lines and threads of light between them shimmer, forming an interconnected link between us.

My vision shifts back to the lab.

"Stay strong, everyone!" I say, but only Franxis sees my lips moving. The comms in the gear are set to receive incoming messages only. They're silencing us as much as they can, but some things they cannot take away.

I transfer, *Stay strong, everyone. Hold onto each other.*

One of the Red Guard steps forward and stands between the operating tables. "Divs," he says, looking to both Harjaz and me. "Dull them. Deep."

Harjaz says. "I'm not going to dull her—"

He immediately raises his boot high. "Then we will!" he growls. His and several other red boots hit the floor, and a flash moves from under each foot into the crystal bases of the operating tables.

Zinwara and Casey both gasp. Casey's eyes roll back before his eyelids droop and close as the force of the dulling divination pulls him under. Harjaz, Franxis, Ehsan, and I leap to catch them as they fall through the foundation of the mindfield. Thiia and Aaliyah reach for us and catch us, but it is as if we've all fallen over some cliff. Casey and Zinwara sink to a low place, but the six of us catch them before they can drift any deeper. Their bodies lie stiff on the tables, barely breathing, and in the mindfield, they lay several levels below us, suspended by our light-threads.

Across the table, Franxis strains to hold Casey from sinking lower. I look across to Ehsan and see the same effort across his face. I strain to stabilize the psybridge, restrengthening our connections, but Casey and Zinwara remain in the low place.

They've got us where we can't defend them—only stabilize them! Thiia's transference is strained with anger and fear. *Can either of you divs dull the Guards?*

It's taking all I've got to keep Zinwara from going under, Harjaz answers. *This much dullness could shut down their hearts and brains if we don't hold them.*

Hold fast, Harjaz, Ehsan says.

I discern that the expression is a reminder of the bonds Harjaz has with Ehsan and Zinwara. It hits me that although they've been apart for some years, they have a history that strengthens them. I worry that my short but intense time with Casey is not enough to strengthen our own bonds.

Franxis senses my concerns. They signal a reminder of my own capacity to hold us, and it's enough to help me quell the fear.

I transfer, *Everyone, hold fast!*

In red and orange combat gear, one of the twin Sages stands next to the garnet column. Around his neck are layers of gold chains secured to his armor. A crystal shard hangs from each chain.

I transfer as calmly as possible, *If that Sage grasps any one of those crystals, he will unlock the power of the EDB frozen inside.*

In his bony hands, the Elder who joined us in Ecuador carries the ornate silver coffer containing the extradimensional ring. His eyes fall on me without a glimmer of recognition, and my heart sinks under the weight of betrayal.

Ferand turns her face up to the rows of crimson robes in the amphitheater. Her eyelids softly close for dramatic effect, and the lights of her implants flash and grow brighter. The colors of the nanotech cube brighten, shifting into more luminous tones of orange, then red. The swarm of bots ascend, pouring up from the cube as the synthezoid cirrostratus cloud billows from them. The sweet chemical smell of ozone drifts into our helmets. Seemingly per Ferand's mental commands, the nanobots reshape their position to form a larger, taller screen. The contours of her face emerge from the screen, and its mouth moves. Her voice amplified through the collective nanobots shouts, "Ave eversor!"

"Ave eversor!" the crowd responds.

Ferand opens her eyes, but her mouth remains closed in a tight smile as she speaks through the screen of fluctuating nanobots. "Hail the Crimson Chain! We are here to seal a wound… to spare the great ones, those who excel, who dominate. Tonight, we not only save the planet we will rule from an extradimensional threat, but we take the first great leap necessary to save the worthy from the clutches of entropy. Tonight, we overthrow death." A murmur of pleased sounds moves through the cult in red, the Crimson Chain. "Let the weak and poor have disease and age." They respond with laughter. "Let those who shirk the natural order of the universe flail in the dirt and dust of their ancestors' graves. Woe is not for us." She gazes into the crowd. "Throughout history, many have tried to become the great conqueror, to purify the human race, to rid our world of the inferior, the weak, the unnatural. They did not have the proper tools for the job. They could not rid the world of their own weakness, their own entropy. Our forebearers saw the coming of this day ten generations ago, yet their arcane magic which brought us here has become fallible, corruptive." She pauses, as a murmur of agreement comes back. "You feel it too. Your forebearers who've lived in you have begun to wither. The power they once brought to you has dwindled—"

What the fuck is she talking about? Carmel transfers, and we all realize that she and Mira are in the mindfield with us, witnessing what is happening in the lab.

The cirrostratus and screen of nanobots parts like curtains as Ferand passes through. The giant, nanotech face looms behind Ferand as she walks toward the operating tables. Franxis struggles against the locked gear with rage until Thiia reaches out to help them steady their focus back on Casey.

Ferand looks at each of us as she continues, and intensity builds in her voice. "The power to overthrow death and entropy was called into this world by generations of our forebearers. It has been bestowed to the undeserving at random. One hundred and eight years ago, a power our forebearers were promised, a power we were promised, was scattered across the globe. To this day, the undeserving rise up… holding our power… They call themselves divinators." As the cloud-surrounded nanotech follows her, Ferand steps back toward the garnet plinth. Ferand continues to speak through the screen of hovering microbots. "These divinators, the Risen, are but another test of our commitment, our intelligence… a final test… The tools to restore order, to shape our destiny are before us. Our time has come to pick up those tools, to seize control of the Risen, to become what our world needs… its conqueror."

The robotic arm jerks, quickly moving in closer to Casey.

In the mindfield, Casey stirs. He is trying to reach us, but he cannot transfer from so far under. This is why Ferand wanted us here. She needs them alive, but so deep that they can't access their Levels.

Franxis stands across the table at Casey's feet, tears running down their face. Ehsan strains as much as Franxis as they both try to lift Zinwara and Casey to where the rest of us have gathered in the mindfield.

I signal for them to stop trying to wake Casey and Zinwara up in the mindfield. *Their pain. They can't shield us from it. It'll hurt but if we let it disrupt us, we'll lose them.*

Casey stirs in the low place. Another figure approaches them. The Shadow peers down on him and the Unlit in Casey's body roars.

I breathe deep. Energy from Six flows down into me, and I see the patterns the Unlit holds, the programming from various consciousnesses. An ancient echo arises, a signal. It will keep hold of the minds it touches. Until annihilation. The knowledge rocks me.

Ferand's voice is amplified through the nanotech. "Our bloodline anchored in the past, redefined in the present, will shape the future we desire. Our forebearer's old magic has given way to science and technology, but a prophesy from generations past tells of a doorway made of that which captures light and that which refuses light. We will shape that doorway with zin-spectrolite crystal grown from the wounds of this world and the Unlit containing extradimensional consciousness. Through that doorway, I will enter my new body. A body that will transcend entropy. I will be the first, and you, the worthy, will follow." She pauses as palpable excitement builds in the crowd. "The time of the crimson prophecy is now."

The robotic arm lunges forward. The scalpel-laser glows bright red and cuts deep into my lover's body. The hook-ended wires pry apart his skin, connective tissue, and muscle to reveal Vinea's gift of benevolent energy glowing between the bones of his forearm. A shadowy substance shifts inside the luminous chamber.

"The Supremacy is near. So close now…" Ferand looks on as the nanotech swarms into a cloud above us. "I can touch it."

The swarm of tech descends on Casey and Zinwara.

It carves into the zin-spectrolite crystals growing from Zinwara's body. Bit by bit, the nanotech breaks away the crystals. We scream inside of our helmets, and inside our minds, we struggle to hold our loved ones steady.

The laser-scalpel retracts, and a frequency disruptor and sonic emulator emerge from the array of tools. The disruptor's grating signal grows increasingly high-pitched, and Vinea's benevolent light, her offering, is shreded. Light bounces off of the uncovered void and it slithers upward, expanding from depths within itself. The sonic emulator whirs a signal similar to the one generated through Casey's implants, directing the growing Unlit's movements. There is so much of it. The undulating void hangs over Casey's inert body. Light slips around it, curving away in refracted beams. A shifting shadow falls over my lover.

The psybridge around Harjaz quakes. He cries out. Aaliyah braces him and gasps when she sees the nanotech digging closer to Zinwara's skin. The horde of tiny bots break away shards of the beautiful crystal until only the rocky chunks fused with Zinwara's body tissues are left. They shatter each piece smaller and smaller until it is small enough for them to attach into each microdrone's tiny casing.

A pool of blood gathers under Casey's arm. With the wires holding his arm open, his body inert, his healing factor remains only semi-active. The bleeding has stopped, but the sight of the open wound tears through my heart. I feel the same in Franxis, and we shine through our light-threads, compassion for each other, compassion for Casey. His body is present, but his mind is remote.

We hold fast to Casey and Zinwara as the clashing sound of the disruptor and emulators force the hovering Unlit into the space between their physical bodies. More robotic arms with disruptors and emulators emerge from the floor and descend from above. They surround the undulating void of Unlit. Their signals keep the recalcitrant substance from setting upon us.

A wave of shadow-smoke moves within the void. The Shadow seems to peer out at us. It directs its chilling gaze into Casey. It wants him.

Casey's body jerks. In the low place, the Shadow's eyes fall on him. His mind freezes. The familiar colors of his traumatic memories begin to swirl around him. Franxis and I try to warm his heart. He tries to reach for us. I feel him slipping away and strain to hold fast to him. I cannot let him slide further away.

I shout at Ferand, "This won't work! What is in the Unlit cannot be erased!"

Franxis shouts, "It cannot be reprogrammed!"

We're all shouting for her to stop, but with our helmets up, comms off, Ferand ignores each screaming face. As she turns away, we realize it's too late.

The twin Sage glares at us as he waves his fingers across the collection of crystals on his chains. With a sinister smile, he threatens to grasp any one of them and unload its force on us.

"No, Sigrund." Ferand's command halts the sadistic Sage. "Not yet. But soon."

Ferand tilts her face up, reaching toward the top of the red garnet column. The pillar descends into the floor slowly as the black veil pools at her feet. When the top of the column is in line with her hands, Ferand scoops up the object under the veil. She keeps her face turned up, and Sigrund grips the fabric.

Her buzzing, discordant voice arises from the swarm of nanotech, "Do not look at the mask."

Sigrund turns away, pulling the veil from MaalenKun's reassembled, golden mirror mask, and we look away quickly. A maddening cry comes the amphitheater. It is followed by another and another as several of the cultists look upon the mask of dis-existence. Those who did not heed Ferand's warning scream wildly as they lose their minds. They faint or drop dead. Everyone near them steps around the fallen bodies, looking on, but gazing around the mask.

Across the psybridge, we hear one of the Red Guard aboard Old Girl yell, "What the fuck is that?"

Fear grips Carmel and Mira as they peer through the cockpit window. The cloudy interior of the rift stirs. Within, some large thing moves.

The Eminent's klaxons blare. Helixx Ops has spotted the Titan.

A rush comes from the faraway Sages as the four stations sound alarms about the movement in the rift. A cascade of divination moves through Pyaar and Arun and into us. As if the Sages are with us, our nimbuses appear above us and our Levels begin to integrate. Luminous sacred geometry and glowing mandalas shift and expand secretly into the space above us. I reach Six, and Franxis looks up at me with confidence. The halos harmonize their sacred song patterns.

Oscar... Franxis transfers as the harmonic song moves between and through us. One end of their thin mustache curves up as they smirk. *Turn it up.*

We pour the song into the low place, channeling it towards our loved ones. The music spills around them like a shield.

Harjaz and I begin attempting to reverse the Red Guards' dulling force, but with the nanotech poised to literally shred Casey and Zinwara, it feels too risky. Instead, we siphon off the flow of the force coming from a few of the Reds, letting it secretly pool away from our loved ones.

Ferand takes quick glances at the mirror mask. Each time, her implants flash white, and her head jerks back as if by some jolt controlling her neck muscles. The sharp movement looks incredibly painful, but she repeats the process again and again.

Soon, phantoms are ripped free of her body. The unmoving Elder Sage still clutching the coffer, slings away the ghosts of Ferand's forebearers. The screeching phantoms disappear into the ether.

Her ancestors were literally inside her! Thiia says. *I thought it was a metaphor!*

At the window, three copies of Vy Anh urgently direct different people in the holographic projections of their comms. One of them looks back toward Ferand, and an unleashed phantom shrieks through the air toward her. It lands in her body, and she falls to the floor. Her body seizes as two Red Guard drag her away by her flailing limbs. The remaining two acolytes continue an urgent coordination of more wings to defend The Eminent.

Ferand again looks into the mirror mask, and with no more ghosts to exorcize, the Elder Sage begins to pull pieces of her mind free of her physicality. My mind flashes to the night we banished Bakkeaux, the blue light which Arun pulled out of us to defeat Bakkeaux. I realize why some of us did not survive. The blue light is life force. She is killing her old body.

Ferand's knees wobble. She slumps to the floor. She grunts and hisses as if frustrated with her body's weakened state. The Elder Sage continues to pull, but Ferand's consciousness recoils into her body. She pants, looks toward him, and he nods. She raises the golden mirror and gazes into it, and the lights of her implants glow white hot and shine on the surface of the mask. She lifts it directly across from her trembling face and holds her gaze steady in its distorting reflection. She inhales so sharply that the sound precedes her voice through the horde of nanotech. She strains to command, "Take me!"

Sparks fly from her implants. Her head is snapped back with a sharp crack. Her limp body collapses.

The bright light of her consciousness is ripped free of her body. The Sage casts it across the laboratory. The undulating void parts. Her mind sails into the center of the Unlit. Its blue light is engulfed in shadow-smoke.

The disruptors and emulators stutter, strengthening and easing their vibrations to pull extensions of the Unlit away from the core. Rivulets of the light-refusing substance stream out like thin threads. The opposite of a heartstar. The nanotech swoops down on the end of each rivulet, capturing the Unlit within the zin-spectrolite crystals. The space around it quivers as the union of tech, crystal, consciousness, and Unlit pulls into itself.

The vibrations slow, growing dark and still. An ominous, hovering orb.

We are being watched by something within the strange fusion.

Ferand's ambition, greed, and entitlement have blinded her. She's created a doorway into our world. She's accidentally built an interdimensional distans. A malevolent being in a hidden dimension, has seized control of the shape-shifting body.

We feel the Shadow staring out of the strange orb. It looks into us.

I quell my scream to prioritize sending the awareness throughout the bridge to my crew, to the Sages. Our network trembles with fear and frustration.

With only a trace of life-force left in her human body, Ferand weakly slides her head on the floor. She looks back at the orb shimmering with stolen zin-spectrolite. It grows smaller as the nanobots pour from its underside and gather into the shape of a feminine form. Ferand smiles weakly and shakes with feeble laughter as her new body approaches her old. But no. Her face slowly conveys a growing terror. Something about the new form is not what she planned.

It kneels and gazes down on Ferand, slowly reaching its hand out, as if to touch her face. Instead, it picks up the mirror mask of dis-existence and holds it out to Ferand, inviting her to destroy the remaining mental tethers to her body.

"Ave eversor!" The chant builds within the crowd. Soon the Red Guard and Ferand's Sages are chanting it too. "Ave eversor!"

Ferand peers into the mask, and as it unhinges her mind, her face conveys a sudden terror. She has failed. She screams. The Sage whips the last of her consciousness free of her human body, sending it into the shape-shifting horde.

The buzzing tech moves quickly, cutting through the air. A spray of red mist flies up from Ferand's neck. Blood is speckled across the nanotech body. Ferand's blonde head rolls away.

"Ave eversor! Ave eversor!"

The nanobot figure reshapes its bloody blade back into a hand. It raises the golden mask, and we look away. Reflected in the silvery cover of the coffer, I watch as the shapeshifter lifts the mask, tilts its head, gazes at the reflection of its terrifying new body. The shapeshifting horde brings its lips to the mind-splitting mask, and countless tiny bots crawl across the reflective golden surface. The mask cracks as the nanotech breaks it into millions of tiny pieces which disappear into the crawling mass.

The fluctuating nanobots shake off the offensive droplets of Ferand's blood. The synthezoid cirrostratus billows forth as the form rises slowly from the floor and lifts into the air before Ferand's pooling blood can reach its feet.

Our minds buzz, and a vision is forced into us. It wants us to see. Ferand's consciousness, a smoky blue avatar of light, is stretched and broken. The pieces drift. She screams as the void consumes her, stealing her knowledge of our world.

The buzzing stops, and we again hold fast to each other, to Casey and Zinwara.

The shapeshifting nanotech turns its featureless face toward the crowd. "Crimson Chain! You have heard my ancient call! You have drawn me to your world!" The discordant voice rises, grows stronger. "I am the conqueror of countless realities!" It rises into the air and hovers. Its lights glow through the crystals, bouncing off the Unlit, emerging as sharp needles of golden fire. Beauty and terror. "Bow before your destruction and savior!"

"Ave eversor! Ave eversor!"

I turn away, and Casey is with me again.

In the mindfield, our loved ones emerge from the low place. They lie before us, weakened.

Casey smiles and transfers, *In all those songs merging, I heard yours. Your heartsong.*

We hold fast to each other with our hearts even as our physical bodies are bound.

The amplified, harsh voice coming through the nanotech weaves into our mindfield, and we all realize that a portion of the Unlit remains in Casey and he in it.

"We are not done, you and I."

Casey recognizes the voice, and it shakes him to his core. The Shadow.

It speaks to all of us, but especially Casey and Zinwara. There is no fear in me as we move in to hold them closer to us as they tremble.

Its voice becomes louder as it invades our mindfield. ***"You cannot stop me."***

We brace.

"Give it all to me," its horrifying voice demands. It bursts into a flying swarm of shimmering tech diving onto Casey and Zinwara's bodies. It moves into Casey's open wound searching for the remaining Unlit. It carves away at the remaining zin-spectrolite crystals, pulling Zinwara's flesh and nerve away with them.

Zinwara loses a good deal of blood from the gaping wound stretching from her shoulder up through the side of her face. Her blood pools in the increased gravity of the operating table. A rush of healing comes through us from the Sages, amplifying Zinwara's healing factor. Her wounds close, and for a moment, we feel the Sages power with us.

Unable to find the Unlit within his physical body, the swarm draws back from Casey's wound. It knows, as Casey does, that there is more Unlit within him, but he hides it.

A piercing peal moves along the psybridge as MaalenKun begins to dig its way into Casey's mind. The psybridge begins to quake as Casey's empathic powers begin to transmit his pain and fear.

Our psychic hold on their consciousness begins to slip.

I gaze into his green and grey eyes. I confess, *I saw you long ago, the moment I got this power. I knew you would be my future. I didn't know how, but I knew you'd be important to me.*

"I know," he says. He smiles, blinking slowly, and I want to steep in the beauty of his face. "I heard it in a dream."

The Shadow roars at him, drilling into his mind.

The mindfield quakes.

I strain to maintain the psybridge.

Our light-line thins to a thread.

I will not let the song end.

Negative, unseeable space spreads around us.

There is only me and my lover and the kiss I place on his lips.

Hold fast, Oscar. He lets me go, takes one step back, and disappears into the nothing.

ꝏ

Written in the private journal of Mira Adivar by Carmel Arais Kosse

sometimes the tear
in my eyes
catches the light
just right
and for a moment
a rainbow
in the periphery
shines
before the tears trail
down my cheeks
a glimpse of
some beautiful thing
heralding release

ꝏ

CASEY

This is not the low place. This is not a mindfield. This is something else.

I am alone.

Space spreads out from me. It somehow feels empty and vast yet full and infinitely close. Seeming opposites come together in this place. I've glimpsed this place before.

This is where I am held, a reality where I am apart from the world, yet a part of the world.

I cannot stay.

The realm shifts, becoming somewhere else as I draw myself closer to another presence. It has become a place of subtle chaos. Fear wavers in the atmosphere. I find groves within me from the many times Franxis has anchored me within myself. I follow those groves, the pattern they've set for me, and I stabilize myself. I reach for Oscar, and a steadiness comes from within my heartstar. The consistency of support through familiar light-threads and lines, from Franxis, Oscar, other friends, centers me. I am still, though the world around me trembles.

Faintly, I hear the sinuous movements and the voice of the Shadow. It's looking for me, but disrupting Oscar, Franxis, my crew mates. Their mindfield quakes. Their psybridge loosens. I need to draw MaalenKun away from them.

I sit. I close my eyes. I bring together the tips of my thumbs and index fingers. I do not reach, but I allow my own mindfield to unfold into the subtle chaos. I reveal my presence, and the fiend redirects, moving quickly, growing closer until it is with me again.

Hints of Ferand's voice dissolve in the mix of clattering assertion. ***"Surrender, Casey Isaac."***

I look within me, finding small traces of its light-refusing body. I do my best to make peace with the knowledge that my mind could be forever integrated with this impetus.

I open my eyes, and MaalenKun sits in front of me. Wisps of refracted light leak from the swarming nanotech, the form in which I can perceive it.

"I am far more than this." The fiend turns its face of scurrying nanotech toward its own humanoid body. "I am not of your world, yet I take form in your world again. What name did you give me?" I feel an invasive psychic gleaning as it reaches into my mind. "MaalenKun, prince of the maelstrom. A poetic name, though I have no gender, nor do I want one. Perhaps the power in that previous body led you to believe I was the male heir of some dark force. To be more accurate, I am all dark forces embodied in immortal Shadow." It pauses, measuring the effect of its words on me as I do my best to quell my fears. "That previous body was built in another world for another purpose. It was defeated by you divinators." It lifts one of its hands and gazes at it through its eyeless face. "This one is… taking some getting used to." The zin-spectrolite crystals and crystallized remains of EDBs glow in shifting patterns like an oil-slick on water, both enchanting and toxic. "It has potential, but I want something you have."

My voice trembles. "What do you want with me?"

It does not answer but tilts its head to the side as if listening or pondering.

Tiny reflective grains of gold surface and gather. The broken pieces shift with the movements of scurrying tech.

"Casey Isaac, I want you and your world to break."

As the bits of golden mask emerge and reform its shape, it distorts my reflection. Again, the alien force within my body and mind begins to pull at my memories. Stronger now, the fiend gathers acute knowledge of my trauma. The curves of the mirror mask are reshaped into my own features.

I lower my gaze, willing myself not to flee.

"You remember well our first encounter. You reached for me to claim this power for your own." Lies. "And my crown stung you for that offense. It was in that moment I realized who you are." As it discreetly gleans my mind, searching for details about my unique attainments, it continues speaking in an attempt to distract me or convince me. "That was the beginning of your transformation. You received the Unlit, which remained hidden until your presence in the rift altered it. It was meant to be my gateway into this world... through you, yet you resisted. Your empathic power, as Ferand called it… has prevented me from taking over your form by strengthening your heartstar." It chuckles. "A boon for me." It lifts both hands now and gazes at them. "Your organic body is weak, fallible. I'm pleased that I did not take it. This body will be stronger, more capable. Through it, I will extract the power of divination and with it, conquer your world." It shivers with the realization that its words are unsettling and unexpected. "Through the ritual of the Crimson Chain, I can take you as I have Ferand… but only if you are willing. A part of you will not only survive, but you will escape the conquering of your world." It lifts memories in my mind: my self-abuse, turning away from myself. "And you want to leave this world... don't you, Casey Isaac?"

There is some truth to its words. So many times, I've been tired of fighting.

The synthezoid cirrostratus billows from the nanotech and snakes around me.

"Time after time, you are broken..."

Shadows and echoes of memories emerge around me. MaalenKun's sting, Usain's death, defending my life during Bakkeaux's attack, a needle in my arm, meth in my veins, my father's fists, the spit on his lips as he throws me away.

"Time after time, you think you are saved..."

The psychic assists from Sages and Vinea to subdue the Unlit, my crew, my chosen family embracing me, Franxis, Oscar. Oscar.

Waves of insecurity, unworthiness, self-doubt, self-loathing swirl within me. More waves of grounding energy, assurance, affirmations, each temporary yet powerful, rise to meet the heavier waves. They crash into each other. Each impact is jostles me.

Its voice speaks with more truth. "All of the pain, all of the pleasure... You are tossed about from one to the other..." But that hint of truth dips in and out. "What is Risen... will fall..." It uses that truth to manipulate. "Your love will only bring you loss... There is no place for you in this world."

A flicker moves in me, and I gaze out beyond the mask, through the void, deep into the Shadow. I pull in towards my heart center. I move beyond truth and lies. Beyond duality. I go in and in.

It hisses, "Give up... let me reshape you."

Within me is integration, interconnection to everything, ever. I am Held. I am never-not Held.

My heartstar glows brightly with a rainbow array of interconnections. Shining most vibrantly are the light-threads and light-lines to Oscar, Franxis, my crew, the Sages who have guided me. Countless thin light-threads reach in all directions, towards every living being. The rays of light gather within me like a glowing cloud. A carillon of heartsongs vibrates through the light rays, turning harm toward harmony, chaos into quiet, at the very center of my being. A place of belonging. The place I've been fighting to find my whole life.

I look through my interconnected heart at all the suffering in the countless lives inter-being in the expanse around me, and a sweet almost ache, a yawning in my chest, signals the expansion of my heart. I am not alone in my suffering.

Strength and care for community, resilience and rage against injustice become luminous sparks. The light flows from every living Queer person into my heartstar. I couple it with my own resilience, sync my empathic power, infusing divination, and send it back.

I see the interconnection of not only living Queer people but a constellation of compassionate connection reaching back throughout the ages to ancestors who integrated their support into the world for future generations, for me.

We are a legion of lovers shaping bright faith for a future of freedom.

Experiential faith, bright faith, arises. I lock it in. A luminous glow extends from my crown. Wisps of shifting and stretching rainbow lights fluctuate through the steady glow. My mind expands to witness halos of spectral light multiply across the sector, illuminating each Queer person's crown.

My spectra halo shines brightly. The resilient divination of an unshakable bright faith.

I stare into the mask. In its golden reflection, millions of colors fluctuating around my head. Rather than feeling the mask pull at my mind, I feel anchored in my heart. I am shielded in the sanctuary of a multitude of interconnections. MaalenKun's mirror mask of dis-existence cannot penetrate the spectra halo.

The multitude of light-threads, the glowing cloud of interconnection pours from my blazing heart toward the leaf Vinea bestowed upon me. The cloud pours into the leaf. A potent power sings within my awakened heart and surges down the length of my arm. Singing an unleashed roar, the well-lit force, a diversity of colored light beams, flies from around my fist. A cascade of energy glimmers and shines extending from my fist like a blade of colorful light. A spectra blade.

Mask twisted in rage, the Shadow bellows.

Without hesitation, I drive the rainbow lightning of the spectra blade into MaalenKun's deceptive mouth. The mask and the nanobots explode in a shower of lustrous glitter. The fiend is cast out of my mindfield.

Through the falling glitter and a faint veil, I see Zinwara seated before me. The similitude of our individual mindfields emerges as the twinkling dust from the exploding nanotech fades. We've cast the fiend out of our minds. With MaalenKun no longer between us, dividing and deceiving us in our individually held realms, the veil falls.

Zinwara sits across from me, a spectra blade shining brightly from her extended left arm. Our positions are so similar to each other's. Our hearts glow brilliantly, and I feel that she has had her own realization of resiliency based on her heritage. She sees within me how I accessed the strength of our Queer Ancestors and smiles with commonality. She sighs, and a single tear rolls down her cheek. I reach for her hand, and she reaches to take mine.

From the void behind Zinwara, our Black Elder appears and places her hands on Zinwara's shoulders. I feel two hands on my own shoulders. Our Black Elder leans toward Zinwara's ear, and the Sage mirroring on my side says in their melodic, yet strong voice, "I will be with you soon. Rise."

Yahima.

I inhale sharply, awakening to see Oscar's full smile burst across his face, setting free a few tears. At the foot of the table, Franxis laughs through tears that fall inside their helmet. A wave of relief moves through our psybridge as our loved ones no longer strain to hold us from falling deeper.

The Helixx Corp MedOps realize we're awake, and they turn up the gravity restraints.

It's MaalenKun! I transfer. *Different body, same threat!*

Zinwara's awakened voice transfers to all of us: *The gravity restraints are too strong. I can't teleport off this table!*

The increased power of the restraints keeps me from moving my head, but I can move my eyes to see over Franxis' shoulder.

The Helixx Elder removes the silver cover from the coffer. The extradimensional ring shines inside; its festoon is still wrapped in Vinea's energy. Vinea and Yahima can see us through the energy. They're boarding Lacassine.

I signal that Yahima is on her way.

Tell her to hurry up, Carmel transfers. *We need help out here!*

The accompanying image of a Titan emerging from the parting mist within the rift sends chills through our collective.

MaalenKun reaches an arm scurrying with nanotech toward the clear coffer, and the Elder Sage removes the lid. The ring floats in place as the Elder Sage steps away with the coffer. A stream of tiny drones pours from MaalenKun's buzzing hand and onto the ring. The drones crack apart the festoon. The nanotech reshapes the festoon into a single, pointed, golden fingernail as the ring slides down the shapeshifter's finger.

MaalenKun turns toward the large window, peering towards the rift. It raises its arm toward the tear between worlds, and I feel the Unlit within the stolen zin-spectrolite swirl violently. A high-pitched peal comes from the ring, and the invisible border of the rift is loosened but not unlocked.

Something is off. It senses me watching it through the Unlit, and it turns back to stalk towards us slowly as if it is questioning whether or not I can affect the power of the ring through my connection to the Unlit.

In my left hand, I feel a twitching. I sense the source of the movement and reach to find Harjaz. All of his focus is on moving one finger. He strains, attempting to touch the divination-channeling sensory pad of his glove to the network of tech embedded in the armor.

Harjaz's technopathic power, Aaliyah transfers hurriedly. *Oscar, strengthen the psybridge. Casey, sync our strength and send it to him.*

As I feel Oscar doing his part to strengthen the psybridge, I feel doubt arising in me. I transfer, *I don't know if I can.*

Zinwara seems far more confident than I am. *Enhanced strength is our divination flowing through us, Casey. Focus our strength through Harjaz.*

It's the same as when you shared Liam's shields in Ecuador. Oscar's transference rings with certainty as he draws from Five to make true. *You can do it!*

I focus on channeling everyone's enhanced strength through Oscar's psybridge. My empathic power unites with Oscar's attainments. I loop our strength back through the network. It merges with a flow of divination from the others. The synced divination, a wave of strength, rushes towards Harjaz, towards his index finger.

We strain to send him our strength. A big push for one small movement.

The locked, armored glove snaps. The divination-conveying pad touches his gloved hand. He reaches his power into the embedded tech to hack the code that locks him out. I couple Harjaz's technopathic divination with our strength, reverse its direction, and guide it back through Oscar's psybridge. An array of multicolored divination traces luminous paths throughout the circuitry within the gear, unlocking and disabling restraints, moving into the operating tables, powering down the gravity restraints.

Oscar's heads up display quickly scrolls welcome text. All systems are unlocked; Helixx Corp Ops are shut out.

Harjaz and Oscar let go of the pooling dullness they've secretly been siphoning off the Red Guard. They sling it back toward them with force, throwing several guards to the floor.

Thiia and Aaliyah step down from the crystal platform and close the space between themselves and their divs. Ehsan places a hand on Zinwara, Franxis reaches out to touch me, and our comps speed up our healing factors. Zinwara and I reach for Oscar and Harjaz. Oscar locks the psybridge in stronger as I loop my empathic powers through it. Our divination flows to our Accompaniment—for the first time, our comps have more than the power to anchor us. They're receiving some of our unique attainments. There is a power shift within us as all of our Levels and abilities harmonize. The rush of divination brightens our minds, bringing centeredness and power.

A growing spectra halo expands around each of our heads, bright with colorful streaks of fluctuating lights. The vision I had is realized. I sense spectra halos lighting up all over the sector, uniting us with every Queer person, channeling a protective power to us.

I catch a glimpse of Mira and Carmel. Their spectra halos shine brightly.

Carmel reaches out as if to touch Mira's spectra halo and instead, caresses Mira's face. "You're so beautiful."

Carmel embraces the surge of divination. She quickly shakes off any unease and begins looking through us for something.

I look up to see the elaborate array of colors radiating around Oscar's handsome face. His crooked smile shines down on me. "Can't wait to kiss you, Casey."

"I was thinking the same thing," I reply.

Our spectra blades flash brightly, cutting through the straps binding Zinwara and me to the tables. I pull my arm away and the hooks pull through my flesh and hang, dripping blood from the smoking robotic arm. With so much divination flowing through us, the wound quickly closes and heals.

"Stop them," MaalenKun says. "I'm not done with them. Especially that fa—."

Bamf! Zinwara is across the room driving her spectra blade into MaalenKun's head, literally cutting off its hateful speech before it can finish. A cascade of broken crystals and short-circuited nanobots falls to the floor.

The cultists gasp and scream.

Zinwara signals a reminder within me. I've done this before. I aim, focus... *Bamf!* My spectra blade lands in the midst of the nanodrone horde. A spurt of deadened crystals, sparks, and tech sprays outward.

I swing again, and the nanotech dodges. My spectra blade connects, but only grazes the tech. Already, the shapeshifter is learning to dodge our attacks.

We swing again and the nanotech separates, parting around the spectra blades. We miss as the tech swirls.

MaalenKun scatters into a thin cloud before sweeping across the room towards Sigrund. The swarm clings to and climbs over his body. He snickers in our direction as two Red Guard descend on us with their swifts raised.

They fire several times, but the blade guides our arms, knocking each stun-bolt out of the air. They rush us with their sonic cannons leveled. They fire, and we are violently pushed back and knocked to the floor.

Sigrund grips one of the crystalized EDB remains around his neck. In a blue-pearl flash, he teleports away with the nanotech.

Klaxons blare, and red lights flash throughout the laboratory. For a moment, everyone in the lab looks towards the window to see the Titan's hands, pushing through the loosened barrier of the rift. Its face of lights brightens as it peers out at the wings guarding the rift. A dreadful purple-black glow builds along the Titan's arms.

With our comms active, Oscar has us dialed in to Old Girl's frequency. Oscar calls to them, "Captain—?"

Through Oscar's superpositioned psychic sight, we see the Red Guard onboard the Old Girl right behind Carmel and Mira. The two guards look at each other, having obviously received an order from The Eminent command. They raise their sonic cannons as Mira whips around screaming for Carmel to duck.

Electricity flies up from the comm and nav computers. Crackling white and blue energy hits the Red Guard. Mira falls back shielding her eyes. The power surge causes Old Girl to go near dark before the Red Guard drop to the floor, unconscious.

"What the fuck was that?" Mira shouts.

"My apologies," a disembodied robotic voice glitches through the ship's intercom.

"Who the fuck?" Carmel shouts. "Is that AI on my ship?"

The robotic voice distorts, managing to digitally slur only, "Hello, I'm Lilly."

Oscar says. "It was going to be a surprise."

"Only because Lilly just saved our asses," Carmel begins rerouting power to the main engines. "I'll let it slide."

Purple-black lightning flies from the Titan within the rift. Several wings are hit, and their shields are breached. The wings immediately explode or go dark.

A sudden *bamf!* comes from the hall of the Old Girl, and Mira gasps to see one of the twin sages rushing toward them. Runar.

A flicker of warning moves through the space between Franxis and me, and I turn toward them to see the first of the Crimson Chain cultists swooping down from the amphitheater. A tall, broad man tackles Franxis, their spectra halo leaving traces in the air as they fall. Thiia and Aaliyah rush toward them. With their arms glowing with div-strength, they easily pull away the large man and toss him back towards the throng of crimson robes spilling down from the ampitheatre.

A Red Guard throws daggers of fire at Ehsan. He casts his shield in time for the flame to bounces off and hit the drape which had set atop the red garnet pillar. "Yesss!" Ehsan yells.

The guard rushes him, sonic cannons raised.

Bamf! Zinwara teleports across the room, and in a fraction of a second, an awareness of the spectra blade's power rushes throughout the psybridge. The blade sings of its power to cut through layers of existence, subtle or physical. Zinwara is given a choice, and we all see it unfold in the short time it takes her to lift her spectra blade. She swings her spectra blade up quickly as she slides underneath the guard's raised arms. The dancing rainbow blade cuts through the cannons before they can unload. Although the energy of the blade does not touch him, sparks and sonic concussions fly from his loaded cannons in all directions, breaking his arms. He crumbles to the floor.

Zinwara lowers the multicolored point of the flickering blade inches away from the guard's face. She seethes, "Any of you come for my fam, and I'll make sure you bleed."

I'm surprised to see Ehsan flick his wrist and knock the downed guard unconscious.

Harjaz and Oscar stand in defense positions with their backs to each other. Their divination and tech shields merge as the crowd of cultists moves in. I focus on the space around them and will my body to be there. *Bamf!* The mostly white faces look momentarily surprised to see me suddenly standing alongside Oscar. The surprise quickly shifts back to rage. I hold up the vibrating spectra blade, its multi-colored energy pulsing loudly.

"Just let us go," I tell them. "We don't want to hurt you."

Seven Red Guards push their way through the crowd and surround our shield. One of them sneers, "She's not done with you." They raise their arms, sonics charged and incursive divination surely tapped.

At Six, Oscar's foresight is just beginning to emerge. Oscar senses him coming before the rest of us. Oscar pulls me close to him, his helmet snaps down, and his lips land on mine. Ignoring the noise of faces shouting at us and fists landing against the shield, I return my lover's kiss.

"Sorry to interrupt," Arun smirks at us.

"It's okay, I saw you com—" Oscar doesn't have a chance to finish. Arun places a hand on each of our shoulders as Pyaar appears and wraps her arms around Harjaz.

Suddenly, the red robed crowd is full of giants, their images stretch long, and we are falling. Only the cultists aren't getting bigger, we're getting smaller and smaller. We see their shocked expressions as we fall below the barrage of sonic blasts, lightning bolts, and beams of heat. With our shield gone, their attacks land amongst themselves. They have to bear the force of their own aggression. We grow small enough to fall through the floor. Flashes of tiny quantum lights fill the space around us, and after a moment, the narrow service corridor lined with pipes and cables underneath the lab, stretches into view around us.

"Did not see that coming," Oscar says, looking dazed.

The Sages vanish again, and the commotion above us continues.

"They should've taken us out last!" Harjaz shouts.

"No… no!" Oscar shouts but not in response to Harjaz. He groans as he staggers with disbelief as he witnesses what is happening to our friends near the rift.

Runar clutches various crystals chained around his neck as he advances on Mira. She unloads her sonics on him, but with a wave of his hand, he redirects a blast back into the cockpit. The impact dents the central panel of lights and switches. Holoscreens glitch and flicker.

Mira hears Carmel shouting for her to stand down.

Mira shouts, "What?"

"GET DOWN!" Carmel shouts, but the Titan has already reached another hand toward them. Its robotic, stony grip wraps around the ship's shields.

The force rocks the ship, and Runar falls to the floor. Mira leaps from the cockpit towards him. He clutches one of his many chained crystals, and as she lands on top of him, her fist drawn back about to strike, his hand moves through her armor, between her breasts, and into her body.

"I could tear your heart out," he growls, "But I've found something more interesting."

He retracts his hand from her body, and she breathes a sigh of relief, but the breath catches in her throat when she feels his hand pull the chain around her neck. He smiles wickedly as he draws out the ring set with the crystalized remains of Bakkeaux.

Mira shakes her head slowly. "Don't," she whispers.

"But..." the wicked Sage whispers. "It's too tempting."

He closes his fist around the gem, his eyes rolling back as he seizes the surge of new power. A rippling vortex flies from the Sage's forehead and plunges into Carmel's head. Her spectra halo provides only a small amount of protection from the sage-amplified attack. Carmel seizes and screams while Oscar and I cast a shield to prevent the vortex entering the psybridge. Runar draws the vortex back out and holds it only inches away from her head.

Oscar falls to his knees. "Casey, you have to teleport me out there!" he pleads.

I kneel down next to him and prop him up with a hand on his shoulder. "I'm sorry. I can't make it that far."

"N'guwe, come in!" Harjaz says over his comm. We both look up at him. He has allies left on the station in his ear. "Prep rescue ships for Old Girl! Redirect all ships to crystalize the light-refusing substance on the Titan's body! And tell Scire's Sages to aim for its fucking head!"

Runar pulls the chain drawing Mira closer to him. Her eyes stay on Carmel holding her aching head, trying to recover. His stinking breath lands on her cheek. "You're going to do everything I say, Mira Adivar. Or I'll pull this chain halfway through your neck. I'll leave it lodged in your throat. You'll die slowly while you watch me destroy your wife's mind."

Mira shakes her head, and they stand slowly. With pattern recognition from Six and the knowledge of her lover's heart, she secretly begins rebuilding Carmel's damaged mind.

"Now," Runar growls. "You're going to tell that Titan my boss wants a word. She's eager to speak with it."

Mira has to let go of Carmel, but she does so, knowing that Oscar is there to take over.

Kneeling in The Eminent's secret corridor, Oscar closes his eyes and forms a mudra for focus. He tries to reorder Carmel's mind.

Mira focuses her divination on the Titan, and the giant illuminated mask of lights turns toward her, peering into the ship within its clutches.

Several crux-wings from Scire sweep down, aiming their chargers on one of the Titan's arms. Crystals form along its arm as streams of the Unlit are captured. The arm freezes in place, but the Titan doesn't attempt to move it. The Titan reaches several more arms out of the rift, batting at the wings even as clash-wings pummel it with powerful sonic blasts.

On nearby Scire, the primary, Haven-linked charger expands like a flower's petals opening to the light, rotating toward the Titan's head.

Mira's focus is intense. She strains to connect her mind with the Titan.

"I've got its attention. Where's your boss?" Mira says through clenched teeth.

Runar smirks as his free hand clasps another chained crystal. "The Supremacy is near."

Another blue-pearl flash fills the cabin as Sigrund, cloaked in the scurrying nanotech of MaalenKun, appears behind him. The swarm of tiny drones peels away from the corrupt Sage and glides over the electrocuted Red Guards into the cockpit. It gazes out of the window.

The shapeshifter turns its head. "Surely, you recognize me, Mira Adivar. I saw your power from within the nanotech you helped Ferand test. Did you not see me, your destruction and savior, as I drained Divs of their power before your very eyes?"

Why doesn't it drain Mira's power right now? Oscar asks.

Through the Unlit I see the answer. *It can't use it the way she can! It needs her!*

Oscar urges, *Use that advantage, Mira!*

Perhaps sensing our transference, the fiend's head tilts to the side as if it is listening. Golden fingernail shining, it lifts its hand wearing the extradimensional ring, the key. An otherworldly, high-pitched peal fills the cabin.

I see into MaalenKun through the Unlit. It's connected to the Unlit within the shapeshifter. I glimpse concern in MaalenKun's mind. It can loosen the border of the rift as Vinea did, but it cannot open or close it fully without more power.

The edges of the rift crackle and hiss like live wires. The space within the opening shimmers, hardens, and the Titan roars, lodged in the breach, caught in MaalenKun's grasp. The Titan's arm, covered in crystalized Unlit, shakes. Dust floats into space as it breaks free from its cracking stone body. The lights of its mask flicker wildly. Bolts of purple-black lightning crash into but not through the hardened edge of the rift. MaalenKun turns its hand around and suddenly loosens the boundary. The Titan stumbles. It turns its face of lights towards Old Girl, perhaps sensing the key being used against it.

MaalenKun turns toward Mira. "Tell the Titan to surrender its Unlit. Tell the Titan to step through the breach... and bow to me."

Runar tugs on the chain reminding Mira that he can easily rip her wife's mind to shreds.

"No." Mira's spectra halo fluctuates as she shakes her head. "I won't help you bring that thing into our world."

Weakly, Carmel murmurs, "That's my girl."

In the corridor, Arun and Pyaar land next to us. They've brought Thiia, Aaliyah, and Franxis. There is significant exhaustion in the Sages' eyes. They kneel next to us, training their focus on Carmel and Mira.

Carmel thrusts her reach violently through the psybridge. Oscar is unsettled by a familiarity with what she reaches towards. Thiia tries to help Oscar heal Carmel's mind, even as Carmel grasps around them.

Amidst a blue-pearl flash, Zinwara and Ehsan appear. Harjaz slings his arms around his old friends and pulls in staggered breath, shaken with relief.

Aaliyah rushes to Zinwara, checks her skin through the tattered uniform, and sees that her boosted healing factor has already sealed up her wounds. Zinwara meets Aaliyah's eyes and without saying a word, but gasping lightly, she acknowledges her pain. Aaliyah is quick to pull her in close and hold her. Zinwara's body trembles briefly as Harjaz places a hand on her back, and she cries on Aaliyah's shoulder.

MaalenKun nods toward Runar, and the vortex flies into Carmel's head again. We shield and brace again to stop the mind-ripping force from reaching everyone, but the pain of not being able to shield Carmel grips our hearts.

Perhaps, it can hear MaalenKun through the Unlit. Perhaps, it can struggle against the boundary trapping it no more. The Titan thrusts forward. MaalenKun flicks its ringed hand again, and the breach loosens enough for the Titan to tumble forward. Covered in frozen streams of crystalized Unlit, its stone arm shatters. Aside from its mask of bright lights, the lights of its mechanical parts flicker off and go dark. The shield on Old Girl's port side wing blinks off. The crumbling stone and robotic claws crash into and through the ship's wing.

"Mira..." Carmel says weakly as the vortex continues to bear down on her. "Shields up!"

Old Girl's klaxons blare as the ship slowly breaks apart.

Mira breaks the chain around her neck, snaps up her helmet, and fires her sonics on Runar, knocking him down. Runar maintains the vortex assaulting Carmel. Mira fires another sonic blast toward MaalenKun, but the swarm disperses around the pulse which lands against the buckling dashboard.

Mira unloads her sonics on Runar. With his other hand, he grips the crystal that empowers permeation. Each blast passes through his body, pounding into the ship underneath him as metal creaks all over the ship.

Sparks shower down throughout the cockpit. The ship's integrity is compromised. It is slowly falling apart, unshielded in the crumbling remains of the Titan's hand.

The movement pulls hard at all of us, and I realize what Oscar knows. He hangs his head, as Carmel pulls a specific attainment from Arun. She turns in her seat even as her body stretches through her gear, shattering the armor and tech as she becomes a giant to face the Titan.

MaalenKun turns and swarms onto Sigrund who grabs the power intoxicated Runar, and they teleport away.

More arms reach from the Titan as its body pulls through the unlocked breach. They bat at the murmuration of wings sweeping down on it. Cannonwings unload sardonyx blasts which break away large chunks of the Titan's arms. Purple-black lightning crawls along one arm, and the Titan slings it through space to destroy a cluster of wings. Scire's charger fires but beams from the mask of lights disperse the Haven-sent divination.

Carmel gently closes one giant hand around her armored and shielded lover as if she were gently holding a small bird. Carmel pushes the remainder of Old Girl apart, and before the cold of space can creep into her giant body, she pushes Mira free of the wreckage, free of the Titan's reach. Carmel's searing pain moves throughout the psybridge, and we brace to shield each other. Carmel tries to hold her breath in as long as she can, but after a few minutes an icy cloud of her final breath escapes her lips. She claws at the Titan. Her body tries to breathe. The intensity of her pain brings us all to our knees. It begins to bleed through the boundaries of the shields and grips us.

Oscar signals one last time to Carmel, and Carmel signals back the same note of love. He draws the psybridge back, and although he does not want to, he lets her go.

Amidst the wreckage, she slowly turns her giant, naked body towards the invading Titan, and her brilliant spectra halo eclipses the rift. As the heat is pulled from her, as ice crystals form in her giant eyes, as her skin turns a whitish blue, she grips the Titan's face, the mask of lights, and pulls it away. The mask cracks, scattering pieces and sparks, killing the lights. From the Titan's gaping neck, a torrent of Unlit pours into space.

Scire's charger lights up again, and the floating river of Unlit is crystalized. Streams of Unlit gush down the multiple arms, hardening as the crystals grow. The Titan's arms shatter, and its headless body falls back through the open rift, breaking apart as the remains disappear in the hazy half-glow.

In my mind alone—not shared through the bridge—I hear MaalenKun's metallic scream. I feel the fiend's fury rushing towards me in an emotional backdraft, and I shield myself from it, extinguishing the flames of rage that slip through the shield. Franxis senses me struggling with something they cannot see, and they send me support and stability until the hellion's fury fades. MaalenKun looks through the distance between us, sensing my presence still connected.

The shattered remains of the Titan and wrecked wings slowly drift around Carmel's body, cold and still aside from her drifting hair and fading spectra halo.

Wings from all stations sweep down on floating rivulets, streams, and globs of Unlit. Their chargers light up, and the drifting Unlit is crystalized, rendered inert, repeatedly.

Clash wings from The Eminent hurtle through the frenzy, striking the other wings with forceful sonic blasts. The Eminent itself lists hard in the direction of the battle over the remaining Unlit.

"We need to get off of this ship!" Zinwara is the first to her feet, pulling Aaliyah up. She speaks in a way we can't ignore, assertively but gently. "Let's move, everyone. Let's go."

Even as we stand and regroup, our vision remains superpositioned with Mira.

As we run through the corridor, we sense Mira firing her thrusters, flying toward Carmel's giant, frozen body, floating in space. Mira dodges remnants of both Old Girl and the Titan. Carmel's body quickly shrinks back to its usual size but remains stiff and icy. As Mira reaches for her deceased wife, she sobs. In Carmel's frozen hand is the chain that was once around her own neck. Before it can slide off the chain, Mira catches their wedding ring, saving it from being lost in the debris around them. Mira wraps her arms around Carmel's frozen body and looks for a way out of the chaos. She cries louder, unsure of which way to go as the ships battle and explode all around her. Shards of crystals and wreckage hang on every side.

"We're here, Mira." Yahima's voice comes through all of our comms.

Lacassine's wings retract and rotate around the stable cabin as the nimble saffron and orange wing weaves through the drifting wreckage, toward Mira clutching Carmel's body. Inside Lacassine's cockpit, Yahima sits cross-legged. The luminous form of Vinea is stretched all around her. The glowing spores twirl around a spectra halo fluctuating brightly around Yahima's crown.

There is heartache in Yahima's voice. "Mira, take hold of my wing, dear."

Mira puts Carmel's frozen body between herself and the wing of the crux, and Yahima pilots them through the detritus as Mira softly sobs. A heavy but sweet ache of empathy moves from Vinea through all of us. Vinea cries softly over her friend's pain. Thiia gently offers Mira accompaniment.

We're lost in the maze of service corridors. The Sages are weak after having divination pulled out of them. Zinwara's lodestar is unreliable after trauma. I could run ahead but I stay by Oscar's side.

I have to help get my crew off this ship.

Franxis, then Thiia, fall back. Franxis moves quickly to take their gear off. "My gear's hacked!"

"Wait!" Thiia urges as she scans the message in her HUD. "The gear technician is giving us directions. Can we trust him?"

"Yes," Oscar replies.

Everyone else's faces say that they are wary to trust anyone from Helixx Corp.

Oscar assures us, "We can trust him."

The gear technician directs us to the shuttle harbor, but at the ladder leading out of the service corridor, we hesitate.

Aaliyah asks, "Won't the harbor be crawling with Red Guard or Crimson Chain?"

Ehsan adds, "Could be a trap."

"Only one way to find out," Zinwara says. Before Aaliyah or Ehsan can discourage her—*bamf!*

Traces of Zinwara's spectra halo hang in the fading blue-pearl flash where she stood.

Arun gazes at the fading lights of Zinwara's halo and says, "Huh, I thought these halos… were more like our aura."

"It appears the radiance is less than subtle," Pyaar says wearily.

"I don't do subtle," Ehsan quips, in spite of the heavy mood.

After a few moments, the panel at the top of the ladder is pulled away. Zinwara and the thin technician who brought the gear into Laboratory Hebe peer down at us. A spectra halo glows around the technician's head.

"We're clear," Zinwara says.

We quietly and quickly make our way to the largest sightseeing shuttle.

As soon as he has the door to the shuttle open, I grab the technician by his collar and swing his lithe body away from my crew.

"That gear! You trapped them!" I roar.

I pull my fist back, even as I hear my crew protesting. Oscar reaches for my arm, but when we hear the roar of the blade come loose, he recoils.

"Casey!" Franxis shouts.

The blood rolling down my skin, dripping off my arm, makes it clear to me. Everyone else is frozen. The Unlit, raised like a weapon, vibrates with intensity.

"Casey." Oscar places a hand on my shoulder. He signals that my eyes are reflecting the light, that I'm not seeing clearly.

The technician whimpers and croaks at the end of one of my arms. The weapon I've drawn for vengeance pulses and refuses light at the end of my other arm. As the small man gasps and groans, the knowledge of his disability becomes apparent. He's mute.

The implants on the sides of his head flash, and a flat robotic voice comes from a comm unit on his neck. "I didn't know… please, don't… I can help." His halo shines with dancing rainbows, and I'm reminded of our commonality.

I release my grip on his uniform.

"I'm sorry," I say. I will my implants to dial up the frequencies from the citrine and black tourmaline crystals. The Unlit retracts and moves back into me.

"You have every right to be angry," the robotic voice says as the technician looks into my eyes. "Had I known their plans, I would've helped you sooner."

"Would everyone please just get on the ship?" Pyaar says from the open door. "We can work it out later."

The small technician bows meekly and shies away from me.

"Oscar…" I turn towards him, horrified by my own actions, by the threat of the Unlit still inside of me. "Vinea's energy… the container is broken."

"Casey," he says, putting both hands on my shoulders. "We need you to hold the Unlit steady." As he speaks, fear grips my throat. "Hey…" He turns his warm eyes on me. "You can do it. We got you, okay?"

I smooth his beard and gaze into his sad eyes. My fear fades into the light of compassion. "Okay."

As he puts his arm around me, we step into the shuttle and the door closes behind us. My crew signal their confidence in me despite their sorrow. As I gaze at the flowing colors around their heads, as I pull my lover in his heartache closer to me, I realize that I've found my people.

I release my fear, the Unlit is stilled, and my love holds me as we brace for liftoff.

ꝏ

excerpt from directive sent by Griselda Harris Ferand to Hebe Lab personnel, Red Guard, Helixx Sages
10 June, 2138 17:00 (Greenwich standard)

"Due to the extremely rare resources within their bodies, I ask that everyone keep both divs Zinwara Osei and Casey Isaac alive during and after harvest. It is likely that their bodies combined with their rare attainments will one day be able to again grow the zin-spectrolite crystals and prepare more of the Unlit for human consciousness. For this reason, *they must remain alive and in our custody!* Once we've got our first harvest, consider their friends expendable. Ave eversor!"

ꝏ

OSCAR

Our unexpected ally plugs in security codes to open the plasma-grid airlock. The small shuttle passes through the yacht's shields, and we finally leave The Eminent.

Most of the battle over what is left of the Unlit is on the other side of the huge yacht. We're packed into the small ship that was obviously not meant to transport nine people. With only a few seats, Casey and I stand toward the back, holding onto whatever we can, including each other.

"Got them on comms. Crazy asses are still on Scire." Ehsan holds out the holoscreen projected from his gear towards Zinwara.

"Kirra! Horatio! Are you okay?" Zinwara asks.

"We're gonna make it, but Red Guard are taking over all harbors," a gruff but jolly, and very Irish voice replies. "They best not set foot on The Queen!"

"Did they stop you?"

"You know us." Horatio chuckles. "Love chaos as cover."

"Once you've got it, go! Got a feeling I'll need you nearby, but do not wait for me on that station! Take The Queen a safe distance out. I've got to take care of something."

"Heard that, Captain."

Zinwara smirks at Ehsan, and he winks an iridescent painted eye at her.

Zinwara notices Casey watching them. She laughs lightly. "I once told you our secret reason to stay on Scire was to snag that prototype hyperdrive." She shrugs. "Wasn't lying."

"And what is it you've got to take care of?" Franxis asks.

"All of you." She nods with sincerity towards Franxis. "And we got a hellion to slay."

A loud thud comes from the storage compartments in back, followed by a scuffling and a thump.

"What the…?" Franxis says, jumping up from their seat, sonics whining.

Fearing another breach of the Unlit, I step between the storage compartment and Casey.

A muffled "Ow!" and a long sigh comes from the compartment. Inside, a familiar but muffled voice spits, "Fuck!"

The compartment door slowly opens, pushed by a hand with manicured red nails. Vy Anh manages to maintain her decorum as she crawls out of the storage cabinet. A spectra halo fluctuates around her crown.

The mute technician looks at Casey, jerks his head toward Vy Anh. "Still want to punch someone? Go for it."

The whine of another sonic builds, and I turn to see Ehsan with his cannon leveled toward our stowaway. Vy Anh raises her hands and lowers her eyes.

Vy Anh's forehead is bruised, and her sleek dress is singed at the hem. She brushes her long black hair out of her face, and I see that several of her fingers are crooked and swollen.

"What are you doing here?" Franxis snarls.

"Same as you. Getting the fuck off that ship," Vy Anh replies. "But I—" she shrugs and forces her painted lips into a taught smile. "—needed a pilot."

"Should we just knock her out?" Ehsan asks, and Franxis lifts their sonic higher.

Vy Anh winces.

"Not necessary," I reply.

Franxis and Ehsan both act overtly disappointed as they lower their sonics. They keep them audibly charged to make a point. Harjaz keeps his sonic raised.

"Any weapons on you?" I ask her.

She shakes her head slowly.

"Comms?"

She taps her implants. One of them blinks, but the other looks cracked and dull. ""Our implants had us connected to Ferand's, but not that new body... I hope." She swallows hard and tears swell in the corners of her eyes.

I hear truth in her voice. "Injuries?" I ask.

She holds up her hand with crooked fingers. "I'll live."

"How many of you are there, Vy Anh?"

"Just the three," she replies ruefully. "Clones, obviously."

I smooth my beard again. Thiia looks at me with tears in her eyes. She juts her chin toward me. We're thinking the same thing. I must step up. With Carmel gone, I am no longer First Officer. I am captain of my crew. I nod at Thiia. Pride and heartache fill her eyes and our light-thread.

I speak firmly but kindly, as Carmel taught me. "Franxis, keep an eye on our stowaway. Harjaz, pilot. Thiia, get us in touch with Captain Commander Maarama."

They move quickly. Harjaz replaces the technician in the pilot's chair, and Thiia launches several holoscreens.

Thiia announces, "Stealth signal to Mani coding. We'll be connected soon."

The technician stands awkwardly nearby, and Franxis shoots him a disdainful look until he retreats to the back of the shuttle, near Vy Anh.

"Hold onto the back of my seat." Despite her blood, which he helped spill, staining her clothes, Zinwara speaks to him with care.

The technician grips the back of Zinwara's chair. His implants blink, and the robot voice comes through low volume. "I'm so sorry."

"Just hold on," Zinwara says.

I glean that Zinwara is holding back her anger. She wants to spare the technician because he helped us escape. She'd rather take her anger out on Vy Anh, but she resists because we're not in the clear yet.

Aaliyah reaches for Zinwara, and Zinwara clasps her hand, welcoming the show of affection and solidarity.

Thiia calls back, "Station Scire broadcasting on all channels."

She taps the screen and Captain Commander N'guwe's rushed voice comes through the ship's audio. "—all personnel. Again, this is Gala N'guwe, former Captain Commander of Station Scire. Any allies left, resist! Fight Helixx! Don't let them—!"

Her voice is cut off, and a chill of worry moves through us.

Harjaz breaks our silence. "Rendezvous with Mani in ten. They're headed toward The Eminent, so we'll be headed back this way once we're on board."

"I have Maarama on comms," Thiia announces.

"Captain Commander Maarama, this is Div Kenzari."

"Happy to hear your voice, Div Kenzari." Her Māori accent is thick. Her voice is firm and steady, but raspy, with a streak of maternal softness. "Div Adivar, is on Mani, in Medical. Physically, she'll be right. Sage Yahima and your extradimensional friend are with her."

"Captain Commander," I ask. "Do you know what's happened on The Eminent?"

"Fucking place. They're evacuating. Even their sightseers are packed. All headed planetside. From the manifests, looks like it's not the staff, it's heaps of tourists." I realize we must've gotten to the shuttle harbor just before the cultists. "More urgently, The Eminent, as I'm sure you know, is moving in on Station Scire. Holt was cooperating with her Helixx Corp bosses, but she was shut down by Gala N'guwe and the allies she's been gathering since a Sage predicted conflict. They're holding off The Eminent for now, but it's heavily armed. They've got Sardonyx cannons aimed on Scire. Griselda Harris Ferand has targeted her own station."

"Captain Commander, Ferand is not really Ferand anymore." I sigh, running both hands down the sides of my beard. "Ferand built a body of nanotech incorporating a highly volatile extra-dimensional substance. In doing so, she might've awakened a being's consciousness that was sort of within the substance." I look towards Casey, and he nods agreeably. "We believe it is using the new body, much like a distans bot. It's a consciousness we've encountered before. It's MaalenKun."

"Not a name I wanted to hear again." She begins typing on a holoscreen off projection.

"That's not all, Captain Commander," Casey says as he stands next to me. "MaalenKun wants something on Scire. They're not going to fire on the station."

"What do you think their plan is?"

"It's having a hard time controlling the rift from within its new body. It wants a power boost. MaalenKun is going for the Haven."

I add, "Tell N'guwe to evacuate. Let MaalenKun take the station."

There is a long pause from Maarama.

"Get our Sages ready in Mani's Haven, Captain Commander." I unfold my arms as my confidence rises. "And we'll need mission gear for two."

"This is the most insane plan I've ever heard, Kenzari," Captain Commander Maarama says as we step off the shuttle. "You sure you're up for it?"

"I'm sure."

Maarama nods solemnly and turns to the rest of my crew. Her gentle smile spreads above the moko kauae tattoo on her chin. "Kia Ora. Welcome to Mani everyone. Nice halos, by the way."

Amongst the small crowd of Ops and divs gathered around Maarama, I notice more spectra halos. Shep Silva, one of her station captains, and Kaipo, her comp, nod acknowledging their strangely visible halos and ours. A couple of armored Div Guards with spectra halos and stun batons step forward.

Captain Silva sternly addresses our passengers. "Zipeng, Vy Anh, you're going with these officers. Zinwara Osei, Casey Isaac, and their crewmates have requested a process of restorative justice. For now, you'll be placed in custody."

I add, "Vy Anh needs medical treatment right away."

When the guards both look towards Captain Silva, he nods firmly. "Of course."

Zipeng, the meek technician bows his head in apology again. Vy Anh turns away from us quickly. The Div Guard escort them both away.

"Ferand's acolyte?" Maarama asks, looking at Vy Anh's back.

"Used to be," I reply.

"UNAF is moving into place to round up her friends fleeing her fancy yacht."

"Cultists. Call themselves the Crimson Chain. Part of a conspiracy to literally turn divs into harvest, so that Ferand could occupy a body of her own making. Instead, they've brought a monster into our world."

"And Ferand?"

"You'll see on our obsidian cubes. That thing beheaded her."

"Hmmm... not how I thought she'd go out," Maarama mumbles.

She looks toward the plasma-grid airlocks. "Let's get out of here before Scire's evacuees start coming in." Maarama looks over my shoulder, nods sympathetically at Thiia and Pyaar. She turns to the rest of us. "You lot, let us know if you need anything."

We follow as she and her comp lead us out of the harbor, down the corridor.

"How's Mira?" Thiia asks as we step onto the enormous elevator.

"Stubborn as hell," Maarama replies. "Her foresight has made her very much aware of your plan."

"She said she wants to join you," Kaipo interjects.

"I said 'no.'" Maarama adds.

"She said she'll grieve later," Kaipo adds.

"I said 'no.'"

Kaipo lifts his eyebrows. "She said if we don't get the ring back, a power-hungry cult will have the ability to send EDBs all over the world."

Maraama meets my eyes. "I said, 'Well, okay then.'"

The elevator doors open onto the operations bridge. As we cross the bridge, we notice several fluctuating spectra halos amongst the crew's flurry of activity.

"I take it you know why our Queer crew mates are glowing?" Maarama says.

"I've got a pretty good idea, ma'am," I say. "I'm not sure how to explain but Divs Isaac and Oseii tapped into every Queer person's resiliency and rage for a unique glow up. It's added protection, we believe."

"MedOps checked them out and they're fine, so I put everyone here back to work. Can't spare to lose them at the moment, even if they are a little freaked out." She scoffs. "Got all of UNAF in a tizzy with these pretty lights all over. Even Queers out in the wops got 'em."

"You mean...?"

"Risen, unRisen, all over the sector, Kenzari." She cocks an eyebrow at me. "Only Queer folks."

This explains why Pyaar is the only one of our crew not bearing the spectra halo.

"We have more wings, including Cannons coming from Eagle and Yerum," Captain Silva says to Maarama.

"Get those pilots patched in. I want all cannon-wings surrounding that posh boat." Maarama speaks and marches quickly. "Convert all auxiliary power to the Haven. Tell our network of remote Sages we're almost ready."

"Heard that, ma'am."

Maarama adds, "We've got Sages in Havens at Yerum and Eagle, multiple Sages all over the sector—all ready to boost you for this, Kenzari."

Sliding doors open for us and most of Maarama's entourage falls back, but Kaipo and Silva stay close to her. She steps into the foyer with us. When the doors close behind us, it's quiet.

"You just lost your captain, so I'll ask you one more time, Kenzari." Maarama gazes into my eyes with care. "Are you sure about this?"

"Absolutely certain," I answer.

"So, this EDB's got a shape-shifting body, who knows what powers, and a teleporter," Maarama says.

"It has two teleporters, Captain Commander. Helixx's twin Sages. They're incredibly dangerous, and I'm pretty sure one of them is psychotic." Zinwara stands a bit taller as Maarama gazes at her bloody attire. "Zinwara Osei, indie Div, The Queen. You might've heard about me? Had big crystals growing out of my face until a short while ago."

"You don't look like your pics. Without the crystals, yeah." Maarama motions to one of the Ops in the room. "I take it the standard armor is for you and the modified armor is for this handsome fella?" She gestures towards Casey.

Captain Silva says, "Ma'am, The Eminent is positioned to dock with Scire. They're about

to bring reinforcements onto the station."

Maarama turns to Casey and Zinwara. "You two better get that gear on."

Casey and Zinwara change quickly into their Mani-issued mission gear. Her courage glows brilliant blue and gold in their auras. His aura is more muddled with worry. While Franxis puts an arm around him and pulls him close, Casey meets my eyes, signaling that he is with me. Through our light-line, he sends me compassion for my loss.

"Div Isaac," Captain Silva says. "Your armor has been modified according to Div Kenzari's requests. Your crew will have access to your gear. If there is a breach from the Unlit, they can throw your shield up. If the armor is damaged, nanotech will reseal it. Like any gear, it can get damaged, but you and your crew are more protected this way. I trust this'll ease some fears and help keep you steady."

"Thank you," Casey says.

A technician hands each of them an amp pack and extra swift cartridges to clip onto their belts. I look over our crew as they strap on their amp packs and holsters, sliding in loaded swifts.

The gravity of what we are about to do weighs on me. We can't just crystalize this enemy. The Red Guard will undoubtedly aim to kill. I look at my crew, knowing any one of them might not make it back. I might not make it back. Casey senses the burden. He secures two of the swift cartridges to his cross-chest belt and holds out a swift to me.

As I clip on the weapons, hesitation rises within me. I quash the urge. I know I have to focus on extracting Murtagh and the Elders, getting the ring, and getting my crew back to safety. I cannot get weighed down, not while others are counting on me.

Casey's eyes meet mine, and I remember seeing them when I became Risen. For one hundred years, I looked for him, my future. Now, our future is threatened. There is no assurance. Before I can reach up to smooth my beard, he takes my hand. He shakes his head slowly. Together, we settle my nerves and align ourselves to support our crew in every way we can.

We have each other in this fight. We are each other's reason for fighting.

Before the doors slide open, I feel her reaching for Thiia and me. Tears trail down her cheeks as she rushes past the Captain Commander, away from Yahima and Vinea. As she slings her arms around me, I sync her into our psybridge again. Thiia wraps both of us in a warm embrace.

Thiia whispers soothingly, "Mira."

Mira nods vehemently and wipes away a falling tear. She is still in her mission gear. "I have to come with you."

Thiia and I both nod in agreement.

We hold each other, psychically acknowledging that we do not have the privilege to be with our sadness and grief at the moment. We assure each other that we will let the tears pour when we are back.

"Oscar, hold space on the psybridge, please. I'll be syncing up as well," Yahima says over their shoulder before they kneel in front of Pyaar and Arun. The two seated Sages reach out. Yahima's beautiful hands hold theirs. Yahima soothes the aches and pains of their physical and mental bodies, further re-charging their energy.

All three Sages become radiant. Our psychic connections vibrate powerfully as the Sages add their strength to our psybridge. They rise together, standing tall in their saffron and orange mission gear.

Vinea, in her humanoid form, drifts across the floor of the room. Captain Commander Maarama watches unfazed, but Captain Silva and Kaipo shrink back away from the extradimensional being. My crew's energy lifts at the sight of Vinea joining us. She places her misty arm around Mira's shoulders, comforting her.

Another tear streaks down Mira's face, but Thiia and I both have her hands, and she doesn't let go to wipe it away.

Mira raises her voice to the group. "Everybody, I know you've already got one ring to get, but I would appreciate getting my wedding ring back from that sadistic Sage!"

Casey reaches out and places a hand on Mira's shoulder. He smirks and addresses everyone, "And please, let's stop calling those assholes Sages."

Maarama looks up from a holoscreen. "N'guwe's resistance fighters are prepping escape pods. Scire's remaining Sages are still in the station's Haven."

Kaipo looks up from a tablet and nods confirmation. "Red Guard are taking Scire's harbors. They'll soon have every way on the station locked down."

"Not every way," Casey replies with a smirk.

I turn back to the rest of my crew, my family. "It's okay if any of you aren't up for this. Just say so now." I already know. They're not backing down. "Y'all need some grand, motivational speech, right now?"

"Nah," Ehsan says.

"We're with you, captain," Franxis says.

Yahima looks to Casey and Zinwara. "My spectra energy speaks to me of itself. The spectra blades are psychological weaponry. Be wise with these powerful weapons, divs." Yahima tilts their head down a degree, looking at us all with serious eyes. "That said. We cannot always keep our hands clean."

Zinwara says, "My lodestar showed me something when I knew I wanted to stop the Red Guard, but not kill them. Their Sages have pushed aside obscurations that would prevent them from accessing their Levels. That was an old UNAF technique that got banned because the obscurations remain strong. If we can release those obscurations, they'll move back into place cutting them off from their Levels."

I'm relieved to see several nodding heads. Casey is not one of them, and I sense his self-sabotaging sense of lack.

I catch his gaze, bow my head ever so slightly, and add, "We've got each other on this."

He nods, and I sense him quelling his insecurities, tapping into resilience and rage, expanding his confidence. He adds, "Bright faith."

Captain Commander Maarama looks at us with absolute confidence. "Go get that ring back." Maarama looks Mira in the eyes. "Both rings."

Captain Silva and Kaipo flank Maarama. Their spectra halos glow brightly. Maarama watches us with admiration as we step onto the elevator. When the doors close behind us, I reach for Casey, and he holds my hand tightly.

In sync, we all signal our mission gear simultaneously. Eleven helmets snap into place, and Vinea coos as if pleased.

I command the lift: "Rise."

The elevator walls descend, and the twelve of us stand in the Haven's effulgent pale light. Sight of Vinea is almost lost in the effulgence. The glowing spores swirling around her are the only visual indication that the luminous being is still with us.

Four Sages sitting on their tech-embedded crystal plinths tone down the white glow of the room so that we can see them and Vinea. Zinwara rushes toward Our Black Elder.

Our Black Elder rises from her crystal plinth and moves quickly to embrace Zinwara. She whispers, "Our halos. Well done, my child." She embraces Zinwara, and their spectra halos merge, growing brighter. When they release each other, their halos slowly move apart, leaving traces of their connection in the air.

Our Black Elder's psychic embrace further integrates us into the powerful psybridge strengthened by Sages near and far. The connection is incredibly potent. It rises and settles within us. Our individual obscurations and boundaries minimize and move low.

One of the Sages on a quartz plinth lifts their hands, and a holographic projection of the battle outside the station descends into the room. A losing battle spreads out before us. Crimson clash- and crux-wings fire on Scire ships piloted by N'guwe's resistance fighters. A battle for remaining Unlit goes on amidst the growing amount of wreckage. The Eminent docks with Scire, as if it is holding the station hostage to keep the UNAF Cannons from firing. Eight Cannons glowing hot with sardonyx charges surround the yacht in their crosshairs.

Moving further from the fray, The Queen heads towards Luna.

Our Black Elder returns to her plinth. She slowly waves her hands towards the projection of Scire. She explains, "The Scire Sages have given us access to the Haven video feed." The view expands and zooms into the other Haven.

Murtagh and the two Elders sit atop their crystal plinths powering Scire's charger while simultaneously reaching toward us with a guiding force.

"Scire Sages are prepared," Our Black Elder gently says.

Sigrund and Runar teleport into and out of Scire's Haven, leaving behind a Red Guard with each flash of blue-pearl light. After several flashes, twenty Red Guard surround the Scire Sages, protected by a spectral shield. The blue-pearl flashes stop. They know that with too many amped up and unfocused Red Guard, the Haven will be inhibited. Finally, the twins teleport in with no Red Guard. MaalenKun's swarming nanotech body peels away from the corrupted Sages and reshapes itself into a humanoid form.

Vinea growls low, and Mira reaches out a soothing signal.

In the holographic Haven, stolen zin-spectrolite crystals shimmer over the surface of its body. Through the extradimensional ring, it begins to pull in the effulgence of the Haven, amplifying its power. Ripples move through the billions of tiny shifting bots as refracted light fans out around MaalenKun. It lifts its arm. The extradimensional ring glimmers on a finger tipped by a gold nail.

Our Black Elder waves her hand, and the projection pulls away from the Haven's interior. Scire's charger expands, taking aim at the rift. Mani's own charger moves to target Scire.

One of the Mani Sages looks toward our crew and speaks softly, "Prepare yourselves."

We move close to one another.

Scire's charger fires into the rift. We moderate our fears to stay focused as we watch the edges of the rift expanding as MaalenKun widens the breach between dimensions. The space around the rift quakes. A pulse rocks the universe, shaking the station us as it moves through us. The powerful psybridge uniting us is the only thing that holds steady.

A Mani Sage looks toward Pyaar, a flicker of doubt in his eyes. "Even with so many Sages assisting us, it will be difficult to teleport so many."

Vinea replies, "Only one."

And we leap into her body of light. From just within Vinea's brilliant body, Casey wraps his arms around me, and together we watch the holographic projection as the rift grows. Scire's charger shuts down at the precise moment Mani's lights up. The Mani Sages brighten with divination as they open the light beam for Vinea, and she stretches thin as thread clinging to the Sage's light.

I look into Casey's eyes, momentarily stunned by his grey-ringed green irises. My memory of that future vision is looped into the present. Him. Now. As if it was all meant to be. The universe unfolds the only way it knows how.

The perception of our bodies becomes stretched long. I hold fast to him.

Vastness ahead of us shifts and shapes rise from nothing into our view. MaalenKun wearing the mirror mask of dis-existence reaches out with the extradimensional ring, the key to the rift. It calls forth terrible creatures from distant dimensions. They look like storms.

Thunderheads turn towards the nanotech body driven by the Shadow. Unseen eyes fix on it. A hurricane calls back in thunderous scorn that it will not obey, and a Shadow sweeps across the sky, swallowing and silencing it. Out of fear, many more sentient storms heed MaalenKun's call. Tentacles of cyclonic wind reach toward the rift, and within the rift's half-light, Titans stir.

I reach for Casey as we are fully enveloped in Vinea's effulgent body of light. Streaks of spectral radiance dart around us. Glowing spores dance between us, reflecting off his helmet shield before all physicality fades. Everything about my being becomes nearly indiscernible. I can feel only a hint of my body, too spacious to be physical.

A radiant warmth moves near me. Casey. Luminous bands of ruby, gold, emerald, sapphire, violet, and white fill our eyes. He radiates his heart into the vast spaces within me, and I loop my love back towards him. We circulate it between us, merging body and essence, movement and stillness, passion and compassion, sex and heart. The power of our connection reaches secret places within us beyond our lifetimes. Ahead I see his radiant body merging into rainbow light and moving into mine.

There are no boundaries between Casey and me. For the first time, I sense the Unlit within him and a voice, calling, weakly.

Casey Isaac… The voice is weary, but undeniably Griselda Harris Ferand. *We can end it, but we must work together.*

A super-conscious knowing flashes within us. If Casey chooses not to help her, Ferand will remain in the Unlit, tormented for an unfathomable stretch of time. If we can open a psybridge within the Unlit to Ferand, she might be able to cross it with the last of her life force.

He chooses mercy.

Within him, the Unlit reverberates with Ferand's war-like scream. I see her drawing in all her will, the remnants of her lifeforce, and she focuses all of her remaining power on one small place within the nanotech body.

Casey lets me go.

In the pull of the light beam we ride, he surges ahead. Colorful quantum flashes burst around us as the teleportation jump succeeds. Within Vinea, we've ridden along the Sage's divination from Mani's Haven, into and through Scire's charger.

Casey leaps from Vinea's sudden presence on the ceiling of Scire's Haven, arm extended. Around his fist, his spectra blade sings with millions of brilliant colors. MaalenKun's mirror mask betrays the being's shock as the spectra blade slices through MaalenKun's outstretched hand and down its arm. Sparks, broken tech, and crystals spray upward. Ferand severs the shapeshifter's ring finger. The ring flies free of the nanotech, and its rift-unlocking peal fades.

Before his feet even hit the floor, Casey sweeps his spectra blade back up through the nanotech body's shoulder. The rainbow lightning carves through the nanotech, leaving behind a clear-cut space. Casey reaches the blade up, and the falling extradimensional ring musically clinks down the flowing light rays until it slides down onto his finger.

Ferand's war-scream is coupled with Casey's painful cry as they access the knowledge of how to control the rift.

Without hesitation, Casey reverses the command given to the ring, seizes control of the space the rift occupies, and forces the borders to rapidly fold in on themselves. The approaching storms are shut out. The half-light of the dimension within the breach is cast out of our world.

The rift is finally closed!

Another gravity wave shakes the universe.

Scire rocks. The twins and the Red Guard stumble.

Ferand's life force vanishes leaving a fading sense of joyful release.

The shapeshifter claws for Casey. Zinwara's spectra blade comes down on top of MaalenKun's head, splitting the mirror mask. She drives the blade of shifting colors through the core of the horde. Sparks fly around the colorful array of her spectra blade as she bisects the weakened swarm.

The broken bits of mirror mask shape-shift and haphazardly reform. The body lunges the mask forward. Reflected in the golden mirror, the spectra halos only brighten. The resiliency channeled from Queers all over the sector into the spectra halos steadies us. The mirror-mask of dis-existence has no power over us. We know exactly who we are and how to hold ourselves strong.

Zinwara and Casey swing, and with each stroke of the radiant spectra blades, more of the monster crumbles and falls to the floor. The stinky-sweet, chemical fragrance of the synthezoid cirrostratus mixes with the burned smell of the damaged tech. I find Harjaz reaching toward me, and I draw his divination through our psybridge, passing it to Casey and Zinwara. Their spectra blades land in the shape-shifting horde and the billions of tiny drones are afire with colorful sparks lighting up the circuitry with technopathic divination.

MaalenKun's body explodes!

Casey and Zinwara are thrown across the room as broken, glittering pieces of nanotech scatter through the air. Casey cries out as the extradimensional ring flies from his hand and is lost in the chaos of oncoming Red Guard.

Harjaz lands on the Haven floor and sends his technopathic divination through the technology embedded in the floor and up through the boots of the Red Guard. Circuits glimmer with divination as Harjaz disables their shield generation and comms. He reaches for more, but it doesn't connect. He glances at me without blame but with a concerned acknowledgement: when I pulled divination from him and sent it to Casey and Zinwara, I pulled most of what he had. He can't shut down the Red Guard easily.

Franxis' boots land next to Harjaz. "No worries, guys." They level their sonics toward the red armor. "We got this." They fire, sending Red Guard crashing into each other.

Murtagh and the Elders redirect their divination, surging the Haven-amplified power back into themselves. Murtagh drops one foot down from her crystal plinth and touches it to the Haven floor, slamming into the Red Guard with a powerful dulling force.

Gripping their chained crystals and quickly levitating, the twin Sages dodge the dulling force. From her position on the ceiling, Vinea catches both twins in her outstretched vines and pries their hands off their prized crystals.

Half of the Red Guard stumble. Some fall to their knees before struggling to get back up. One of the Red Guard goes down completely, unconscious from the heavy energy. The other half of the guards redirect the force and sling it back. With added psychological protection from our spectra halos, the Reds cannot easily dull us. The dulling force moves across the floor, through the crystal plinths, hitting Murtagh and one of the Sages. They fall unconscious to the floor. The other Elder remains seated in meditation, unshielded and vulnerable.

Vinea drops each of us boots first. As each of us fall into the Haven, our nimbuses expand and rise to integrate our Levels with the Haven connection maintained by the Elder. When Yahima's and Arun's boots touch down, the Sages turn up our psychic connections so that our powers begin to flow more freely from our Levels.

The nanotech scattered along the floor begins to gather in various clusters, and we move quickly to protect the Scire Sages before MaalenKun can pull itself back together.

The Red Guard fire their swifts, but each bolt either bounces off of a shield or is cut down by the multicolored flash of a spectra blade. They reach their minds towards us, and their aggressive strength pushes against our psybridge. It's apparent that their training is different from ours and that they have no qualms about killing us.

Vinea's misty vines hold Sigrund and Runar aloft by their arms, preventing them from grasping any of the crystals chained around their necks. Their feet kick wildly above the floor as they struggle against her grasp. Mira and Thiia drop down from Vinea and step towards the immobilized twins. Thiia and Mira raise their whining sonics. More vines fly down and wrap around the twins' crystals and chains. Vinea tugs at the clusters of jewelry.

"Fuck you!" Sigrund seethes.

Runar adds, "And your dead wife!"

All four sonics unload. The blasts connect against the twins' chests as Vinea lets go of their arms. The chains pull tight and break away. A few of the crystals spill to the floor before Vinea hides the rest of the dangerous jewelry deeper within herself. The twins raise their sonics, but Casey and Zinwara are there to disable their lifted cannons with the brilliant ends of their spectra blades. The two set upon the sadistic pair, driving their spectra blades in, willing the energy to not harm their flesh, but instead, they destroy most of their gear, their physical weaponry.

A red blur slams into Casey and Zinwara, knocking them away from the twins. The Red Guard who launched herself at them like a cannonball slams them into the wall before they can fight her off.

Mira pulls Runar up by his collar and sneers, "Where's my ring, asshole?"

Across the room, Arun faces down two oncoming guards calmly. Arun looks at another Red Guard quickly moving toward Franxis. Through Arun's insight and my own awakening Level Six, I see the same tethered obscurations within the Red Guard's mind.

"That's where you need to hit them," I message Zinwara and Casey, signaling sight of the obscurations.

"Make it quick, please!" Franxis quips as a Red Guard rattles their shield with glowing orbs shot from his hands. Thiia moves behind Franxis to couple their shields, but another Red with her shield raised moves in behind the other. The second guard raises her foot, ready to slam dulling force through the floor under the prismatic shields.

Bamf! Bamf! Casey and Zinwara teleport to within striking distance of the Red Guards. They drive their spectra blades into the guards' subtle bodies, cutting the cords that keep their toxic traits obscured and shifted aside. The dense globular obstacles ascend and weigh on the Reds subtle bodies, pulling their minds down, blocking their flow of his divination. They cry out with frustration. Casey and Zinwara twist the blades, disabling their tech, locking their gear.

The screams of two Red Guard cut through the air from where Arun has thrown them. They crash into nearby Red Guards who were getting too close.

"Let's get these Sages out of here," Pyaar says, guiding Franxis and Thiia toward the shielded Sages near the crystal plinths.

As Casey and Zinwara, teleport around the room, repeatedly disabling Red Guards, Harjaz pulls me toward the control panels along the wall.

"Come on, handsome," he says. "Let's get the escape pods ready!"

Ahead of us, Aaliyah looks up from biometric scans on a holoscreen, "Get down!"

We're confused, but we immediately duck as Aaliyah shoots a signal past us. She transfers, *Zinwara! There!*

A flash of blue pearl and Zinwara is nearby, driving her spectra blade into a Red Guard who had been invisible and poised to attack. The guard falls forward in locked gear.

Zinwara winks at Aaliyah and says, "That was hot." Then, she teleports away.

"I like you two together!" Harjaz says as we pass Aaliyah.

Aaliyah gives Harjaz a smile.

His own smile broadens. "After forty years together, that's the first smile she's ever given me."

"She's finally warming up to you."

Recovering from our attacks, small clouds of the remaining nanotech begin to gather and rise into the air. The deadly bots move in clusters, strategically dodging and rising above the skirmish as they gather. Vinea swipes at it weakly. It's clear that she is weakened from the teleportation jump from Mani. MaalenKun changes direction. The cloud of specks amidst the cirrostratus cut through the effulgent light, and a few sparks fall as the wounded MaalenKun swirls and weaves to gather its body again.

Casey runs faster than I've ever seen anyone run. He swings the spectra blade toward MaalenKun, and when the swirling horde of nanotech dodges, Casey teleports a few feet out to meet the fast-moving fiend with the brilliant sword of rainbow lightning. More of the tech falls away, sparking and smoking. Casey doesn't give up pursuing MaalenKun until one of the Red Guard barrels into his path and slams into his shield with enough force to knock him down, but not before Casey extends the spectra blade and lets the guard land on it. He is the last of the Red Guard to fall. Casey pushes him away and begins to pull himself up.

Pyaar stands over the fallen Scire Sages holding a prismatic shield strongly in place as Thiia and Aaliyah check the unconscious Sages' vitals and attempt to wake them.

Mira stands nearby looking up towards Vinea, "Can you carry the unconscious Sages?"

Vinea replies, "Not safe. Feel weak. Energy unsettled."

I run towards Casey, but he looks up from kneeling, holding out a hand to halt me.

We both feel it. A flicker on the edge of Casey's periphery. It seems familiar to him, but he meets it with dread. It is like a message sent from behind the veil of our reality. It is a warning.

We notice a trembling through one of our light-threads, a line that extends from our hearts to one of the Red Guard lying near the twins.

The swirling waves of nanotech descend near the twins, and they cast a shield around the tiny bots as they gather into a kneeling form. MaalenKun reaches its arm towards one of the still conscious Red Guards in locked gear. It opens its fingers wide. The guard seizes as he fights against whatever is being done to him. Through Six, I can see the guard's aura, his consciousness, and life force being siphoned away from him. The flow of energy is pulled into the swarm of tech. The crystalized EDB remains within the nanotech flash bright and glow with reawakened energy. The light slips away from the Unlit within the zin-spectrolite crystals and shines out in prickly-looking grey beams.

Sigrund and Runar's psychic reach becomes stronger. We see them beyond the shimmering borders of our psybridge, moving towards a gloomy figure.

I start to ask, *Is that…?*

Casey replies. *The Shadow.*

As they did when we tested the nanotech, the twins open a path for the consciousness controlling the nanotech swarm. The Shadow, MaalenKun's true form, uses the energy taken from the Red Guard to move into their mindfield. A clattering discord shakes us all.

We realize that the protection our spectra halos provide might not be enough to keep a being as powerful as MaalenKun from invading our minds.

The nanotech reshapes itself into a humanoid form, and the mirror mask emerges from the horde of scurrying bots. At its feet, Sigrund and Runar pull themselves up to their knees. They look around the Haven, at the Red Guard disabled on the floor, at us ready to fight.

Casey springs forward, moving fast with divination glowing throughout his body. He raises the spectra blade.

MaalenKun's head tilts as Casey quickly approaches. A pulse moves from within the nanotech horde as the Shadow unlocks a power within the crystals. The atmosphere of the room cracks with a thunderclap that jolts us.

The white atmosphere of the Haven peels and stretches before pulling apart like plastic.

For a moment, I fear that the being has cracked the Haven, exposing us to the cold of space. But it is the psybridge that has been cracked. And the Shadow has pulled us into its mindfield. Grimy shadows hang all around us. The atmosphere is heavy in places, rippled, too thick to move through in places. It is as if invisible folds of space have been shaped into vertical peaks and valleys. The ripples waver pushing against us, rocking us, and we struggle to stay on our feet. The remaining effulgent light of the Haven is pulled between the folds of space, and the room grows dark.

We stammer, looking through the smoky and foul-smelling mindfield for each other. I hear Thiia's voice crying out, Yahima calling to her, signals of Harjaz's frustration with escape pod hatches jammed after the gravity waves rocked the station. But I cannot find them. Their voices, their signals, are muddled and distorted within the folds of space.

I sense the twins psychically scanning the space as if looking through turbulent waters, and I try to quell the fear that they will find my crew before I do.

I focus on drawing divination from Level Five, desperately trying to make true as I whisper, "I am with you always… I am with you always…" I repeat the words, extending my reach from my heart to my crew, my family, my lover, and as I sense my connection to them the desperation changes. "I am with you always…" Confidence comes. "I am with you always…"

I sense them reaching for me.

A constellation pierces the darkness. Our luminous heartstars radiate bright faith, and I see each of my crewmates. Yahima and Aaliyah are trying to wake the fallen Sages. Thiia and Mira are poised to protect them. Harjaz works at the control panel with his old friend, Ehsan watching his back. Arun and Pyaar hold a shield strong around them. The rest of us are scattered about the room, in the thick of MaalenKun's superimposed mindfield.

Between us and the rest of our crew stands MaalenKun. Undulating darkness shrouds it, swirling around its mirror-mask. Sinuous, inky smoke curls amidst the nanotech. The twins, unable to see our heartstars, kneel next to MaalenKun.

Zinwara pushes her way towards them, using her lodestar to navigate the waves of rippling space. Searching for a clear shot at teleportation.

MaalenKun raises its arms over the twins' heads. It pours a small portion of itself onto their third eyes. The tech arranges itself to place crystalized EDB remains against their skin. They immediately draw power from the crystals and set upon Zinwara's mind.

The twins claw at the constructs they helped Zinwara build to restabilize her level at Four. As her anger flares with their betrayal, as she berates herself for having trusted them, her lodestar goes dark. The twins lift her traumatic memories, inject doubt, and suddenly, the blue-pearl light doesn't flash around her, but sputters out, and she remains in the same place. Her eyes go wide. She cannot teleport, which means Casey can't draw the ability from her either.

Zinwara grits her teeth and continues pushing towards the twins. Ehsan drops to his knees, psychically steadying her as best he can against the Sage-level assault.

MaalenKun turns the mask towards Casey. It glides toward him in serpentine movements. It reaches out a hand with fingers growing into long pointed claws crawling with nanotech. The space around Casey folds in tighter until he cannot push forward.

He instead kneels, but not to the Shadow. He kneels for meditation.

Its voice feels as if it rises from within our hollowed guts, as if it has invaded us to speak from within our very being, leaving us feeling violated and without protection. ***The Shadow will cover earth and sky. Your world will fall beneath eternal darkness. All that you are will be consumed by the Shadow the light cannot touch.***

What I hear in its voice, coming from with me, chills me until my awareness of it quivers out through the remnants of our psybridge. Mira screams with the prescient knowledge it awakens in her. Pyaar screams, Arun winces. Because it is Truth.

It turns toward Casey and speaks from the nanotech. "Casey Isaac, give up, and you will be spared. Let me reshape you."

Casey's spectra halo grows brighter. "I will not give up who I AM."

Franxis steps to Casey's side. Together they stare down the monster. Franxis places their hand on Casey's shoulder. The force of accompaniment moves throughout our psybridge, giving us all assurance.

"You can't have him," Franxis says. "He belongs here. With us."

The mouth of the mirror mask opens, bearing golden teeth as the Shadow screams through the nanotech. Another pulse moves through its body, and another thunderclap shatters the rippled atmosphere.

The twins fly through the open space, Runar towards Zinwara, and Sigrund turns his amplified, psychic attack onto Pyaar.

Without a spectra halo protecting her, Pyaar crumbles and drops the shield. Sigrund wraps his bony fingers around her head, slicing into her mind with psychic razors. Arun drops the remainder of the shield and lunges for Sigrund. He casts a shield around the crystals on Sigrund's forehead and strains to pull away the tech embedding itself deeper into Sigrund's skin. With glowing fingers, Yahima reaches through Arun's shield, through Sigrund's body, and reverses his healing factors. The tissue around the nanotech touching the crystals rots, and strands of decaying flesh break away as she closes her fist around the crystals and pulls them away. Skull and nerves exposed, Sigrund flails and falls back. Yahima releases the nanotech into the spherical shield, and Arun tightens the sphere until it crushes it into dust.

Flying psychic razors of hot white light find their way through Zinwara's shield as Runar lands against it. She drops the shield, swings the spectra blade towards him, but misses.

Ehsan runs towards them, sonic whining, but Runar throws a whirlwind of psychic razors into his mind. Pain rips through their comp-bridge. Zinwara's entire body screams with an agony that becomes rage, reigniting her lodestar.

She desires only the defeat of her enemy to protect her loved ones. With a golden curving line of direction, her lodestar shows her the obscurations within her enemy. Her lodestar shows her where to strike him, how to cut off his access to Sage Level.

Runar flies, extending a hurricane of psychic razors toward her. She catches the blades in her spectra halo and swings up. Runar's own momentum sends him crashing headfirst into her spectra blade.

She cuts at the binds holding his obscurations. The dense obscurations dam the flow of divination. He's cut off from the power to access the crystals on his forehead. The obscurations collapse releasing the toxicity of his racism and queerphobia to implode into self-loathing that consumes his mind. He howls under the calamity of his poisonous thoughts.

She raises her foot glowing with divination and kicks his chest plate, driving him down with a heavy dulling that leaves him nearly unconscious.

The twin sages writhe and groan, too weak to stand. Their psybridge unravels and the power from it slips away from the Shadow.

We all focus our attention on the monster rising into the air in front of Casey and Franxis. Harjaz touches the control panel, hacking the power output of the Haven, and turning up the power. The white light of the Haven begins to pierce the flowing folds of MaalenKun's mindfield.

We might not be able to kill the Shadow hidden in lower dimensions, but we can destroy what it uses to move in our world. Each of us prepares to attack the body of nanotech as it spreads into a murmuration around the floating mirror mask.

Bright faith surges within us. We simultaneously shape the mudra for accessing the heart. Casey draws from Murtagh, and together they find the light-thread connecting us to the deadly extra-dimensional being. We extend those beams of light toward it. It pushes back, but without the Red Guard or Sages to draw power from, it's weaker. Its mindfield superimposed onto our reality is folded in on itself, forced back to where it came. The shroud of smoky darkness disappears within the waving murmuration of nanotech.

"This body… a puppet," it says, words fading. "You cannot destroy…"

Waves of the murmuration fall away. Bands of the nanotech and crystals fall to floor inert. What remains moves in clusters in the air.

Still fading the Shadow says, "Your world will fall…"

A flash of prescience sweeps through our psybridge cutting our rising joy and confidence short. With weary eyes that have seen ahead, Mira looks to Casey, then me.

ꝏ

A flash of gold rushes across the room, through the air, into the cupped hands of the Elder Sage. Amidst the chaos, he had focused on obtaining one thing as he meditated atop the power-enhancing plinth. The Elder's hands close around the extradimensional ring.

The nanotech swarms toward him, reshaping what's left of the mirror mask. Pyaar scrambles toward the crystal plinth, trying to cast a protective shield around the Elder. MaalenKun retaliates sending psychic needles into her mind. It begins to pull what divination it can from her. Her shield wavers and fails as she falls backwards.

The swarming gusts of tiny buzzing drones and shiny stolen crystals are on the Elder before any of us can reach him. It coils around the Elder's perfectly still body, wrapping around his shoulder to turn the mask on him.

"Why can I not see the other ornaments? Where have you hidden them?" the shapeshifter hisses as it begins to siphon away what it can of the Elder's divination. .

The Elder's spectra halo shifts to a brighter, paler violet. His hands remain closed around the extradimensional ring.

"Give me the ring," MaalenKun snarls.

The horde descends on the Sage's unshielded hands, digging into the Elder's soft skin. Flecks of blood dot the Elder's robes, yet he remains still, holding the ring tight. His halo glows a brilliant white. MaalenKun's body of nanotech scurries like an army of hungry ants. They tear into the Sage's flesh, and still, he does not move. Arun and Yahima scramble to shield and pull away the violent tech, but there is so much of it. It evades their grasp. A pulse like a gravity wave moves through the psybridge as the Elder drops away from the Levels and our connection is weakened. His nimbus descends and rotates slowly above his head. Red drops grow into streams as the Sage's blood soaks his robes, trailing down the crystal plinth and onto the floor of Haven.

The swarm peels away from the bloody bones, empty hands.

The Elder's body remains upright and still as his blood continues to spill and pool on the white floor. As his nimbus vanishes, his heart emanates an eerie and heart-breaking melody, the song of uncommon compassion.

"*Mahasamadhi*," Pyaar says reverently as she gets back to her feet, weeping into her hands. "Even under violent assault."

The awe and defeat bring me to my knees. I turn away from the Sage's body as Pyaar, her face streaked with tears, reaches toward him. We turn to see the other Scire Sages finally waking, roused by the Elder's final breath that shook their Levels.

Stunned, I watch the horde of tech I helped create sail across the room towards the weakened twins, still grinning after watching MaalenKun kill the Elder and seize the ring. My heart sinks, but I get up.

Sigrund reaches for something shining on the floor. I recognize the ring. He closes his hand around it. A surge of power rushes through him as he unlocks the power of Bakkeaux. Beneath the bloody, rotten wound on his forehead, his eyes widen, and he turns his hateful gaze towards Casey. A cyclonic tendril sputters forward from his third eye, but his forehead wound is ripped open further. He screams, unable to aim the mind-warping cyclone. He rushes towards Casey.

The tendril hits Franxis, and they scream. Franxis reaches for Casey.

Casey springs forward and slams his fist into Sigrund's red chest plate. Stopped in his tracks the cyclonic tendril sputters out. He chokes up a splatter of blood. The jagged Unlit pierces through his back. Casey's face is twisted. Brassy yellow reflections shine in his eyes. He pulls the Unlit back through the Sigrund's chest, and his dead body falls away from him.

Its reshaped mirror mask screaming to lead the horde, MaalenKun hurtles around us.

I hastily transfer, *Casey! Get control! Pull the Unlit back so I can seal your gear!*

He cannot hear me. Casey grits his teeth and pulls his arm back, poised to strike with the jagged void. As I run towards them, I pull from both Casey and Harjaz. I run fast with my arms outstretched, but MaalenKun is faster. It swarms onto him, dodging his unruly strikes, clinging to his armor, attempting to capture the Unlit. Casey hisses and cries out as the nanodrones pour into the tear that the Unlit has made in his gear. The Unlit tears through his skin and gear, up his arm to his shoulder, and across his chest toward his heart. It hangs over him in wildly moving craggy outcrops.

He knows he's lost control, and that it's costing him. I feel his heart break, and defeat pours into the cracks. He cannot steady himself. He cannot call the Unlit back within. He slings his arm futilely trying to shake off the swarm. MaalenKun digs deep into his wounds, causing Casey's body to seize as nerves are hit. The Unlit flings into an uncontrolled surge. It sweeps from his arm and chest around his body.

We run towards him, firing our charger cannons trying to crystalize the Unlit before it can hurt him more, before MaalenKun can get more of it. Swaths of the deadly substance spreads outward from his wounds. Our charger beams land. Crystalized Unlit flies. And Casey flails in the chaos.

I pull divination from Harjaz. I place my hands on Casey's armor and send Harjaz's tech-hacking divination through it. The array of colors flies from my hands and seeps through Casey's gear into the nanotech. A small amount of the nanobots fall away from Casey, and my heart sinks.

Franxis reaches up with one bloody hand and grips Casey's bleeding arm, sending steadiness into him. The gushing Unlit hangs in the air above them.

The frenzied swarm flies into the Unlit to steal it away.

Harjaz places his hands on Casey's back and a charge of his divination moves direct from its source through us. More of the nanotech sparks and falls away. Franxis breathes deep, sending Casey all of their stability. Yahima appears next to us, places their hands on Casey, and aligns their own Sage Level with the tech-hacking divination. Arun is next to join us, then Zinwara. I feel Mira and Thiia's hands on me, steadying me. Ehsan and Aaliyah add their support. Vinea weakly flows down from the ceiling, surrounding us with her mists, as if to hold us. The Sages amplify the connection to the source, drawing out more of the technopathic divination.

The Shadow sweeps toward Casey along the psybridge. He panics, and I reach for him. With a clawed, shadowy hand, MaalenKun reaches into the Unlit and pulls up Casey's trauma. Memories of abuse and abandonment crash through his mind. His sense of failure is amplified as memories of Usain and how Casey had to defend himself are pulled up. The Shadow twists Casey's sense of the past. Casey begins to believe that he deserved to be a loner, that he never deserved Franxis' friendship, our care, my love.

Franxis strains to speak. "Don't listen to it, buddy."

I say what I know to be true. "We belong. And you are exactly who we need you to be."

Casey's eyes flash from brassy discs back to their beautiful grey and green. He reaches up. We all reach up. We Rise together.

We are the channel to send the divination through our unified Levels and into Casey. The nanotech flashes with prismatic sparks as it is slowly forced out of his body. It hovers around us in deadly clumps, trying to make its way back to the exposed Unlit.

Arun and Pyaar cast a prismatic shield around us. They form a sphere, protecting us from the nanotech. They strain to hold it. Ehsan, Thiia, and Aaliyah double down on their accompaniment. With her spectra blade bright, Zinwara watches the nanotech slipping across the shield.

Casey cries out in pain with his whole body. Some of the Unlit creeps back into his wounds, but dangerous barbs prickle up from his wounds.

Give up, Casey Isaac, the Shadow hisses through the Unlit within him. ***You are mine.***

Casey's mind wavers. His nimbus sway as if he is about to slip away from the psybridge. Franxis and I both reach for him to anchor him, but he's lost in his pain. He stumbles as if he is about to faint, and we brace him. Careful not to touch the Unlit, we take the risk to hold fast to him.

The nanotech moves as if it is weakened. It flies in clumsy clumps, scattering itself across the locked armor of whimpering Red Guard.

"Fuck. It's going to suck them dry," Ehsan says.

"It'll regain its strength," Yahima adds.

The nanotech begins to shake off the technopathic divination, gathering itself along the borders of the shield, looking for any weakness, any way to get through.

Pyaar shuffles toward us with the Elder leaning on her. Both offer their divination to enhance Casey's healing factors, and Murtagh raises her weak hands to turn all of our heartstars. Enervated, Vinea slowly transforms into her humanoid form and reaches out her misty arm to place her hand on Casey. Vinea's glowing spores move along her arm and begin to swirl and dance along the edges of our light-threads beaming from our heartstars.

"Heartsong," she says. "StarTemple gate."

Mira gasps. "Vinea's showing me… There's pattern. A specific placement—a harmony—of our heartsongs. Murtagh, can you see it?"

"Yes," Murtagh says, shaping a mudra. "I see."

As Murtagh turns our heartstars to align with each other, the music of our heartsongs comes out of chaos and into harmony. Within our light-threads, Vinea's glowing spores illuminate an emerging pattern.

Mira recalls Vinea's words from Ecuador, "Your music… You're music…"

A viridescent flicker moves along each light-thread and light-line. The glimmers spread across what appears to be thin strands of glass-like light. The strands rotate to reflect more of the Haven's light. The thin beams meet, forming an equilateral triangle which rotates at the center of us. More strands of invisible light stretch forth from the edges of the shape. Synchronized lines and curves of glassy light spiral and expand. The luminous threads create music as they weave in, out of, and around one another, finding harmony. Light rays and musical notes adhere to each other, forming sacred geometric patterns, shape-shifting elegantly. Prismatic sparks glide the length of each thread, each pulsing and turning shape. A massive, moving tetrahedron within musical light formations grows before us. The shapes expand and open outward like a blossoming lotus.

The world around us vibrates. A pulse invites us to move, but we don't know where to.

"StarTemple," Vinea coos.

There is no delay from any of us. We pour our care through the light-lines opening the gate to the StarTemple. The Shadow looms at the borders of our psybridge, held back by our force of will. It watches us, reluctant to move toward us, as if some force beyond the gate we hold open, frightens the Shadow.

As the sacred geometry of our radiant nimbuses rotate above us, a realization moves within us all. The gate to the StarTemple, the sacred geometry formed by the power in our connection, shining and shapeshifting in the light of our heartstars, is a nimbus, the halo of some meta-being.

"One who weeps for all," Vinea softly replies in a soothing voice.

Awe moves through us, yet for once, I do not feel the tendency to steep in the beauty before my eyes. I feel urgency and conviction.

Casey winces as the jagged Unlit expands up from his wounds.

Growing stronger with each cluster of tech returning from a now dead Red Guard, MaalenKun pounds against the prismatic shield, slipping over its edges, casting its shadow onto us.

The Shadow inside the Unlit shrieks, and Casey goes down to his knees. It rages in his mind, quaking the psybridge. I reach for him, and see his mind thrown backwards through time. (He's getting out of his father's truck. He's afraid. He has to move into the unknown. He's afraid to do so alone.)

Our crew strains to maintain the shield, to keep the gate open.

I hold out my hand to Casey. "I got you, Casey."

He looks up toward our crew, then me. Weariness and defeat drain from his face. His eyes begin to radiate bright faith. His implant lights flicker, and he wills most of the Unlit back into his body. He has enough control of it for me to take his hand.

As our chosen family holds the gate open, Casey and I step into the center of the shifting sacred geometry. Our crew shapes their hands into the mudra for accessing the power of the heart. I feel their focus on love: love of friends, love of lovers, love of love itself. Their heartsongs become aligned with a song coming from the temple gate. The light-line between my heart and Casey's sings the song only we can hear.

The gate opens.

The glassy rays of light twinkle, chiming like the strings of some otherworldly harp. An emerald glow, like a green star, shines from within.

Casey asks, "You're coming with me?"

"I'm always with you, Casey."

With our eyes open, our hearts bright, we pass through the halo of the one who weeps for all.

We enter the StarTemple.

We fall.

ꝏ

from the personal, hand-written journal of Oscar Kenzari
10 April, 2138 (Greenwich standard)
on assignment aboard Helixx Corp vessel, The Eminent

I think I felt it when I heard Franxis talking about him.

Franxis knew I'd read the AARs, but I wanted to know what they felt before the encounter.

When I asked about their div, the tone of their voice changed to adoration. Franxis spoke about his wit, his heart. They described him as a lovable loner, friendly without a lot of friends. The way Franxis looked at me when they said they "couldn't wait" to introduce us made me suspect they'd picked up on my budding curiosity.

It's been over fifty years since I've had any real interest in romance.

I had begun to feel that after a hundred and forty-eight years, even though my biology hadn't changed much, my mind and Leveling up had somehow phased out that desire.

If it weren't for my crew, my family now, I'm sure I would've become lonely and hardened.

So, of course, I get to a new station, I'm up for having some fun. I reactivate my Joynr profile. Every message I get seems the same as so many before, which is fine, but every message reminded me that I want something else. Something inside me had shifted, and I knew it. Still, I opened Joynr for one more scroll through the profiles before deactivating my account, and that's when I saw his pic. I remembered seeing his eyes from my century old, prescient vision. He was my future.

When he walked in that door, my heart lit up. I finally see those eyes, playful and sexy, and I steep in his beauty. I knew right away. I'd do anything for him.

CASEY

Inside the luminous viridescent light, we fall slowly.

We cannot see our loved ones who hold the passage open, but we see the shifting glass-light architecture and at its center, a small opening to the white light of the Haven. The green glow of the StarTemple surrounds us, seeming to go on forever.

Tones of viridescent light extend from our heartstars in all directions.

"Casey…?"

The massive gash up my arm and across my chest is searing hot. The Unlit still extends up from the bloody laceration in spiky barbs. It's violently resisting the green light we're falling through.

"I'm okay," I answer, knowing he can tell I'm not. "Nothing to worry about, I guess. Except falling into this endless green whatever this is."

"The light. Is it coming from us or into us?" Oscar asks.

A voice comes through the rays of light, mighty and musical. "We."

The vibration of the word rattles our gear on our bodies.

Ah, the voice, delighted and welcoming, says in our minds. *Human.*

We psychically reach out, and while we can sense a presence, we cannot fully psybridge the being. Oscar unfurls a psybridge wide, but it doesn't hold, disappearing into the glow.

We feel the Presence gazing upon us. We open ourselves further to the array of green lights, allowing them to enter and spill from our heartstars. The Presence accepts us, and the light bends and curves around our bodies, slowing our descent. We slip along the flowing streams of light and come to a stop, landing on the pillowy surface of light made semi-solid.

The Unlit hides away within me again. My arm, shoulder, and chest heal faster than usual. My damaged gear seals itself with patches of nanotech. Oscar gazes at me with concern as I breathe heavily. He runs his fingers through the back of my hair, and I'm so grateful he isn't afraid to touch me. I need him close. His weary eyes meet mine, and he softens with heavy sigh.

I lift my arm to inspect the damage. My holoscreen tells me that most of the systems are operational. The charger and sonic on my right arm are destroyed. The armor is compromised. I fear my vulnerability. The lights shift around me, psychically highlighting the benevolent energy of the environment. My heart feels more radiant than ever. A rush of endorphins brightens my mood.

Oscar launches a holoscreen to find our location, but it displays one word: "Unknown." He checks his holoscreen to see that my gear is sending a clear signal. He's making sure he can take control of it if the Unlit breaches again.

I keep expecting him to smooth his beard, but he doesn't.

"Oscar… are you?"

"I'm maybe a little drunk on all this light. But I'm okay.

"Same." I smile apologetically. "And… The Unlit is subdued."

He pulls me close and holds me tightly. "Thought we were going to lose you."

Over his shoulder, I look up. The gate, with our friends on the other side, is far above us.

The voice says, *They are safe for now, yet their battle is not over.*

The temple softly sings. Within the chorus, ebullient escalations taper into tender measures. Multiple songs weave into and out of harmony drifting and expanding, becoming more obvious before more faint as they stream past us. Rolling underneath it all is a steady *AUM.*

Shifting streams of jade, emerald, and malachite flow around us. Without losing any radiance, the tones of light have become semi-fluid, then semi-solid, and finally soft but sturdy underneath us.

Oscar presses his foot down once, twice, testing the firmness of the structure beneath us. His spectra halo is luminous with rainbow colors against the green around him. He slips and falls into my arms.

"You're drunk."

He laughs. And we feel relief.

Green streams of light slip over us as I embrace him, hold him, kiss him.

My heart swells, aches in a way that opens it more. Sweet thrills move throughout my body. Chills move up my back. Our breathing is heavy on each other's lips as we bring our foreheads together and steep in the feeling of connection around and within us. I tilt my head to the side, and he kisses my cheek before rubbing his beard across my neck. My breath moves in quick and out with light laughter.

"So sensitive," he teases.

"Must be this place."

"Do you…?"

"Yes…" He grins, knowing what I'm going to say. "But… our friends."

Time is different here, the voice says with a knowing tone. *It has been barely a second where your friends stand on the other side of the gate. You have time for each other.*

His gear slackens, and I signal mine to release. We pull off the armor and drop it aside, letting the weaponry we know we don't need here land quietly against the soft flowing light. We skillfully and quickly peel each other's clothes away, letting each brush of our hands against each other's bare skin arouse and delight. He traces his hands along the jagged scar, new but quickly fading. His breath against my shoulder exhilarates me. We embrace with the temple's liquid-light rays flowing around us, passing over our bare skin and through our spectra halos.

He presses against me. He breathes next to my ear, and the closeness of him feels inadequate, even though he can feel my quickened breath land on his lips.

"Have we built up enough pleasant anticipation?" I joke.

He grabs the backs of both of my thighs, pulling me towards him. Seeing his crooked grin, I smile and chuckle, lying down into the glowing soft light. The solid, flowing light shifts underneath us, contouring to our bodies. As the temple holds us, I wrap him in my arms and legs.

Tones of various greens––evergreen, emerald, jade––slip over the curves of our bodies.

"We're naked within aurora borealis," I whisper.

"Why do you always get me naked whenever there's an emerald light show," he quips.

"So, I can steep in the sight of you."

My words almost make him shy, but instead, he allows himself to hear the truth in them. I feel not through our psybridge, not through our light-line, but in my own body, my own heart, how much he wants me, and I belong.

Our heartstars radiate as we move chest to chest. I pull him closer, and he moves inside of me. I finally have him close enough. He thrusts, slowly at first, building to a stronger rhythm. He notes the movements of my body, my face. I see him integrating divination from Six, a pattern recognition. He finds the rhythm and angle of our bodies coming together that I find most pleasing. He keeps his hands on me, holding fast to me, guiding my lips to his, looping his sensations into mine until they are merged. My body relaxes deeper as I let go, trusting and releasing, allowing him to move me.

I feel him moving with me, being moved by making love to me. Something moves deep within me. He moans close to my face. My body rocks as something falls away from me, as if we've cast off invisible weight. We pour our passion, care, sex, love into each other. We find ourselves in moving each other. Together, we move our bodies, breath, and bliss.

"Closer," he says.

I pull him into a kiss.

His pleasure is mine, mine is his. Boundaries dissolve.

Our synchronized orgasms fly through our bodies like a torrent of light. Our lips stay close together, and we breathe into each other. Layers of the surging climax pulse through us. He tightens his arms around me as if he is holding on to stay close. Just when I think we've both reached the peak, the surge rises higher with each thrust, and our joy flares through our midlines like rays of light. With each rush of the orgasm, the Unlit is pulled through and away from me. I feel my eyes flash brassy yellow, but no fear stirs in us before the reflected light fades. Again, he gazes into my grey and green eyes. I keep my eyes on his, releasing an ecstatic sigh. I feel only our joy, as the void, wafts of shadow-smoke inside liquid glass, is cast out of my being.

We both see the Unlit pulled away by bands of semi-solid light. It hangs a couple of meters away, bound and contained.

He exhales a very satisfied moan. I breathe heavily, smiling at him. We sit up. He kisses me, eyes open. I smooth the edges of his beard and adore his crooked grin.

The Unlit fades into the background.

ꝏ

The StarTemple shapes itself around our embrace. Passing songs drift around us conveying delight. We both smile at each other knowingly, acknowledging the temple's awareness of our lovemaking within it.

We bask in radiant *jouissance,* in pleasure and afterglow.

I kiss his shoulder lightly and breathe in his scent. He smiles his crooked smile, and I see the tiny reflection of my spectra halo on the surface of his eyes.

A deep sense of reverence moves around and through us.

The warmth of his body against me feels like home. Relief and release spreads through me. The presence of the StarTemple guides me to a new awareness. What I have found has always been with me, it is not dependent on this handsome man in my arms, but my own action in accepting and receiving another.

We sit up, and he tilts his head back as if he is too exhausted to hold it up.

"No more div-endurance?" I laugh.

"Just super relaxed… super pleased." He smirks, cocks an eyebrow up. "We could stay here if we didn't have a fight to get back to."

"It's only been seconds there," I say. "But now that the Unlit is out of me, we should go."

The green liquid light binding the Unlit guides the shifting shape back towards us. Green temple lights slipping over its surface keep it restrained.

"Come to me," a sweet but powerful voice calls from within the green glow.

The light around us swirls into semi-solid shapes and a massive wave rises before us. The wave grows wide and infinitely tall as the swirling jade, emerald, and malachite lights shape a massive wall of flowing liquid light. Other green light rays, sea green, green pearl, slip over and around the wall.

Oscar reaches for his gear, and the temple's song becomes joyfully bubbly. Music, laughing.

"No need for artifice," the sweet voice beckons, full of caring. "Come as you are."

A ripple of sound moves from within the wall. The liquid light parts to reveal a passage. Evergreen, jade, celadon, and more slip around and over each other, becoming distinct luminous rays which flow freely along the surfaces of the cavernous passage.

We follow the direction of the flowing liquid-light. The foundation beneath us sinks ever so slightly underneath our bare feet. As we walk, he reaches out a hand to the cavern walls, and the streams slip through his fingers and over his hand, gliding over each other, merging, blending, and separating again. He looks at me with wonder in his eyes.

Ahead of us, an opening to a large cave yawns wide. A light green glow within the cave brightens, becoming so pale that it is almost white. Our perception shifts and we can no longer discern whether the flowing liquid light is moving into or out of the cave. I reach out to touch the wall but find that the void of the Unlit is by my side.

Floating, fluctuating, the murmuration of shadow-smoke within the void appears to move in a current independent of whatever moves the liquid glass boundary. This thing is no longer inside of my being, wreaking a havoc that I have to constantly negotiate and repair.

"Come." The voice vibrates differently, along the edges of the space.

We step into a cave so still and quiet that we hear only the low hum of *AUM* and gently flowing water. A stream of blueish green waters quietly flows across the gently sloping foundation. At the walls of the cave, the waters merge with the flowing liquid light, and beyond the translucent border they become pure viridescent light rays. The array of light shines out into the endless expansion of the glow.

A gentle figure kneels on the other side of the flowing stream. Her green, hooded robes flow with thin rivulets of flowing green hues. Her bright, green eyes blink slowly. Dark ringlets of hair cascade down one shoulder. Around her crown glows a halo of every green light beam. Her spherical aura around her is a pale green light bordered by a rainbow, a multitude of colors. She holds a large amphora across her thigh, pouring a thin thread of a glimmering solution gently into the bourn.

She lifts her head slowly, and a soft smile moves across her round face.

Her gentle gaze meets mine, and we see her for who she is, the one who weeps for all, the bearer of the star-gate nimbus, Eternal Emanator of the Heartstar.

Enrapt, awestruck, stand naked before her.

She bows her head as a greeting. Oscar and I bow our heads.

"An ancient gesture, yet your ways of reaching me are novel…" Her voice is melodic, soft, uplifting. "For humans," she says with a touch more smile. "Humans rarely open the gate to the StarTemple the way you have. And never before have they under such distress."

"We had a little help," Oscar replies.

"Ah, the effulgent one." She smiles. "You know her as Vinea. She is the child of resilience from a world consumed by the Shadow. Few of her kind escaped. Your kind is, as you say, lucky she did."

I'm happy to hear the humor in her voice.

"Are you the one who cries for all?" Oscar asks, although we both already know the answer.

"I AM," she replies. "I AM movement within all hearts. I AM the hand that touches every sage. I AM the light that illuminates the guru, the sadhu, the wali, the saint, the Bodhisattva… I AM the All-Mother of the Universe. Within all divine avatars, I AM. The rising star of many names. I AM Karuna, Rahm, Compatior, eternal and ever present... search your own heart. I have always been there." She says with a touch of humor, "I have many names across the cosmos." She looks toward the amphora. "My collected tears… no need to shed them in front of guests." She gazes down toward the waters with eyes full of empathy. "The waters of life." A bittersweet smile moves across her lips. "Both an endless stream."

She glances toward the hovering Unlit. "It's finally out of you, I see." She shapes several quick mudra expressions, and the void is forced into a sphere. The shadow-smoke inside condenses into a smaller sphere as it yields to her silent commands. "I was expecting to remove this from you here near the waters of life. You would have certainly seen me shed tears then." She smiles. "But your passion in pleasure, your love-making, has spared me the tears. You have added to the light of the temple, the emanator of all heartstars. Your love will go on and on, shared into the power of life." She shrugs. "It is always this way… yet proximity to so much love in the temple has cast out what the light does not touch."

I ask, "What is the Unlit?"

She calls the sphere of Unlit closer to her and stares into it. A fire glows in her eyes; flames flicker in the depths of her pupils. "It is the semi-conscious remains of collapsed realities, coded with ancient anger and shame, primal fear, absolute entropy. It bears the terror, malice, and deaths of countless realities in inertia. Within, the Shadow has placed an extension of itself, a dark consciousness."

"How do we stop the Shadow from destroying our world?" Oscar asks. "How do we save our friends?"

"The one you call MaalenKun is the Primal Shadow, consumer of cosmoses. Nearly eternal, the Shadow infects the depths of lower dimensions. Untouched by light for millennia, it seeks to destroy your reality as it has countless others. It has taken the remains of those realities and weaponized the Unlit with fear, hate, and rage. The sentient storms sent to disrupt your lives are agents and heralds of the Primal Shadow. The discord that dominates your world has made it an easy target. In the chaos of the storm, it is more difficult to see the light. This gives MaalenKun the opportunity to harness your world's emerging fear, hate, and rage, as it has done before in many worlds." She smiles ever so gently. "However, an intervention has been made. Your world is the first to meet these attacks with resistance. Amidst the tempest, you have begun to embrace a power you call divination. Your unique attainments afford you the opportunity to defy this arcane threat." She turns her compassionate eyes onto mine. "Casey Isaac, your empathic divination saved you from the Unlit that existed within your being, but the Unlit keeps a psychic tether to everyone it touches. The wound from the sting of MaalenKun's crown is a well. To save those you love, you will need to peer into that well. Do not fear what the void holds. You will be connected to the Unlit until time's end. Realize what this means… knowing MaalenKun perhaps better than any other being in your universe."

I'm almost offended. I don't want to hear any more about the reservoir of Unlit that can be accessed through my hurt. How am I supposed to live with this?

Compassion moves from her heartstar to mine, and my emotions are settled.

"The way is not easy. It takes lifetimes of training, even for near immortals such as yourself."

"Whatever it takes, we'll do it," Oscar says. "Together."

She slowly closes her eyes and bows her head.

I nearly plead, "Can we… force the Shadow to meet the light or something?"

With a graceful gesture, she draws the sphere of Unlit toward her.

"Only a bearer of diamond light, perfectly alone, can cut the void and force the Shadow into the light. It cannot be pacified, yet it can be destroyed by the light of the eternal diamond."

A white light emits from her heartstar engulfing the Unlit. It resists her light, casting away various green light rays. But not all of her light bounces off the void.

I worry our being here will disrupt the perfection of her presence. I open my mouth to ask if she needs to be alone, and the mental constructs of "alone" fall from my mind.

Before they close, I see compassion filling her eyes. A soft light builds behind the smooth skin of her forehead, and her third-eye opens with a ring of bright blue circling an ultramarine spark. Her own heartstar illuminates, a reflective light. At the edges of everything—her body, the amphora, the solution of her tears flowing, the endless stream of life, the countless swirls and streams of light, my body, my lover—tiny, invisible light beams angle toward her breast, the beginning and end of each ray moving towards her heartstar into infinity.

I am in awe of what is before me. The light of compassion swells and envelopes Oscar and me. Our separateness falls away easily, as if every aspect of our beings are looped into oneness. I'm encouraged to let go of everything, and though I can glimpse what is beyond that action, I cannot let go. I must remain, I must get back to the people I love, I must use my power to defeat MaalenKun, the Shadow. Everything rushes back. A sense of purpose anchors me within my body.

The Unlit void clings to the open space, slowly dragged towards her radiance. The sphere condenses around the shadow-smoke as its borders disintegrate with static. The Light touches the shadow-smoke. With a faraway cry of pain, it unravels.

Brightest light surrounds us.

Through my consciousness tethered to MaalenKun, I feel the Shadow churning in the depths of the lower dimensions. Enraged, it roars. It feels the loss of the part of it that was destroyed. It rears its force and throws its darkness across vast dimensions towards the StarTemple.

The foundation underneath us lurches. The waters of the stream slosh violently. We open our eyes to see the swirls and rays of light falling away as the curves and walls of the cave tremble and part. The temple quakes. Its songs begin slipping out of harmony. Discord at the unseen temple borders threatens to break through.

A rippling sound grows louder in the distance.

Her booming voice fills the temple. "The Unlit reaches from the depths of dark worlds to cast its shadow on the StarTemple." Her tone shifts. "Make haste, divinators! Your loved ones need you. The Shadow sets upon them!" Some force builds within her tone, and the ferocity rattles us. "I must defend the Waters of Life! Do not look upon me now!" A fire builds in her eyes. "Go now!" She stands and tilts the amphora, spilling her remaining tears into the waters of life. "Godspeed, Lovers."

Thunder crashes through the temple. The Shadow.

We scramble to our feet and run towards the rippling passage. As the walls tremble around us, the swirls of various green liquid lights spill becoming less solid, back into light rays drifting out into the space around us.

Righteous rage rattles her battle cry as her towering body rises from an ocean of turbulent green light. She draws a sword of fire from an emerald scabbard. Tears streak her cheeks. Blood drips from her extended tongue. Her dark hair swirls in wild wind. The flame of her sword reflects in her black eyes.

Oscar pulls on my arm, and I look away. "Don't look at her, Casey. Run!"

I fix my gaze forward as we run through the trembling green cavern. The thunder intensifies, coming closer. Swirling green liquid light slips from the walls, becoming less and less solid. We run through them even as they melt away into fast moving rays of light. Oscar stumbles, and I pull him up. We run but fall as the foundation underneath us becomes less solid. The temple is beginning to let go of its solidity. He pulls me to my feet.

"Your implants!" Oscar shouts. "Call your gear! It's synced to your implants for emergencies!"

In the periphery of my vision, I see the lights of the implants flashing as I psychically will my gear to me. Moved through the space by its thrusters, the pieces of armor splash through semi-solid light. I yell at him, "What about you?"

"Just get your gear on, Casey!" He shouts over the crashing sounds as the invisible borders of the StarTemple's internal glow are pummeled by the Shadow.

Thunder hits, and it's as if we've both been punched in the chest.

Thiia and Franxis strain, crying out for help.

We both hear Zinwara's scream.

A terrifying vision rushes through Oscar's psybridge. The nanotech has broken the borders of their wavering shield. Runar is recovering, crawling towards them.

The giantess, the fierce one, moves within the glow, and light rays spark as they crash against each other. The ground dips below us. The sword of fire moves through the glow, parting the light with thunderous urgency. As the flaming sword lands against its target, both the temple and our ears are filled with the familiar metallic shriek of the Shadow.

I stumble to catch the gear, and as soon as I touch it, it opens to me. The psychic uplink begins immediately, and before I've even got the suit sealed, the holoscreen is up, shields ready. I will the suit snug to my body and snap the helmet up. My heads-up display pings Oscar's gear ahead of us, twenty meters away in the green glow. The damaged gear glitches and the ping is gone.

As the walls of the cavern come crashing down like towering waves of thunder, I wrap my arms around Oscar, pull him closer, and signal the thrusters. Designed for one person, the thrusters are not enough to lift us both into flight, but they give us an extra boost. We run, bounding further with each step, propelled by my thrusters through the winding passage as its walls fall behind us. Each thundering collapse lands closer. Cascades of light rays break apart, exploding against each other. The last of the towering light waves fall in the wake of our spectra halos.

I let Oscar go near his gear. My feet sink further into the light than they did before. I gaze up at the gate and notice the asymmetry forming as the light wavers around it. "I don't know how much longer they can hold it. Let's hope the thrusters can make—"

The foundation under my feet rocks and tilts. I fall to my knees and scramble to turn towards Oscar.

His gear lilts and rolls as the foundation underneath it slips back into light. He lunges for it. His gear, the amp pack with thrusters, is swallowed by the infinite glow. He scrambles backwards. He hold just the arm of his gear.

"Oscar, what are you doing?"

Even in my suit, I feel my hair stand on its ends. My gut hollows. I crawl towards him.

His warm eyes are full of apology. "Don't hate me." His heartstar glows bright. He lifts the holoscreen and presses a single button.

My suit, controlled by his holoscreen, pulls my arms in at my sides. My tears land on the helmet shield. "NoNoNoNo!"

"Forgive me, lover."

He activates the security features of my suit.

The crashing sounds of the temple, the explosions of colliding light, the battering Unlit at the temple borders, all fade into the background.

He says, "I love you."

"Take my gear!" I sob. "Oscar—!"

My words are cut off with another tap from his finger into the holoscreen. The thrusters in my gear fire, and my body is forced upwards. I let him push me away. My heart wrenches as he seems smaller and smaller.

The ground gives way underneath him. The green light of the temple engulfs him.

My HUD shows no sign of him. I try to turn around, but he's set the controls of my gear to stay on course for the gate. A giant flame sweeps by as the sword of fire is swung towards an enemy I cannot see. I look up toward the temple gate and a wave of emerald light conceals it momentarily. I fear we will both be lost in the endless glow and with us all that was learned about MaalenKun. If I don't make it out, Oscar's sacrifice will have been for nothing.

I weep, rising quickly, as the temple shakes around me.

A loud strike pops across the invisible borders in the temple's glow, and a massive length of the sacred geometry that formed the gate crashes down, parting the streams of green glow as it falls. The shimmering, thread-like lines and shapes of the broken gate begin to crash through the light of the temple.

The crashing remnants of the falling gate narrowly miss me. Several towering pieces fall towards me as the closing gate grows closer. I will the prismatic shield up, and it flickers around the damaged gear on my arm. Another thunderous hit from the Shadow breaks away a piece of the gate, and I feel Zinwara fall to the Haven's floor.

I sense Harjaz forcing himself to let go of the gate to place his hands on Zinwara, sending enough technopathic divination into her to repel the nanotech attacking her. Large sections of the gate fall, breaking against each other like crashing glass. The gate wavers and near closing as Franxis falls away from the group.

My mind whirls.

A steadying force moves through my spinning thoughts and catches me, holds me. Franxis.

Through my empathic divination, I pull from Oscar, and even as he falls, he gives me the power. I lift my hands. I push Oscar's divination attainment, his ability to connect with each other, towards our loved ones, and re-strengthened, they force the edges of the gate to remain open.

His voice comes through my mind with calm. *I'm with you, Casey. Always.*

ꝏ

Through an exploding shower glass-like light, I exit the collapsing gate of the StarTemple.

The nanotech swarms over their bodies! It's draining them of their life-force, their power.

Each ray of my heartstar expands outward as if reaching for help. I cannot feel them connect. My heart is shattered. I feel only loss. Void. Fate is flaying my heart, but my crew reaches for me. My family pierces the void. Their embrace draws forth the last of Oscar's divination running through me. His psybridge network is alive with a brilliant array of colors. I pass them the rays of my spectra blade. Light-threads grow to light-lines and expand into radiant channels. Our heartstars shine as bright as suns.

Where once the pain of the Haddyc sting and the toxic energy of the Unlit lived within me, glows a dazzling array of luminous beams.

With her lodestar bright on me, Zinwara sees my effort. Together, we push each radiant beam of the spectra blades through the psybridge. The power of the spectra blade moves through the remains of Oscar's network. The array of colored light beams touch our hearts, spread over their bodies, and rip through the attacking nanotech.

Though most of it is destroyed, a large throng of the tech slings itself outward, escaping.

In our midfield, we send millions of spectra light rays towards the descending Shadow. A torrential upswing of protective divination crashes into the Shadow. As millions of colored rays pierce it, the Shadow shrieks. Above us, an explosion of sparks rips through the nanotech swarm, and in our mindfield, the Shadow screams the sounds of bending metal as the spectral blade cuts the darkness, dividing it in two. An unknown amount recoils in the lower dimensions, and the aspect that occupies the stolen zin-spectrolite crystals and Unlit within the nanotech screeches as it is cut off from the well of its power. Unable to draw from the ocean of Unlit, the Shadow within the nanotech flails, screaming with rage. Broken zin-spectrolite crystals and smoking tech cascade down around us.

A dense cluster of the nanotech falls to the floor with a loud thud, and a smaller, slimmer, weaker version of MaalenKun's humanoid form emerges. Portions of the mirror-mask turn to gold dust and fall away. Unable to swarm into the air, it drags itself across the Haven's floor toward the weakened twin Sages.

Amidst the waves moving through the tech struggling to keep the form together, the extradimensional ring rises to the surface before the swarm swallows it again. Zinwara, rushes towards it with her spectra blade raised, but with a sudden thrust, the cluster of shimmering nanotech throws itself onto Runar.

A single crystal glistens in Runar's hand. He squeezes his fist around the quartz streaked with blue-pearl, and in a distorted flash, he and MaalenKun are gone.

The ring is gone.

I snap my helmet back and stumble. I gasp for air, bend over the sharp pain in my gut, and try to steady myself. I stifle a flare of guilt, signaling to Franxis that Oscar saved me from being lost in the crumbling temple so that I could return with what we learned of MaalenKun.

"Where's Oscar?" Mira asks, desperation creeping into her voice.

Oscar is gone, replaced by a hollow emptiness we all feel.

"You were gone for less than a minute." Thiia says. "Casey, where is he?"

The sound that escapes my throat is a strained cry, beyond language, but communicating so much. Harjaz puts his arms around me and keeps me from falling. Yahima places a steady hand on my shoulder.

The Sages do their best to stabilize us in our defeat as our nimbuses slip away from integration and back over our heads each hung low. Oscar's psybridge fades away, our shared divination energies retract from our crewmates. The lights of the spectra blades return to Zinwara and me alone.

Franxis cries out, clutching their side and stumbling. The look on their face is of shock and pain. Aaliyah rushes to them.

"No!" Aaliyah shouts, and my blood runs cold.

Franxis' face turns pale, their eyes transforming into brassy-pink discs.

ꝏ

I realize we are losing more than the ring when Franxis pushes away Aaliyah and slumps further to the floor. Thiia lunges to catch Franxis. Yahima rushes to them. I feel frozen, unable to process what I'm seeing.

A small swath of Unlit slithers into a wound in Franxis' side. As I watch it retreat, my heart aches with the awareness that when I lost control, the Unlit used the power of my rage to pierce the body of my best friend.

I shine through our light-line, and Franxis meets my heartbreak with forgiveness. I kneel and cradle them in my arms. My tears fall on their cheeks.

Yahima and Aaliyah check Franxis' wound.

The colors of Franxis' halo have slowed and grown faint. Their eyes are brassy pink reflections. The Unlit is unfazed by their healing factors.

Ephemeral spores of golden light sway gently around Franxis' body. Several leaves of benevolent energy drift down from Vinea's outstretched palm and fall onto and around Franxis' hand, pressed against a bleeding opening in their armor. The ephemeral leaves sink into the gear and move into Franxis' body. We all feel the relief rise in Franxis, and we ride the wave of hope before it crashes down as we realize that the energy from Vinea can only relieve a fraction of their pain. Vinea's benevolent energy cannot contain the Unlit within Franxis as it did within me thanks to my empathic power, a power I could maybe send into Franxis if Oscar were here.

Aaliyah pulls Franxis' hand away from the growing bloody spot in their abdomen. "This will hurt," she tells Franxis. She places a blood-stop pack to the wound and squeezes out the gel. Franxis barely winces as the gel expands and hardens, stopping the blood flow.

Thiia removes and sets aside Franxis' swift and ammunition.

Yahima holds out their beautiful, healing hands, and concentrates over the wound. "It's causing internal damage."

Franxis grinds their teeth, and sucks in air sharply as their body jerks. Their breathing becomes irregular. They're trying not to show how much pain they're in to spare my feelings.

"Can't hide anything from me," I say gently as I push Franxis' hair out of their sweaty face.

"Shit hurts," Franxis says through clenched teeth. Tears slip down the sides of their face.

"It's moving," Yahima says, voice urgent but low.

"Fuck." The word trembles out of Franxis' mouth. They maintain eye contact with me, and unexpectedly, they laugh in wheezes. "Ooh… It's got a potty mouth. Called me a cock-sucker-pussy-licker."

The laughter coming from me is half sobbing. "Total disrespect to your non-sexual orientation."

Pyaar looks towards Arun, and he nods. The Sages reach through the psybridge and shield our crew's psychic connection to both Franxis and me. We feel more held than blocked by their shield.

"Murtagh," Yahima asks the weary Sage, "Turn Franxis' heartstar to halt the Unlit's movements. The way we did with MaalenKun."

Murtagh sets about turning the energy of Franxis' heart to immobilize the thing attacking them from within.

Tears slide down Franxis' cheeks as their dim heartstar rotates. The light-line to my heart glows brightest.

Yahima says, "It's slowing it down."

Franxis tries to restrain the sound but lets out a long, painful groan.

The entire station jolts and quivers. The Haven quakes around us. Klaxons sound off in the bridge below, but only flashing red lights indicate the alarm in the Haven.

"That was an explosion," Harjaz says.

I cannot take my eyes off Franxis' eyes. Around me I hear snippets amidst the hurried movements. Harjaz says something about AI sealing off sections of the station. Aaliyah calls for a stasis chamber, but they find it's jammed in its storage port. Ehsan works to free the chamber, and Arun works to unlock damaged doors leading to the escape pods.

"Might be lights out soon okay, Franxis?" Aaliyah says, and Franxis nods without looking away from Casey. "We'll wake you up when we can get this thing out of you."

Franxis cries out again, arching their back in pain, shutting tight their reflective eyes.

A closer explosion rattles the station.

I put my head against Franxis' forehead and feedback fills our comp-bridge. MaalenKun's distorted, cacophonous voice snarls at us from the Unlit within Franxis. ***I am never-ending... You cannot break this bond, Casey Isaac! You are mine!***

No, Franxis answers. They highlight the heartsong coming through our light-line. *This is the bond that cannot be broken.*

Another explosion rattles the Haven. The biggest yet. This time it's not just a harbor being blown. Critical structure has been compromised. Red lights flash around us and alarms blare in the distance.

Harjaz reports, "They've blown Scire's stabilizing center! Lower levels already gone! AI is sealing off sections. Station's crumbling from the bottom up!"

I hold Franxis' limp hand and cry as the colors of Franxis' spectra halo fade further. Franxis closes their eyes slowly, and I shake their body until they weakly open again.

Throughout the station, the voice of Scire's AI announces, "Life support compromised... evacuate immediately... Life support compromised..."

ꝏ

I pull Franxis closer to me, wishing I could cast out the enemy inside them as easily as Vinea did with Runar. I glance up occasionally to see others working to get the stasis chamber and escape pods online.

Franxis' eyelids are too heavy. They can see through the brassy pink reflections that have replaced their kind eyes, but their gaze drifts.

The station's alert system repeats, "Life support compromised..."

With my best friend dying in my arms, every repetition of the warning flays my heart.

Our crew moves around us, and the crystalized remains of Vinea's energy meant to relieve Franxis' pain crunch under their boots.

"Life support compromised..."

I keep reaching forth with my empathic divination trying to enhance Vinea's benevolent offering, steady Murtagh's aid, amplify Yahima's healing energy. All of it is failing. I'm only able to buffer a fraction of the pain they're feeling. I'm not as skilled at buffering their pain as they were with mine. I need Oscar to strengthen our connections.

Franxis groans. Their eyelids droop. I shake them again. Sweat beads across their pallid face. As is their spectra halo. Their thin mustache curves up as a brief smile rises and falls away. Their brassy pink eyes narrow with another surge of pain.

We reach for each other through our comp-bridge, our psychic connection strengthened over a hundred years by our friendship. They have already let go of all of their other divs. We are alone together in our connection, and it is full of love.

The first time we met, Franxis immediately began tending to my wounds as South Los Angeles fell around us. They kept me calm when my divination, just beginning to manifest, healed those wounds before our eyes. I piloted us both to safety as the dusty space-cloud descended its vortexes around us, forever altering the world's perception of how bad things could get. We've been together since then, facing terrors.

Fear and guilt flood me.

"No." I shake my head harder. "No."

An outpouring of steadiness, compassion, and love moves through Franxis and into me. The stabilizing stream dwindles as the station shakes around us.

"Evacuate immediately... Life support compromised..."

Their face twists in pain. Their breath slows.

"Casey," the Elder leaning on Murtagh calls to me. "Let go of everything else and be with your friend."

I drop all of the offerings being poured into Franxis, catching them before they slip away from our bridge.

"Casey…" Franxis' eyes widen as they peer deep into mine. I look past the other-worldly brassy discs in each of their eyes. Franxis draws me in through our connection, so I can feel their voice close to my heart. "You are so powerful in your love… Thank you for allowing me to accompany you for a while."

The words crush me, for in the moment, I feel I don't deserve them. I pacify my insecurity, refusing to let it invade the moment. My love holds me steady. Franxis signals assent and urges me to listen.

The faint sound of a bell sounds across our comp-bridge. Franxis slips away. I shake them, but their eyes slowly close. The mindfield withdraws from them. I cannot hold them.

From the corners of my tear-filled eyes, a flash of brilliant circuitry moves through the stasis chamber. Harjaz exclaims, "Got it!"

Harjaz and Pyaar push the hovering chamber to us. Aaliyah and Yahima rush to pull Franxis away from me, slinging off Franxis' amp pack. As the chamber lid opens, I cannot help but feel that it looks like a coffin.

With Franxis' body inside, they close the lid, and Aaliyah hastily pushes in a sequence on the stasis chamber's control panel.

My mind spins.

The AI repeats, "Evacuate immediately…"

"We have to go," Yahima says, pulling me to my feet.

Another explosion rips through the station, but I can't shake the hollow feeling I'm bearing. The sounds of bending and breaking metal remind me of Haddyc screams, the rift opening that started this all. And this is how it ends, with Station Scire, my home for decades, crumbling. My love and my best friend both torn away from me.

As the others board escape pods, Thiia wraps her arm around Mira's shoulders and guides her into the pod next to me and the stasis chamber.

The mag locks release the pods, and the engines fire. The three pods rocket away from the crumbling station.

I look at Franxis through the metaglass window of the stasis chamber. Their spectra halo moves slowly, growing dim. I reach for our comp-bridge but feel nothing. It's gone. The anchor that has held me for a century vanishes. A lump swells in my throat. My chest tightens. Pain grips my heart.

Across the lid of the chamber, Thiia places a firm hand on my arm. "Let it go, Casey."

I wail.

A gravity wave slams the escape pods, tossing them about, but they recover quickly. Hurt and loss moves in all of us when we look out the window to see a second extradimensional breach surrounding The Eminent. Its rippling edges move toward the cracking station as the surrounding Cannons retreat from its expanding borders. Several sardonyx blasts pummel The Eminent's shield as the new rift spreads around the yacht. The undulating borders of MaalenKun's controlled rift move through what's left of the station. Scire's massive crystal energy array explodes, sending a fireball against The Eminent's shields. With the undulating edges collapsing inward, The Eminent disappears into the closed rift along with half of Scire.

MaalenKun, Sigrund, and hundreds of the inimical Red Guard vanish.

Another gravity shockwave moves out from the brief rift's closure, rattling our small pods. Large chunks of station wreckage are sent sailing through the sector. Scorched remnants of Scire spray outward through space. The broken pieces of my old home clatter against our shield, but none of it breaks through.

With its own prismatic shield turned bright, The Queen moves through the blaze to receive us.

ↀ

The vihara doors slide open, and I step into the softly lit space. Ahead, I notice a familiar glow coming from the alcove where Franxis lies in stasis. The small alcove entrance encourages everyone to enter quietly with a bowed head.

Inside, the Vihara Elder and Vinea sit in meditation. Swaying floral-shaped mist billows from her crown like sacred, ephemeral dreads. Her glowing spores gather and hang in place around both of their crowns.

Thiia stands from the bench on the opposite side of Franxis' chamber. My heart swells and falls apart. I take her hand.

We look into the small window of the chamber to see Franxis' pale, unmoving face. The Unlit within them has remained frozen, unable to harm their body further, but no one knows if the Unlit is reaching Franxis' mind. Their spectra halo fluctuates slowly.

I wonder why I came here. I worry that the shuffle of my feet, my breath, even my sad thoughts will disturb Vinea and the Sage's meditation. When the tears come, a sob catches in my throat. I drop Thiia's hand and duck out of the alcove before releasing the sound.

My sobs don't echo in the specially designed vihara. The vibrations meet the sound-buffering, rippled surfaces on the columns, walls, and ceiling. The reverberations barely come back to us. It's so quiet here, I can't avoid the hurt I'm feeling.

Thiia rubs my back as I lean forward with my hands on my knees. I'm sure I'm going to throw up. My gut feels queasy, my heart feels sunken. Trying to shake off my sadness and worry, I reach for Franxis out of habit. But I don't find them. I find only heartbreak.

When I finally stand up, Thiia pulls me into a tight hug. I hesitate to return the full embrace, but she holds me tight. Giving in, I wrap my arms around her and cry. She radiates care through the light-thread connecting our hearts.

I ask, "Why aren't you at the memorial?"

"It doesn't start for a little while longer. I wanted to get Vinea here safely. She's still not a welcome presence to most of the Station Mani crew who don't trust any EDBs. For that reason, she won't be at the memorial. She's been coming here to meditate with the Vihara Elder. They're searching the knowledge of the universe for a solution.."

I turn towards the alcove opening. Vinea's shifting lights glow inside. "I don't understand why all of our efforts to reopen the StarTemple gate keep failing. Murtagh says that we might not be able to access the gate with our heartstars alone—maybe it had something to do with MaalenKun being there, maybe it was Oscar's psybridge network." I huff, "I hate feeling powerless." I lift my hands, fingers curled in frustration amongst wisps of colored light around my head. "I was a direct line for channeling the spectra halo through every Queer in the sector." I close my fist, sending a familiar surge through my arm, unleashing the spectra blade. "I can manifest this fucking rainbow sword." I sigh, opening my fist, letting the spectra blade flash away. "But I can't get back the people I love the most."

Thiia nods with understanding. "Carmel is gone, but we'll get Oscar and Franxis back. I know we will. We will get them back." Thiia glances up at my spectra halo and half-smiles. "Our resiliency is what became the spectra halos. Zinwara thinks rage against injustice became the spectra blades."

I sigh. "Ugh… So it's because of the oppression put on people like us that we have these powers?"

"Not the oppression, but how the challenges of oppression were faced," Thiia says. "If we created something beautiful and powerful out of all that, we'll do the same with the challenges we now face." Thiia flashes a gentle smile. "I've been meaning to tell you. I guess now is just as good of time as any." She reaches out and takes both of my hands and squeezes them gently for emphasis. "Casey, I would be honored to accompany you, to share your fate for a while. However long it takes until Franxis is back with us. I'm here for you as your friend, as your family, and I can also be your comp."

"Thiia…" I look in her gentle eyes.

"Listen, Casey."

I hang my head again. I'm not sure I can hear whatever it is she has to say. I don't know what to say to her. I shake my head, ready to tell her that I'm sorry.

"Listen," she says again, and I realize she isn't asking me to listen to her.

I look up, and she taps her fist against her chest. Her heartstar shines brightly.

I listen to my own heartstar, searching through the various light-lines leading to our crew, my family. It's there. The song between my heart and Oscar's. I gasp, and bittersweet tears come.

"You hear it?" Her voice pleads for confirmation.

My voice wavers with relief and joy. "I hear him."

Thiia laughs through tears. "We'll find him. Together."

"Together."

Realizing the risk of hope, I choose not to embrace it. Instead, I turn to those who have been building each other up, relying on each other. I turn to the heartsongs of my crew, my family. Bright faith.

ꝏ

A gently flitting hand catches my attention. Ehsan waves as he, Zinwara, Harjaz, and Aaliyah make their way to us. Walking with them are the other crewmates from The Queen: Horatio and Kirra. Horatio gives me a friendly smile. Kirra's grey tribal tattoos curve up her neck and across her face, making her stern expression more intimidating. Zipeng is with them. Timid, he nods. I force a smile back.

I glance around the crowded room. High-definition camera drones aim their lenses to the low stage. The memorial is being live-streamed so people all over the sector can mourn together. There is standing room only in the large space. Many spectra halos shine in the crowd of heads. I see a few faces in the crowd gaze at me, and they turn to each other, whispering excitedly. There are several holographic attendees, lots of decorated Ops, people in uniforms from almost every station department.

Captain Commander Areta Maarama sits alongside the two other Captain Commanders from other stations. Gala N'guwe nods towards me, and I nod solemnly.

In the cluster of saffron and orange uniforms, I see the familiar faces of the Scire Elder, our Black Elder and other Mani Sages. Murtagh, Pyaar, Arun. I notice another familiar Sage. It takes me a moment to realize that Yahima has cut off their long hair. Yahima smiles gently, and without their long hair framing their face, I'm even more awestruck by their beauty.

Yahima, Pyaar, and Aurn approach our group. All of our spectra halos grow brighter with our reunion. The Sages reach for the rest of us to embrace us. There is a moment of surprise to be offered an embrace from Sages who traditionally do not touch anyone unless necessary. I welcome the affection when Yahima takes my hands.

"Not everyone can pull off a buzz cut," I say. "But this works for you."

Yahima tilts their head. "A change was necessary." Yahima shrugs one shoulder, and their mood shifts to a bit more reverence. "Our hair, in my tradition, holds our past thoughts… and I needed to let go of my old thinking habits. I misplaced my trust. I did not see the ruse." Yahima bows their head with eyes closed. "I should have known better."

"The responsibility is not yours alone, Yahima," Mira says. "None of us could foresee Ferand's schemes." Mira offers Yahima her hand, and they take it. "You didn't fail us."

"No one here is at fault," Thiia says.

Kirra looks away briefly with a clenched jaw.

"If we need to blame someone," Ehsan says, gazing at Kirra, "We can blame Helixx Corp."

"The Crimson Chain," Thiia adds.

"A small group, but one with a lot of power," Arun says.

"A lot of racism and homophobia too," Ehsan quips.

"That makes sense," Arun replies. "People with strong biases are easier to manipulate."

Thiia says, "Ferand was powerful enough to fool us all."

"Well, not Carmel," I quip. Mira is the first to laugh. "But she stood by our sides."

"That is where I will be from now on," Yahima says.

I can feel the truth in their voice.

"It's time," Thiia says to Mira. "Should we start?"

"This would be a lot easier with Oscar here," Mira says.

Thiia puts her arm around Mira. "He's with us."

Together they ascend the steps to the pedestal where Carmel's body has been lain.

Harjaz gently places his strong hand on my back. As the room grows quiet, he whispers, "How are you holding up, Casey?"

I answer honestly, "It's tough, Harjaz."

"If you need anything…" he says. "And, I don't mean, I mean, you know, non-sexual, I mean, anything. If you need anything. Like as a friend—"

My body shakes as I try to suppress laughter, drawing some looks from the audience. Mira smiles gently at me as if to say any amount of joy despite our losses feels like a shared win.

I reply, "Thank you, Harjaz."

He blushes.

Mira takes Thiia's hand.

A UNAF flag with its image of the globe and olive branches symbolizing a wish made long ago for world peace is draped over Carmel's body. Two divs in decorated uniform draw back the flag and begin folding it into a taut triangle.

Mira gazes at them with her heartstar bright as they hand her the folded flag. Without pause, Mira steps toward the pedestal and lays the flag at Carmel's feet.

A white cloth covers Carmel's still body. Everyone takes in the sight of the iridescent circle printed on the cloth. The symbol subtly reflects a multitude of colors. Carmel is the first div to be memorialized with the symbol of the spectra halo.

Mira reaches out and touches the cluster of blooming jasmine vines encircling her wife's body. I glean an echo of her intention as she takes in the fragrance of the blooms to strengthen the memory of this moment. With dignity, she embraces the difficulty, hurt and hope, the movement of life, even as she must move on without her lover, her wife.

I imagine how Oscar would see her, support her. I see him steeping in the beauty of the moment though it hurts.

Their spectra halos intermingle as Mira and Thiia turn to face the crowd.

Thiia pauses and looks around the room before speaking. When she opens her mouth, her voice is clear and steady. "We are here today to memorialize a magnificent woman, our crewmate, our friend, our family, and a loving wife, Captain Carmel Arias Kosse. Carmel is said to mean the garden of god, Arias means gift of god, and Kosse, beardless." Light but genuine laughter ripples through the crowd. "And she was indeed without a beard." Even Mira laughs lightly. "She was indeed a gift, and like a garden, that gift grew as she gave her friendship and her service. Although she could also be fierce in withholding her friendship when she felt those she loved were not treated with kindness, Carmel had the power to fully love someone immediately." Thiia looks over at me and the rest of our crew. "She also loved the people of the Earth, even if she wouldn't admit it." More laughter, polite and low. "And she was keen on redirecting anyone who did not align with love. Carmel was a first-generation United States American, a Jersey girl. Her parents brought with them from Croatia their own homophobia, and even though they refused to accept their beautiful daughter, she never gave up on them." Thiia's voice wavers ever so slightly. "In an effort to wake up her parents and folks like them, she began making documentaries, starting with a film about Queer joy in the face of struggle. That's how I met her. She followed me around for a month, and then, I followed her around for over a century. She was always trying to make the world better, even before Rising. It's been a profound honor to have worked with Carmel, to have been led by Carmel, and to have embraced Carmel as my family. On behalf of Carmel's family, we thank you for being here, and we thank you for loving her."

Mira reaches out and takes Thiia's hand, and something moves within me. I feel their dignity and sadness, their grief and honor. All of their various emotions begin to reveal themselves so clearly to me. I feel something I never named emerging with me, a deep respect for the bonds of chosen family.

Thiia sniffs and clears her throat. "We would be remiss to not mention that our beloved friend Oscar Kenzari is unable to be with us today." Thiia turns to me and conveys confidence with a nod. "The three of us have had the privilege to know and work with Carmel, since before Rising. I had to look it up in an old comm system to be sure, but she hired Oscar for her documentary crew exactly one hundred and eleven years ago today." Ehsan whispers a sound of amazement as others in the crowd do the same. "I'd say that's an auspicious number. She'd tell me it was just a number… but then, she would joke about us being destined to find each other." I'm reminded of Franxis joking that I was their destiny, and I smile. "Then, she'd get serious and tell me that whether it's destiny or not, we've got a job to do. She was not one to shy away from the job when things got tough. She'd simply steady herself and her crew." She pauses and sniffs again, steadying herself. "At these memorials, we often don't speak of how our loved ones died." She looks towards Mira who nods at her encouragingly. She turns back at the cameras live streaming. "It angers me that the news channels have overshadowed Carmel's heroic act with stories about the world's richest woman and whether or not she lives in a nanotech body." Her voice is forceful, concealing anger. "It would be a mistake to not speak of Carmel's sacrifice today. To sacrifice is to 'make sacred.' To hold something as sacred is to regard it with great respect and reverence. Our lives are sacred. Carmel knew that. Carmel Arias Kosse was a hero."

The divs in the crowd stomp their boots on the floor, drumming celebratory agreement.

"As immense pain gripped her body, Carmel made a great sacrifice, heroically prevented a catastrophe, and with her final move, saved countless lives, including the life of her loving wife." She pauses to let the words land, shifting her tone to something more reverential. "That invading titan was defeated because Carmel fiercely loved her wife." She turns to smile at Mira. "We will not forget that, and we ask that none of you forget Carmel's sacred act." I look over and see every captain commander nodding. "She'd be pissed if we forgot." Polite laughter. "We honor her memory by leading ourselves and each other forward, waking each other up, protecting each other in spite of and because of the risk—" She looks at me and my heart shines brighter. "—and loving fiercely."

We all pause for a moment in silence.

Tears well in my eyes as I realize I must lower my defenses, drop my guard, and open myself to fully receive the love these people are offering me, a love I will have until the end.

Zinwara takes my hand.

Mira gazes out into the crowd. "My wife, Carmel Arias Kosse, was not shy about expressing how she felt about someone. It's true she loved fiercely, but also… stubbornly. And I admired that about her. She had a way of growing and learning from loving and not loving alike. She got to a place where even not liking someone helped her realize compassion for them. She would say things like, 'Oh! It must suck for them to have a mind like that. Bless their heart.'" More laughter from the crowd. "In one breath, she could call someone an idiot and wish them well—and mean every word of it." Mira pauses and smiles. "People have asked me what it was like having foresight and if it made our relationship easier. It did, and it didn't. I could see the stubbornness and arguments coming and brace myself, but I had to create space for Carmel to live her life. I realized, I could learn to love better by growing with her and not ahead of her. Since she saved my life and countless others, I've wondered why I didn't see the end coming, and now, I realize that I never looked ahead to see if it was coming. I never tried to see our end… because it never will end. She will always be with me." Her tears have stopped, and she gently smiles towards all of us. "She will always be with us."

Mira nods at Pyaar, who steps to a control panel on the wall next to the stage. Pyaar taps the holoscreen, and a portion of the wall at the back of the stage slides open.

Thiia wraps her arms around Mira's shoulder and Mira leans into her embrace. The colors of their halos integrate as they lean on each other and watch the platform move into the open space.

A metaglass shield lowers and quietly seals the body inside the cremation chamber. Per Carmel's will, her cremation is visible, unhidden. The red light inside grows bright, and we bow our heads. In just a few moments, the sardonyx rays turn the flag, the flowers, and the body to ash. As the light dims, we return our gazes to the chamber in time to see the fragile remains of the symbol of the spectra halo drift up from the ash and reflect a prismatic flash before it slowly turns to dust.

Mira places a hand over her heart, and as if to hold the beautiful lightthreads there, she closes her fist and taps it against her chest. Thiia does the same. One after another, the mourners do the same, a spontaneous salute to our interconnection. My crew hold their fists close to their hearts.

I hold my hand at my heart as if I am holding all of them, including Franxis and Oscar, closer.

ꝏ

The Queen stands upright, aimed at the stars. And he is glorious.

Thiia follows my gaze. "He's beautiful."

I turn towards her and smile. "He's home."

Zinwara says, "The UNAF does not know about the launch, but soon enough, they'll know that we completed the hyperspeed technology."

"They'll be coming for us," Ehsan snickers.

We snap our helmets up and step out of the shuttle, onto the docks.

The ship is impressive, even to me and I designed it. The new paint job shines in the launchpad spotlights. The hull, fuselage, and stabilizers are aubergine, but the nose, stabilizer edges, and bay doors are bright magenta. Stripes of neon pink run down the sides from the tip of the nose along the fuselage. Rhodolite garnet ngars along the length of the highliner catch the sunbeams.

Thinking I'll have plenty of other opportunities to see the ship, I instead watch the upturned faces of my crew. Their eyes are a little more open than usual. Some of their mouths hang slightly open too. I smile with tempered delight, allowing myself to move forward while wishing Oscar and Franxis were here to see this. I see several of them scrolling through their HUD, taking in details about each feature of the ship.

As Zinwara calls out each feature, the holographic model in our HUDs highlights the various parts. "The Queen, he/him pronouns, is equipped with advanced pilot psychic interfacing, military grade AI, high-density Ulloah shields—" Mira smiles at the new name for our advanced shields in honor of Liam Ulloah. "Stealth and cloaking capabilities, two fully rotating sonics on the top and undersides—smaller than but more powerful than a clash-wing's, sardonyx cannons on the port and starboard sides, two deployable drones, and of course, the length of him is lined along the borders with reinforced, ngar chargers. In the bay, there's a small shuttle and room for the updated Lacassine. And last but not least, my personal favorite—" she taps a comm button. "––The Halos."

"That's our cue!" Horatio's cheerful voice comes through our comms. He and Kirra pilot the two small pod ships, Halo 1 and Halo 2, out of a nearby hangar. "These little things are nimbler than a crux with a Sage piloting. No offense, Sage Yahima."

Yahima laughs. "None taken."

"They look like little Saturns," Aaliyah says.

Zinwara voice relays her smile. "Secured by div-manipulated electromagnetism, the halo's rings reposition through intuitive interfacing with the pilot and can spin around the circumference of the spherical ship, instantly aiming the most powerful pink quartz ngars ever developed in any direction."

Kirra keeps her pod-ship steady, but Horatio seems excited to humor us. He spins the crystal ngars over the top and bottom of the sphere.

Horatio adds, "The metaglass sphere is lined in a grid of thrusters. These little ships are quick and can change direction in a fraction of a second."

Horatio's Halo zips forward and he weaves around Kirra's Halo in a fluid corkscrew pattern.

"Stop showing off!" Kirra growls.

Horatio says, "You've made The Queen a finer ship, Div Isaac. He's finally complete."

"Just pulled down some ideas. Div-tech indies really refined everything." I try to sound humble.

"Seven blessings on you. Let us polish that halo a bit, Div Isaac!" Horatio says.

"Just upgraded the highliner and added a bit of flare."

"I love flare," Ehsan whispers loudly as nudges me, winking a pink eyelid.

We ride the independent shipyard's small rover up to the boarding ramp and onto the elevator platform.

"So..." Harjaz narrows his eyes. "We pissed off the Helixx Corp army, an interplanetary cult, and a world-eating sentient Shadow that could show up at any time—"

"Let's not forget those Titans. They're not MaalenKun's friends, but I'm pretty sure they're problematic," Ehsan says.

Mira nods. "The one that destroyed Old Girl might've been going after MaalenKun, but it also seemed fine with destroying our world to do so."

"And you want us to leave UNAF?" Harjaz asks.

"I'm ready to go after MaalenKun." Aaliyah asks, sounding far surer than her div does.

I answer, "We'll work with the UNAF when necessary, but we won't answer to them. We won't have them telling us where to go, where to stay, who our team is. We decide."

A few of them look uncertain.

Mira steps to my side. "Carmel's legacy shows me that leading with love makes us stronger. We want to prioritize what we love. We want to bring back Oscar and Franxis." Mira turns toward Vinea. "And we have to make sure the Crimson Chain doesn't get the other ornaments. The Sages who took them to flee Helixx Corp are no longer with the UNAF. They've gone rogue."

"Rogue Sages." Ehsan nods approvingly.

"And who's going to captain this new crew?" Kirra snaps.

Zinwara signals support, but outwardly shows no signs. She lets Mira meet Kirra's abrasiveness as a test.

"I will," Mira says. "Per Zinwara's request, I will captain The Queen."

As if the rest of us aren't on the same comm channel, Kirra turns on Zinwara. "How are we letting this outsider take over for our captain? We don't owe them—"

"I owe them," Zinwara says.

"You don't have to stay, Kirra," Ehsan says softly and directly. "But I'll be staying with our Captain Commander Zinwara Osei."

"Ah! HAHA!" Kirra beams, "I'm with you, Commander!" Her smile immediately drops from her voice. "Though I do not understand your every choice."

"My lodestar tells me…" Zinwara takes both Harjaz's and Aaliyah's hands. "We are the way. This crew, this ship. This is where I need to be."

The elevator stops and we step through the airlock channel towards The Queen.

Mira spins up a holoscreen from her mission gear's gauntlet. "Captain Commander Osei," she says. "Would you like to have the honor?" She stretches her arm and brings the screen closer to Zinwara.

Our chosen leaders share a smile and nod, acknowledging the task before us all. Zinwara taps the unlock sequence on Mira's holoscreen. The port door on the side of The Queen slides open.

Zinwara gestures toward the open door, "This is your design. Lead the way, first mate."

I bound forward through the open door, leading my crew into our new home.

When we're all strapped in, Thiia opens a line to the control tower. "Aashray Control, this is The Queen. We are seated and ready for liftoff."

The harbormaster's voice comes back. "Checking crew vitals, ship psychic interfacing… He seems to like your pilots well enough." Thiia laughs. "You're twenty until lift off, Queen."

Harjaz lifts the ascension panels on the holoscreens in front of our pilot seats.

"You ready for this, Casey?" Harjaz asks with a bit of concern in his eyes. "You look a little nervous."

I start to answer, but I'm interrupted by Thiia as she opens the comms ship-wide.

"Casey Isaac, you asked us if we would join you on this journey. You asked us to leave behind the structure and organization most of us have been a part of for over a century. You asked the crew of The Queen if we could buy their ship." Zinwara and Horatio laugh. "You asked us if we would help you defeat an extradimensional threat that weaponizes the world's hatred and chaos." Thiia looks up to the cockpit, meets my eyes, and listens intently. "With all of the hatred and chaos in the world, how do you suppose we do that?"

I close my eyes, bow my head, and breathe slowly. I wonder what Oscar would say, but a glow in my heart tells me use my own words. "Because of and in spite of the hatred and chaos, I ask you to join me. The Shadow weaponizes our hatred and fear. The Crimson Chain, the Red Guard, Sigrund, MaalenKun... The Shadow… We will face them again. We'll weather many storms. We'll align ourselves with those we can trust and defend ourselves from those who wish to tear us apart." I feel the power of my crew's heartstars aligning. "Bright faith will be our weapons, our method, and our superpower. I know that with you, as a team, we can fulfill the promise of divination: truly shaping the future."

Harjaz looks back at me with a sparkle in his eyes. He pauses for a moment, "Heard that, first mate!"

Thiia beams, "You know I'm in."

"From here on out," Mira says with conviction.

Through the intercom, we hear Vinea cooing from the Augur.

Mira chuckles. "Vinea says she's with us!"

More laughter from the deck below, even from the Sages above us.

"The Queen's looking better than ever… also, I kinda like you lot now." Zinwara says with a touch of dry humor. "You already know I'm in!"

"Thank you, Captain Commander."

Ehsan laughs and says, "Big purple and pink spaceship? No place I'd rather be."

Aaliyah smiles toward Zinwara, "I'm where I want to be."

Kirra says. "If my mates are a part of your crew, I'm with you too, yeah."

Arun's voice comes over the comm, "I'm with you—all of you."

Yahima's voice is musical and dignified. "This is only the beginning."

Horatio nearly sings. "Cheers to the new crew of The Queen!"

There's a longer pause as we all feel the sentiment.

Pyaar's voice comes through cheerful as always, "Forgive me, everyone." I look over to see Mira smiling and nodding, having predicted Pyaar's response. "I'm with you for this mission—however, I feel I must continue working with Station Mani. After all, you'll need someone on the inside. I will be there to support you, as will our Black Elder, Murtagh, and more. You'll have our full support in any way we can assist."

"Thank you, Pyaar. I'm sure we'll need you," I say.

Thiia announces, "Countdown from thirty has begun."

The song only he and I can hear, the song made by the light-line between our heartstars, harmonizes with my sense of direction. For a moment, I close my eyes, bow my head, and listen.

I remember his voice, *I am with you, always.*

I open my eyes, I hold out my hands, and catch the ascending piloting crystals. "Let's make something beautiful out of the future."

ꝏ

I walk the ruddy landscape alone yet connected. In my chest, longing couples with contentment. I miss him. I want him back with me, yet I honor the sacrifice he made. I do my best to hold it all as red dust and stones crunch under my boots.

Beyond the mountains on the horizon, sunlight moves across icy clouds which appear iridescent, mother of pearl. I gaze up at the bluish orb filtered through the golden Martian atmosphere. Earth and all of its chaos is so far away.

The Martian moons, Phobos and Deimos, make their orbits across the sky. Phobos, the spirit of fear, is a small shape floating peacefully in the vast sky. Lights of small lunar mines blink across its cratered surface. Deimos, god of dread, is so far away that it is only a tiny light, almost disguised as a star.

Oscar would have appreciated this view. He would've steeped in the scene as I told him that my own fear and dread are present, but small like the Martian moons. After a sufficient steep, he'd then remind me that they are still there, both the fear and the dread, and that they're bigger than they seem. I can see the corner of his mouth turning up.

I assent, nodding my head to no one.

I laugh to myself and feel a note of joy coming from my comp-bridge. Care shines through our light-line, and I send care back to her. Without any verbal transference, Thiia seems to know what I feel whenever I think of Oscar, without any intentional signals. We both hear him now. His heart song, at least. We are the only ones who have heard it for months, but none of us have lost faith.

There have been times when our failed attempts to reopen the StarTemple gate have left me reeling or sobbing. Thiia and Harjaz have picked me up off the floor of The Queen many times. Vinea has been patient with our questions. She explained calmly, and as she spoke, I heard that unlike the rest of us, her voice carried no tones of desperation. Mira's voice settled next, then Arun's, and Yahima's. The assurance I heard in the voices of our most prescient crew-mates created a new foundation within me. I knew I wouldn't backslide into the sadness or self-blame that had entangled me before Oscar.

I know now to take all that he gave me, build on it, grow from it.

"The StarTemple is eternal, as immortal as the force of life. Its radiance continues to flow into all beings," Mira had said, unpacking Vinea's words. "The gate is temporal, coming only when the music of the spheres harmonizes to manifest the sacred geometry. It will open again, as it always does."

"And Oscar?" Thiia had asked.

"Perhaps he is with the one who weeps for all."

I had wrapped my arm around Thiia's shoulders as she leaned toward me. "Listen," I whispered, guiding our attention to our light-lines singing in harmony with Oscar's song.

We're still listening, searching.

Thinking of Franxis, I look back towards the blue orb that is Earth. I wish

I could hear their heart-song. I yearn for my own heart to be enough to open the gate to the StarTemple, to channel the power of aloneness that the one who weeps for all used to destroy the Unlit.

I'm struck by how alone I must appear on the Martian landscape.

I bow my head as I walk towards the ruddy outcrop ahead. I look over the jagged surface and find a long ridge horizontal to the ground. There is so much of the rock underneath the ground below me, so much of which I am unaware. As I look at the dual moons, I feel no fear or dread in the uncertainty, only humility and faith.

I open the pouch on my belt and tap the bottom. Without much gravity to restrain it, the palm-sized chunk of quartz which once served as Old Girl's piloting disc floats up. As it spins in low gravity, the crystal that Oscar used to guide his ship and crew reflects the soft lights from my gear and sparkles brilliantly along its broken edges. Gravity begins to pull the sparkling rock back down and lands in my hand. The weight of it reminds me of all that feels heavy on my heart and all of the compassion I hold to keep from crumbling under that weight.

"Martian Armed Forces might come for you if you leave that Terran stone out there, first mate. What do we do then?" When she jokes, Mira reminds me of Carmel. She watches over me from The Queen, still in orbit.

I smile. "Don't let me go, captain."

I'm nearly overwhelmed with the fullness of gratitude. With a sigh, I close my eyes, and feel into it. I allow myself to hold loss without complaint or indulgence, and the sweetness of what I've found spreads through me. Bittersweet.

I try to shine my care through the light-line between me and Oscar. I try to find him through our light-line. The ray of light curves back into my heartstar. The only sense of direction that it gives is back into my own heart. I hear his song, faint but present. I signal gratitude for the support he has given me, the support he taught me to give myself. I let go, not knowing if the signal can reach him, but happy to feel it myself.

Sweet and bitter.

As I pour out the essence of my thoughts into the light-line, compassion for myself awakens in my heartstar. The warmth is coupled with joy as I wonder if the compassion is from my heart alone or if Oscar is highlighting my heartstar from deep within the interconnection of all hearts at the StarTemple.

I think of his sexy, crooked grin, his nervous habit of smoothing his beard. I remember every freckle on his skin, the constellation of him. I steep in the memory of our synchronized breath, the integration of our auras, our movements, how we moved each other, body, breath, bliss. We were moved by loving each other.

Memory brings with it a gentle smile.

I allow myself to continue being moved by loving him, to feel his song emanating within my heart.

My longing for him is softened by an awareness of interconnection.

I look back out across the dim landscape. Dawn is coming on the Martian horizon. The still mysterious flicker that keeps coming back moves on the edge of my vision. I realize I won't see just what it is for some time. I hold space for it, inviting it to be. A light ray bends as if some being moves just behind the fabric of my reality. Questioning stops.

I feel at peace.

A glimpse of the future unfolds without visuals but with feeling.

I feel myself loving.

I steep in the felt-echo of the brief glimpse of what will be.

Morning sunlight falls on the broken quartz piloting disc. It moves over its green surface and reminds me of the flowing viridescent tones of the StarTemple.

With both hands, I place the green quartz onto the ledge along the outcrop. I press it down, settling it until the Martian gravity holds it still. I remove my hands slowly.

I head back towards Halo 2. On the meta-class canopy, the reflection of my spectra halo shines back at me. I take one more look at the starry sky, the distant blue orb, the dual moons, the ruddy landscape, and the glimmering crystal on my lover's altar.

I pull down from Five the power to make true, and I whisper, "Closer."

ꝏ

urgent message to all crew of The Queen from First Officer Thiia Bacelar, June 28, 2150, 1:14 (Martian standard)

"All crew, return to The Queen immediately! We found something! We think it's him!"

ꝏ